The Peace of Freysdal

A Light-Twister Novel

The Peace of Freysdal

A Light-Twister Novel

Michael Richards

LODESTONE BOOKS

Winchester, UK
Washington, USA

JOHN HUNT PUBLISHING

First published by Lodestone Books, 2023
Lodestone Books is an imprint of John Hunt Publishing Ltd., No. 3 East Street,
Alresford, Hampshire SO24 9EE, UK
office@jhpbooks.net
www.johnhuntpublishing.com

For distributor details and how to order please visit the 'Ordering' section on our website.

Text copyright: Michael Richards 2022

ISBN: 978 1 80341 257 3
978 1 80341 258 0 (ebook)
Library of Congress Control Number: 2022937878

A CIP catalogue record for this book is available from the British Library.

Design: Stuart Davies

UK: Printed and bound by CPI Group (UK) Ltd, Croydon, CR0 4YY
US: Printed and bound by Thomson-Shore, 7300 West Joy Road, Dexter, MI 48130

We operate a distinctive and ethical publishing philosophy in
all areas of our business, from our global network of authors to
production and worldwide distribution.

For my wife, Adrianne

Prologue

Artor lowered the unconscious guard to the ground and closed the door, blanketing the stairwell in darkness. He steadied his breathing, then hurried downward, keeping his balance by trailing his long, narrow fingers along the roughhewn stone wall. The cool air smelled musty, like an old cave. He jerked his hand back from a cold stream of water trickling down a groove in the stone. It was the only sign of the savage storm raging above. Not even the earth-rattling thunder penetrated this deeply. The muffled thud of his soft boots was the only sound—that, and his pounding heart.

The storm in his several minds was just as severe, where dozens struggled to convince those that doubted of the rightness of his plan. Ever since his youth, he had known he would change the world. He wouldn't let a few weak minds dissuade him from his destiny now. He set the dubious to simple exercises, confident they'd soon come around, and focused his free minds on the task at hand.

Artor had read every book about the prisoner, studied his attacks, reviewed his capture, and examined all that had been learned during the man's sixty-two years of imprisonment. The histories said his power was beyond measure. Nineteen members of the True Council had united to subdue him—three had died in the process. Artor, however, was more powerful than any member of the True Council.

But even with all that had been learned from the prisoner, the most important question remained unanswered. It *had* been asked before, but only by weak people bound by outdated laws. But broken laws could be mended. Several minds recoiled at that thought, but most assented.

The air grew stale and heavy the deeper he went. The dank odor became oppressive. It wasn't a cave he had entered. It

1

was a crypt. He took comfort in the energy radiating from his pockets and willed his heart to be still.

Expecting another step down, he stumbled when instead he found the floor. Straightening, he felt for wards, but knew he would find none. Buried deep and isolated from any sources, the prison was dug here for this prisoner.

Artor stiffened at a dry grating sound. In the glow of his sources, he could make out the stooped figure of a filthy man. Knobby, age-spotted hands clutched the iron bars of his cell, holding them for support. His patchy gray hair partially covered his face and hung to his shoulders. Artor couldn't tell where hair ended and beard began. The man shook on unstable legs, setting his hair and tattered robes swaying.

"I said, 'hello,'" the man rasped again.

An intense chill seized Artor's heart. A handful of minds shouted this was a mistake. He fought down the urge to retreat and focused all his minds on why he was there. Slowly letting out a breath he hadn't realized he was holding, he took a step forward. The prisoner was no threat—he was old and weak, barely clinging to life. Discomfort radiated from his posture, and he shielded himself from the glow of Artor's sources.

"Hello."

Artor coughed to hide the quaver in his voice. He had wanted to sound threatening but found that harder than he had imagined. Several of Artor's minds pitied the old man. How could this bag of dusty bones inspire such fear in the council? He barely held his own weight. A few minds shared contempt for the council.

"It has been several years since I've been spoken to. Has the council so decayed that they now accept children into their ranks?"

Most of Artor's minds wanted to withdraw, but the few that could tolerate the grating voice noticed the insult and stoked the rest. Indignation overcame discomfort. At twenty-four, Artor had left childhood behind long before. Who did this mangy menace think he was?

"I am not a member of the council." Artor's voice reflected the heat in his minds.

The old man took no notice. "No? Has the council fallen then? Surely, they wouldn't allow a mere boy down here."

"I am here on my own. I've come for some answers." That time, threatening came easily.

The old man's eyes narrowed, and his dry voice took on irritation. "I've told the council everything I know."

"As I said, I'm not of the council, and I'm not bound by their laws."

Artor folded out a lump of heat too intense for anyone but him to handle. The strain on his minds removed all vestiges of fear. The old man let go of the bars and staggered back, surprise replacing defiance on his face.

"Tell me where it is."

The man smiled, then let out a blood curdling laugh.

"You're a fool," he croaked.

A rhythmic thumping told Artor people were coming. He needed an answer now. "Tell me where it is!"

Artor set the lump swirling, in preparation for releasing an attack, but then something impossible happened. Artor no longer controlled the lump of energy. There was no struggle—he had it, then he didn't. The lump began to concentrate, intensifying beyond anything imaginable. Artor's heart froze. The older man straightened to his full height and suddenly seemed imposing. He stopped laughing and his eyes, illuminated by the lump of heat and Artor's sources, shone with ferocity.

Near half of Artor's minds gave over to panic. One cheeky mind recalled the description of the prisoner's immeasurable strength, but the rest ignored it. Artor stumbled backward. He drew on his sources, desperately folding, forming, and spinning energies, to launch an attack on the older man while simultaneously building defenses.

In the split second it took to form his attack, Artor saw the stolen lump of heat move into the keyhole of the cell door. The lock exploded into blinding white molten droplets. The old man tore energy from Artor's sources to deflect his attacks, then stole the flow sustaining his shield, and used it to pin Artor to the ceiling. He felt like a kitten in the maw of a wolfhound.

Artor struggled to protect himself as a whirlwind of flames roared around him. He screamed for help. His robes ignited and burned his skin. The flames vanished as quickly as they appeared, but Artor continued to cry out in pain.

He instinctively reached for his sources to heal his wounds, but they felt miles away. Powerless, he watched as all five floated away from him. They settled in the prisoner's outstretched hand. He gazed at them, wide-eyed like a starving man at a banquet. Artor writhed in pain against the rough stone ceiling, certain he was going to die.

Relief washed over him as two members of the True Council appeared, surrounded by layers of protection, including several that Artor didn't recognize. One opened his mouth, but before he got a word out, the old man began an assault. Drawing, folding, forming, streaming, splitting, and spinning energies from and through the stolen sources with such ferocity that it was a blur. The onslaught was unbelievable. The two held their ground, countering and giving their own. But in mere moments, large stones tore free from the stairs behind the council members. Their attacks evaporated in a single, blinding flash as their heads were crushed with a deafening crack.

The two collapsed, along with Artor's hope for survival. Swirling flames consumed the bodies, leaving only bones and ten stones that rose and slowly circled the old man.

Artor watched through the pain, in fear and amazement, as energy flowed from stone to stone in an intricate pattern and then poured into the old man. The gray hair receded and turned black. The beard turned to dust and settled on the ground. The wrinkles disappeared, the skin pulled taut against strengthening muscles, the eyes cleared. Dirt fell from his skin and clothing. The old man was transformed to a young man in a matter of seconds. It was unheard of. All that remained of the former wretch were the tattered robes, and those he cloaked in an ornate cloth of light.

Pain shot through Artor's burned body as he hit the stone floor. The vibrant man examined his fingers and said, "I don't know where it is, but when I find it, I'll send you a message." His voice was deep and rich. He tossed a fingernail to the ground, then strolled up the stairs.

Artor Joans remained motionless on the ground where he had fallen, knowing he had changed the world.

Chapter 1

Surviving Research

Jaren slowed as he approached the big brick building. Made with the thickest walls in all of Freysdal—if the ascending western slope of the valley could still be considered Freysdal— the research facility was situated far from any other building. Several years earlier its predecessor had been in the center of town until an accident destroyed the original building, killing everyone inside and damaging surrounding buildings. As the story went, it had only been *Hel'dig's* blessing that Hairth hadn't been there that day.

Jaren shivered despite sweating from the uphill run. Thinking of his owner, the man for whom Jaren was carrying an urgent message, always made Jaren's heart skip a beat. Even with the dramatic increase in "urgents" over the past few days, his chest still tightened when his normal schedule was interrupted with a message for Hairth.

A dark-skinned guard recognized Jaren and waved off his warrant. Jaren replaced it in his satchel and took a final deep breath of fresh air before stepping into the facility. The acrid air still tickled his nose, and when he finally did have to breathe again, he coughed, holding the edge of his segg, the rough sack-like uniform of the thralls, to his mouth.

Jaren moved through the cavernous building, dodging the researchers bustling about—some with peculiar contraptions or smoking pails, others just with noses high up in the air. Jaren paid these kinds only enough attention to avoid bumping into them. Despite his many visits, he never grew accustomed to the research facility with its curious instruments, loud banging, heat pouring from enormous furnaces, and intense smells that irritated the nose and lungs. Gables and large windows in the roof allowed light into the long building and tall stacks brought cool, unpolluted air in from outside while others let big billowy clouds of smoke escape into the sky.

Jaren marveled at all the lights, strange contraptions, colorful liquids, and puffs of smoke. Looking for Hairth meant he had to look at almost everything, and some of it was pretty amazing. Jaren turned a corner and narrowly avoided crashing into someone. The poor fellow stumbled but Jaren caught him before he hit the ground.

"I'm sorry," the man said as he righted himself.

"Mosj?" Jaren asked. The maintenance man's normal smile was gone, and his cheeks were flushed. If it hadn't been for the big ring of keys on his belt, Jaren might not have recognized him. Just a couple weeks earlier, Mosj had helped Jaren get into the locked admin building.

"It was my fault," Mosj said in an unsteady voice. He wiped tears from his red, puffy eyes, and then said, "Oh, hello, again," as he recognized Jaren.

"Are you okay?" Jaren asked, concerned that their near collision had injured Mosj.

"Oh," Mosj laughed weakly, wiping another tear from his cheek, as he shook his head. "I'm fine. Just got some dust in my eyes while repairing a storage cabinet—who knows what's in this place's dust. I need to get some water to try to rinse them out." He forced another laugh and rubbed his eyes as he maneuvered past Jaren.

Jaren watched Mosj continue his rushed departure, narrowly avoiding another collusion, then, resumed his own search for Hairth. As Jaren continued deeper into the facility, he heard Hairth's voice. Jaren's heart skipped a beat for the hundredth time since getting this "urgent."

"That's incredible!" The deep voice was distinctive, even amidst the hammer falls and roaring flames of the research facility. It was coming from a small walled-off room. Jaren knocked on the door, pushed it open, and said,

"Hairth, sir…"

"Jaren, from admin," Hairth finished as he turned to Jaren. "Another urgent?" He sounded discouraged but took the message. He frowned as he read it but smiled at Jaren when he looked up again.

"Come and see this." Hairth stuffed the message in his robes, and beckoned Jaren into the room.

"Do you not have a return message for me to carry?"

"No, no, this was bad news, but nothing terrible—and nothing to be done now. Come see this!"

Jaren felt relieved. The flurry of urgents made him worry about what was happening, but Hairth's quick dismissal set his mind at ease. He turned his attention to the room. He hadn't noticed before, but it was full of people. Hallumon, the Associate over resources, had a long morose face and stood leaning against a large shelf opposite Hairth. He was wearing light green robes that looked like they were made for a larger man. The skin hanging loosely on his gloomy face looked like it was made for a larger man, too. Despite his appearance, he was always kind when Jaren delivered messages to him.

Jaren did not know any of the other ten or so people in the room. They were watching Hairth or staring at an assembly on a table in the center of the room. A woman beside Hairth gave Jaren a cross look but smiled when she looked at Hairth. She kept adjusting the orange and red ropes on her segg.

"Jolinda, tell me more about this."

"As I was saying, when we focus the energy from the heat source through the cold source it creates these…well, we're not exactly sure what they are."

On the table stood two wooden candle sticks and a curved piece of thin metal, like a bowl on its side. The first candlestick sat in a slot cut in the bowl, so that it held a stone-like ball in the center of the dish. The second candlestick held a rock in line with, but about a foot away from, the ball.

Hairth was moving his hand in front of the rock, fast then slow then fast then slow, back and forth. "Amazing." Hairth's green eyes shone, like a child opening a gift. The others in the room smiled, too—except Hallumon, who just looked bored.

"Try this," Hairth said to Jaren, as he continued to wave his hand fast and slow.

Jaren frowned in uncertainty but waved his hand in imitation of Hairth.

"No, not there, here." Hairth took Jaren's wrist and moved his hand closer to the assembly. Jaren moved his hand toward the rock. His jaw dropped and his eyes widened. Then he smiled, too. It *was* amazing! It felt like his hand was pushing through water, then hot air, then water, then cold air, but it was all just air—not wet at all. He squeezed the water-air and it seemed to ooze out of his hand—but he couldn't see anything there.

"How is this happening? Why have we not seen this before?" Hairth asked, fingering the contours of the water-air.

"We've never been able to concentrate and direct so much energy before. Gerald improved the reflector material and Crostalin improved the shape, and...well, this was the result."

"That's perfect," Hairth replied. "We'll need to upgrade my rings."

"Yes, sir," a balding, pale-skinned freedman said.

"We also need to see if these improvements can be done on a large scale at a reasonable cost." A man and women nodded vigorously then began whispering to one another. Turning back to Jolinda, Hairth asked, "Do you understand what's going on?"

Jolinda's expression faltered, "Not exactly, sir. We believe that something about the mixture of cold and hot is...thickening... or...stiffening," Jolinda struggled for the right word, "the air."

"Stiffening the air...?" Hairth's long, gray eyebrows drew closer together.

"Yes, sir. We know it depends on the strength of the two energies. For example," she slid the second rod closer to the first until they were almost touching and gestured to the air. Hairth raised his hand and moved it toward the assembly. He stopped and slowly made a fist. Again, he turned to Jaren, his eyes wide. "Try it."

Jaren lifted his hand to pass it through the air, but this time found a glob of...air...that was as stiff as heavy bread dough. He could move his fingers through it, but only slowly.

Jolinda clearly wasn't happy about Jaren's presence, but she did appear pleased with Hairth's response. "We're using an unrefined cold source, but if we switch to a refined source..." she grabbed Jaren's wrist and pushed it away from the assembly. Then, she picked up the rock and nodded to a man wearing a thick leather apron. He extracted another small stone-like ball from a dull metal box. "...the air will become solid." Someone handed Hairth a hammer, and his smile quirked a bit.

Jolinda took the ball and as she went to place the refined cold source on the stick, a wave of heat blasted Jaren's face and a bright flash of light hurt his eyes. Everything seemed to slow down. Jolinda screamed. Terror slammed into Jaren's heart. He squeezed his eyes shut as he instinctively turned away from the table and covered his head, a terrible *bang* rocked the building as screams rippled outward. An oppressive dread filled Jaren's mind—the weight of it tugged at his body, threatening to crush him. He pushed back against it, barely able to keep upright. The smell of smoke filled the air.

Time resumed and some of the closer screams choked off, others continued unabated.

"What in Thadren?" Hairth whispered. Jaren slowly opened his eyes. That pressure still threatened to crush him, and he felt unsteady on his feet. Strange lights, as if given off by a bright torch, danced on the walls. Sounds, like distant thunder, filled the room.

"How is this possible?" Hairth asked.

Jaren looked to Jolinda for an answer. She lay crumpled on the floor, smoke rising from where her hands should have been. Jaren gasped at the sight, and the pressure pushed past him. He collapsed and darkness crowded in on his sight. A rising shout filled his ears…then nothing.

Chapter 2

Waking in the Clinic

Jaren woke with pounding pain behind his eyes and a slowly fading whining in his ears. His tongue stuck to the roof of his parched mouth. He tried to speak, but just coughed. He heard talking but could only slowly make sense of it.

"Marigold, get some water."

Jaren looked toward the commanding voice, but his sight was so blurred that it was like he forgot to open his eyes. He blinked several times, and slowly his vision cleared to reveal a girl with brown eyes and large brown curls framing a heart-shaped face. She placed a hand on his forehead, then took him by either side of the head and peered into his eyes. He smiled at the softness of her touch and felt his eyes close.

She released his head and he struggled to open his eyes again. A plump woman with narrow eyes handed him a cup of water. The first swallow went down rough, but the second was a relief.

"Jaren, my name is Haerlee. I'm the healer," the curly-haired girl said.

The healer? Jaren narrowed his eyes. He had delivered several messages to the healer, and she was *not* Haerlee. He looked around the room, trying to make sense of things. He lay on a pallet on the floor, surrounded by bandaged and moaning people.

"You were in an accident."

Yes—the urgent for Hairth. Memories came back, and Jaren recognized the balding man from the research facility. Bandages covered half his face and all of his chest. Jaren thought he recognized others as well, though all were covered in bandages—some more, some less. One man—or woman, Jaren thought—covered from head to toe with bandages moaned with every breath.

"How are you feeling?" Haerlee asked. "A little confused."

"Any pain?"

"My head hurts."

Haerlee nodded and handed him a piece of what looked like tree root.

"Chew on this, it will help with the pain."

Jaren closed his eyes. He chewed on the bitter root for several minutes. The fog of confusion began to clear as the pain left. Opening his eyes again, he could see that it was, in fact, the clinic, but the floor had been cleared to make room for pallets. Everyone there must have been injured in the accident. A shocking thought struck Jaren, and he cautiously looked down at his own body. There wasn't a bandage on him anywhere. It made no sense. He looked for Haerlee to ask why he wasn't injured.

She stood a few feet away at a small table, grinding with a pestle and mortar. She surveyed the men and women, lips compressed and eyebrows furrowed like she was looking for something she couldn't find. Her segg looked good on her, which was odd since seggs were designed to look bad, but something else seemed out of the ordinary. Jaren squinted until he saw what it was. The crest on her chest was not Hairth's. He had seen thralls in Freysdal that belonged to someone other than Hairth, usually a trader or one of Hairth's Associates, but they were rare. In Freysdal it didn't matter, though. All thralls were treated like humans, and everyone who entered Freysdal agreed to follow that rule.

Jaren lifted his squinting eyes from the crest and found Haerlee glaring at him. His cheeks turned red. Yes, he had noticed her pleasant shape, but that wasn't what he had been staring at! There was no way to explain that without making it worse, so he just looked away, all but forgetting his question.

The door opened and a large, dark man stepped in and surveyed the room.

"Shut the door!" Haerlee hissed at him. He ducked his head, stepped in and gently shut the door.

"Sorry, of course."

Jaren's eyes widened. The man was at least a foot taller than Haerlee, and his arms were bigger than her legs. Even if she didn't recognize him for who he was, the fact that he was wearing lavish robes should have told her his position relative to her. But Jaren did recognize him. He was Deaelestran, Hairth's first Associate.

"He's awake." Haerlee said, as if answering a question she knew was coming.

Deaelestran looked toward Jaren. "Is he...?"

Haerlee cut him off, impatience in her voice. "He seems fine, though I could never tell why he was unconscious in the first place. Just watch him and bring him back if he worsens."

Deaelestran smiled and revealed big white teeth. "Yes, ma'am."

Jaren gawked in amazement. No one talked to Deaelestran like that—except maybe Levi, and he was usually wearing a sword and a whip when he did it. Jaren looked between the two to see what would happen next, but Haerlee just looked at Jaren and said, "Well, don't keep the man waiting. You do know who he is, don't you?" Jaren clamped his gaping mouth shut. Of course, he did. Did she?

He hopped up, shrugging off the lethargy and confusion of moments before, then paused for a jolt of pain in his head to subside and stretched his muscles a little as he walked toward Deaelestran.

"Jaren?"

"Yes, sir."

"Hairth's been eager to talk with you."

Jaren felt his heart skip a beat, and thought his legs would give out, but before he could react, Deaelestran stepped out through the door. There was nothing for Jaren to do but follow.

Chapter 3

Becoming Hairth's Apprentice

Deaelestran smiled as he approached Hairth's office. An ancient woman with more wrinkles than face sat by the door, looking at a ledger on a counter in front of her. Without looking up, she pointed at an entry.

"Sir, you're not on the schedule."

Deaelestran leaned down to be in her view. "Ruth, you know Hairth wanted to see Jaren. He's not on the schedule because Hairth didn't know if…" he glanced at Jaren, "…*when* he'd wake up."

Ruth just frowned at Deaelestran in response.

"He's right, Ruth," said a young girl who sat beside Ruth. She had a pale complexion, wild black hair, and eyes that were too far apart. "You put the note in the other ledger, on page two-hundred-forty-seven, in the middle of the second column." Ruth raised an eyebrow at her. Jaren glanced at the girl's ropes and frowned. When he was a Blue, he never would have spoken so boldly.

Jaren worried that Ruth's brittle bones might snap as she opened a second, larger ledger. She drew a stubby, gnarled finger down a list of mostly crossed-out notes in a neat script. Her finger stopped and tapped on one line, then read, "Admit Jaren."

Then, turning to the Blue, she said, "Remarkable, Tobie! Just where you said it would be."

But then she lifted her wrinkly face to look at Deaelestran and said, "But how do I know this is Jaren?"

Deaelestran tossed his hands in the air.

"Ruth, you know me. I'm telling you it *is* Jaren."

"I do know you," the woman croaked. "And I know all about your Oiandan trickery."

Deaelestran grimaced at the slur, but before he could reply, Tobie interjected, "It's him."

Jaren narrowed his eyes. She had said it as if she personally knew him.

"Have we met?" he asked, uncertain.

"Well, no. But I know who you are. You're Jaren, from administration. You live in Dragon Hall. You put on green-yellow five months ago. You've got two sisters you suspect were captured with you. You come from Eirenburg. Your performance was mediocre on the aptitude tests, except for reading and endurance where you scored above average, and social intelligence where you scored below..." Tobie noticed Jaren's glare and trailed off. "That was the only area where I did poorly, too..." her voice was a squeak.

"How do you...? I don't even...Mediocre?" She winced at his tone. Jaren was flummoxed. Below average social intelligence? He didn't need a test to tell him he was awkward. He kept to himself so others wouldn't notice. Deaelestran snorted softly, and Ruth just smiled at Tobie.

"She's got a great memory," Ruth said.

Tobie smiled at Ruth, took a deep breath, and straightened her petite frame—the perfect Blue trying to project confidence. Then, to cap off the effort, she raised her narrow chin and replied in a steady voice,

"I read your file. It's got your test scores, and more. Mediocre means average, or, that you're about the same as everyone else— it's not a bad thing. From your grades at school, I expected you to know the word."

Jaren could feel heat rising in his face.

"I *do* know what mediocre means," he said.

"You are not on the schedule, but since it appears you are Jaren, Hairth will see you," Ruth continued, her smile the only evidence the intervening exchange had taken place.

Deaelestran straightened and smiled like a child that had just snuck a treat. He started to lead Jaren through the door when Ruth cleared her throat,

"Sir," she almost sang, if croaking frogs could be said to sing, "the note says nothing about you."

His smile dropped and he gave her the stink-eye. She didn't even look up, just closed the ledger and put it back where she had gotten it from. Deaelestran threw his hands in the air again, groaned, then turned to walk away.

"Don't worry. You'll have better luck with Hairth than I have with Ruth." The woman made no indication that she had heard him, though Tobie smiled.

Hairth's office wasn't fancy—a simple desk with a few plain chairs were the only furniture. A window looked out across Freysdal, and from the second-story room, Jaren could see Freysdal's growing wall. The unfinished half still showed the original red clay brick, like the rest of the buildings in Freysdal, and the upgraded half showing the heavy white granite towering even higher. Thumb-sized masons scurried around, moving huge white blocks up the scaffolding as they went.

The only decorations in the room were a simple blue-and-yellow-patterned rug and a painting of a younger Hairth with a woman holding an infant. Jaren studied the grain of the wood floor. The boards were smooth, and stained a rich brown color, though in front of Hairth's desk some raw wood showed through from wear. Hairth and Hallumon, the long-faced Associate over logistics, were standing in the worn area. They had noticed Jaren come in but hadn't stopped their conversation.

"He arrived last night," Hallumon said, scratching at a thick bandage wrapped around his arm.

"Were the precautions I described in place before he arrived?" Jaren glanced up at Hairth and almost gasped aloud when he saw that the left half of Hairth's face was bright red and brown, with a little pink beneath peeling curls of blackened skin. Jaren reached to his own face, but quickly lowered his hand.

"Yes, all of them. We also have guards posted per your instructions."

"What was Levi's response?"

"He thinks you've successfully mounted a lion. So long as you can stay on, you'll be unstoppable. But beware that you don't fall asleep."

Jaren gave up staring at the floor and examined their shoes.

"I've got some fresh game to tempt that lion with. And, despite what Levi may think, I've been riding this lion for close to twenty years. I haven't fallen asleep yet and I don't plan to now. I just need this lion to help me raise a baby tiger, and then I'll dismount easily." They both turned and looked at Jaren. Hairth smiled, but Hallumon narrowed his eyes.

"I hope you do have a baby tiger, and not just a stray cat," Hallumon said as he walked past Jaren, brushing his shoulder with his bandaged arm.

Once Hallumon shut the door, Hairth gestured Jaren to one of the simple wooden chairs as he took the seat behind his desk.

"Jaren, from admin, it's good to see you up and about. We were pretty worried about you. Please, please, sit down."

Jaren took one of the two seats in front of Hairth's desk. The wood was polished, and the arms felt smooth under Jaren hands, but quickly became slick as the sweat from his palms dampened the surface. Jaren scrubbed them on his segg, though it made little difference. His heart was pounding.

"Cherry. It's a fruit-producing tree. Makes little red berries that can be sweet or sour."

Jaren scrunched his face in confusion. It was not what Jaren had been expecting Hairth to say—not that he knew what to expect from Hairth. The knot in his stomach tightened.

"The desk. It's made of cherry wood. Marvelous stuff. Starts out light-colored and darkens to this reddish color with exposure to sunlight. My wife had this desk made for me over twenty years ago with wood brought in from the other side of Dragon Desert. Do you, uh, know much about wood?"

Again, Jaren was uncertain how to respond. Sweat beaded on his brow. He shook his head.

"No," Hairth paused, gingerly scratching at a brown patch of skin on his cheek, "No, I don't suppose you would." Hairth looked at the parchment and strips of paper on his desk, shifting from one to another as if he were looking for something.

"Yes, so, to the point. I've transferred you from Paul directly to myself. You will be my, uh, apprentice. There's a lot for you to learn, so you will be busy. I'll have you working with my Associates at times and in training at other times. Wood is not important for you, but radiance is. Do you know much about radiance?"

Jaren sat there, bewildered. Had he heard right? No, he couldn't have. But he had. And, as he tried to determine if he was imagining it all, he noticed Hairth's head tilted in concern at Jaren's silence.

"Yes, sir. No, sir. The only thing I know about radiance is what I've learned here." Great impression. Jaren berated himself. Impression? Why did Jaren care what impression he made on Hairth? Clearly the man did things for his own reasons—if there were reasons at all. At this point, Jaren could not confidently say that Hairth had all his documents filed correctly.

"Well, tell me what you do know." Hairth appeared to have regained the composure Jaren expected.

"Yes, sir. I know that you, or your workers, rather..." Jaren said workers and not thralls because that's how they were referred to here, in Freysdal, as often as not. Most of them were thralls, but there were plenty of freedmen and a few freemen among them. "Your workers make radiant items for people."

"That's true, but not what I was looking for." Hairth cut Jaren off. "What do you know about *radiance*?" The emphasis he put on the last word and the way he peered across the desk made Jaren push back against his seat a little. What was he supposed to say?

"Well, sir, I know radiance is energy—or something—that comes from rocks. It, the rocks, that is, can be refined and used to make radiant items."

"So, we start with the basics. You can read? Good." Hairth handed Jaren a small book. "'Fundamentals of Radiant Materials.' It was written by a partner of mine—Derek from Enrich—shortly before he passed away. Why don't you go into the conference room and start reading? I have one more thing to deal with before we can start on your, uh, training. I'll have Ruth call you in when I'm ready."

And with that, Hairth picked out a parchment and began reading, for all the world as if Jaren wasn't sitting right across from him. Jaren sat for several seconds, unsure of what had just happened, but when Hairth just kept reading his papers, Jaren stood, with the book in his hand, and left the office having no more answers than when he had entered.

Jaren closed the office door behind him. Ruth seemed to be napping in her seat, and the wild-haired girl was engrossed in a large book on Ruth's desk. Neither so much as glanced at him as he walked past.

The conference room was cavernous. A large table, big enough to seat all of the Associates and more, sat in the center of the room. Chairs sat in rows at the ends of the tables, and others lined the walls. Jaren took a seat by the door. His mind kept trying to understand what had happened over the past few days, but it felt like trying to assemble a large puzzle with only a handful of pieces—and those pieces didn't even seem like they were from the same puzzle. Jaren shook his head, opened the book Hairth had given him, and began reading.

In this work I present the fundamentals of radiant materials, or sources, as I have determined them from my twenty years of exploration and examination together with one Hairth of Crotsdum. I have divided the work up into a number of sections. The first deals with the history of my explorations and the manner in which I came into contact with each of the radiant materials. The second gives a summary of the nature of radiant materials—that is, why they are different from seemingly identical materials that have no special energy. The third examines the five radiant energies that have been identified thus far. The fourth is a catchall that contains cautions for interacting with sources, methods identified for testing materials, and potential approaches for practical uses of sources.

Jaren was intrigued by the book, though Enrich understated the dangers of radiant materials. "Care must be taken when strong sources are brought in close proximity with one another, as doing so may greatly amplify the release of energy." Jaren reread the statement as he recalled the intense heat of the fireball that had injured so many in the research facility. "... greatly amplify..." indeed! Jaren also bristled at the off-handed discarding of his closely held beliefs. "Those who view radiance as evil are either ignorant or dim witted." And "Despite what the bumpkin may say, one should expect no more corruption of moral values or mental capacity by handling radiant materials than he should from handling other forms of soil, stone and ore." Jaren scowled. It had taken well over a year for Jaren to realize that being around radiant material or even handling it is not what corrupts Light- Twisters, but rather controlling the energy. Even though he had already come to those conclusions himself, it was still insulting to have someone else—even someone dead—mock him for his formerly held beliefs. Those feelings, however, soon gave way to the pleasure of satisfying curiosity. After fifty pages, Jaren felt like he was an expert on radiant materials, and he was barely halfway through, though he did wonder about the author's honesty given the fantastic beasts he described encountering or hearing of.

"Jaren," Ruth's gravelly voice sounded from the doorway, "he's ready for you."

Chapter 4

Facing Danger

Hairth stood behind his desk, wearing a wide smile that would have been inviting without the healing burns across his cheek and forehead. He motioned Jaren toward a seat.

"Jaren, I've got a few questions for you, and then there's someone I would like you to meet." Hairth sat down, resting his clasped hands on his desk.

"What do you remember about the accident?"

Jaren recounted it as best he could, wondering why Hairth asked, since he had been there himself. He ended with, "I didn't see Jolinda at the clinic. Is she alright?"

Hairth shook his head. "We're not sure if she'll survive. They had to remove her hands—what was left of them—and most of her body was burned, too. Several assistants are treating her in her own home because she needs so much more attention."

Jaren stared in disbelief. How did he escape injury?

"Do you remember anything else? Like, right before you passed out?"

Jaren shifted uncomfortably in his seat. Hairth was always imposing, but with patches of skin peeling off his face and only one eyebrow, he was intimidating.

"Sir, I...don't know what else to tell you." Jaren shrugged. "Everyone became quiet, there was that deep rumbling, and strange lights. Then everything went black."

"Yes, but what was going on inside of you?"

Jaren opened his mouth to speak but was not sure what to say. He wished he had more of the root Haerlee had given him for his head. The memory of the oppressive feeling returned, and as if the thought summoned it, the feeling, though weaker, also returned.

"He's asking how you felt, boy." An ice-cold voice sounded from across the room. Jaren knocked his chair over as he jumped to his feet in surprise. Hairth calmly turned toward an empty chair in a corner of the room. Like a solidifying shadow, a tall, skinny man rose from the chair.

"Did your bowels burn? Did your bones ache? Did your mouth water? Did you taste sulfur? How did you feel?"

The man wore a long, dark robe that trailed behind him as he walked toward Jaren. His face was pale. Thin, black eyebrows overhung deep recessed eyes. A long, narrow nose projected sharply from the face and hooked down, giving the distinct appearance of a vulture's beak. Wide sleeves concealed his hands, and an unworn hood added substance to otherwise weak shoulders.

Frozen by his shocking appearance, Jaren did not move as the man grasped his chin with long, narrow fingers and drew Jaren's face close to his own.

"So, boy, how did you feel?" His breath was foul.

"I ... ," Jaren stammered, summoning the control to pull away from the man.

"Joans," Hairth said in a firm voice.

Joans scowled but returned to his seat. Jaren had to pull his eyes from the vulture-like Joans as Hairth began to speak, excitement returning to his voice.

"When I saw that first bright pulse, I knew something was terribly wrong. Heat and cold source don't make light, they change the air." Hairth balled his fists and struck the ring on his right-hand middle finger against the ring on his left-hand ring finger. A sharp crack sounded through the room and then a breeze rushed over Jaren. "Someone replaced the cold source with hot—whether by accident or intentionally. I should have noticed."

Joans snorted at this comment. Then, apparently alarmed by his own outburst, he cleared his throat and swallowed. Hairth ignored him.

"Like everyone else, I covered my eyes and turned away from the light. I knew I was a dead man. My life has passed before my eyes so often, that it doesn't happen anymore. Instead, I did envision Deaelestran sifting through the ashes trying to determine how many there were among the dead. But it didn't happen." Hairth paused, and with a sharp intake of breath said, "What I saw instead was incredible. Even now, I can hardly believe it."

"Nor can I," Joans muttered, but loud enough for Jaren to hear.

A twitch in Hairth's eyes said he had heard Joans, too. He continued.

"A ball of...fire...swirled where the fixture had been. There were no flames, though, just spinning red and yellow light. The fire seemed contained like it was within a glass ball. I reached my hand toward it, but only felt small amounts of heat coming off it like little puffs. I looked around the room wondering if I had died, but, because I was not buried, that I was stuck on my journey—stuck in the moment that I had died. Some near me were hurt, but many were fine. Slowly, the shouting stopped. The room went silent except for the moaning of the few who were hurt. Everyone had turned to look at the fire—everyone, that is, except you." With these words, Hairth's unwavering gaze made Jaren squirm in discomfort. "So, Jaren, I ask again, how did you feel?"

That pressure —the weight sat solidly in Jaren's memory, but he wasn't sure how to describe it. He tried anyway.

"Scared...burdened...heavy."

"Scared?"

"Yes...scared."

"Burdened? Heavy?" Hairth repeated but looking to Joans instead of Jaren.

Joans snorted. "Yes, of course 'scared,'" he said, imitating Hairth's voice. "Heavy and burdened for sure. You and your people think you know so much about radiance, but you know less than fish know about air."

Joans stood and began quickly pacing. His hands were wrapped behind him, his head down—almost as if he were talking more to himself than someone else in the room.

"Feelings. Feelings indeed. Oh, no you are right, it is by feelings. But very different kinds of feelings. Certainly, food is food. But there's a difference between a pastry and a crust. A tender, seasoned loin and an old fish. A well-aged wine and a draft from a chamber pot."

Joans was almost shouting by the end of this rant, and spittle flew across the room as he said "pot." Then, quite unexpectedly, Joans lunged toward Jaren and wrapped his icy fingers around Jaren's chin again, lifting his face so Jaren looked into his gray eyes. He tightened his grip and Jaren opened his mouth to alleviate the pain. Unfortunately, this just allowed Joans more leverage and he squeezed harder, cutting the inside of Jaren's cheek against his open teeth.

"Are you scared now, boy?" he whispered in Jaren's face.

"Joans!" Hairth called from behind the desk. Jaren tried to strike at the man, but something was holding his arms to his sides as if the air were stone.

"Joans, don't make me..." Hairth said more, but all Jaren's attention was focused on Joans' other hand.

A small orb of fire had appeared, exactly as Hairth had described it, pulsating and swirling above Joans' hand. He brought it toward Jaren's face. Jaren desperately pulled back, but the air was solid again.

In a calm, emotionless voice, Joans asked, "Are you scared now?"

And Jaren was. Joans brought the orb closer. It burned Jaren's face. Panic started to overwhelm him, the burden intensified, and the heat diminished. Jaren watched as the side of the ball facing Jaren flattened, and then drifted away from Jaren's face. Joans dropped his hand and the orb shot away from Jaren, disappearing as it went until it vanished before running into the wall.

"Bones of *Mah'van*," Hairth muttered, collapsing into his seat.

"That is not fear, my boy. That is fire," Joans said, as he turned and walked back to his seat as if nothing unusual had happened.

When he sat, he smiled—a real, kindly smile, and asked, "Now, do you taste anything, smell anything, feel or see anything that is unusual?"

In confusion, Jaren looked at Hairth, who was staring at Jaren, with wide-eyed anticipation. Jaren found himself rubbing the scars on his wrists and stopped. He had been released from his invisible bonds. Hairth nodded, indicating that Jaren should answer the question.

"I...felt heavy," Jaren stammered, opening and closing his mouth trying to work away the pain. He could taste blood from his cheeks but was there something more?

"Kago root?"

Joans laughed. "Ah, spice...how quaint. The heaviness comes with all uses, but spice for heat is funny. It will go away as soon as your minds understand."

Jaren, still confused, looked once again to Hairth for clarification. He sat perched on the edge of his seat.

"In the research shop, when you stopped whimpering, the orb began growing and shrinking. Puffs of heat would come off with each cycle. Then, when you uncovered your face and turned to look, the orb dissolved, as if the glass ball had shattered. The heat burst out and burned those of us that were close by. As I turned, I saw you hit the ground."

Hairth looked at Jaren expectantly, his eyes bright. But Jaren didn't understand.

"Don't you see?" Hairth asked, jumping to his feet.

Joans scoffed, "Of course he doesn't."

"You're a *Light-Twister!*" Hairth almost shouted.

Jaren gaped. Hairth beamed. Joans studied his fingernails. Dust motes in the air sparkled against the dark wood paneling, as daylight poured in through the window, warming Jaren's segg. Despite the warm heat, he felt cold inside. It could not be true.

Hairth and Joans were speaking, but Jaren couldn't process what they were saying. He just kept hearing "You're a *Light-Twister!*" over and over

Hairth clapped his hands together and said, "Then it's settled!" He was beaming at Joans now, and Joans wore a crooked smile. His eyes, partially obscured by the shadow of his prominent brow, focused on Jaren like a falcon on a rabbit.

"Jaren, think how you'll be able to help Freysdal as a trained Light-Twister."

Hairth rubbed his hands, clinking his rings together.

"You will start training with Joans right away. With any luck, you'll be able to help defend Freysdal before my enemies strike."

Joans broke his gaze at Jaren to roll his eyes at Hairth. "Don't get your hopes up. Not all lumps of clay can be turned into masterpieces. Some are only fit for chamber pots."

"I'll take whatever I can get—a chamber pot is better than nothing when you need a vessel. Until we know which it is, I'm hoping for the finest porcelain."

"Porcelain, indeed. In that case, I'll keep the temperatures high." Joans' lips couldn't decide between a wicked smile and a frown. "Come with me, boy."

Joans turned from Hairth's desk and walked out of the office.

Chapter 5

Making Sense of It

Sunlight blinded Jaren, and a warm breeze made sweat bead on his forehead, but he just shivered. He followed as Joans hurried down the street. This had to be a mistake.

Jaren made no effort to catch up, and Joans didn't slow. In fact, Joans never even glanced back. Jaren considered fleeing, but where would he go? Escaped thralls were executed. Plus, Hairth was negotiating to purchase his recently found sisters. If he left, he'd never see them again.

People stared as they passed Joans in his trailing dark robe. Jaren's spine tingled, like when he saw a bad wound, as he realized Joans' robe never touched the red ground. Oh, brittle bones! Jaren couldn't possibly be a Light-Twister.

They passed out of the town and headed up toward the research facility. Joans marched right past the guards. For a wonder, they parted, giving him a wide berth, but otherwise ignored him. They did nod to Jaren, though. He didn't offer a warrant, and they didn't ask for one.

The familiar stench of the research facility was overshadowed by the heavy smell of wood smoke. The damage jumped out at Jaren as soon as he passed through the doors. Black soot stained the ceiling in a large, jagged circle above where the accident happened. The tall columns that supported the ceiling were scorched on one side, as if the builders had used logs that had been lying across a fire. There was also a change in the atmosphere—people wore gloves and leather aprons—they moved more slowly and with more care.

Jaren stopped mid-stride and blinked in surprise. Tobie was there, staring, with eyes slightly too far apart, in puzzlement as

Joans walked past. Her curly hair had been pulled back and was tied in a bushy tail with a red ribbon.

"Who is that?" and then with incredulity, "Is his robe floating?"

Jaren tried to say something, but nothing came out. What could he say? He turned to follow after Joans.

"Hey!" She followed after him, and tugged at his segg. "You don't have to be rude. Your file says you have a pleasant disposition, I'm going to have to tell them you've changed since your last update."

The irony of the statement hit him, and Jaren let out a bitter laugh. If she knew what else they'd have to change in his file, she wouldn't want to be anywhere near him. He *was* being rude, though. Could two uses of radiance have changed him already?

Jaren stopped, and Tobie ran into him. The answer hit him, and everything became clear. He *hadn't* used radiance! What happened in the office was a trick. Sudden relief settled on Jaren as everything fell into place. Hairth knew that his enemies were spying on him. He brought Joans in and was using Jaren as a distraction while he executed some other plan to protect Freysdal. It all made sense. Jaren's involvement was just a fortuitous coincidence that Hairth was weaving into his plan.

"Are you alright?"

Jaren smiled.

"Better than you can imagine."

Joans had turned down one of the aisles, and Jaren resumed walking. Tobie kept up with him.

"Good. You just looked a little...I don't know...concerned." She only paused a second before asking, "Who is that guy you're following?"

"His name is Joans."

Tobie stopped and grabbed a handful of Jaren's segg. In a loud whisper she asked, "Artor Joans? Do you have any idea who he is?"

Hairth's big distraction, Jaren thought. Joans had stopped at a long table and was handing a rolled parchment to a Yellow. Would it ruin Hairth's plans if he told Tobie about them? He decided it might.

"Not really."

"Me neither, but he's *somebody*."

"What do you mean?" Jaren turned to Tobie.

"His file is enormous, but it's restricted."

"Restricted?"

"Yes, no one is allowed to look at his file."

"No one? Then why have a file for him, and how do you know it's enormous?"

"Obviously some people can look at his file. I was told to review everyone's file except the restricted files, and his was one of the largest."

Jaren shrugged.

"It's just that..." she shrugged, too, and Jaren noticed her segg was too big which made her look smaller than she actually was, "...well, I don't like mysteries. I've been able to learn about most of the people with restricted files—the Associates, of course, Prestare of House Krandor, Natalia Estareet, Dristan of Pinnutuck—but no one talks about Artor Joans. *No one*." She tried to put weight into the words with the look she gave Jaren, and then said, "And now I find you trailing behind him. What's going on?"

He knew why Joans' file would be restricted, but the words "Light-Twister" would fit on a single sheet of paper. What else was in there?

"I don't know. Hairth asked me to be Joans' assistant." There, that seemed like a good story.

The Yellow returned pushing a cart stacked with five dull metals boxes. The man strained as he lifted one onto the table. He opened the lid and withdrew a grayish ball that resembled the source that caused the accident. Joans plucked it out of the man's hand and cackled. The Yellow recoiled, as did Jaren and Tobie. Joans placed the ball in his robe and gestured impatiently at the other boxes. The man retrieved the second box.

"Ploomun boxes?" Tobie asked, more to herself than to Jaren. "They stop the energy from strong sources."

Jaren nodded. He had just read about ploomun—a thin sheet of it reduced the energy passing through it, and a thick enough plate could completely stop it.

"How do you know about ploomun?" Jaren asked, trying not to show his repulsion at Joans greedily snatching another source.

"'Fundamentals of Radiant Materials' under the heading 'Potential Approaches for Practical Uses' under the subheading 'Transportation Safety.' On the second and third pages of that subheading, Derek Enrich addresses the danger of transporting sources. An accident led him to search for a material that could interfere with or contain radiant energy."

Jaren turned back to Tobie. Her oversized segg with tight blue ropes gave a false impression of a waist. She didn't talk like a little girl. But she was.

"A donkey pulling a cart laden with sources was startled, and the cart overturned. The sources tumbled together and caused a fireball that consumed the cart, the donkey and the man driving it. Enrich and those further from the cart were severely burned. Many of those who were closer died, and were buried—at least, what was left of them was."

Jaren imagined a pulsating ball of fire, like the one on Joans' hand, large enough to consume a cart and its donkey and shuddered. He looked at the blackened columns and thanked

Hel'dig for his luck. No, not luck. Joans must have been there, too, to stop the accident from being worse. Why hadn't he stopped it completely? Maybe if he had, the ruse wouldn't work.

"He's a Light-Twister," Tobie said, and clapped her hand over her own mouth. Then, speaking to Jaren through spread fingers, "You have to tell me what you learn."

Jaren just said, "I've got to go."

Joans swept by as if he and Tobie weren't even there. Jaren followed after him, but Tobie didn't move.

Chapter 6

Training in a Cabin

Joans led Jaren further up the mountainside, weaving through trees like he knew where he was going. The view of Freysdal was soon blocked by pine needles, and the smell of sap replaced the acrid odors of the research facility. Jaren mentally rehearsed how he would explain that he had figured out the plan and was willing to help.

The slope leveled out and a clearing in the trees revealed a wood frame house. The thatch roof was old and gray, compacted to the point where Jaren doubted it kept rain out—not that it rained often in Freysdal. Tall grass and weeds filled what once might have been a small yard.

Joans stopped at the edge of the clearing. He wiped sweat from his forehead through his stringy, thinning black hair, and muttered, "I would have expected him to keep it up."

A quiet sound, like a stick swishing through the air, pulled Jaren's attention to the tall grass. It was falling as if a wide scythe was being thrust through it. The cut grass rolled up, flew over the house and unrolled in an even layer over the old thatch. Joans nodded and walked forward. Jaren followed, feeling both dismayed and impressed by Joans' use of radiance.

The front door swung open of its own accord, though it creaked loudly in surprise. Inside, dust, illuminated by the sudden appearance of a sphere of white light, floated in the air, then froze. It swirled, gathered into a small, humming whirlwind and twisted past Jaren, pulling at his segg. It slipped out the front door and collapsed in the freshly cut yard.

Joans patted the sources bulging in his robes, "Yes, these will work nicely." Pointing to a chair, he commanded, "Sit."

Jaren moved to the chair.

"Joans, sir, I've figured out what's going on."

"What are you talking about?"

"I know I'm not a Light-Twister, and..."

"Pah! Of course, you're not, you clay-eating mucker," Joans interrupted.

"Yes, sir. I'm happy to play my part in Hairth's ruse."

"Ruse?" Joans lifted his eyebrows. "What do you mean, ruse?"

"You know, sir, pretending I'm a Light-Twister."

"No one's pretending you're a Light-Twister, boy, but you do have the potential to become one. How much potential you've got is yet to be determined. Hairth might try a ruse if you are as weak as I suspect, but for now, I will teach you as much as you can learn, as fast as you can learn it."

The crooked smile returned. Jaren's stomach sank. His relief disappeared—swirling out the door as the dust had. He collapsed on the seat and put his head in his hands.

"What kind of response is that? Do you have any idea what radiance can do for you?"

Jaren tried to ignore the horrible thoughts about what light-twisting would do to him. A firm pressure on his chin lifted his head. Joans was leaning forward, skeletal fingers clasped behind his back, staring directly into Jaren's eyes.

"Radiance will change your life."

Jaren pulled his head back and scowled, repulsed by the thought of radiance touching him again. Joans straightened and scowled in reply.

"What do you know of radiance?" There was an edge in his voice.

The question was the same as Hairth had asked. Jaren knew more this time. He tried to keep sullenness out of his voice but didn't manage it well.

"Radiance is power released from sources of light, bio, heat, cold, and force."

"You were doing so well when you started, but then you just kept talking." The edge in his voice had become anger. "Radiance is power," Joans said. "Repeat it."

Jaren stayed silent. A force as hard as stone moved his lips and tongue, and bands crushed his chest, squeezing air past his vocal cords, making him screech out an almost unintelligible, "Radiance is power."

"Radiance is power, boy, power!" Joans repeated.

Jaren stared in horror. Had that really just happened? He touched his lips to see if they were bleeding.

"Energy comes from these," five metallic balls floated out of Joans' robes, "Radiance is not just energy, though, it's the ability to control that energy. Radiance is power to force nature to do *your* will. Radiance is power to force *people* to do *your* will. Radiance is power. Without it, Light-Twisters are no more than ordinary people."

Jaren's heart raced in fear as he processed Joans' words.

"Sources offer the powers of heat, cold, light, force, and bio." As he spoke, waves of heat and cold passed over Jaren. A sheet of blue light flickered into and then out of existence, leaving a Joans-shaped after-image in Jaren's eyes. A push, like a strong wind without the wind, tipped Jaren back in his seat. Each of the four experiences was both startling and revolting, but the fifth was astounding. The residual pain in Jaren's lips and throat vanished, as did a headache he'd grown accustomed to.

"The limit to their combinations is unknowable." Flakes of gray materialized in mid-air, then gathered into a small, dusty ball. The ball congealed into clay. The clay spun, opened up, and smoothed into a thumb-sized vessel. Thin lines, like spider silk, peeled off the spinning vessel, leaving intricate stylizations of the word "power" etched into the surface. The free-floating lines twisted into a thin, solid curve which attached itself to the edge of the vessel, forming the handle of a tiny teacup. A brief wave of heat pushed past Jaren and a puff of steam surrounded the cup. When it cleared, the teacup had turned white. Then, colors swirled through the cup—blues and reds, peach and gold—until they settled, filling the etching in an elaborate design. It was the most impressive piece of art Jaren had ever seen.

"Beauty can be created from nothing...and can be destroyed just as spectacularly."

With a sharp clink the cup broke apart and large gaps replaced the etching lines. The pieces began to glow, then flew through the open window and slammed into a tree. An oppressive burden struck Jaren right before an explosion shook the small house. Echoes reverberated across the valley. When the dust settled, Jaren could see a gaping, charred hole, the size of a head, through the center of the tree. The smoking trunk and scattered chunks of burning wood brought a terrible admiration to Jaren's heart.

With that kind of power, he could return home with his sisters. No one could challenge him. Jaren immediately felt disgust at the thoughts. His sisters wouldn't go with a Light-Twister—especially not once the radiance made him cruel.

Joans never varied from his deliberate pacing, not even when the blast shook the house.

"Very few can control the power of radiance, but those few are always granted other talents as well. We begin our training with the first talent. A Light-Twister can manage multiple thoughts simultaneously. To develop this skill, we'll start with simple exercises. First, we'll tie mental to physical and learn to move our body parts independently. The many minds of..."

Joans droned on, and Jaren tried to sort through his thoughts—one at a time. Hairth and Joans were mistaken. He *could not* control radiance. But what should he do? If he trained hard with Joans, but was never able to control radiance, then

Joans and Hairth would have to admit that he was not a Light-Twister. On the other hand, what if even small exposures to light-twisting could corrupt him? Part of his mind shouted at him to resist every effort to train, but a quieter part whispered that he could do incredible things with the power Joans had just displayed.

Pain seared Jaren's back and flooded his mind with memories of being whipped. He jerked forward, away from the pain, and twisted to look behind him. No one was there.

"Did you do that?" he demanded of Joans.

Joans glanced at Jaren as if only remembering he was there. Another stripe slashed across his back. Jaren shouted and staggered forward. He pushed down memories of his captivity, but the pain brought them close to the surface.

"Stop it!" Jaren shouted.

More strokes followed. Jaren tried to run but was caught in thick air. Stroke after stroke came, and the memories broke through just as the tears did. Images of stocky men in leather armor laughing as they whipped. Heavy manacles offering the only protection from the biting stripes, but also chafing his wrists and ankles.

"Stop it, please!" Jaren pled between sobs, hanging limply in the air, "Oh, *Mah'van*, please stop."

It stopped. The air released Jaren and he collapsed to the ground, the tears still streaming.

"Get up!" Joans ordered.

Jaren lifted himself off the rough floor and stood before Joans, feeling as broken as he was the day he had been sold.

"When I speak, you will listen. This is your only warning. Next time you will be punished."

If Jaren weren't already in so much pain, he could have kicked himself. The peace of Freysdal had settled so thoroughly in Jaren's heart that he had forgotten that to outsiders he was just a thrall. Joans was not of Freysdal, and he was a Light-Twister whose radiance use had corrupted him.

"I hate to use pain when teaching. Let's start over." A cool wave passed over Jaren's body and the pain disappeared.

"Sit."

Jaren carefully took his seat, surprised when there was no tenderness. He gripped his knees to stop them from shaking. He took deep breaths. His heart slowed and he gradually began to feel steady again.

"Good. Good. As I was saying, we'll start simply. First, we learn the pointer."

Joans took Jaren through a series of increasingly complex exercises, starting with moving the index finger of each hand in a specific, but different, way. Jaren kept his humiliation and anger in check, trying to focus completely on the imbecilic exercises Joans demonstrated. Once Jaren mastered the first, Joans added a third finger with a new movement, then a fourth. He included wrist and ankle movement. Jaren began struggling with the addition of the wrist movement and could not manage to add his ankle without losing control of one of his fingers.

"Well, at least you're not totally incompetent," Joans commented. "Your goal is to be able to control every joint and every muscle independently—something someone of your talent may never quite accomplish, but even the weakest can improve on what they've been given."

Joans repeated the exercise, mocking Jaren for each mistake, but Jaren was able to add wrist, ankle, and eyebrows by the time they stopped. Jaren did exactly as he was told, never more, and channeled his anger, like he had so many times before, toward his hatred of Thralldom.

"Developing physical control will help you in forming. Eventually, lumps, streams, shells, and all forms of energy will feel like extensions of your body. Until then, you practice with the body you have. Our next exercise will help develop your mental abilities so you can design and direct your work. Can you read?"

Jaren nodded, and in response, Joans again forced air out of his lungs, and made him say, "Yes!"

"Can you do arithmetic?"

"Yes," Jaren said through clenched teeth.

"Prove it." Joans withdrew from his robe a small book and handed it to Jaren. "Open up to any page and read." Jaren obeyed.

"Braces can increase the strength by transferring the load to the various structure elements."

"Now, count the vowels and announce the sum every four words...without slowing."

". . . but if misplaced, the six load may be transferred seven to weaker elements, thus eight weakening the entire construction twelve."

Jaren continued reading. Joans made the tasks more complex—summing words, counting the consonants, multiplying the consonants by the vowels in each word, then summing those results. Jaren was surprised that he rarely made a mistake, but Joans acted like each one was a huge embarrassment. After what felt like hours of mocking, Joans nodded and told him to stop.

"You are in an interesting position," Joans said, replacing the berating tone with a gentle lecturing voice. "Most Light-Twisters are discovered when they see sources. They then need to be trained to control the energy. You, however, have already controlled energy, in a very crude fashion. However, you seem completely blind to it."

Jaren shook his head in frustration "I'm not a Light-Twister."

Joans' boisterous laughter made Jaren wince. "You've just done exercises only a Light-Twister can. If the two times you've avoided radiant damage were flukes, then you are the most incredible non-Light-Twister ever, and I'll eat a pile of rocks. No, you can learn to control radiance, and, as I was saying, the training is backward from normal. We need to help you learn to see, something that I have never heard of being done before, but..." Joans' finger tapped his chin, "...it shouldn't be too difficult."

Jaren felt exhausted. He suppressed a sigh and looked out the window.

"You felt the burden, an oppressive feeling, at both the accident and in Hairth's office?"

Jaren nodded to the open window, then quickly answered vocally.

"Have you felt it at all during training here?"

Another involuntary nod followed by a simple, "Yes."

"When?"

"When you destroyed the tree."

"Not when I cut the grass or made the cup? No? Maybe an affinity for heat."

He held up a source in front of Jaren's face and explained, "This is an extremely refined heat source—just short of the size for self-folding."

Self-folding?

"I can sense the source. It's like a bright lightball that I see without my eyes. Now, if I gather the energy and fold it back onto the source, compressing it over and again, the source becomes brighter. Can you see anything now?"

Jaren looked around but couldn't see anything out of the ordinary.

"Goat-brained boy. Not with your eyes, you must sense it. Feel for the burden."

Jaren sighed. He did not want to "feel" for it. He did not want to be a Light-Twister. However, he also did not want to be beat by Joans again. So, Jaren took a deep breath and paid special attention to what he was feeling.

He closed his eyes, and considered his feet on the rough wooden ground, his bottom in the seat, and his back on the chair. He considered memories of the pain he felt moments earlier but felt no longer. He felt the scratchy segg against his skin, the cool air from the window and the heat from the sun-warmed roof. He let himself feel the worry about the day's revelations, the anxiety about his proximity to Joans. He felt his exhaustion compete with his fury at being demeaned by Joans, and the seething, barely-suppressed rage at those who had captured him. He felt the continued excitement at the prospect of seeing his sisters after so many years. But there was no oppression, no weight on his mind or heart. He shook his head and opened his eyes.

"Nothing? I've accumulated so much heat that I could melt a stone the size of a horse. Let's try this."

Jaren started when a translucent, golden glowing sphere, slightly larger than a man's head, appeared in the air.

"I can see it!" Jaren shouted in excitement, simultaneously repulsed by his own excitement.

"Of course, you can, flea brain. I'm containing all of the heat energy, but I've filled the heat with a bit of light, so you can see it with your eyes." Jaren stood to watch as the ball floated out of the window, stretched end-to-end to form a thick rod a pace long before disappearing into the smoldering tree trunk.

Jaren's breath caught. The oppression struck him violently, like someone kicking him right in the center of the chest. The trunk flashed impossibly bright, and Jaren stumbled back against the wall opposite the window. The house moaned. A roar like the mountains crumbling into the valley shook the air. Jaren staggered back to the window. The oppression was gone, replaced by incredulity and pain in his back from striking the wall. The smoldering trunk was no more. In its place was a crater two paces wide and one pace deep. The surface of the crater was smooth, like river stone. For ten paces in every direction from the crater, the trees of the forest lay down on the ground like weeds pushed over by a swollen river after a heavy rain—in every direction, that is, except for toward the house. From the crater to the house, the foliage was undamaged. If that protective region was not there, Jaren was certain, the house would be a pile of rubble, with him and Joans on the bottom.

"Very good," Joans said. "I presume you felt the burden?"

Jaren nodded, still taking in the damage wrought. The sound of rain pounding the thatch filled the house, but it wasn't water that was falling from the sky. Pieces of earth and tree were plummeting from above.

Joans chuckled. "Yes, you did well deflecting that energy—taking control right as I released it. If you hadn't, we'd be in pretty bad shape."

"What? I saved us?"

"Don't be a fool. I had defenses ready to protect myself, but I didn't need them."

"How can I do something without knowing what I'm doing?"

"I'm not sure. How does the Jay-hawk know to copy the Jay's call? How does the stone striper know how to build a nest? So, how do you feel now? Has something changed?"

Jaren rubbed his chest. The pain was not physical, but there was something that hurt inside him—like the hollowness when his parents died or when his brother Ben never came home.

"Yes, that's it," Joans said, nodding toward Jaren's chest.

"What you're feeling is the strain of controlling energy. You directed a very large amount, like deflecting a barrel of water rolling down a hill. It's either the heart or the head that feels it, sometimes both. Now, do you see anything? Can you sense the power? Feel with the pain in your chest."

Jaren tried.

"It feels like the pain is...stiffening."

"Good. Now, search outward, with that stiffness in mind."

Jaren took that stiffened pain and stretched it forward, like stretching his legs after too many deliveries. He pushed outward. The tension increased as the pain expanded around him.

"I can feel something. It's like it gives way when I push it."

The experience was indescribable, and curiosity drove him to reach further, wider, feeling through the entire room. His head started to ache, but he kept reaching. Something near the ceiling quivered as he pressed up against it. It slipped away from him, like flotsam sliding past a cupped hand in water. Five rigid masses all but immovable rested on Joans.

"That's it. Now, open your eyes."

Jaren hadn't even realized that he had closed them. He opened them and marveled at what he...saw. In truth, he didn't see anything different about the room. The stiffness in his heart somehow created an additional awareness that overlaid everything he could see. When he closed his eyes again, it became a feeling again.

"You have found your radiance-sight—it is like sight or taste or touch, but it detects radiant energy. Right now, your mind is unable to process it entirely, so it is trying to give you understanding with the abilities it knows. With time, it will become distinct."

Jaren opened his eyes and stared at the light in the ceiling. He could see the white light with his eyes and could see and feel something else in the same place. A small string of the same stuff led down to Joans' robe. Jaren gasped. The five sources Joans carried were like strange sunlight shining through the woolen cloth. Joans was smiling at him, but it wasn't the oily, creepy smile that Joans had displayed earlier.

The reality of the smile stung Jaren more than the whipping ever could. His bruised heart sank. His mouth felt full of sawdust, and he wasn't sure he could stand. Sitting heavily, Jaren dropped his head in his hands. It couldn't be.

"It is quite a lot to take in in one afternoon. Let's be done for today. I will see you here, tomorrow, right after third bell. You sit there and relax as long as you need..." Joans fell silent, then walked over and awkwardly patted Jaren on the shoulder on his way out. Jaren twitched at the touch.

The lightball blinked out. Tears ran down Jaren's face. With the sources gone, Jaren could tell himself he hadn't "seen" anything, but he knew it was a lie—and he knew what he was destined to become. Joans' volatile behavior was like a prophecy of his own future. Kindness was foreign to Joans. He had mercilessly beaten Jaren mere hours ago. True, he had healed him as well, but that didn't erase the memory of the pain.

Returning anger displaced sorrow, and a small, quiet part of Jaren watched as the rest of him imagined using power like Joans' for revenge.

"Is this who I am?" the small part asked through the tears.

Chapter 7

Moving Out

Shadows stretched down the side of the valley when Jaren finally left the abandoned house. He looked away from the crater as he climbed over the trees lying in his path. The smell of burnt pine still filled the air. The fading light and growing shadows obscured the path, but he knew, if he kept moving downward, he'd eventually reach Freysdal.

Jaren carried a profound loneliness, heavier than any stone, down the mountainside. He hoped, as he stepped out of the forest, that the weight would be lifted, taken by the peace of Freysdal. A part of him knew it was foolish to hope, but even that doubting part was surprised by what happened.

"Broken bones," Jaren muttered in shock.

The darkness settling across Freysdal was punctured by thousands of pinpricks of unholy light. The bluish white of lightballs sitting on night posts and betopping torches reached his eyes, but his heart saw twisted light. Unnaturally, it shone through solid walls and people, like bright sunlight through a bedsheet hung out to dry, even when Jaren closed his eyes.

In somber reflection after Joans' departure, Jaren had sought to explain what he'd experienced. He had clung to one possibility—that Joans was responsible for everything. He caused pain and healed it, could he not also cause the "burden" and remove it? Joans could have manufactured everything to continue the ruse. At the edge of the forest, however, the light that only his heart could see pierced his remaining hope.

With head hung down, Jaren descended the hill, past the research facility which looked like a smoldering bonfire of radiant energy. Sources shone through walls and roof. People passing between him and sources cast peculiar shadows. It was disturbing, so Jaren turned away and kept walking. Except, turning away did no good. He could still "see" it, even from behind.

He clenched his jaw. It was not fair—hadn't he suffered enough for one lifetime? He reached out and shoved the energy away. The stiffness is his chest rang like a bell in response, and he gasped. The ringing moved up into his head, a reverberating headache that beat against his heart. The pain slowly subsided.

The mountain's shadow was crawling across Freysdal. Jaren passed the dining facility. He had no appetite and no desire to interact with people. He recognized an Arentash Blue-green, Youlanie, coming his way. She often smiled at Jaren when they crossed paths which always made him smile, even if only at his feet. This time, though, her smile seemed malevolent, illuminated as it was by a weak source within a necklace she wore. Jaren grimaced and turned down a side street.

He walked by more people he recognized, but, praise *Hel'dig*, he kept his head down, and no one noticed him. They were all just going about their lives, oblivious to the anguish Jaren was feeling.

He passed a pair of Reds staring at the mountainside with puzzled expressions, squinting against the shadow that covered the valley. They were not the first he'd seen looking that way. Jaren paused to look for himself, but just as quickly turned away.

"It just appeared, right after that thunder."

"Buildings don't just appear. It must have been there before."

"Have you ever noticed a house there before?"

"Well, no…"

The older of the two men locked eyes with Jaren. He dropped his gaze and hurried past. Jaren couldn't help but feel like everyone he passed eyed him with suspicion. He hurried the rest of the way to the barracks but pulled up short when he reached his room.

"Where's my stuff?" Jaren asked in surprise.

"It's about time," an irritated voice answered.

Jaren turned to see a boy near his same age with curly brown hair on the next trunk over. Red marks appeared on his cheeks as he lifted his head from his hands. He cleared his throat, stood and stretched in an exaggerated fashion, like he was trying to make sure Jaren knew how long he'd been waiting.

"Where's my stuff?" Jaren repeated.

"That empty chest? It's in my room. They probably threw your pallet away. Come on. Dinner's getting cold." The boy started walking, but Jaren grabbed his arm.

"Wait. What?"

The boy stopped and looked at Jaren. "You are Jaren, aren't you?"

"Yes, but..." The confusion must have shown on Jaren's face.

"You're kidding, right? They didn't even tell you? This is rich. Best week of my life. First, two girls show up—don't get me wrong, I like girls—but neither seems quite right in the head. Then Mom moves them into the spare room and tells me some stranger is moving into my room." The boy turned and walked toward the door. "Come on. You're moving in with me."

Worst week of *his* life? Jaren just stood there, but when the boy stepped out of the door, Jaren realized he had no clean clothes and nowhere to sleep. He ran after him.

He followed the boy as he made his way toward the back of Freysdal, but he didn't try to catch up. He slowed as he passed the last of the buildings that made up Freysdal proper. Everything further up the valley was still Freysdal, but it was mostly farms and families.

The entire valley was in shadow. The vast openness made Jaren feel a little tense. A few houses dotted the gentle slope, illuminated by the glaring light and surreal glow of lightballs. He followed the boy up the dirt road and watched as he walked into a house just off the road.

As Jaren approached the house, he could smell the roasting meat and vegetables and could hear talking. The smells should have been appetizing, but they made his stomach turn. He waved his hand through the energy that shone through the walls. It cast a shadow on his chest, like it was sunlight coming in through a window. There were several lightballs in the house, and something odd. It looked as if they had two plates of weak source slightly overlapping each other. Jaren couldn't understand what they were for. He paused, staring at the plates, and was struck by the door swinging open.

"Watch it!" the boy said. He sounded even more sour than at the barracks. Thrusting a bucket into Jaren's hand, he said, "If you're going to share my room, you can share my chores, too."

Jaren followed him to the river and filled his bucket. He had so many questions running through his mind that he briefly forgot the dreadful pit that had settled in his stomach. As soon as he realized he wasn't thinking about being a Light-Twister, he started thinking about it again.

"Kehvun," the boy said.

"What?" Jaren asked.

"Kehvun. My name is Kehvun." He still sounded irritated, but some of the edge had gone from his voice.

Jaren poured his bucket of water into the barrel on the porch and followed Kehvun back down to the river.

"Mom says that you're a 'good boy.'" His voice went high to impersonate his mom, "But let's get something clear right up front. They are my parents. It's my house. I may have to share my room with you, but nothing else. You don't touch my stuff, and I won't touch yours. You got it?"

The edge had slowly returned as he got on a roll.

"Yeah. I got it," Jaren replied, an edge entering his own voice.

"Good. You stay out of my life, and I'll leave you to your sisters."

Jaren stopped, sloshing water on his legs in the process.

"What did you say?"

Kehvun stopped, too.

"I said, you stay out of my life."

"No, after that."

"What? I'll leave you and your sisters alone. That's all."

"My sisters?"

Kehvun set his bucket down and folded his arms.

"Look, I was nice about it in the barracks, and I understand that being made Hairth's apprentice and all could go to your head, but I'm trying to set some clear rules here, and I don't appreciate you mocking me."

Jaren felt like he'd had cold water splashed on his face—not just his legs

"I'm not mocking you."

"Right. You expect me to believe that no one told you that you were moving in with us? Or, that you didn't know your sisters have been in Freysdal, living in my house, for days?"

Jaren put his own bucket down and stared at Kehvun.

"Is this some sort of cruel joke? Are you working with Joans?"

Jaren wouldn't put it past the mad Light-Twister to do something like this to him.

"If it is a joke, then someone is playing it on me. Ella's cute enough, but she says strange things, and May just doesn't say a word."

Jaren blinked, and tears rolled down his cheeks. He dashed past Kehvun and rushed up the stairs. He didn't even announce himself at the door, he just ran in looking for his sisters. He barely registered that Maullie, his former teacher, was sitting at the table along with a large man who looked like a taller, filled out version of Kehvun. Another woman sat beside Maullie. She stared at her hands in her lap and didn't lift her head. A third woman was rushing toward Jaren, and it was only after she shouted his name and wrapped her arms around him that Jaren recognized his sister.

Ella pressed her face up against Jaren's chest and squeezed him tightly. He returned the hug, surprised at how short she was, and felt the tears continuing down his cheeks.

"Ella," he cried through the tightness in his throat.

They held each other until Kehvun opened the door and almost ran into them.

"Watch it," he snapped, and almost as quickly the man at the table barked,

"Kehvun!"

Ella pulled back from Jaren and wiped tears from her eyes. She looked more like a woman and hardly like the little girl he remembered.

"Jaren, Ella, why don't you come sit down at the table," Maullie called. Ella squeezed Jaren's hand and brought him along to the table.

As Jaren started to sit, the man partly stood and extended a hand to Jaren.

"Gerald, this is Jaren. Jaren, this is my husband, Gerald."

"Welcome to our home."

"Thank you, sir." Jaren said, recognizing Gerald as soon as Maullie mentioned his name. Jaren had made several deliveries to Gerald. He was one of Hairth's Associates and was over material processing or something similar.

Jaren couldn't believe that he was sitting with Ella. With a sinking feeling he realized the unknown woman at the table was his sister May. Her eyes were sunken and bordered with dark circles. Her hair was short, poorly cut, and stringy. She didn't look dirty, but like she had only recently been washed for the first time in a long time. If Jaren squinted, he could kind of see a ragged version of his sister in her. Oh, *H'ust* what had happened to her?

He felt a hand squeeze his and looked over to a smiling Ella. "Not all owners are as kind as Hairth."

May never lifted her head.

Kehvun sat down and began filling his plate. Gerald cleared his throat, and in a very flat voice said, "Jaren, Ella, you'll have to excuse Kehvun. Sometimes he forgets that other people exist."

Kehvun looked up at his father, a spoonful of sauce balanced over the center of the table. He gently set it down, then plunked down onto his seat with his arms folded across his chest. Gerald raised an eyebrow, and Kehvun's glare softened, and he dropped his hands to his lap. Gerald just nodded, then turned to Maullie.

"Mother, are you ready to start?"

Maullie nodded, and everyone began dishing up food. Jaren felt like he was in a dream. How many times had he imagined being reunited with his sisters? And now here he was, sitting beside Ella. It was surreal.

"We got our assignments today," Ella began, as if this were any other day, and they were all just a normal family. Jaren smiled. It was just like her. She was always comfortable around people, and everyone liked her. With one small caveat, of course. "I'm going to be working in lightball production and May will be in maintenance. I met with Trizzella—she's the Green that will be supervising me. She showed me…"

Ella continued talking about her new job as everyone began to eat. Jaren listened, though his heart sank as his mind drifted to his own experiences. Maullie and Gerald listened politely, but Kehvun's overwrought eye-rolling and utter disinterest was distracting. Maullie glared at him, but he only stopped when Gerald snapped at him. Ella didn't even seem to notice.

Jaren shifted to rub his back against the slats of his seat. He was searching for some evidence of the abuse he had received earlier—bruises or sensitivity—but there was none. He had been whipped as savagely as ever he had been by...he blocked the recollection... .

"...dying the fabric..." Ella trailed off, and Jaren brought his attention back to her.

"What happened to you?" Ella asked. All eyes turned to Jaren. Well, almost all—May's were still trained on a roasted potato chunk she was pushing around her plate, and Kehvun's eyes had to finish rolling first.

"What do you mean?" Jaren asked in surprise. Could she possibly know? Trying to be nonchalant, he continued, "Nothing. Nothing at all."

"You have that look on your face you get when something awful has happened."

"I don't have a 'look.'" Jaren's face burned as he became defensive, but he tried to keep calm. Could he be fighting with his sister within the first twenty minutes of their reunion?

"Yes, you do—it's the same look you had when Petreola ran away. Your eyes looked like that for weeks after Mom and Dad died, and almost as long when we knew Ben wasn't coming back." The litany of horrible experiences disarmed Jaren and he couldn't hide his despair.

"There. That's the one." This time even May looked up.

Jaren didn't know how to respond. What would they think if they knew he was a Light-Twister? It would break May completely. Fortunately, Gerald came to the rescue.

"This morning, Jaren was chosen as Hairth's apprentice. It was quite a surprise to most of us, but I'm sure it was more surprising to Jaren."

Heads turned to Gerald and then back to Jaren. Another pit formed in his stomach. He had forgotten all about his new assignment. It was just a cover, but he would need to work to make the ruse effective.

"Yeah, uh, it's pretty stressful."

Everyone reacted a little differently. Ella narrowed her eyes at him. May returned her attention to the nimble chunk of potato — perhaps the red sauce made it difficult to capture — and Maullie turned to Gerald as her face recovered from the shock. She whispered something. He made hushing motions with his hand. Kehvun stuffed his last piece of roast into his mouth. The food was terrific, but Jaren's appetite hadn't been much to begin with. He stood.

"I'd like to go to bed now. Thank you for dinner."

Kehvun jumped up, obviously ready to be away from the table, too.

"I'll show you."

Jaren felt exhausted as he lay on his pallet, but he couldn't fall asleep. He lay there for over an hour just thinking. It seemed like weeks since he had woken in the clinic that morning. Eventually Kehvun came in the room and went to sleep. Jaren's thoughts were still churning.

There he was, in a room with a stranger, in a house with his former teacher and another of Hairth's Associates. He had inexplicably fallen unconscious for days and was Hairth's apprentice when he woke. He had been reunited with his sisters — not following the normal process, but because he was a despicable Light-Twister. Kehvun began breathing deeply, and Jaren's thoughts kept going.

In the quiet, he heard Gerald say to Maullie, "I really thought we would get some clue."

"So did I."

"But you heard — the boy..."

"Jaren."

"Yes, of course, all Jaren knows is that he was made Hairth's apprentice. That's no more than we do."

"Tell me again what Hairth told you. Why does he want Jaren to stay with us?"

"He just said Jaren needs stability, a home with two adults to watch over him—two adults that he could trust without question."

"But why?"

"I don't know, but I trust Hairth. I know he trusts us, too. So, whatever is going on, this must be important."

"I know. I know. It's just that the only times Hairth has asked me to act in so much mystery have been very serious—like when he maneuvered the council to grant thralls rights, or when he purchased the mine. How could this boy...*Jaren*... possibly be..."

"Just trust him."

"I do. But, can he afford to divert his attention when..."

"Trust him."

Chapter 8

Waking to a Snake

Jaren jerked awake to an awful scream. His pulse raised, and eerie other-light assaulted his senses. Kehvun gasped, then screamed again, writhing on the ground while clutching his arm.

A thick rope of darkness undulated across the wooden floor toward Jaren. He scrambled off his pallet and backed against the wall. Pressure weighed down on his pounding heart and head. Radiant energy bent around the creature, lighting it with an unnatural glow. It was a red and black snake with a narrow, triangular head. It slithered onto the pallet and coiled in on itself. Jaren screamed and pressed against the wall. The sound of running steps distracted the snake, and Gerald swooped in and slashed it with a long knife before it could strike. It twisted and rolled in two halves, little jets of blood spurting from its writhing corpse.

"Did it bite you?" Gerald asked Jaren.

He shook his head. Maullie rushed in with a lantern, flooding the room with harsh light. She dropped to Kehvun's side. He screamed again, and Maullie tried to gather him in her arms.

"Gerald!" Maullie cried.

Sweat covered Kehvun's pale face. His eyes, half-open, only showed white. The arm he had been grasping lay limp at his side, and two thin trails of blood ran down his hand.

Gerald pulled the limp body from Maullie's arms and dashed through the door. Maullie ran after, taking the light with her. The shadowy snake's contortions had slowed to intermittent loops and rolls. Jaren kicked the remaining half off his pallet. He pulled his knees against his chest as he sank with his back against the wall. The burden on Jaren's chest left and the radiant luminance spread out even again, but Jaren's heart still raced and ached.

"Jaren?" Ella appeared in the doorway with another light. She covered her mouth. "What happened?"

"The snake bit him." He gestured toward the athetotic forms. "It tried to bite me, too."

"But the chicks haven't hatched."

Jaren stared at her. She returned a confused look, and Jaren looked away. Sometimes Ella said things that didn't make any sense—apparently, she hadn't outgrown that in their time apart.

"Are those common around here?" Ella asked, as she shivered and gathered her oversized robe around her. It must have belonged to Maullie. The snake half made a final flop and stopped moving.

"I've never seen one before." Jaren had seen plenty of snakes, but never one this thick around and never with a pattern of black and red rings.

Neither spoke, and, as if the silence was too much for the crickets and cicadas, they began to fill it. Some toads joined in. Then a soft, rhythmic creaking, setting the tempo, came from down the hall.

"May!" Ella darted out of the room, leaving eerie darkness again.

Jaren tore his eyes from the lifeless snake and followed. May sat curled up, rocking back and forth in the corner of their bedroom. She had buried her face in her arms, like she was shielding herself, and was quietly moaning. Ella crouched beside her, stroking her hair, and began to softly sing a lullaby. Tears came to Jaren's eyes as he remembered his mother singing the same song when he was afraid. Oh, what he wouldn't give to have her there now!

The wide neck of May's sleeping clothes laid bare faint white and pink scars crisscrossing her sun-darkened shoulders and back. Jaren could almost still feel the welts from his encounter with Joans, though he knew those had been healed. Anger welled up inside him, and he struggled to suppress a memory of a thralltaker. Repeated blows with the whip cemented the man's face in Jaren's mind's eye. If ever he saw that man again... No, Jaren would not bear those thoughts. The peace of Freysdal relieved him of that burden.

"May, it's okay..." Jaren started, but Ella interrupted. "She can't understand you when she gets like this." She began singing softly again.

Jaren left the room and sat down in front of the stove, trying to clear his mind, but failing to do so. He felt sorry for Maullie, his former teacher, even if he wasn't connected to Kehvun or Gerald. What would happen if Kehvun died? Jaren pictured the lifeless form in Gerald's arms, but quickly pushed that thought away.

Jaren reached out and touched the energy coming from the stove. His chest felt tender to the burden, like a sore muscle, as the energy resisted his touch. Recognizing what he was doing, Jaren recoiled. But though he didn't touch it, he couldn't stop *seeing* the energy. The sources' arrangement produced an odd display of energy that drew his attention. The sides facing each other produced more energy than the sides facing open air, and where the two plates overlapped, they produced significantly more energy.

Jaren's ears perked up. Distant shouting grew louder. He jumped up and ran to the door. Cool air rushed past his legs. Moon and starlight showed a form running down the road.

"Jaren! Get the snake!"

What? Was there another snake? Jaren scanned the ground. Ella joined him at the door. They could see Maullie now, running and breathing heavy as she shouted, "Jaren! Bring the snake!"

Understanding, he dashed into the room, and hesitated only a second before picking up both snake halves. He ran out of the door toward Maullie. When she saw him coming, she slowed, then stumbled and fell to her hands and knees.

Jaren ran to help her, but she batted away his hands and panted out, "Take it to Haerlee!"

Her panting turned to sobbing, and as Jaren ran toward the lights of Freysdal, he heard her cry, "Run! My baby is dying! Run, oh *H'ust* run!"

Jaren ran harder than he ever had before. The pain in her voice spurred him on. The two snake halves swung like beefy whips with each stride. Her cry echoed in his mind long after her voice quieted.

Chapter 9

Healing Bites

The clinic shone like a torch in the night. People dashed in and out, shouting as they went. Outside, men, women, and children wept, consoling one another. Why were so many people at the clinic?

Jaren dashed in, squeezing past a large man rushing out, and stopped just inside the door. The clinic was full to overflowing. Along one wall stood many of the burn victims he had seen the day before. They were shaking their heads and covering their faces. Pale, sweat-covered patients now filled their beds, with others kneeling beside them, holding their hands or stroking their hair. They were offering words of reassurance or begging their loved one to hold on for just another minute. A foul stench—like rotted meat—made Jaren gag, but he had to keep breathing hard because of his run.

"Snake!" someone shouted.

Haerlee rushed over to him, "Whose is it?"

Jaren frowned in confusion.

"Who did that snake bite?"

"Oh. Kehvun. Gerald's son."

She tore the headed half from Jaren's hand and started shouting for Marigold. A plump girl wearing an apron over her segg took the snake from Haerlee and disappeared into the crowd. Jaren looked around for Gerald but hoped he wouldn't see him. He didn't know what to say or how to offer support if Kehvun died. Some of the patients already looked dead.

"Jaren! Did you bring it?" Gerald's voice rang out, ragged and unsteady. The man's face was a dusty, tear-streaked mess. He cradled Kehvun's limp body as he sat on one of the pallets.

"Yes, sir."

"Oh, *H'ust*, let it be in time!"

Jaren squeezed his way through the room to Gerald. A large black bruise had formed on Kehvun's arm, and Gerald was pressing a wad of moist pulp directly on top of the bite. Kehvun's face was gray, with a bluish tint around his lips and eyes. His head lolled as Gerald gently rocked. Tears continued down Gerald's scruffy cheeks. Jaren wanted to comfort him but wasn't sure how. He chided himself—he was acting like Joans—and placed a steady hand on Gerald's shoulder.

Jaren gazed around the room and realized that every patient had large bruises—some covering entire limbs, others were fairly localized. Were they all there for snake bites?

"Snake!"

Jaren looked at the entrance to see Hentoya, Hairth's Associate responsible for selling Freysdal's products, bent over his large belly, trying to catch his breath while holding out a limp snake as Haerlee approached.

Marigold materialized out of the bustle. She placed a large bundle on the pallet and unrolled a cloth, revealing a small bladed knife, a long, narrow spoon, and some strips of white cloth.

"Please lay him down and put that pulp aside." Marigold stretched Kehvun's arm out from his body and examined the bruise. Jaren could see it creeping up his arm. On inspection, it wasn't truly a bruise at all. Rather, it was a dense, blackish-blue spider web that extended from the bite, with thicker, darker strands near the bite, and thinner, lighter strands further away.

Marigold began making shallow cuts along the webbed lines. She worked carefully, but occasionally cursed when she drew putrid smelling, blackish blood. After scoring all the webbing in a band around his arm, she scooped a thick, creamy green poultice from the jar and spread it over the cuts. She then stretched and squeezed the skin, ensuring the poultice got into each cut. She concluded by wrapping the poulticed cuts. Then she repeated the whole process on the next band of skin. Kehvun didn't move, even when she drew black blood.

"Will this heal him?" Gerald asked as she worked.

"This will counteract the poison. He is young. That's a good place to start." Marigold finished the rest in silence and left. The three sat for a long time, then Maullie came in, her eyes red and puffy, her cheeks still wet with tears.

"Is he..."

"He's got a good chance."

Jaren's legs ached from the hard run and the days of unconsciousness as he stood to go, but that pain was insignificant compared to the discomfort of watching Gerald and Maullie. As he stepped away, Maullie grabbed his hand, squeezed it, and whispered, "Thank you!" Jaren kept his eyes down as he made his way out of the clinic. Even in her extremity, she had thanked him.

As Jaren reached the door, a familiar voice called out, "What are you doing here?" He looked up to see Tobie running her hand through disheveled black curls. Her fingers caught on a knot, and she winced as she pulled through it. Her wide-set, light brown eyes watched everyone entering and leaving the clinic.

"Oh, hey. I'm..." He paused, unsure of how to continue. Then, he shrugged and held up the snake-half he somehow was still holding for her to see.

Tobie scrunched her face. "You obviously weren't bitten, so...I hadn't heard that any snakes got into the barracks."

"I..." but she interrupted as he pushed through the door.

"No, don't tell me. Let me figure it out!" She followed him away from the clinic into the night. The cool, fresh air, with a hint of pine, was a relief from the putrid smell of sick blood and sweat-bathed bodies. The noise died to a soft rumble as the door behind them closed. Her face relaxed.

"Umm...they brought admin runners like you to retrieve the snakes since you can run for so long?"

Jaren just looked at her, then tossed the snake body out into an open square. Let the birds have it.

"Oh alright, I can't think of any good reason for you to be here."

"I've got to go," Jaren said, and began walking. He didn't want to talk about it, and certainly not with her. She wasn't bad, but tonight she made him uneasy—like he was an oddity she was examining.

"I'm headed in this direction, too."

Jaren sighed but didn't say anything. Tobie had to walk fast to keep up with him. He didn't rush, but he didn't slow down for her either.

"What have you learned about Joans?"

Jaren stumbled at the rush of anxiety that hit him. He had forgotten all about being a Light-Twister and Joans.

"Nothing. He just...sits there and mutters while staring at his sources. Sometimes he sends me to get him stuff."

"What kind of stuff?"

"I don't know. Stuff."

"Well, has he done any radiance in front of you?"

"No." Jaren felt his frustration rising. Luckily, Tobie seemed to sense it, too. They walked in silence for several minutes.

"Crazy with those snakes..." Tobie started up again. Jaren grunted in reply.

"I was just reading about them a few days ago. They are only found in Mohis and Votna."

"Wait," Jaren interjected, "You mean they are not from around here?"

"Oh no, of course not. If they were, Haerlee would have known how to counter the poison, and she wouldn't have needed me."

"You've lost me. Were you treating people?"

"No. I just told Haerlee how to do it."

"And you knew this because you had read about it in a book a few days ago?" Jaren started walking again.

"Yeah, thirty-eight days ago, to be exact. Very interesting snakes. They normally live in secluded areas, eating small animals. But when agitated, they become very aggressive, biting anything that moves. A single snake, if riled up, can kill a small herd of livestock. That's what makes them such good tools for assassins."

"Assassins?"

"Yeah. Assassins are people who kill other people for money."

"I know what an assassin is."

"Oh. I just thought...Well, never mind. Yes, they are used by assassins, but what I read made me think they were only used in areas where the snakes are indigenous—so it can look like an accident."

"Indigenous?" "Yes."

"No—I meant what does 'indigenous' mean?"

"Oh. Sorry, I just thought...Right. Well indigenous means the native inhabitant, as opposed to being moved there from somewhere else. For example, the Pinnutuckans are indigenous to this area, while you, me, and almost all the other thralls are not."

"So, you're saying someone brought those snakes here to try to kill people?"

"No, that's not what I'm saying." Then her eyes opened wide. "But, maybe that is what happened!"

Jaren and Tobie walked in silence for a minute, but then it was Jaren's turn to ask a question.

"So why were you at the clinic tonight?"

"I told you, I was telling Haerlee how to treat the bites."

"Right, but how did you know people were being bitten?"

"Oh. Haerlee sent an apprentice to get me out of bed. That's why my hair is so crazy." She raked her fingers through the tangles again. Jaren didn't mention that her hair looked the same as the last times he had seen her.

"Okay, but how did Haerlee know that you would know how to treat the bites?"

"We run into each other now and then at the library and we discuss what we're reading. She's always looking at things about herbs and cures. She happened to be there when I was reading a book on the snakes of Thadren."

"And why were you reading about snakes?"

"Oh, it's just part of my job."

That struck Jaren as odd.

"And what, exactly, is your job?"

"That, um, is something I'm not supposed to talk about," and with that, Tobie darted down a side road, her little legs pumping at a quick pace. She turned and shouted, "You've moved in with someone...Gerald." It wasn't a question. She turned and kept walking. Jaren watched her go, puffy hair streaming in the wind. She was a strange one.

Chapter 10

Folding, Shaping, Shuddering

The burden pressed against Jaren, but it no longer hurt. He focused on a round lump of energy. It was not dense, but it was getting there.

"Folding would be faster," Joans said as he flipped a page in the book he was reading.

Folding energy felt to Jaren like trying to squeeze water between his hands. It was remarkably faster, though every time he tried, the energy just slipped away. If he could manage to take the energy coming from a source and fold it back into the source, then the output from the source would significantly increase. He could then take that energy and fold it again, producing even more energy. In theory this could go on forever. In practice, Jaren could hardly hold the energy coming off a source naturally. So, instead of folding, Jaren did his best to just capture and hold on to the energy leaving the source. Jaren's jaw popped as he stifled a yawn.

"Finally! At this rate, you'll be useful in about twelve years." Joans continued reading, reclining on a cushion-covered pallet, and all but ignoring Jaren.

A thin rod of light energy slid from Joans' robe and pierced Jaren's lump of heat before he could move it. The lump jiggled as Jaren struggled to keep it together, but it split in two. A pulse of heat flashed in Jaren's face as the energy was released.

"Do it again."

Jaren obeyed without a word. Inwardly, though, he imagined twisting heat and cold energy to form a solid rod of air with which to thump Joans as he had done to Jaren. Unfortunately, juggling water would have been easier.

Jaren began collecting energy, imagining that the burden in his chest was creating an invisible net around the source. He knew he could make the net tighter, could capture more of the energy, but he was unwilling. He feared that the more energy he manipulated, the more the energy would manipulate him. But it was hard to resist. Light-twisting was exhilarating.

"Fold!"

Jaren sighed. He started to fold, but the denser energy pushed through the net, breaking it and releasing a small puff of warmth. Joans clucked, and Jaren erected his net once more. He yawned again.

"Keep yawning, boy, and you'll use all the air in here. Didn't you get enough sleep?"

Jaren glared at the back of Joans' head. His mottled scalp showed beneath thinning, black hair. Jaren's net slipped, releasing another puff of heat. He focused, and, working through the burden, reinforced the net. All of Freysdal was talking about the snakes. Joans must have heard…or maybe not. Did anyone speak to Joans? Regardless, strokes from solid air awaited if Jaren didn't answer.

"No, sir. My roommate was bitten by a snake."

"What?" Joans sounded surprised. Perhaps he hadn't heard of the snakes.

"Your roommate was bitten, so you didn't get enough sleep? Was he moaning all night or are you just so soft-hearted that your sympathy kept you awake?"

No, Joans had heard. He was trying to provoke Jaren. But Jaren wouldn't let him. He pushed on the energy, and it slowly took the shape of a brick. Keeping most of his concentration on the shape, Jaren replied,

"No. His screaming woke me, and I had to run the snake to the clinic to save his life." The form wobbled, but a little extra focus firmed it up.

"The snake bit him while he slept? Was he outside?"

"No, the snake got inside," Jaren raised the brick to avoid Joans' spear of light. The spear peeled itself in two and sped back toward the brick.

"So, you think you're a hero now?"

Jaren pushed the brick sideways. It wobbled like a waterskin. One spear curved away from the brick and toward Jaren's face.

"No," was all he could manage before a burst of light flashed in his face followed by a wave of heat from his disintegrating brick.

"Good. You're not. You didn't save your roommate. The herbalist did. You're lucky you didn't poke yourself with the snake's fangs while you ran. Now focus and try again."

Jaren had lost track of how many times he had done this exercise. Training had started with moving each joint independently. Then moved on to arithmetic while tapping out complex patterns. Throughout the exercises, Joans droned on about the superiority of Light-Twisters. Jaren wasn't sure if the lecture was supposed to teach or distract him. Regardless, he felt like he progressed through each exercise quickly.

Joans had next demonstrated how to collect energy. He had seemed surprised when Jaren had held heat on his first try. But when Jaren failed folding repeatedly, Joans' smug expression returned.

Jaren formed another heat brick. When the light spear came, he reached out and grabbed it. Once he wrested control from Joans, he let the spear go. There was a tiny flash of light. But Jaren had already returned his attention to the brick and began forming it into a cone.

"Better," Joans said before piercing the cone with a faster spear, "but not good enough. What does the herbalist say about your roommate? Will there be permanent damage?"

"She can't say." Jaren tried folding again, but this time he set up a second net to catch the increased energy output. "She says she'll know better in a couple of days." The trick worked.

Another spear flew toward Jaren's freshly formed brick. He captured and released the spear. The bright flash momentarily blinded his eyes, but not his radiance-sight. He stopped two more spears—each faster than the previous—as he worked through the cone, then he forced the cone into a rod. It wasn't perfectly straight, but Joans nodded, and Jaren released the energy.

"Like a potter, a Light-Twister's skill starts with his ability to make the right shapes." Joans folded heat and cold until he had two lumps as dense as stone. Each lump flattened out like a long sheet and then kinked up and over. Joans brought them together and then rested one end on the floor. He released the energy, but there were no waves of heat or cold.

"Each potter has his own style and techniques, but masters create functional objects that are also works of art." Joans stood and began climbing into the air. "A novice, with a little practice, can copy a master's design. But they lack the finesse and the beauty."

Joans head brushed the ceiling.

"Of course, many techniques require more finesse than a novice can muster. The beauty possible with such intricate designs is limitless."

Faster than Jaren could track, Joans drew out a staggering combination of energies. Staring down his sharp nose at Jaren, he spun and formed, shaped and turned until the energy was an immense multi-hued blob behind him. Joans released some of the energy and the blob sank inward, revealing a large throne of radiant metal, ornately decorated with sparkling jewels. Joans adjusted his black robe and sat down. Another released bundle of energy revealed a glowing vase on a marble pedestal.

"Master, these skills, even as weak as you are, and you can wield power beyond belief."

Jaren's momentary awe shattered. He did not want power. He wanted peace and safety for himself and his sisters. Light-twisting might give him the power to provide safety, but his sisters would never feel peace around him once they knew what he was. He felt his heart sink, and it wasn't from the burden.

Joans continued speaking as if giving a great discourse to a large crowd on the superiority of Light-Twisters and their right to rule. Jaren listened just enough to avoid getting whipped, but the topic worsened his melancholy. To distract from his misery, he thought about the previous night. Was it coincidence that Tobie had read about those very snakes so recently? How many people had been hurt in the attack? The bite victims were all Associates or their family members. Maullie had called it a decapitation strike. Was someone trying to eliminate the leadership of Freysdal?

Joans was wrapping up his speech. The vase and throne had vanished, replaced by an invisible spiral of stairs which he was descending.

"So, you see, you must first master the basic shapes and how to move them. You must increase your capacity until you can manage dozens of lumps. After that, I will teach you how to combine energies to achieve different effects."

Jaren nodded, ignoring his internal protests. He would do the minimum necessary to avoid punishment.

Joans demonstrated twenty basic shapes, and then told Jaren he was on his own until he mastered them. Joans then threw out a blend of energy and vanished. Jaren watched as five sources floated to the door, stopped, then returned. Joans reappeared as suddenly as he had disappeared.

"I suppose you'll need these." Joans withdrew the sources from his pockets, placed them on the table and vanished again.

Jaren saw that light and force energy were included in the mix, but beyond that, he had no idea how Joans had vanished.

Jaren stared at the sources. He felt like a small child on the hearth. The flames were mesmerizing, but he knew enough that if he played with them, he'd get burned.

"Practice!" Joans voice filled the house. A twist of heat and cold energies streaked out of the sources and swung toward Jaren. The burden pressed heavily against him as he caught them. He could feel the energy writhing to get free of his grasp. He was struggling with Joans for control. Rage at the abuse he'd suffered boiled in his heart. He would not be whipped again today. The energy pulled free from his net, but he formed it again. With an effort that left his head ringing in pain, he jerked the energy free from Joans' control and released it. Joans was folding the sources again, but Jaren put his own net around the heat source. A lump of cold was already formed, but Jaren fought for control of it as well. After a second, it released. Joans had given up, but Jaren had no idea if the madman had left. So, he began practicing.

Chapter 11

Committing to the Cause

Jaren barely heard fifth bell as he put the last arch on a "rainbow" of energies. He released the energy very carefully after separating each piece, rubbing his head where he had hit it with a solid chunk of air he had unintentionally made earlier.

He left the sources on the table and made his way down to Freysdal. Only a hint of the burnt pine scent remained. Cool air filled his lungs and drove out the radiance's corruption. The burden was still there, but he no longer felt like he was beneath a pile of rocks. Instead, it felt like a proper burden—a yoke intended for him to bear. That he was becoming comfortable with it repulsed him, but the air somehow lifted the regret and disgust and filled him with contentment. Passing out of the trees, the peace of Freysdal once again settled upon him—until he remembered Kehvun.

Would Maullie and Gerald expect Jaren to go to the clinic? Surely not—he'd just be in the way. The house lay through Freysdal, the clinic on the other side of the valley. Jaren took a few steps toward the house, then stopped. He turned toward the clinic, then stopped. A turn and a few more steps toward the house then a turn and another stop drew the eyes of a pair of Yellows who were talking at the corner.

"Do you need some help?"

"No." Jaren's cheeks colored. He put his head down and hurried past the pair—toward the clinic. He hadn't decided to go there. It was just the last direction he was facing. As he moved through Freysdal's streets, the curiosity and wonder in that morning's conversations had shifted to fear and dread by evening.

"…trying to kill the Associates…"

"…if Hairth is killed, who will own us?"

"No, *Lo'jem* put the house up there to show we live too close to one another."

"…he said with his dying breath that there's an army marching toward us right now…"

"Maybe we should leave, while there's still time…"

"I don't want my son to die in the next wagon train."

"No, that house has always been there. The thunder just made you look in that direction."

Jaren understood their anxiety. The peace of Freysdal had been shaken. It was wobbling like his earlier lumps of energy, but it was much more stable. For every worried expression, there were two reassurances, almost all with the same words,

"Hairth will protect us."

As Jaren approached and entered the clinic, he was surprised by the clamor. It sounded as if he were approaching a party, not a place of healing. People were smiling and laughing. Some were embracing. A plump freedman woman wearing a flour-coated apron was wiping tears from her eyes, a huge smile filling her freckled face. She took a little girl whose wild red hair was a small copy of her mothers and squeezed her tight to her chest. The girl's knee-length skirt revealed a leg wrapped in bandages. Hentoya, the plump Associate over sales, had one arm around the woman and the other around the girl.

Even though he expected it, Jaren still felt surprised to see an Associate in most of the groups—either injured or comforting a victim. He wasn't sure how he had missed that the night before.

"Jaren!" Hairth's baritone voice called. Jaren's heart leapt, and he turned to see Hairth gesture toward the door with a bandage wrapped hand.

"You were attacked, too?" Jaren asked, as he followed Hairth back out of the clinic. It suddenly made sense why his morning meeting with Hairth had been canceled.

Hairth looked from left to right, and then said in a hushed voice, "I prefer not to refer to it as an attack. All the adults recognize it for what it is, but let's let the children continue to believe it was an accident, eh?"

Jaren's face colored, but Hairth gave him a kind smile.

"I'm frequently the target of attacks, but this is the first time anyone has gone after my Associates." Looking at his bandaged hand, he added, "But this was close."

Hairth's smile faded as he glanced back at the clinic. The skin on his face had improved a little, but the patches of brown and bright pink still made Jaren flinch.

"The peace of Freysdal failed four people last night, and left hundreds questioning. Until today, this intrigue has mostly been a game for me—can I outwit my enemies? But they're no longer satisfied with just me. They're trying to undermine everything we've built here."

His voice could chisel stone, and his face was set as hard as one. Jaren took a step back. He had never seen Hairth so angry. Hairth looked at Jaren, and the anger drained from his face, replaced by sadness.

"I'm sorry. I don't mean to burden you with this. You've got enough of a load to carry without additional concerns. It's just that my enemies are watching. They will soon know your name, if they don't already. I hadn't thought there would be any threat to you...but...I'm sorry. After last night, I feel a new sense of urgency. How is your training going?"

Jaren looked down. The toes of Hairth's dark leather boots poked past the hem of his blue robe. Jaren wondered if he'd now be a target, too. His throat tightened as everything over the past day and night and day came rushing through him. He was exhausted. He rubbed his eyes to hide the tears, but he couldn't keep the frown from his face.

Hairth reached out and put his thick arms around Jaren and pulled him tight against his shoulder. Jaren was startled at first and instinctively pulled back, but the embrace was warm and comforting, making it that much harder to hold back the flood of emotions.

"It's okay, son. You're safe. Freysdal will keep you safe." Jaren wept into Hairth's robes. Hairth just held Jaren's head against his shoulder with his bandaged hand.

After a few moments, Jaren took a deep breath and stepped out of the embrace. As Hairth watched the people going in and out of the clinic, there were tears rolling down his cheeks too, and his voice broke as he spoke.

"I can't fail them, Jaren. I can't let them down—not like I let these people down…like I've let you down." Hairth let out a long breath and his voice steadied.

"*H'ust* has bestowed a great power on you. I know I'm asking more than I should. This is an awful weight for one so young. But I need to know if you will help me carry it. Not just for me, but for Freysdal, and for all it stands for. To end Thralldom, to spread our peace—the peace of Freysdal—to all of Thadren. Will you help?"

A fire ignited in Jaren as he listened to Hairth. His revulsion at Joans' description of power was matched by the draw of the purity of Hairth's request. He would carry this burden. He would become powerful and ensure the peace of Freysdal— even if it meant his own personal descent into the darkness of light-twisting. The peace of Freysdal would remain a beacon for him in the shadow that would eventually swallow him, and he would ensure that whatever cruelty entered his heart, it would always be directed at those who threatened that peace. He nodded, not trusting his own voice.

"You're a strong young man. Now, tell me how your training is going."

Jaren had never considered the burden Hairth carried. He was wealthy beyond imagination. He had his own soldiers and town. He was surrounded by people who revered him. However, all of that came with a price—an enormous responsibility. Hairth bore it with such grace and kindness that Jaren could not add to the burden. If Hairth could carry his burden, Jaren could too, so he chose not to speak of Joans' abuse.

Instead, he told of the progress he had made—his ability to see energy flowing from sources, and his nascent ability to control it. He explained the exercises that Joans had given him, and the plan—as best as he could recall from his haphazard listening—that Joans had laid out for his development. He even collected light from one of Hairth's rings and made a bright flash in the approaching dusk.

Hairth clapped.

"That's fantastic! And I'm jealous. I've worked with radiance for decades, but I have so little control of it. I've built all of Freysdal by selling lightballs, but there is so much more that could be done—so many ways to enrich people's lives. But research takes time. Maybe, once you are fully trained, you will be able to help with that. The items we could develop with your talents could change all of Thadren."

Hairth was all smiles—almost giddy—in sharp contrast to his tear-stained eyes, burnt face, and bandaged hand.

"But this is serious and also dangerous for you. Soon enough you'll be able to protect yourself with radiance, but even then, radiance may not always be available. You also need to learn to protect yourself without radiance. From now on, you'll spend first bell with me. At second bell, you'll train with Levi. At third bell, you'll train with Joans. It's clear that I need better security, and since you're my apprentice, everyone will assume you're to help with that."

Levi? Jaren's commitment to bear the burden suddenly wavered, and he dropped his eyes. At least with Joans, he could take some comfort in knowing Joans would probably heal any physical damage he caused. With Levi, that wasn't a possibility.

"Levi isn't that bad," Hairth said.

Jaren just sighed, and then nodded.

"Good! Very good!" Hairth, smiling once more, turned and headed down the road in the growing darkness.

Jaren's mood was significantly more depressed as he entered the clinic the second time. He resurveyed the crowd and noticed that Levi was not among the victims or visitors.

"He probably caught the snake and ate it raw," Jaren muttered as he looked for Kehvun.

"Who?" someone asked over the noise in the room.

Jaren turned to see a tangle of dark hair obscuring Tobie's face. She was leaning against the frame of the door, also surveying the room.

"Who what?" he said loudly to her.

"Who ate a snake raw?"

Jaren flushed. How had she heard that? "Oh, nobody." He stammered. "It was...I mean that...oh, never mind."

"You were talking about Levi, weren't you?" He stared at her in disbelief. How had she known that?

"He's not here—that's what you were noticing. But why were you looking for him?"

Jaren's tried to hide his embarrassment with irritation. He glared and asked his own question.

"What are you doing here?"

She shrugged. "Haerlee wanted me to see how well the treatment worked. It's really quite remarkable compared to the scene from last night."

She was right. Jaren could hardly believe the change that had taken place. The smell was mostly gone. Those wearing bandages were smiling and talking as if last night had never happened.

"Attention!" The shout was just barely audible over the din, but quiet spread at a second "Attention!"

Haerlee, wearing an apron smeared with blood and gunk cinched tightly around her waist, stood on a chair. Despite the dark bags under her brown eyes, she was still stunning. A man could fall into those eyes and never come out. Even her disheveled hair couldn't take away from her beauty. Jaren blushed as he listened to his own thoughts.

"Most of you are healing well. I'm still concerned about your recovery but keeping all of you here is making it difficult to care for those who still need my attention. I will check on each of you over the next few days. You may not go to work. You will eat and drink as I've told you. And you will rest. If I find that you have not been strictly following my orders, I will require you to return here so that I can supervise you directly."

She stared down at Zmendra, the only Associate in Freysdal who could go toe-to-toe with Levi and sometimes come out on top. Zmendra glared back. But Haerlee didn't back down.

"I have Hairth's support in this, so don't try me."

Jaren wasn't sure if she was saying this to everyone or just to Zmendra, but the fact that Zmendra began replacing the bandage she had been removing suggested she got the message regardless to whom it was directed.

The bustle of people leaving was worse than the racket of them talking. Jaren found Maullie with her arms wrapped around Haerlee, whispering something in her ears. When they stepped apart, both wiped tears from their eyes. Haerlee straightened her apron with delicate hands. She looked Jaren over, then said, "Since your recovery appears complete, you will help take care of Kehvun. He'll be weak for a while yet."

Then something else caught her attention and she stormed off shouting, "Marigold do not let them..."

Jaren glanced at Kehvun, who appeared to be well enough based on the smirk he was directing at Jaren. Gerald and Maullie didn't notice, though. They were too busy beaming.

It turned out, however, that Haerlee had been right. Gerald and Jaren had to support Kehvun for most of the walk home. Before they reached the edge of Freysdal proper, Kehvun's rosy cheeks had turned pale, and a sheen of sweat covered his forehead despite the cool breeze coming down the river. When they arrived home, they gently laid him on his pallet. He was asleep before Maullie could pull off his boots.

Chapter 12

Lying to Family

"Kehvun won't be eating with us," Ella said. May returned the plate to the cabinet without looking up.

The smell of fried bread and spicy meat made Jaren's mouth water. Ella must have learned to cook in her former master's house. Jaren quickly filled a pitcher from the water barrel and sat at the table.

Dinner was like clean-up after a feast day. Everyone was happy. However, the long night and subsequent day had left everyone exhausted, especially Gerald and Maullie. There were great bags under Gerald's eyes and new wrinkles had appeared overnight on Maullie's face. Both would perk up briefly at times and smile at each other, but the weariness always returned apace.

Ella smiled and chattered as usual. She wasn't oblivious — at least, Jaren didn't think she was — but she didn't let the turmoil touch her. She told them all about her new job at the lightball core facility. She told about the people she had met and described how the bases of the lightballs were made.

"Coranton, the manager I assist, pretends like he's a gruff man, but I think he's just unsure of himself. If I can boost his self-confidence, I'm sure he'll be just as nice as a person can be."

Gerald coughed to hide a chuckle. Maullie gave him a haggard look, then smiled at Ella and said, "I'm sure you're right, Ella."

"Did you talk with anyone nice today, May?" Ella asked.

May looked as if she were going to lift her gaze from her lap, but it proved too heavy, and she couldn't quite do it.

"Mosj."

In addition to the surprise that May responded, the name triggered something in Jaren's memory. Yes—the one who had helped him when he had been locked out of the admin building.

"I met him once," Jaren said into the shocked silence. "He was very nice to me."

"Yes. Very kind," May added, finally looking up.

Ella reached out and squeezed May's hand. She wore a soft, sad smile.

"I'm glad you were able to talk with someone."

May returned her attention to her lap and resumed stirring the sauce around her plate.

The rest of the meal was quiet, except for an occasional sigh of exhaustion. Maullie and Gerald then said good night and retired to their room. May helped Ella and Jaren clean up and then silently left for her room. Jaren was tired, but this was his first opportunity to actually talk with Ella, and the hole in his heart for his sisters had not yet been filled by their presence. While these two were his sisters, somehow, they also were not. They had become new people during their years apart. True, Ella had not changed as drastically as May, but even she was different.

"I still don't believe your story about being Hairth's new apprentice." Ella caught Jaren off guard.

"What are you talking about? Of course, I'm his new apprentice. You heard Gerald say it."

"That's not what I meant. Something is wrong—I can see it. There's more going on than what you're telling me."

"I don't know what else there is to tell you."

"So, you say, but I'm going to figure it out."

"Ella, I don't want to argue with you." Jaren sighed, and then sat down heavily in the blue-cushioned chair. He winced—the padding was not as good as it appeared. She was right, of course, but he couldn't tell her.

"If you won't believe me, will you at least trust me that I'm trying to do what is right?"

Her hands on her hips made it clear that had not been the right thing to say.

"If you're trying to do what is right, then why not just tell me what it is?"

Jaren leaned back. Ella could be stubborn at times, but he never remembered her being so direct. He looked at the ground. His palms were sweating into his segg, and his heart was racing. In his mind he could hear himself telling her the truth. Panic engulfed him. He couldn't do it, and yet, in some odd way he couldn't stop himself. Jaren opened his mouth...

"You control radiance," Ella said, her voice flat, her posture unchanged.

Jaren's heart sank. His mouth went dry.

"How did you know?" he croaked out. He didn't dare look at her. He couldn't stand to see her horror or tears streaming down her cheeks. All these years waiting, hoping to be reunited, only to discover that her brother was a monster just waiting to claw out from his gentle exterior.

"I've always been able to tell when something was wrong, and you've always been a terrible liar."

Her tone still hadn't changed. She was irritated, but he expected more—a reaction or something.

"Yes, but...but...how did you know...that...you know?"

Before she spoke, he had been ready to tell all. Now he couldn't even bring himself to say the words. She began tapping an impatient bare foot.

"Look, I can see it in your face. Your smile never reaches your eyes—it's like they are always sad. You respond slowly— like you are moving through cold honey—like you're always distracted. Your shoulders are hunched down, and you walk like a man who's lost a child."

"All that tells you…"

"Yes," she cut him off, "All that tells me that something is wrong, and if you don't tell me what it is, I'll…well, I don't know what I'll do, but believe me, you won't be happy with it."

Jaren jerked his head up in shock. There was an intensity in her eyes that said she meant every word, but there was no horror, no tears. His mind perked up, like it had been pulled up along with his ears. What was she saying? She knew, so why was she asking? The voice in his mind pointed it out to him— she doesn't actually know.

She hadn't heard herself say it—it had been one of her strange outbursts. Her odd interjections had never been so clear— and certainly never so…relevant. What had just happened? Somehow, the crazy part of Ella knew something true that was impossible for her to know.

"Why are you looking at me like that? You have no right to be angry with me. I'm not the one hiding things here."

Jaren hadn't realized it, but he had been scowling in contemplation. The verbal slap brought his mind back to the issue at hand, and the sudden relief of his secret staying— well, secret—relieved his mind, and sent it racing in search of a solution.

He shook his head slowly and lowered his eyes.

"It isn't just that I'm Hairth's apprentice, though that's part of it." Jaren heaved a big, fake sigh. "Hairth is worried that he himself is in danger. Since I'll be around him so much, he wants to make sure I can defend us. He's having me train with Levi."

Jaren paused and raised his eyes just enough to look up at Ella. He tried to read from her face whether he had fooled her.

"Levi is a very hard man," she said.

Hard indeed. He made granite look soft and cuddly. But the way she said it and her narrowed eyebrows said the explanation didn't match the weight Jaren was carrying. He realized that while all of this had been going on, the independent voice in his mind had been searching for and had found a better answer.

"He's so hard, and if that were all, I'm sure it would be fine. But the truth is, I'm worried I'll fail. There's a reason I was sent to admin and not to defense in the first place, and there's a reason I'm not among the people who train regularly with the defenders. I just don't have the aptitude."

He dropped his outspread hands, and let his head fall forward. He hoped he hadn't overdone it, but he was pretty sure he hadn't—mostly because what he was saying was true. His reaction to Hairth earlier that day had not only been because the idea of working with Levi scared him stiff, though it did. It was also because of what he had just told Ella, though this was the first time he had admitted it to himself.

Even staring at the ground, Jaren could see her stance soften. She walked over and put an arm around him. There was the slightest familiarity in her scent. He leaned against her, and she put her cheek against the top of his head. He regretted lying to her, but he knew it was his only choice. It was so nice to have her there with him.

"Oh, Jaren. I've missed you."

"I've missed you, too."

Chapter 13

Sweating on a Rug

Jaren wiped sweat from his forehead as he approached his second lap around Freysdal. Running somehow made everything feel better. Whether it was simply the reminder of his previously uncomplicated life as an admin messenger, finally working off the effect of sleeping for days, or the healing started by his conversation with Ella late into the night, Jaren felt more clear-headed than he had since waking up in the clinic.

Puffy clouds drifted above, shading parts of his run. People smiled as they moved about Freysdal. Finches flittered from rooftop to rooftop in great swirling masses, turning in on themselves before shooting out from within—looking the same as a lump of energy when Jaren folded it back into its source.

Everything about the run was good, but the best part was that no one noticed him. No one pointed to the exposed house in the trees and discussed the thunder and the cloud of smoke. No one worried about snake attacks or invading armies. At least he didn't hear anyone talking about those things. No one saw the lumps of light, like small eggs, floating beside him while he ran. He collected one each time he passed a lightball. He had fifteen, and wasn't sure he could hold any more, which was just as well as the run was almost done.

Apprenticing with Hairth earlier that morning had almost put Jaren to sleep. Hairth reviewed documents and met with people, and Jaren was supposed to learn by watching. The only remarkable thing was a visit from a man in a long black robe with a cut and fabric Jaren had never seen before. It had high, peaked shoulders and a splash of dark green in the collar. It shimmered as he walked, almost like it was made of water. Hairth and the man greeted one another like old friends, and Jaren was asked to step out—the only meeting he wasn't allowed to listen to. He considered asking Ruth who the man was, but as soon as the door shut, she turned her sagging face back to her desk to continue doing whatever it was she did when she wasn't stopping people from going into Hairth's office.

When he had arrived at defense after working with Hairth, Jaren had been curtly informed by an ogre of a Blue that he would be working with a man named Mastiff rather than Levi, and that Mastiff wanted him to run two laps before starting. The insolence of the Blue had been promptly forgotten at the overwhelming relief in not having to work with Levi. Perhaps that also had something to do with his good mood.

The big hairy Blue didn't get up when Jaren entered the building. He just gave Jaren a dismissive glance, pointed down a hall, and then returned to sharpening his belt knife. It wasn't right for a Blue to treat a Green-Yellow like that, no matter how big he was. Jaren released the energy of one of the eggs over his head. A burst of light cast shadows throughout the entry way. The man jerked his head toward Jaren and narrowed his eyes at him.

"What?" Jaren asked.

"Nothing," the man grunted in a deep voice. He looked around again, then turned back to his knife.

Jaren pushed an egg behind the man and released it. The man jerked around, holding his knife ready.

"What is...?" he asked.

Jaren moved toward the hall.

"Did you see that?" the man asked.

"See what?"

As Jaren went around a corner, he released the other eggs to the left and right of the man in quick succession.

"Blistered bones!" the man swore, and jumped to his feet, spinning left then right.

Jaren grinned as he walked through an open door, but then frowned. Had he just abused that man with radiance? Was the radiance already corrupting him? He wanted to throw up.

A man, Mastiff, presumably, was waiting for him in the otherwise empty room. There was no furniture, but training implements lined the wall. The floor was covered in a thick, soft rug, and it smelled like sweaty bodies, despite the open windows on opposing walls. The man wore a smile that pushed his heavy cheeks back and made his face seem wider than it was—which was saying something considering how large his head was. Puffy eyelids made his eyes look mostly shut, but Jaren doubted that very much got past him. Despite his bulk, he moved with surprising grace, and closer inspection revealed that little of the bulk was fat.

"I'm Mastiff. Jaren, right? Are you doing okay? You're looking a little sick."

"I'm okay…"

"That run was fast. Maybe too fast?"

"No, the run was fine, I just…" Jaren shook his head.

"If you can do two laps that fast and feel okay, that's very good. Fighting takes a lot of energy out of a man. Your run lasted about half an hour. Three minutes of intense fighting will drain you just as much. If you're not in shape and your opponent is, all he has to do is wear you down. When you report here each day, you'll change out of your segg and into one of the training seggs and then run the same two laps. Then you'll come find me and we'll get started."

Jaren nodded. Mastiff's voice was rich and clear. His creamy brown skin and impressive height made Jaren think he was from Grallan…or maybe Chorat—though he lacked both the accent and the number of freckles they typically had.

"I'm going to teach you two styles of unarmed combat. One is used while you're standing, and the other after you are down on the ground. If you're only fighting one person and they know what they're doing, you'll end on the ground. We'll start there. It's called grappling."

Jaren quickly learned the purpose of the squishy rug and the reason for the revolting smell. Over the next two hours, Mastiff repeatedly—and effortlessly—forced Jaren to the ground, leaving long damp smears of sweat in his wake. He showed Jaren how to take someone to the ground and what to do once there. Jaren practiced the techniques but using them against Mastiff was like wrestling a stone statue. Mastiff repeatedly promised that the techniques, when properly used, would enable Jaren to take control of much larger and stronger men, but Jaren had his doubts. The training lasted two hours, but Jaren's muscles did not—within the first half-hour he found it difficult to get his arms to do what he wanted them to do.

Mastiff was a remarkably patient teacher. When Jaren struggled understanding an arm bar, Mastiff had him practice it dozens of times without showing any frustration. He simply reset and asked Jaren to do it again, coaching him each time on how he could improve his technique. Mastiff was the exact opposite of what Jaren had expected from Levi, and what he knew he'd get from Joans.

Chapter 14

Practicing Radiance

Jaren could make out the sources before he got to the clearing. They shone through the weather-beaten wooden walls like sunlight reflecting off polished silver, but were dimmed when the energy passed through the stone chimney. Joans had been right. Jaren "saw" the sources, though not with his eyes, and gave it no more thought than he did hearing with his ears.

The grass in the clearing had grown uneven. A few blades even poked up between the downed trees. The smell of smoke was gone, and the smell of pine sap saturated the air.

Jaren opened the creaky door and walked into the old house. He opened the wooden shutters, being careful not to break the aged slats. In the sunlight he could see that dust had returned to the air. Joans' influence was wearing off. Nature reclaims everything. Jaren sat down gently on the old chair at the table and stared at the sources. Something was off. Jaren turned his head at a call from a jaylark, but part of his mind continued to study the sources—seeing them just as clearly as when he had been looking at them.

The sources had been moved. Jaren wondered if Joans had been there earlier. Or was he still there? Jaren began folding lumps of heat and light. He let some parts of his mind practice the exercises Joans had given him but focused most of his attention on the question that had been bothering him all morning. What was he to do? He had promised Hairth that he would train. And he knew if he didn't work hard enough, Joans would punish him. But he didn't want to be corrupted by the radiance.

He nested a sphere of light in a cube of heat within a pyramid of light.

Radiance's contaminating influence had already affected him after just two days of half-hearted training. It was so seductive, but so disgusting.

He successfully braided thin strands of heat and light into a rope that circled the room. Then he fumbled as he tried to move five lumps in different directions while trying to simultaneously vary each shape.

"Focus!" Joans' disembodied voice roared.

Jaren jumped from his seat and whipped around. The voice had no origin, and Jaren couldn't see Joans anywhere. He sat back down and devoted more of his mind to his practice.

Jaren took one small part of his attention and assigned it to the anger he felt at the situation. With the rest, he pushed himself to do more, to do it faster, and to do it with better control. He treated his anger like he treated the energy. He threw a net around it and compressed it into a small shape, which he stowed neatly in a recess near his stomach. He redirected that aspect of his thoughts to join the training, and, in essence, released the anger where he left it. While he knew emotion did not really work like that, he felt better. Jaren focused on Joans' exercises and improved as time passed.

The sun was sitting just above the treetops as Jaren made his way back into Freysdal. His anger had bubbled back up but being out of the house away from those bright sources and walking under the slanting rays of the setting sun helped. Things could always be worse, he tried to tell himself, though it didn't actually make him feel any better.

He ignored the people he passed, only extending greetings to those thralls who outranked him. Soreness from his training with Mastiff was already setting in as he walked toward Maullie and Gerald's. Their home still didn't feel like "home" to him, but it eventually would. Every time he had changed barracks, he had felt like an invader in a stranger's home, but as the peace of Freysdal settled in, each eventually felt like home.

The sun was behind the mountain when he arrived at the house. Without thinking, he filled the water barrel and brought the clothes in off the line. He was the first one back...well, Kehvun was there, but he was asleep. His face still looked pale beneath the brown curls splayed across his pillow. His unbandaged arm was lying outside the blanket. It was a mottled mess of yellows, browns, and purples with little red cuts from the treatment. It was still swollen and looked squishy. Seeing it sent shivers down to Jaren's tailbone.

Jaren sat down to set the table and rested his forehead on his arm for a minute. He awoke to the sound of knocking. He lifted his head and found that the table had been set—except for where he had been sleeping. The kitchen smelled of sweet and savory meats and spicy fruits—the same as the dining hall on the way back from training.

"Come in, come in!" That was Maullie.

Between the night's darkness and the glaring lightball, Jaren couldn't see who she was talking to. How long had he been asleep? He quickly wiped his drool from the tabletop. He tried to stand, then stopped in response to the intense pain in his muscles.

"Thank you."

Cool air seeping in through the open door brushed Jaren's calves as Maullie stepped aside and ushered Haerlee in. Jaren's heart skipped a beat. Haerlee's eyes took in the room, met his briefly, then looked past him. A small half-smile curled one edge of her mouth as she turned back to Maullie.

"So, how is Kehvun doing?"

"He's better, but still quite pale. He's been asleep most of the day."

Haerlee nodded, rubbing her bare arms. The evening air had cooled from the warmth of the day, and it didn't look like Haerlee had brought anything to wear over her rough segg.

"Has he eaten much today?"

"He ate some bread earlier, but nothing more."

Haerlee nodded again. "Yes, that's common. Everyone feels fine, but they are tired, and they have no appetite. The treatment I read about didn't mention this, but as the poison wasn't ingested, I think we need to insist that he eat something. May I check on him?"

"Of course." Maullie walked Haerlee back to Kehvun's room.

"He's so lucky!" Jaren spun around, muscles stabbing again, to see Ella staring toward Kehvun's room.

"What do you mean?" Jaren asked.

"That she was there—he was lucky—and that she knew how to treat his bite." She looked at him and smiled.

"Oh, right, of course. Yes, very lucky." He turned around to look at the closed door. Jaren wondered if he would voluntarily be bitten by a snake to spend more time with Haerlee. He shook his head to clear his thoughts.

"You looked pretty tired yourself," Ella said, still smiling at him.

"What are you smiling at?"

She nodded toward the mirror.

He looked at himself and groaned, but not from the aching pain of moving. Two thick red marks ran across his cheek and to the side of his head from where his head had been resting on his arms. No wonder Haerlee had smiled. He rubbed his skin, but the marks remained.

"Don't worry, they will go away."

"But not before she comes out..." Jaren muttered under his breath.

After Ella set Jaren's place at the table, she began pulling covered pots from a large cloth-lined basket. The savory smells reminded Jaren how hungry he was. He peeked in one and was greeted by steam that smelled of cooked rice.

"We'll get him up to eat some dinner as soon as Gerald gets home," Maullie said as she and Haerlee walked out of Kehvun's room.

As if his name had summoned him, Gerald walked through the front door. He moved slowly and delicately, like he was trying to sneak past someone.

"It's okay," Maullie said, as she laid her head on his chest and wrapped her arms around him. "We need to wake him up to eat dinner." Gerald returned the embrace, burying his face in Maullie's curly, dark brown hair.

"How is he?" he asked Haerlee, who was still standing in the hallway. She smiled at the couple, her hands behind her back and replied, "He's doing well." Her eyes shifted between Gerald and Maullie.

"Are you checking on all of the victims today?"

"Yes. This treatment's new to me, so I'll be checking every day. So far, almost everyone is doing about the same as Kehvun, but I want to make sure they continue to heal."

"Almost everyone?"

"There's one whose bruising looks worse, and he hadn't woken up all day until I came by. He is still improving, though, more slowly."

"How many more do you have to visit?"

"Only four more."

"If that's all, why don't you stay and have some dinner with us?" Maullie suggested. "Unless you've already eaten..."

"I haven't, but I don't want to intrude." "You wouldn't intrude."

Everyone turned to stare at Jaren. He was as surprised by his interjection as everyone else was.

"Jaren!" Ella quietly chided. The glance Maullie shot at Jaren was no less harsh. Gerald just smirked at him. Jaren flushed and lowered his head—he was little more than a guest himself.

"Jaren's quite right, even if it wasn't his place to say it. You wouldn't be intruding, and we would love the opportunity to show you our appreciation."

"That is very kind of you, but it is getting late, and I still need to visit the others."

"Please, we insist," Maullie said, stretching out her hands to grasp Haerlee's. Haerlee gave a resigned smile and nodded in agreement.

Chapter 15

Enjoying Dinner

Jaren found himself staring at Haerlee anytime his mind wandered. When she caught him, he looked away or tilted his head, as if he had been trying to see past her. She smiled knowingly, or perhaps because of the marks on his face. The whole meal was an exhilarating embarrassment. Kehvun's gaunt eyes were similarly drawn to her, but despite his pale face and weak posture, he smiled or winked whenever he caught her eye. She seemed to ignore him. Jaren suppressed his irritation at Kehvun's forwardness.

No one else noticed the spectacle. Jaren wished that Maullie would catch Kehvun and deliver one of her well-known rebukes. However, Maullie simply beamed at Kehvun and repeatedly explained how she couldn't thank Haerlee enough. Eventually Gerald interceded, interrupting Maullie by laying his hand on hers.

"Haerlee, we are grateful," he said, then looked at Maullie, "but we don't want to smother you with that gratitude."

Haerlee softly replied, "My mother called this the burden of the healer—if you fail, you share in the loss. If you succeed, you endure the gratitude."

"Well, then I'll say no more of it, but don't mistake my silence for ingratitude."

Haerlee squeezed Maullie's hand, and both smiled.

"Maullie, I know you run the school and teach. Gerald, what do you do?"

"I develop techniques to refine sources. The ores we use do not contain enough source material without being concentrated, so my shop tries to find better ways to concentrate the materials."

"I'm his apprentice," Kehvun added with a toothy grin that made his ashen face look skull-like. Haerlee glanced at him but turned back to Gerald. Jaren rolled his eyes.

"I had no idea." She paused as if she had more to say, took a breath, and then looking between Gerald and Molly, continued, "Can I ask you a personal question?"

"Please."

"Well, all three of you are freedmen..." Haerlee paused again, and Kehvun again interjected.

"We believe in Hairth's cause."

"Of course." Haerlee looked at Kehvun and shook her head. "What I was getting at is...well...aren't you too young to be a freedman?"

Maullie answered. "Kehvun was born into Thralldom— before there were laws prohibiting that. He was made a freedman the day he turned ten." Haerlee nodded as if it made sense to her, but Jaren was just confused. Maullie continued, "There aren't too many families like ours here in Freysdal. Gerald and I were among the first married couples that Hairth acquired. We hadn't been here long before Kehvun was born. One of the last children born as a thrall."

Gerald nodded. "Several other children had been born as thralls, too. But there weren't many of those. One of the early victories for Hairth was convincing the council that if a woman conceived before she was a thrall that the child could not be a thrall."

Maullie nodded, and added, "That lowered the value of pregnant women as thralls and allowed Hairth to acquire most if not all that arrived in Caidron. Soon after, being born a thrall was outlawed, as well. It wasn't long before there were small children all over Freysdal. When we knew I was expecting Kehvun, I suggested to Hairth that I start a school for the children. I had been a teacher before, and it would help free up some of the women to work while their children were with me. Hairth loved the idea." She turned to Gerald, "Listen to me, telling her our life story."

"No, it's very interesting. My mother and I could both read and write when we got here, so neither of us went to your school. Some of the patients told me about it, and Mother said you were a wonderful lady..." Haerlee's voice trailed off and Maullie placed her hand on Haerlee's arm.

"And how is your mother doing?"

"She's about the same," Haerlee said.

"A perfect heart, a broken mind. The one he'll fix, the other refine."

Maullie and Haerlee both turned to Ella, shock on their faces.

"What did you say?" Maullie asked with surprise, but there was also a hint of anger in her voice.

Ella kept eating her dinner, oblivious.

"She doesn't know what she said," Jaren answered. Haerlee turned to Jaren in confusion, but Maullie understood.

"Oh, did I just say something?" Ella asked, color rising in her cheeks. "I'm sorry."

"It's okay," Jaren said in a soothing tone, then addressing Haerlee he added, "She doesn't mean anything by it. Sometimes, she just says strange things."

"Maullie had mentioned that to me. It's just..." Haerlee looked at Maullie.

"What?" Kehvun asked.

Maullie glanced at Haerlee, then said, "Haerlee's mother is the kindest woman I've ever met. You could say she has a perfect heart. But she's suffering from a sickness that one might call a broken mind." Everyone turned to look at Ella again.

She looked back, unease creasing her brow. "What did I say?"

"Something about a perfect heart and a broken mind," Haerlee said.

Gerald recited, "A perfect heart, a broken mind. The one he'll fix, the other refine."

Haerlee wiped tears from her cheeks.

"Oh, *H'ust* guide me. Haerlee, I'm sorry. I'm really..." Ella's voice trembled, and tears welled up in her eyes.

"She can't control it," May said, putting her fork down and looking at Haerlee's hands instead of meeting her eyes. "She's been saying unusual things since she could first talk. They almost always have nothing to do with anything." Now everyone had turned to May, surprised at how much she had said.

"What, exactly, is wrong with your mom?" Kehvun asked.

Maullie shook her head and Gerald looked like he was ready to slap the back of Kehvun's head. Everyone at the table besides Kehvun realized that it was not a polite thing to say, but Haerlee had already regained her composure.

"I'm not exactly sure. Something is wrong with her memory. Sometimes she's fine for a few hours, but most of the time she can't remember what happened even a few seconds earlier. Sometimes she's able to remember things from a few days earlier, and sometimes a few weeks earlier, but more often than not she can't remember anything that occurred in the past year."

"Isn't there something you can do to help?" Kehvun spoke again.

"Not that I've found, but I won't give up." There was no despair in her voice, only determination. She wiped the final tears from her cheeks.

Kehvun started to ask another question, but Haerlee firmly thwarted him. "Forgive me, but I need to understand what just happened. Ella, are you sure you don't know anything about what you just said? It's too peculiar to be a coincidence."

They spent the remainder of the meal in a futile effort to extract more information from Ella. Jaren felt bad for her. His family had learned to ignore her comments. Their standard conversation had been, "What did you just say?" followed by "I didn't say anything," and then everyone just moved on. No one had ever tried to figure out what it was—it was just something strange that Ella did. But despite her embarrassment, Ella tried to answer their questions. Jaren also felt guilty for not mentioning Ella's comments about his radiance, but he couldn't reveal that.

As Haerlee was preparing to leave, Jaren tried to work up the nerve to ask if he could walk with her to the next families. She had visited everyone in Freysdal proper, and the remaining places were further up the valley. His heart was pounding, his palms were sweating, and in his mind he kept repeating, "Would you like me to walk with you?" He was going to ask her, but then the door closed without him even lifting his head to speak.

Chapter 16

Following Hairth

The following weeks consisted of identical days—apprenticing with Hairth, training with Mastiff, training with Joans, then to the house for chores, dinner, and bed. It was the same routine each day, but it never felt tedious.

Morning meetings with the Associates, their apprentices, and other supervisors set the stage for the day. They discussed making and selling lightballs and the business of managing Freysdal. Every few days brought a new report of an attack on a wagon train. Hairth responded each time by increasing the guard. Eventually, though, Levi spoke up.

"Look, Hairth, you know if you order me, I'll do it, but at the rate we're going, we'll soon have more defenders outside than inside of Freysdal."

The large room rumbled with disapproval.

"What would you have me do? If we cut back on the number of trains, our revenue will drop, which will greatly hinder our work—reducing the number of thralls we can save, decreasing our efforts at influencing others, and so much more. If we don't increase the guard, the trains will just continue to be raided."

Everyone remained quiet, waiting for someone else to speak up.

Zmendra finally broke the uneasy silence. "But, what good will that revenue do us if Freysdal is destroyed?"

Hairth stood and leaned forward over the table, knuckles against the wood. "I've heard no reliable reports of an army gathering, let alone one to 'protect the holy institution of

Thralldom.'" The contempt he put in the phrase was enough to singe Zmendra's braids.

Jaren wondered if Hairth's use of "reliable" meant he *had* received reports, but they just weren't reliable.

"But your network is only so wide," Hentoya said.

"Even as limited as it is, do you think it could miss something as big as an army?"

"And we've had reports from multiple, unrelated sources — peddlers, merchants, new thralls," Roglos, the director of research said.

"Who all heard it secondhand," Hairth replied with exasperation.

"If it's not true, then why are these rumors so consistent?" Tupreet asked.

Hairth threw up his hands. "I don't know. Maybe Estareet is planting these seeds to scare us. I dare say it's working. Hallumon, tell them what you showed me last night."

"Our productivity has gone down ten percent over the past two months. Everything we do we are doing less efficiently," Hallumon stated.

Danneta, Jaren's former boss's boss's boss, chimed in, "Hairth, I haven't reported this yet because we're still compiling the data, but we've also seen an increase in the number of freedmen leaving Freysdal over the same period."

There was another murmur from the hall.

"I need your help dispelling these rumors, but it feels like instead you are accepting them. Our enemies don't need an army to destroy the peace of Freysdal — these rumors are doing it on their own!"

"I wish it were that simple, Hairth," Gerald spoke up. "I've corrected dozens who were talking about this, but they just continue once they think I'm out of earshot. They're scared — they weren't able to protect their families when the thrall-takers came, and they worry that they'll be unable to protect them now. Most are too scared to leave, but there's this sense that staying here is almost as dangerous."

"Is everyone seeing the same thing?"

"I'm not," Levi declared emphatically. He had been sitting, looking uninterested since making his first observation. "My men aren't scared of anything."

That wasn't an exaggeration. The defenders had an excessive measure of self-confidence.

"Yes, that makes sense. Your men are not scared because they feel they can protect themselves and their families." Hairth paused. "So be it. We're down ten percent because of fear. I'm going to give up five percent to increase confidence." Hairth smiled, but the men and women around the table just looked at him uneasily. "Everyone will spend one in twenty days with security, learning to defend themselves."

The announcement brought a brief uproar, but after a few minutes of lively discussion and negotiation—Levi acting as chief complainer—it was settled. Tension left the room and a knot between Jaren's shoulders vanished.

In addition to attending stand-up each day, Jaren would update Hairth on his training, sit in on meetings with Associates, run errands, or follow Hairth around Freysdal.

"What's it like being Hairth's apprentice?" Hans, a tall skinny Souhain, asked during a production tour. The two were trailing behind Hairth and Zmendra as they reviewed the manufacturing of heat plates.

"It's different, I guess. It's been a couple weeks, but I'm still trying to put all the pieces together."

Hans nodded. "I was surprised by how much I didn't know when I was taken as Zmendra's apprentice. I had been working in the coating shop for four years, and thought I understood how Freysdal worked. Then, once I started seeing what the Associates did, I felt like I was a first-week Blue again."

"That's exactly how I feel! I've been delivering messages to these people for years, but there's so much more going on than I ever realized."

"Saydron, whose place I took, came and visited after I had been in the job for a few weeks and made things so much clearer for me. Tell me something you knew before you became an apprentice—especially things that you are questioning now—and I'll tell you what I know about them."

The tour paused as Hairth and Zmendra stopped to watch a man pour a series of small crucibles of molten heat source in heavy molds.

"We've reduced the size of the batches, since the accident," Zmendra was explaining.

"I thought Hairth made radiant items—that's what he said in his welcome speech—but he only sells lightballs," Jaren commented to Hans.

"Yes—I had that same thought. Hairth often speaks of the future as if it is now, or just around the corner. I think it's what keeps him so positive. He does make a few different radiant items, but he actually only sells lightballs. The plates we're making in this facility will go into the ovens that we will be selling in the near future, but he wants to have a large inventory before he starts selling them."

"So, he's built all of Freysdal from lightballs?"

"Yes. It's crazy. But each one costs more than my annual reward, and he sells a lot of them."

Jaren could hardly believe it—one lightball for all the money a thrall earned in a year?

"Who would pay that much for light?"

"People who have more money than they have sense. Tell me something else."

The two continued to talk. Most of what Jaren knew was correct, but he didn't have the whole story.

The visit with Hans was not unique. He gleaned knowledge from each of the apprentices and soon developed an appreciation for their hidden role in getting the work of the Associates done.

The most interesting visits were to the research facility. Jaren understood why Joans belittled Hairth and his workers. They viewed radiance like someone looking at a tree through a piece of straw—only seeing small fragments at a time. But when he considered that they were also like blind people learning to paint, he was more impressed than anything. Most of the time, anyway.

"Sir, you have perfect timing. I'm about to perform a life-changing experiment," an older thrall with narrow eyes told Hairth as he walked by.

Hairth was like a child in the pastry house when it came to new radiant developments, so they stopped to watch the man.

"I'm going to encapsulate a source in the interior of a sphere composed entirely of reflector material."

Hairth's discovery of reflector material was what had made his business possible. While sources released radiant energy, reflector materials—when they were thick enough—acted like a mirror, so any radiant energy bounced right off. Thinner plates would reflect some of the energy, but some could still pass through. In essence, a reflector allowed a non-Light-Twister to fold energy.

"Did you use Crostalin's technique for curving the reflector?"

"Yes. It's a marvelous development."

"What do you think will happen?"

"The energy from the source should be trapped inside the sphere, and it should increase until I open the sphere, at which point it should be released."

Jaren was shaking his head. This researcher didn't understand folding. The first fold just produced twice the energy, but the next fold produced four times, the next sixteen times, and so forth. His sphere wouldn't work quite as well as the folding done by a Light-Twister, because some of the energy would actually release and some would still get past the reflector. However, enclosing it in a reflector like that would extract an unfathomable amount of energy. As the man began working, Jaren softly spoke up.

"Sir..." but Hairth didn't respond, he was too interested in watching the man.

"*Sir...*" Jaren said, a little louder. Again, no response.

"Hairth!" Jaren almost shouted and pulled on Hairth's arm just as the man closed the sphere over the light source. Jaren reached out and put a net around the source. The burden kicked him in the chest, but he could hold it. He breathed a sigh of relief. He had thought he would need to see the source — to sense it — to control it, but he could reach right past the reflector. It was awkward, like writing with your hands under a blanket. You knew the motions to make, but you wouldn't know if they looked right on the page until the blanket was taken away.

Hairth turned to Jaren irritated and asked, "What?"

The man placed his hand in front of the sphere and opened it. Idiot! Jaren thought. He released the light he had collected, and a bright flash lit the room.

The man grunted but frowned. "That's strange. It should have been much brighter."

Hairth had turned back to the man, who was examining the interior surfaces of the sphere. The thrall then pulled out a cloth and began wiping them.

"Sir," Jaren whispered, trying not to draw the attention of the man.

Hairth scowled as he turned back to Jaren. Quietly but quickly, Jaren explained the situation. Hairth's eyes widened as he listened.

"So," Hairth began, picking up the source, "This device works like the chiller or the oven, right? Except that the reflector isn't arranged as two plates with the sources in the center?"

The man nodded, as he continued to clean the inside of the sphere.

"I must not have cleaned off the forming oils well enough. I guess they absorbed a lot of the energy."

"But with those other devices, the energy escapes out of the open edges. With this sphere, the energy won't escape."

"That's exactly right—not until I open it," the man said, smiling at his great invention.

"And," Hairth asked carefully, "how much energy will there be when you open it?"

The man's brow furrowed. "Well, it should just grow..." he began slowly, then stopped polishing and sat down hard as his face paled. "Actually, I don't know how much. Maybe all of it would be freed from the source."

"What would that much light do to us?"

The man made some calculations, and then looked like he might throw up.

"Uh, sir...I need to do a little...that is...I don't think I'll be able to show you this experiment today."

Chapter 17

Becoming a Fighter

"Skill is more important than strength in a fight. However," Mastiff had said, "you are remarkably weak. Let's cut your running in half and work more on your strength."

Jaren hadn't been sure whether to feel insulted or vindicated. He'd been saying for days that he wasn't strong enough. After the first strength training session, though, Jaren wished he had just kept his mouth shut. He had no idea there were so many pointless things you could do with big rocks. And, to make it worse, when Mastiff finally said it was enough, he didn't let Jaren rest. They went right into grappling. Jaren was sure his arms were going to fall off.

Over the weeks, however, Jaren was pleased to see how much he improved. Holds that he thought he'd never get right came naturally a few days later. And despite the intense soreness, he was getting stronger.

"Why are you grimacing like that? Did you sit on a fire ant hill?" Joans flung a blend of energy that Jaren didn't recognize but guessed it would feel like hundreds of fire ant bites. He caught it and released it, wincing as his muscles tensed in response.

"Mastiff was rough on me today."

"Pah. What kind of a teacher intentionally hurts his students?" Joans asked. Jaren couldn't hide his incredulity. Joans saw it and added, "Without healing him when the lesson is over, of course. Temporary pain isn't real pain."

Jaren smothered his blossoming anger. Joans was abusive to the extreme. Yes, he did heal the hurts he caused, but that didn't make hurting acceptable. Jaren chose not to point out that the pain Mastiff caused made Jaren stronger, while the pain Joans caused—even if it was healed—only made Jaren angry. Joans flung an unfamiliar blend of bio, heat, and cold too fast for Jaren to intercept. He prepared himself for pain but sighed when all the soreness drained from his muscles.

"Don't thank me. I only did it so you would appreciate the pain when I inflict it."

Jaren had seen how the healing was done, so the following day when Joans didn't show up—a "practice day" as Joans called it—Jaren began spinning up the same lump. As he was about to apply it to himself, something violently seized the lump and Joans' voice rang out.

"Fool! Never try something on yourself unless you know it perfectly. Watch!"

Jaren recovered from the shock and watched as the lump of healing energy flew out of the window and settled on a chattering squirrel perched atop a toppled tree. When Joans released the energy, the squirrel tumbled to the ground.

"Is it dead?" Jaren asked, discomfort tingling down his back.

"If he isn't, he will be shortly. The blend you made paralyzes muscles in addition to removing pain. Every muscle in his body stopped working, including his heart, and you, fool child, almost did that to yourself."

Without another word, but with a very dry mouth, Jaren began the exercises that Joans had given him the day before, and the soreness of his muscles didn't distract him at all.

In addition to physical training, Mastiff taught Jaren about the human body. They examined the locations and functions of different muscles, joints, organs, and vital blood channels. Mastiff demonstrated how to exploit the weaknesses of each. Jaren was surprised how easy it was to knock someone out by blocking the blood flow through their neck, or how easily legs, ankles, wrists, fingers, and arms could be broken. He was also surprised by how sensitive the various organs were.

The day after Hairth announced the requirement that everyone must train one day in twenty, when Jaren walked in Mastiff yelled, "Defend yourself!"

Surprised, Jaren failed to react as Mastiff plowed into him and pinned him to the ground. With his wits slowly catching up, Jaren was able to avoid Mastiff's first submission hold. But the two only grappled for a few more seconds before Mastiff succeeded in getting an arm bar on Jaren.

"I yield!"

Mastiff released Jaren and helped him to his feet.

"What happened?" Mastiff asked, as simply as Maullie asked students "What sound does the character 'keh' make?"

Jaren was a little frustrated. Wiping sweat from his forehead he said, "I wasn't ready." Mastiff smiled, as if it was the answer he had expected.

"Jaren, do you think I am training you to participate in a sport? I'm supposed to train you because Hairth needs more defense around him, but you and I both know that he's well defended by properly trained guards."

"What do you mean?" Jaren asked, a little uneasy with what Mastiff was suggesting.

"I'm not asking you to tell me anything. I don't need to know why. But you need to recognize that I am training you for some reason. I want you to be able to defend yourself even when you're not ready. In other words, you need to be ready at all times."

"Yes, sir," Jaren replied.

Mastiff again launched himself at Jaren, who had been anticipating another attack ever since the first one ended. They grappled a bit longer this time before Mastiff blocked a blood vessel in Jaren's leg with his knee. Jaren knew that his leg would go numb and become a dead weight within a few seconds, but Mastiff was too powerful to dislodge. Again, Jaren yielded. Again, Mastiff asked, "What happened?"

Jaren shook his head, "You're too strong for me."

"We've been over this. You are getting to the point where strength becomes increasingly irrelevant. Speed is important, and you should be faster than I am. So, think about it—what happened?"

Jaren thought about it and realized he hadn't really been paying attention to the struggle. He didn't have a good answer. After a couple more seconds of thought, Jaren rushed Mastiff, wrapping both arms around his legs, and knocking him to the ground. Mastiff responded as he went down by grabbing onto Jaren's ears, lightly tugging them and shouting, "Your ears are gone!" Then when both were on the ground, Mastiff pummeled Jaren with his free hands as Jaren tried to pin one of Mastiff's legs. Utilizing a pressure point, Jaren briefly stopped the blows, but that exposed his wrist to Mastiff's crushing grip. Jaren knew he was defeated again, and so he yielded.

Standing up, Mastiff said, "That wasn't so bad, but you now have no ears and you're also dead. What happened?"

Before answering, Jaren asked, "Yeah, what was that about my ears?" Mastiff chuckled, "That was something that I haven't taught you. I guess I've been guilty of thinking about sports combat, too. When you're in a real combat situation, anything goes. So far, I've taught you about weak points, but we haven't utilized any in our grappling. While we're training, a quick touch and a shout can be used to communicate what's being done."

The two spent the rest of the session grappling from various starting positions. After each encounter, Mastiff would ask what had happened, and Jaren would review the choices he had made. Mastiff would make suggestions for improvement and the two would practice those techniques until Jaren was comfortable with them and Mastiff was satisfied with his performance.

Chapter 18

Becoming a Light-Twister

"Make each lump as dense and as large as you can, but only use one mind per lump."

Jaren was still trying to get used to having multiple "minds." That's what Joans called them, anyway. At first, Jaren had just thought that he was dividing his focus between different tasks — counting, reading, moving, thinking, and controlling different lumps of energy. But as he became stronger, the distinctness of each mind became clear. Some were stronger, others were better at one task or another, and some even had different personalities, but they were all him.

He was holding twenty-two lumps that varied in size and density. He knew he could control more, but he said, "I think that's it."

"No more? Not even a young mind strong enough to hold a little one?"

A young mind? Jaren sifted through his minds and did find one that was somehow younger. It was weak, but maybe...

"Yes, that's better," Joans said as a small, wobbly lump pulled away from the source on the table.

"Now, give me a minute." Joans muttered some numbers as he did some calculations in his notebook, then looked up and said, "Seventy-three. That is your baseline. We'll measure every few weeks to see how your strength is growing. You should be able to have some idea from the number of minds you have, but this will help you know their strength. We have one more test."

Joans folded out a large sphere of light energy, filling much of the simple house with its bulk. A network of tunnels of varying sizes and shapes appeared throughout the sphere.

"Fold out a single-density light sphere precisely this size." Another sphere, the size of a walnut, appeared.

Jaren copied the sphere.

"Now, your goal is to bring your lump through the examosphere without touching it."

Joans' lump zipped through the channels faster than Jaren could track. Jaren tried three times, but never got through.

"Well, at one hundred twenty-four, your control exceeds your strength. That is unusual, but you being unusual is no surprise."

Jaren had unintentionally used all his minds on the examosphere. He wasn't sure why, but he did not want to give Joans an accurate understanding of his progress.

"Why are you just sitting there? Resume your practice."

Jaren folded out lumps and began running through the exercises, directing the weaker, younger minds to perform the simple steps, and the stronger, more mature minds to handle the more complex steps, but always keeping the strongest minds free to help him think.

Jaren resented Joans because of his caprice. Some days he would rasp at Jaren for mistakes, striking him with cruel blends of energy and stinging insults. Others he was almost friendly. Sometimes he would just rant instead of teaching. Jaren never knew which Joans to expect.

"It's a cruel twist of fate that brings me here! I had such hopes, such plans! Rising from a humble potter working in clay to the majesty of light-twisting. I was going to do what no one had done before, but my promise failed, the order rejected me, and now I'm stuck here, training a mediocre thrall in exchange for sources."

"The order" was often derided in his rants, always for rejecting Joans and that, aside from Hairth, they were the only way to obtain high-quality sources.

Light-twisting fascinated Jaren, even as he was repelled by having to use it. He released a lump of cold in a river rock until thick frost accumulated on it. He held the stone in a wooden bowl, formed a cylinder of heat and cold, and spun them around each other above the cold stone. As he released the energy in the cylinders, an airstream blew into the bowl, melting the frost and dripping water into the bowl. A small lump of force held the stone above the water. He fed a thin stream of energy into each lump as he released it. He had to keep it all balanced. The hardest part was keeping the force vectors aligned so the rock didn't wander around or fall out of the bowl. A lump's size and density determined how hard it pushed, but the orientation of the vectors within it determined the direction. It was unique among the sources of energy and took a great deal more concentration and practice to control well.

Eventually, a small but steady stream of water dribbled from the stone into the bowl—significantly better than the previous day which had seen Jaren with a ball of ice with a stone at its center sitting in a bowl.

"A complete failure," Joans had said.

Jaren had melted the ice with some heat, which filled the bowl, so it *hadn't* been a complete failure.

"You are spoiled indeed if you think you will always have such high-quality sources at your fingertips. You must learn to be efficient. Your life may one day depend on your efficiency."

That speech, and a swift radiant boot to the rump, had encouraged Jaren to be more economical.

He had failed repeatedly that previous day. But with an additional day of practice, he managed the flows correctly, with little effort on his part. He was surprised but knew he shouldn't be. This was how learning worked for him. He'd struggle and fail and struggle and fail, and then one day it would just be easy.

Jaren took a drink from the bowl. The water was lukewarm, so he dropped a small lump of cold in the center. A chunk of ice crackled into existence and floated in the water. He took another drink, but the water was still warm. All the cold had been locked in the ice. He made another lump with the same amount of cold, but this time allowed it to fill the bowl before releasing it. There was no visible reaction, but the water was pleasantly cold.

One day, Jaren came to practice and discovered that the house was empty. He took a lump of light and zipped it about the house. He tried in each corner, beside the door, under the table, in all the chairs, on top of the table, and in the rafters—everywhere Joans could fit. He even spiraled it out of the house several times. Jaren had discovered that light energy felt different when it was inside dense matter rather than air. That is—even when Joans was invisible to the eye and wore no sources, Jaren could still detect him if he passed a lump of light energy through him. For some reason, the same phenomenon did not occur with the other energies.

With Joans absent, Jaren continued his warm-up exercises, but he only used about half of his minds. No sooner had he sat down but the birds outside stopped singing, and Jaren could hear twigs snapping as someone approached the house. Joans strode in. One hand was either shading his squinting eyes or he was holding his head—Jaren couldn't tell which. The other hand scratched at an angry bug bite on his forearm. His greasy dark hair was piled up in a large clump on one side. He looked as if he had just rolled out of bed—including his robe which looked slept in.

"Sorry for being late," Joans said, a thick slur obscuring his words. The slur alone made him difficult to understand but hearing an apology from Joans' lips was incomprehensible. He sat down hard and seemed to mold to the chair. His head lolled to one side. He scratched his wrist. *"H'ust's* bones! What was I saying?"

"Sir?"

"Yes, yes. The order. A pompous bunch of old men. Thinking they know better than..." he trailed off and began to softly snore.

Alcohol was forbidden in Freysdal—it disturbed the peace from properly settling on people who drank it—but that didn't mean Jaren was ignorant of its effects.

"Get back to work!" Joans roared as he jerked himself upright.

Jaren jumped, losing one of the lumps he held. He folded out more lumps and moved through the exercises faster before noticing that Joans was not even looking at him. He could see Joans' fiery expression change to one of confusion.

"Please..." Joans began, "Please, uh, excuse me, Jaren. I do not feel myself. Demons are haunting me."

He made as if to stand but couldn't quite manage it. Instead, he scratched at the bite on his wrist—an angry, raised red area the size of a pea surrounded by a lighter red ring.

One of Jaren's minds, the one most taken by the radiance, spoke up. *I could kill him now. He couldn't stop me in this state.*

Appalled, Jaren passed the control of three lumps to younger minds that had been thinking and directed the freed minds to suppress the insurrection. They were making good progress when the weakest of the three was infected. Jaren sighed and closed the two evil minds. He'd re-open them when he had the capacity to control them.

Joans unsteadily hauled his wrinkly-robed, wiry body out of the chair and sincerely apologized, again, before stumbling back out of the house, mumbling about a giant mesmerizing sloth plant and the quest of the source trail. Jaren shook his head and continued his exercises, minus the two minds.

The following day Joans was there as Jaren arrived and behaved as if nothing out of the ordinary had happened, except for a single off-handed remark about how well he had slept.

"It's time we step up your training," Joans said, as he handed Jaren a segg.

"Sir?" Jaren asked, as he took the segg.

"I've had pockets sown in this segg for you, like I have in my robe. You need to start carrying the sources around with you."

Jaren tried to swallow the lump that formed in his throat.

Chapter 19

Meeting Haerlee's Mom

Haerlee's features came from her mother. Orthania had long, wavy brown hair that bounced when she turned, and a heart-shaped face with cheeks made for smiling. Her eyes were bright and, except for some thin lines around them, she did not look like she was old enough to be Haerlee's mother. She wore a well-fitting segg—at least, as well-fitting as a segg could be—with Hallumon's sigil, just like Haerlee. Jaren looked for signs of her mind-sickness, but he didn't notice anything.

"Orthania, it's so good to see you!"

Maullie threw her arms around Haerlee's mother as the two came inside. She was shorter than Maullie, with features that looked delicate next to Maullie's sturdy frame.

When Haerlee had told Maullie that the snake-bite victims had all healed and she would no longer be making rounds, Maullie had insisted that Haerlee still come for dinner, and suggested that she bring her mother.

"Maullie, your home is so beautiful. When did you get all of these wonderful decorations?"

The two talked as Jaren and the girls got things ready. Despite having recovered, Kehvun did his usual thing—sat at the table and told Haerlee about his day while she helped with the work.

"Dad was talking with Gaprol about an expedition to find new sources. He said it could be dangerous but that I could come."

Haerlee handed Jaren a stack of plates which he almost dropped because he was glaring at Kehvun.

"They think there may be a good force material in the jungles near Butanogato, but there are aggressive people there that only talk in hoots and howls, and they kill anyone who goes there."

Jaren just held his tongue. He couldn't share what he did each day—even those things that happened with Hairth. That was part of the masquerade, so that no one would notice how little time he actually spent with Hairth. Not that anyone cared, besides Ella.

Jaren's irritation continued as they all sat down. Orthania's arrival had thrown off the normal seating arrangement, leaving Kehvun next to Haerlee, with Jaren between Orthania and Maullie. His irritation didn't last long, though. He was swept up in Orthania's storytelling. One story made Haerlee turn redder than Jaren thought possible—she started blushing as the story began, and by the end her face was so red she looked like a tomato.

"...she was so pleased with herself for about half an hour. Berryfoil really is quite tasty the first time you eat it."

The adults and Ella all burst out in laughter—even May smiled a little. In her embarrassment, Haerlee just looked like she was trying to suppress a smile. Jaren glanced at Kehvun, and seeing the befuddled look on his face, wiped a similar look off his own and made himself laugh, too. A quiet mind whispered that radiance was making him cruel by trying to embarrass Kehvun. It was the most sensitive of the minds, and Jaren knew he ought to listen to it, but three others viciously silenced it.

Kehvun asked, "What's berryfoil?"

"You don't know?" Jaren asked derisively.

Kehvun shrugged. That was something else about Kehvun that got on Jaren's nerves. He never seemed embarrassed. Jaren would have turned redder than Haerlee if forced to openly admit his ignorance.

"Jaren," Ella said, narrowing her eyes, "Why don't you explain it to Kehvun?"

Jaren's throat tightened. The laughter had died down, but everyone was still smiling. Gerald was wiping a tear from his eye. Haerlee looked up at her mother, shaking her head. Her cheeks were still a little red, but she had an amused smile on her face.

Jaren swallowed, "I..." All of his minds were racing, except the quiet one that had warned him, but none of them were coming up with an answer. Finally, Jaren listened to the one that had been beat down as it suggested, "I don't know, either. The laughing was contagious..." Jaren lowered his eyes and scrutinized the yellow lentil stew in front of him.

Laughter erupted again, and Jaren's cheeks burned. Orthania gently patted his leg and explained, "Berryfoil is what you give to someone who is stopped up." She made a delicate downward motion toward her stomach.

"I still feel queasy when I smell it," Haerlee added.

Everyone laughed again. Gerald wiped another tear from his eye as the laughing settled down. As everyone recovered from the hilarity, Maullie sighed and commented, "Keeping berryfoil where small children can reach is a risky decision." Gerald nodded and smiled at Haerlee.

Orthania got a wide grin on her face. "I have the funniest story about berryfoil. About nine years ago, when my daughter was just a small girl, she got into my herbs and ate her stomach full of the stuff."

Orthania slapped the table and laughed, but everyone else just looked uncomfortably at the floor or away from her.

Then Maullie smiled gently and said, "That must have been quite a mess."

"It was. It was. I made the poor girl play outside in her skins while I cleaned up the herbs inside. When I went out to get her, it looked like she had been playing in a muddy puddle—except we were in the middle of the dry season." This time everyone groaned, including Kehvun and Jaren.

Through her laughs, Orthania added, "It took a lot of scrubbing to get that little 'muddy' body clean." Everyone chuckled, and the conversation moved on to Maullie's day at the school, and then to Haerlee's work in the clinic.

As everyone finished up their meal, Orthania started to tell the berryfoil story a third time.

"Okay, Mother, no one wants to hear that story again," Haerlee interrupted.

"Young woman, don't interrupt me," Orthania snapped back harshly, then her face softened into confusion. "Did you call me, Mother?"

Haerlee drew a deep breath. "Yes, Mother, it's me, Haerlee."

"It is you!" She brightened as quickly as she had snapped. "You shouldn't be embarrassed so easily. You were just a child. Everyone does silly things as children."

"I'm not embarrassed by the story. But I'm sure they don't want to hear it."

Darkness fell across Orthania's face. "Wretched child! Didn't your parents teach you manners? When I find your mother, I'll make sure she gives you what for." Orthania was looking around as if trying to find her mother.

Jaren wished he could crawl under the table to get away from the thick discomfort in the air.

"Orthania," Maullie began in a gentle voice, reaching her arm past Jaren to lay a hand on Orthania's.

"Maullie, it's so good to see you!" Orthania said, her eyes becoming bright once again, as she looked past Jaren.

"I was wondering if you could tell me about how you met Mark."

"Oh, I was so lucky to have met Mark." Orthania perked up as she told the story of how she and her husband had met.

Haerlee's eyes teared up as her mother spoke. Jaren didn't know anything about Haerlee's father—he had learned it was best not to ask about a thrall's family members who were not safely in Freysdal.

There was little talk that evening after dinner or once Haerlee and Orthania were gone. Instead, a solemn weight pressed down on everyone, hurrying them off to bed.

Chapter 20

Developing Relationships

"Kehvun, finish clearing off that shelf so Jaren can have some space," Maullie told Kehvun for the third time.

"Why? He doesn't even own anything."

Jaren's face burned because it was true.

"Even if he doesn't, he will soon, and he needs his own space."

Kehvun had multiple sets of clothes, toys from childhood, and a nice hunting knife, among other things in his room. Jaren had a couple sets of seggs and his colored ropes that sat in the bottom of his otherwise empty trunk. He also had the sources, but he tried not to let Kehvun see them.

Whatever Jaren had thought would happen between him and his new roommate, it was far from what did. Kehvun and Jaren simply did not get along. The extent of their conversations was limited to short statements like, "Out of my way!" and "It's your turn to get the water!"

Kehvun had taken to calling him "Rail" on account of how skinny Jaren was. Jaren tried to come up with some suitably insulting name in response, but the truth was that there was little about Kehvun's appearance that lent itself to insults— calling him "tall" or "muscular" or "strong jawed" just didn't have the same effect. He once called him "Bonesponge," but May had overheard it and smacked him with a heavy wooden spoon. The others did not let unkind remarks go unchallenged, but the two had both become proficient at waging an unseen war.

Jaren looked forward to leaving each morning to escape Kehvun's cutting remarks. The rest of each day was like a fool's pie—he never knew if he would get a bite of fruit or of meat. He could be sure, however, that boiling anger would punch through his tightly-lidded heart at least once each day. He tended to let it go while doing strength training with Mastiff, but more often than not it was back with a vengeance by the time he was done with Joans. Occasionally, he even felt some bitterness toward Hairth. He had been promised the peace of Freysdal, and for three years Jaren had enjoyed it, but this new life was anything but peace. The frustration continued to build, until one day he could no longer take it.

Orthania joined Haerlee at the house for dinner that night. As usual, she had interesting things to share.

"I grew up near a village that had chased off a Light-Twister who was stealing food. Apparently, he would steal something and leave a radiant image of the item. Once he was gone, however, the radiant image disappeared. It took the people a long time to figure out it was him, but when they finally did, they chased him off for good. He set fire to some of the houses as he escaped. It was a terrible thing. Even though I was only five years old when it happened, I remember it like it was yesterday." She shivered as she said it.

The next time she told the story that same night, she stated that she had been seven years old. The third time she was five again, but the Light-Twister had killed a child rather than torching houses. The fourth time she was eight and he had burned a house with a child in it. She stopped in the middle of the story the sixth time, confused by why she was telling it, and wrapped things up neatly with, "I just hope that I never have to meet a Light-Twister. They're an evil lot." Everyone just nodded in agreement.

Jaren tried not to let the story bother him, but she just kept telling it. He could hear the contempt in her voice each time she spoke of the Light-Twister. By the time she left, Jaren's minds were all agitated.

"Why are you all stone-faced, Rail?" Kehvun asked as they got ready for bed.

"Not tonight."

"What? You need me to get you some berryfoil?"

Jaren snapped. He lunged at Kehvun, pulling his legs out from under him while driving him downward. Kehvun hit the ground hard, shouting as he went down. The wooden floor hurt Jaren more than the training floor, but he ignored the pain. Kehvun shoved Jaren's shoulders, trying to get free, so Jaren grabbed his wrist and rolled him face down, moving more with instinct than thought. All his minds were still grinding at the repeated story and the weeks of insults. Kehvun struggled, but even though he was bigger and stronger, Jaren easily pinned Kehvun's arm in a painful lock.

Strong hands grasped Jaren's shoulders, and before he could react Gerald had him in a submission hold.

"Easy, Jaren," he growled into Jaren's ear, as he added pressure to the hold.

The pain cleared his head and he stopped struggling. Gerald eased him down to the ground. Kehvun was scrambling up, backing away from Jaren. His eyes were wide in surprise. Jaren's face probably looked like he was ready to make a sacrifice to *Mah'van*. Maullie was standing in the doorway to the kitchen with a look of shock.

Gerald loosened his grip, and Jaren jerked free, then ran out the front door.

"Jaren!" Maullie called for him, but he didn't stop running until the house was out of sight.

He scrubbed at the tears running down his face as he caught his breath. He kicked at a stone and pounded his fists. He reached to take hold of heat energy to destroy something, but the source was not in its pocket. The others were still there, but that one must have fallen out when he tackled Kehvun. Jaren's heart sank, and the darkness enveloped him as he moved further and further up the valley road. The air was cold, but he felt hot with anger and exertion.

So many thoughts ran through his minds—and he could focus on each one. How could this be happening to him? Did the gods hate him? Maybe he should just keep running and never go back. Maybe he should just end it all now in a lump of cold rage as large as he could possibly make it. He imagined releasing that much energy over his body. He would be frozen solid. If he did it while he was moving, he'd probably fall over and shatter into a million pieces of icy Jaren—like the story Pribas had told about the ice dragon. They probably wouldn't even be able to tell that it had been him.

It would devastate Ella. And who knew what it would do to May. It would be worse than when they lost Ben. Kehvun would be relieved if he never returned. He'd have Haerlee all to himself, he'd have his room back, and enjoy a larger slice of his parents' time, and...whatever other reasons he had for hating Jaren would be fixed. Another mind carefully considered how it would affect Ella. She didn't deserve that. Nor did Hairth, who was hanging so many expectations on Jaren.

The man was not perfect—Jaren had witnessed that over the past few weeks—but in many ways he was better than most people knew. He did not accept excuses when the searchers failed to find the family members of his thralls. He asked shop leads about their people and did his best to make sure everyone was taken care of. He was liberal with his vast fortune in trying to undermine Thralldom's legal basis. Plus, Jaren had agreed to this. He had not asked for it, but he had agreed to it.

He continued walking until the road narrowed into a lightly worn path amid large rocks. The lights of Freysdal twinkled from afar in the cool night air. With so many minds working on the problems, he had worked through all his thoughts fairly quickly. Several had no resolution, so he put those aside. However, though he knew he should go back, he wasn't quite ready to do it. He turned and peered at the valley wall with his radiance-sight and could barely make out tiny swirls of energy against a background of weak, stationary light. Deep beneath the surface, water flowed in small streams, pulling minuscule sources along with it. It was mesmerizing.

The house was dark when Jaren finally talked himself into going back. He quietly made his way down the hall and into the bedroom using the reflection from his sources to see. As he took off his segg, Kehvun softly said, "I put your ball by your trunk."

"Thank you."

He was embarrassed by what he had done, but was still angry with Kehvun, too. He was proud that his response had come out as gently as it had.

He wondered if Kehvun knew what the "ball" was. Jaren removed his segg, tucked the heat source back into its pocket, and crawled under the blankets. He was so embarrassed. Had Kehvun been lying awake, waiting to tell him about his source? In his minds, Jaren had rehearsed the words he wanted to say over and over again, trying to build up the courage to say them out loud.

"I'm sorry." Kehvun beat him to it.

"I'm sorry, too." It was so much easier once it had been started, and Jaren was surprised to find that he meant it. He was sorry—sorry for the whole situation, sorry he'd interrupted Kehvun's life, sorry that he didn't treat Kehvun as well as he should, sorry that he'd tackled Kehvun.

"How did you learn to fight like that?"

"Mastiff, one of Levi's deputies, has been teaching me."

"Really? He's the one that doesn't have a neck, right?" Despite the darkness, Jaren could see Kehvun moving his hand around his neck to indicate how large Mastiff's was—as wide as his head.

Jaren chuckled, "Yeah, that's him."

"That must be some intense training."

"He's actually surprisingly gentle."

"Well, he must be a good teacher. I wrestle with Dad sometimes, at least I used to before you moved in, and he could never manhandle me like you did."

"I just caught you off guard."

"That's the thing. I could see in your face you were upset. I was kind of expecting you to tackle me." There was a long pause as Jaren pondered the fact that Kehvun had actually baited him. "Like I said, I'm sorry. But I was ready for you, and you still caught me like a cat catches a grassbird. It was incredible."

Jaren was unsure what to say. So, he stayed silent, and Kehvun kept talking.

"It's just...well, life was different before you showed up—before your sisters showed up. At first, I was excited about it. I'd always wanted brothers and sisters, but then when your sisters actually got here, everything changed. Mom and Dad were always talking about them and were always so worried about May and kind of weirded out by the things Ella would say."

Jaren chuckled at that.

"The three of us used to sit up late and talk. We'd play games together. Dad and I would wrestle. We'd tell Mom all about the things that we'd done that day. And then you all came. Now, there's almost no talking. It's like you all brought a blanket of sadness and tossed it over our home, changing everything." Kehvun became more animated as he spoke. His increasing volume and intensity acted like folding energy for Jaren's own anger.

"Look, I didn't ask for this either!" He practically shouted back at Kehvun, readying himself to leave before he tackled

Kehvun again, awaiting his response and preparing potential retorts: "At least you've had your family this whole time," or "Sorry for interrupting your perfect life with my own awful one." But, Kehvun didn't reply right away. He breathed deeply a couple of times and then said, "I'm sorry. This is not the way I wanted this conversation to go. What I'm saying is that I'm sorry for treating you so poorly. I know the reasons I did it were dumb, and I'm sorry."

Jaren's fever-anger slowly went down, and that quiet mind of his told him to accept the apology. The other minds wanted to emasculate that mind, but Jaren held them at bay. He knew that voice was right—it was always right—but it was so hard to listen to it. He said the words in each of his minds and finally verbalized, "I forgive you. And I'm sorry for being unkind too." The anger drained out with the words. They both laid there in silence. Jaren rolled over to face the wall, pulled the blanket up over his shoulder and let his minds wander.

"Hey, do you think I could come train with you and Mastiff?"

Jaren smiled at something other than Haerlee for the first time in a while. "Yeah, I think so."

Chapter 21

Stopping an Assassination

"What do you want me to do?" Hairth bellowed, flinging his arms wide, his eyes burning with frustration in the harsh shadows of the lightballs.

"I get it—we're losing men. Wives lose their husbands, children their fathers. I don't know how to stop it. Please, anyone, give me a better option. Please..."

The fire in his eyes was extinguished by the tears that began to trickle down his cheeks. Hairth's heart was tied up in the lives of the people of Freysdal, and he suffered when they suffered.

"We've been over this before. I can't call on my allies, my enemies are too powerful to directly confront, and we aren't even sure whose men they are. I can't call upon the city garrison because the "bandits" are only attacking *my* trains. And lastly, I refuse to give up on Freysdal and its ideals."

Hairth's features hardened. He was usually kind and gentle, just like a mother bear was kind and gentle until someone got between her and her cubs.

"No. We will beat them at their own game. Levi, increase our listeners network. We need all the information we can get. Also, get Dashvah and Theohbul to consider ways that our wagon train scouts can be more effective." Hairth detailed a number of other actions that the Associates were to take to reduce the chances of defenders being injured or killed, and then he closed the meeting.

Jaren shared a worried look with Kehvun before Gerald came up and put his arm around Kehvun's shoulder and led him out of the room. Jaren smiled to Haerlee as she made her way out, and he turned to follow Hairth back to his office.

"No, sir, I locked it, just like I do every night. And you're quite sure you didn't pull out your schedule this morning before your meeting?"

Ruth squinted at Hairth—Jaren assumed her eyes were bad, but it was possible that was just the way she looked at everything. She had to be the oldest person Jaren had ever seen. Her skin had more wrinkles than a slept-in robe, and her hair was long, stringy, and pure white. Her voice was like rocks tumbling around in a polisher, with the same occasional squeak from the axle.

"Ruth, I know you say I've got a key to your desk, but I don't know where it is. You probably just forgot to lock it when you left last night."

Hairth was patting Ruth's gnarled hand. She snatched it back from him like he was a snake about to strike.

"I may be old, but my memory's sharp. I locked this desk last night and someone unlocked it and pulled out your schedule." She pointed a finger right at the center of Hairth's barrel chest. It looked like she was poking him with the stub of a twisted and bumpy tree branch.

Hairth gently took her hand in his and began patting it again. "I'll have Levi come see if he can tell who broke in."

Ruth gave a grunt and a solid nod that Jaren worried would dislodge her white head from her frail neck. Hairth walked into his office. Jaren followed, nodding to the guard as he walked past. He was a new addition. Levi had insisted that with the heightened anxiety Hairth needed a guard near him, not just at the building entrances. Hairth didn't argue, though Jaren heard him grumbling about it to Deaelestran.

Jaren sat in a sturdy chair against the wall, facing Hairth. This had become Jaren's seat. When people met with Hairth, they sat across the desk from him, and Jaren sat here, behind them, so he could watch Hairth and the other person without actually distracting them. This morning, instead of visitors the day started with reviewing reports.

The first discussed the progress on building the wall—it was just over halfway complete. The completion date had slid due to poor-quality stone from the quarry. This stone was being diverted to other, smaller projects within Freysdal, though there was more than could currently be used. Hallumon and Hentoya were jointly suggesting that Hairth consider selling the stone in Caidron, where stone was in high demand.

"Humph. We should be able to make those deliveries without our trains getting attacked. We may even be able to do them without guards."

A shout, a thud, followed by a shrill scream and the sound of pounding footsteps tore Jaren's attention from the report. He looked up to see Hairth rising from his seat. The door burst open, and Jaren instinctively pushed backward. He would have toppled over had his chair not already been against the wall. Two men in dark robes, their faces masked, rushed into the room. Each held a long blade in his hand. They rushed toward Hairth. Jaren watched them, fear holding him to his chair. Fortunately, Hairth was not similarly frozen. He shouted at the men while at the same time hurling his own chair at the first intruder. The man tried to deflect it with his blade, but the long knife was no match for the heavy flying chair. The man's body absorbed the blow and he toppled backward. Without breaking his stride, the second assailant— robes trailing behind like a flag—leaped over his fallen accomplice, knife outstretched and thrusting toward Hairth. But Hairth was more agile than his large body suggested. He side-stepped the lunging man, pushing the wrist of the knife hand away, thereby moving the blade further from his body. Hairth rotated with the attacker and delivered a blow to the back of the man's neck. The man dropped onto Hairth's desk and slid over from his own momentum. But the other assailant had recovered and was advancing toward Hairth, whose attention was on the man scrambling back up right next to him. Jaren's minds were all paralyzed—except one, which was screaming at him.

"Help me!" Hairth shouted.

Jaren jumped from his seat and charged at the first assailant, the reports scattering all over the floor. The man started to turn at the sound of Jaren moving, but he didn't have time to do much more. Like he had practiced so many times on Kehvun in the weeks they'd been training together, Jaren plowed into the man's legs. The force drove the man toward the desk, but since he was no longer facing the desk, his legs were bent the wrong way. There was a pop from the man's knee as he careened sideways. The man screamed. Jaren's head was down, so he couldn't see what happened, but there was a sharp thud as the man hit the desk and then collapsed. As soon as Jaren hit the ground he rolled away. He knew he wasn't prepared to grapple with a man holding a knife. He flung himself up from the floor, readying himself for both the man he had tackled and the one on the other side of the desk. But he found that Hairth was the only one standing, and he was gazing downward. The man Jaren had tackled lay still on the floor.

Hearing more pounding footsteps approaching, Jaren turned to the open door, ready to charge again, only to see Freysdal guardsmen led by Laodosus rushing in.

"You're late!" Hairth said grimly. The man at his feet groaned and Hairth gave him a good kick. The man stopped moaning.

Laodosus was one of the men Jaren had met in Levi's shop. He was hard-bitten and not one to smile. His face looked like someone had used it to test hammers. He walked over to the man Jaren had tackled and gave him a push with his boot. The man didn't respond. Laodosus gestured to the men that followed. One of the guardsmen rolled the man over as another left the room. An irregular dark spot covered the wood where he had been lying and his robes were wet with blood. The man's knife was buried at an angle in his stomach up into his chest. Jaren suddenly felt very faint.

"Doesn't look like you needed our help," Laodosus wryly commented. Firm hands grabbed Jaren's shoulders as darkness closed in. He would have fallen without Laodosus' support.

"Whoa there. Bring that chair here."

One of the guardsmen brought the chair and Laodosus helped Jaren down.

"How did they get in here?" Hairth demanded.

The guardsman that had left the room returned, shaking his head. "They're asleep, too." Laodosus nodded, then answered Hairth.

"Two of our gate guardsmen were found asleep at their post. When they couldn't be awakened, Levi sent teams out to find all the Associates and ensure their safety. Shran and your secretary are also both unconscious."

Jaren felt sick. The room felt unsteady, and he was having trouble keeping his eyes off the dead man, blood still oozing from him onto the floor. He took a deep breath to try to steady his nerves.

"Even if they could knock out the men guarding the gate, how did they get in? Our guardsmen wouldn't open for them unless they knew them."

"Unless someone was already on the inside to let them in," Laodosus suggested. Hairth shook his head. The thought of a traitor within Freysdal felt about like the thought of eating eggshells.

Turning to Jaren again, Laodosus placed a hand on his shoulder.

"This was good work. It's lucky you've been training with Mastiff, or these two might have succeeded."

Jaren looked at Hairth, whose large hand scratched at his upper lip, his green eyes focused fully on Jaren.

"Yes. You saved my life."

Chapter 22

Lying to Maullie

Jaren couldn't get outside fast enough. He avoided looking at Ruth and Shran laid out on the floor. Regardless of what Jaren tried, the image of the man with the knife jutting from his chest moved from one mind to another like they were passing around a drawing of it. In all his talk about mastering focus, Joans had never talked about minds running amuck on their own. The scene kept replaying. The men rushing in. His panic. The fight. The scream and the thud. Laodosus asking and answering questions. Hairth's praise and encouragement that somehow conveyed a sense of disappointment.

He stepped into the brisk morning air, still panting, and began folding out lumps—assigning one to each mind, except for the oldest mind. They began their exercises. Forming, spinning, combining, and dividing. A banging door made Jaren jump, and he lost three lumps. No one noticed the puffs of fog and the waves of cold.

A young peddler in a simple brown robe had set up his greenwood wagon as a shanty-shop. A pair of freedmen and a Yellow and Red were examining the pots and pans, bolts of cloth, and other essentials he sold. The peddler at the counter turned and looked in his direction, but Jaren moved away before he made eye contact. He kept walking. He wanted to get away from everyone.

He failed to wrestle away an image of knives sticking out of Ruth and Shran. That imagined scene proved the pebble that caused the rockslide. Jaren turned behind a building and emptied his stomach. He leaned his shoulder against the rough red blocks of the wall and cried.

An elderly Yellow turned down the street toward him. Jaren looked away and ran in the opposite direction. The wind blew his tears down the back of his neck. His heart was pounding, his breathing uneasy. He needed to get out of Freysdal.

He reached the perimeter road and practically fell to the ground. He sat against the sloping valley wall and forced his minds through the exercises. He closed his eyes and focused on the otherly light of the sources in his segg and the lumps he was controlling. He steadied his breathing and listened to the wind.

"Jaren?"

Jaren opened his eyes to see Maullie walking toward him. He stood up and wiped at his face again.

"Hi, Maullie, I was…just taking a break during my run," he lied. And she knew it.

"What's wrong?"

Jaren tried to talk, but as a wave of emotion washed through his minds, the younger ones lost their focus. Maullie rubbed her exposed arms and looked around as waves of cold brushed up against her. Tears began streaming down Jaren's cheeks again. He couldn't stop them. The eyes of the dead man, the strain of the fight, imagined knives in Ruth and Shran all shifted between his minds.

Maullie wrapped her arms around him. She pulled his head down to her shoulder, held him tight and whispered in his ear. "Hey. It's okay. Whatever it is, it's okay."

Jaren wanted to laugh but couldn't stop crying. She had no idea. If she knew what had happened and what he was, she would be trying to get away from him, not comforting him. The laughter came out as choked sobs.

"Oh, sweetheart. Talk to me. What is going on? You know you can trust me."

At that, Jaren pulled away. He wanted to stay close, wanted to tell her everything, but he knew—in all of his minds he knew—

that she would be revolted. She would recognize how he had changed and would know what he was destined to become.

"I'm fine," Jaren said through his sobs.

Her eyes were filled with compassion. She really believed what she was saying about trusting her. It made the truth that much harder.

"I'll be okay. You don't need to worry."

Jaren took off jogging down the perimeter road without waiting for a response. Maullie did not follow. He ran for at least an hour, and when the bell rang, he went to train with Mastiff and Kehvun, acting as if nothing unusual had happened.

Chapter 23

Learning from May

Jaren closed the bedroom door and slumped down against it. He had made it through dinner. Everyone knew something was wrong, but when it had become obvious he wasn't going to talk about it, Gerald had directed the conversation to a different topic.

Jaren sighed at a soft tapping on the door.

"Please go away."

"I just want a few minutes."

May's voice was surprisingly resolute. He opened the door. She smoothed her segg as she came in, fingering the blue rope around her waist. The reddish mottling in her cheeks stood out against her pale skin. Her hair was tied back, and her eyes searched the ground for something to stare at. She sat on his pallet and settled on looking through the window at the night sky.

Jaren sat down beside her, folding his legs and fiddling with the tassels on his boots.

"Maullie and Ella say something terrible happened today, but they don't know what."

It was one of the more complicated things May had said since her arrival. She took his hand in hers. Two minds dug up memories of holding that hand so many years before. It had been soft. This hand bore heavy calluses. She had made him feel safe all those years ago. Now her firm squeezes did nothing to calm his fears.

"My owner," she grimaced, then took a deep breath. "My last owner was a horrible man." Her face contorted like she smelled rotten meat. Her voice quivered, "He did things..." She trailed off, and it was Jaren's turn to squeeze her hand. His own memories and other thralls' stories of abuse attempted to break into his tightly-guarded minds, but he maintained control.

"He did things that no one should have to live through. Sometimes I wished I didn't. There was nothing to look forward to, and always something to fear. He hurt me..."

She put her hand to her mouth. Her eyes went blank, like the first day Jaren had seen her. He put his arm around her.

"You're safe here ..." he started, but then hesitated.

He wanted to tell her about the peace of Freysdal. But that peace had failed him.

She inhaled and spoke into his uncertainty. "I was so naive. When our parents died, and then when we lost Benjamin, everything was so dark, so bleak." Jaren listened, but he did not let himself reflect on those times. They were not his worst memories, but he kept them buried with all the other awful memories.

"You and Ella eventually began to laugh and play again. You became happy again. That let me heal." She shook her head.

"At first, I used to try to remember that—that things could get better. I hung on to that thought when I would lay on the ground at night unable to sleep. I used it as a shield against the memories of what had happened each day, even while still hurting from it. I told myself that I would heal, and I believed it. My owner would apologize, give me gifts, and go days without hurting me, so that I would let my guard down, and then he'd hurt me again. More than once, he let me escape. I would run for my life. After several hours, I'd collapse and pass out. I'd wake up and realize that I was free! Then he'd step out from behind a tree, laughing. He'd beat me and describe how he had been following me the entire time."

"For the first year I let him trick me over and over again. Then," her body shook as she continued, "I watched as he beat my friend to death. He hit her again and again until she fell to the ground. Then he kicked her over and over until she stopped moving, and then more until she stopped moaning. He beat her to death in front of me—just because she refused to obey him.

He made me drag her body out of the barn, made me cut her foot off to remove her chains because he didn't want to waste the metal and couldn't find the key. He didn't let me bury her either. Her soul is still trapped there. I realized that night that there was no hope. I gave up."

"When Hairth's buyer came and took me away, I knew it was just another trick. I didn't even think of trying to escape because I knew he would just find me again. At one point— as we crossed over a river—I thought about throwing myself in. I could finally get away. But the buyer must have seen something in my face because he said, 'I don't think Jaren will be very happy if you do that.' Your name cut through the darkness. I had never told my owner about you. The tiniest spark of hope flickered in my heart. Then, when we arrived, I saw Ella. I knew I had gone mad. Then you came too. But I still couldn't open, couldn't believe it. I was certain that it was still another trick he was playing on me, and that as soon as I opened up, he would step in and hurt me. Sometimes I see him in the shadows as I walk the streets of Freysdal, waiting to step out and take me back—to tell me it was all a ruse. People tried to tell me about the peace of Freysdal, but it was all madness."

"Then something strange happened. The fog started to clear. I started to believe in the peace. I met Mosj, and Maudilille and Torrea and Stenen. They were all so kind. Maullie and Gerald, even Kehvun, and Haerlee were all so good to me. You and Ella were real. It wasn't a fever dream. I still worry. I still see him when I close my eyes. But he's getting hazy and for the first time in so many years I have regained hope."

Jaren sat silently as she spoke. His anger at his own suffering and situation was replaced with an intense hatred for May's previous owner. One of his dark minds promised he would kill May's first owner, and the others agreed. And they specifically agreed that he would use his cursed radiance to do it. Maybe this was the way to tolerate what he would eventually become — channel his cruelty toward those who deserved it. Maybe it would be like an appetite he could satisfy. A few minds considered that idea while he said to May, "No one will hurt you here."

"I believe you. But I want to make sure you believe it, too."

But it wasn't true for him. "Of course, I believe it," he lied.

"Jaren, if you believe it, then what is wrong? What has happened to you?"

He slowly took his arm from around her shoulder and stood up. He paced up and down the room as his minds reached for some answer — something to say that would satisfy her without telling her the truth — that he was a bar of glowing, hot iron being forged into a weapon for Hairth to wield. Yes, Hairth would wield it righteously, but no one ever thought of how the heating, pounding, quenching, and grinding felt to the sword. Even in his current unformed state, he had already killed a man. Somehow deep inside he knew he would kill many more besides May's first owner. A gentle mind suggested that he simply tell her. He pondered that and then reached a decision.

"I can't tell you."

"Why not?"

"You wouldn't understand." You would despise me, he thought.

She looked at him. Her gray eyes were as bright as he had ever seen them. There was determination in them.

"Maybe not, but at least I can love you. Please believe that you'll heal — I know for myself that the peace of Freysdal and time will heal all wounds."

Jaren forced a smile. She was right, except that he was beginning to realize that he would be the sword that ensured that peace — and the sword itself could have no peace.

Chapter 24

Watching Mama Bear

"Don't talk to me about security! You..." Maullie turned toward Jaren as he stepped through the door. Her eyes flashed with fire and her face was set hard enough to sharpen a knife. Jaren tried to step back but was locked in place by her gaze.

"And you, young man!"

He suddenly wished Ruth had recovered so she could have warned him away from Hairth's office.

"How dare you say you're moving out? You broke Kehvun's heart. I don't care if you've sworn your soul to *Re'hal,* you are a part of our family, and families don't quit." A slight tremor entered her voice, but the hardness quickly returned.

"Now you sit down and keep quiet while I talk to Hairth."

Jaren's heart burned. All morning long he'd been fighting back tears. Telling Kehvun that he was moving out had been so hard.

Hairth put his hands up as if trying to stop a landslide when Maullie turned back to him.

"Security? How dare you! The peace of Freysdal is not just *your* promise. It's the promise we *all* make to everyone who comes here! Did you forget that he's just a boy? A fifteen-year-old boy, Hairth."

"Maullie, I..." But she wasn't having any of it.

"Don't you, 'Maullie,' me. I want some answers."

"I..."

"No! Whatever you've done—or allowed to happen—to Jaren is unconscionable. Look at the floor. Look at it! Did Jaren need to see this?"

Hairth lifted his eyes from the bloodstain to look at Jaren. Jaren looked away.

"Do you remember the first time you saw someone killed? I know you do, because you've told me about it. How could you?! Well? What do you have to say for yourself?"

Jaren looked back at Hairth, who was staring at Maullie like a dog with its tail between its legs.

"I need you to tr…"

"I do trust you!" she roared. "But I'm not convinced you're thinking clearly. Don't you remember why you founded Freysdal? Why you've dedicated your life to eradicating Thralldom? A thrall, not much younger than Jaren, taken from you and returned broken? Yet here you are doing exactly what was done to your childhood friend to prevent it from happening to others. How rich! I'll give you one chance to tell me what's going on, and I swear on my father's bones that if the next words out of your mouth are anything less than the full answer you know I want to hear, I will take my family and we will leave."

Hairth dropped his head. He wasn't an ashamed dog, he was a beaten dog.

"Jaren is a Light-Twister."

The blood drained from Jaren's face. How could Hairth do that to him? He wanted to run as Maullie turned around. He couldn't bear to see the horror in her eyes—not after she said that he was family. How quickly her feelings had changed. She would probably threaten to leave if he weren't put out of Freysdal. She wouldn't even care if he was caught by the enforcers.

But then, she took his face in her hands, and made him look at her. Her face had softened, and a broad smile parted her lips.

"Oh, Jaren! Is it true? A gift from *H'ust*! What a blessing to my family!"

She hugged his head against her, almost pulling him from the chair. A knot formed in Jaren's throat and tears came to his eyes. Did she misunderstand?

"Maullie, there's more. Yesterday when I was attacked, Jaren saved my life by killing one of my attackers."

"Oh, Jaren. I'm so sorry. You poor boy!"

"Why didn't you tell me?" She asked over her shoulder.

"Once people know, he'll become a target. I need it to stay a secret until he can defend himself. He needs to learn to use radiance and that takes time."

Maullie released Jaren and spun toward Hairth. Jaren almost toppled forward out of the chair and Hairth took a large step backward.

"How are you training him, Hairth?" Maullie asked, the heat returning to her voice.

Hairth looked around the room like he was searching for a way out.

"Maullie, how else...? I didn't have any other choice."

"You didn't?!"

He took another step backward, bumping into his desk. "What else could I have done?"

"*Anything* else, Hairth! Joans is a cruel, wicked man!" "He is, but I trust him."

"Trust him?" Maullie laughed grimly. "I'd trust a red-striped viper to watch an infant before I'd trust Joans with anyone I cared about."

"Come on, Maullie, he isn't that bad."

"Right. And what did you offer him in return?"

"A significant quantity of refined sources."

"How do you know he won't just steal what he wants and leave? Not that that would be all bad. How do you know he wasn't the one who sent people to kill you?"

"I have defenses in place that he cannot overcome without risking his own life. And despite what you think, I trust him, and he trusts me."

Maullie harrumphed.

"Did you make your deal contingent on him treating Jaren kindly in addition to training him well?"

Hairth grimaced.

"You stupid, stupid man! It's no wonder Jaren..."

She turned to Jaren, eyes wide in realization, and again wrapped her arms around his head. "I'm so sorry. Joans is a demon."

Jaren pulled away, shaking his head while wiping tears from his eyes.

"He can't help it."

"Of course, he can. We all can choose," Maullie replied.

"No. It's what happens to people who use radiance. It makes them cruel."

"What are you talking about?" Maullie asked, looking from Jaren to Hairth. Hairth simply shrugged.

"Did Joans tell you this?"

"No, he didn't have to. I know the stories—the Light-Twister and the stars; the Light-Twister and the wolves; the king, the thrall and the Light-Twister. Light-Twisters are all evil. Radiance makes people evil."

Hairth scowled. "Jaren, almost half of Freysdal works with radiance. Do you think we're all evil?"

Jaren shook his head, surprised they hadn't thought through this before. "Of course not. It isn't just being around radiance that makes people evil, it's twisting it. It twists you in return."

Maullie narrowed her eyebrows.

"I know those stories you mentioned, but you left out Light-Twister and the widow, and the lost lamb and the Light-Twister, and the mountain of radiance?" Jaren shook his head—he had never heard those stories. "Light-Twister's aren't always bad." Maullie looked at Hairth.

"It's true, Jaren. I've met some very kind Light-Twisters, and if it had been possible, I would have brought any one of them to train you, but..."

Jaren felt like someone opened a shuttered lightball in his mind. The pit in his stomach faded, though the knot in his throat stayed. He'd seen how his new minds were darker. He knew how bad Joans was. But if there was a possibility of charting a different course...

Hairth reached out and took Maullie's hand. "Maullie, I've made some mistakes, but you know I'm trying to do what's best. Freysdal's enemies will soon learn that our peace is not to be taken lightly. Before long, they will know of Jaren."

He paused, and then placed his other hand on Jaren's shoulder and looked him straight in the eyes.

"But the name they will know him by is the *Defender of Freysdal!*"

Chapter 25

Doubting Joans

Jaren tried but failed to keep the smile off his face as he walked into the abandoned house. He had apologized to Kehvun and after a few tense seconds, Kehvun had embraced him. Mastiff taught them the basics of fighting against armed opponents. When Kehvun asked when they would learn to use the weapons, Mastiff answered, "As soon as you can regularly take mine from me."

Unlike Jaren, Joans did not have a smile on his face. In fact, his frown was so deep that Jaren wondered how it stayed on his face. In a sanctimonious voice he intoned, "Today I received a visit from one Maullie Geraldswife—a most exquisite adversary." He paused. "I apologize for the way I've treated you. I will treat you with more kindness in the future."

Jaren stopped mid-step, unable to comprehend.

"Hairth spoke to me as well, with her present. He tells me that you made your first kill yesterday. Congratulations. How did it feel?"

The happiness and confusion both shattered at the question. The knife protruding from the would-be assassin, the pool of blood, the glazed eyes, all came back to him. He grimaced and recoiled.

"Good," Joans said. "When you enjoy killing you know you've lost the struggle. The burden can push a man to cruelty, but it can be resisted."

Coming from Joans, it was like a moth sitting on the lightball saying to another moth, "You don't *have* to fly toward the lightball."

"He also said—and was very disappointed by the fact, I might add—that you used a knife to do it. You do realize that you could have easily stopped both without hurting either."

All of Jaren's minds perked up, and regret ran through each. It was so obvious, but it never even occurred to him. Jaren's minds began suggesting ways he could have done it. The possibilities seemed endless, and yet he hadn't thought of any of them at the time. He shook his head.

"I didn't..."

Joans scoffed as he folded out several lumps of energy.

"As the circumstances seem to direct our course, we will now focus on using radiance against people. Until you are more capable, we will rely on direct radiant attacks."

Joans rose from the table, clasped his hands behind him, and straightened his back. He began the slow pace that he always used while delivering a lengthy lecture. Jaren slouched in his seat and put half of his minds to work on the exercises while the other half listened to and considered what Joans was teaching.

"There are two types of people in the world. Those who control radiance and those who do not. Those who control radiance are very rare. And there is an excess of those who don't." Joans glanced at Jaren from the corner of his eye. "Using radiance against the second group is easy and only limited by your imagination. Using radiance against the first...watch that cube!"

Jaren devoted one of the listening minds to shore up his newest mind who was struggling with the edges of a cube. Each new mind had to learn to do each skill, but with help they progressed quickly.

"Care must be taken with the first group. We will first focus on the easier target."

Joans spun out two treebunny-sized humans of light. One was vibrant and smiling, the other was drab and dour.

"Killing a non-Light-Twister is as simple as dropping enough energy on them in the right spot."

The vibrant mini-person produced a dense lump of heat the same size as his body and incinerated the other person. He repeated the process, freezing and shattering the opponent with cold, tearing him apart with force, and causing strange growths with bio.

"Of course, using light only causes blindness. This whole-body approach is an enormous waste of energy, as much smaller lumps placed in vital organs will do the same trick. Heat, cold, or force lumps in the brain, lungs or heart will kill someone almost instantly. In other organs, these same lumps will still kill, but it will be a protracted and painful death. Again, light is really only good for blinding. As for bio, it causes inconsistent results in different organs, but in vital organs it usually causes death within a few hours."

Each of these was then demonstrated by the little light people. Each made Jaren's stomach curl.

"Smaller amounts of energy can kill if you have proper control. Heat or cold in a major blood vessel will destroy it. Force can also tear small holes anywhere within a body. Some places will just cause pain, others will kill."

Joans' puppets demonstrated these as well.

"Now, you try." Joans folded out a life-sized human illusion.

"I..." Jaren shook his head as he stared at the light man

Joans extinguished the illusion and took a seat next to Jaren. His lips tightened and his eyes looked sad.

"I know this is hard. As I said, when you enjoy it, you've lost the struggle. In time, I'll teach you how to incapacitate an adversary without killing them, but that is hard to do consistently. It is a sad truth, but you will probably have to kill again."

Jaren just shook his head again and stared at the floor, unable to say anything. He jerked forward as something touched his back. He looked and saw Joans pulling his hand away, unease on his face.

"Yes, well…I know it's unpleasant. Why don't you pretend it's a bear instead of a person?"

Joans reformed the man of light but gave him a snout and a shaggy texture.

Jaren's rational mind convinced the others that he had to learn this. He dropped energy into the chest and head.

"Good, now do it while it's moving."

The bear began juking back and forth, rushing toward Jaren. It was harder to time the release right, but with only a few minutes of practice, Jaren could consistently do it.

"Fighting another Light-Twister is infinitely more complicated because they can just take over your lumps."

Jaren had already learned this on his own, but he watched the lesson as Joans demonstrated with the small puppets again. For some reason, he did not feel the same revulsion at killing a Light-Twister.

"Energy cannot be controlled once it's released, so an attack against a Light-Twister must be released before he can take control."

A lump turned from heat energy to a ball of fire as it sped toward one of the men. The man's face showed surprise as his chest was enveloped by fire. The scene reset with the ball of energy speeding toward the man again.

"Of course, a skilled Light-Twister will still be able to counteract the attack."

He formed a ball of cold energy and released it as it reached the fire ball. The scene repeated rapidly with a half-dozen countermeasures saving the life of the man. The attacker increased the number of lumps used and the defender began sending his own attacks until it looked like fireworks at a festival.

"In the end, it is the skill and the strength of the Light-Twister that determines who survives. The more lumps, the larger the lumps, and the more mental dexterity and knowledge you have will determine whether you live. Of these, knowledge is the most important and takes the longest to gain. However, we will start by focusing on skill and strength, as they are easiest to master."

Joans folded out a weak lump of light and sent it streaming toward Jaren. He caught it and returned it. Weeks of trying to protect himself from Joans' capricious rages had helped him perfect that skill

"Good. Again." They repeated the process, adding more lumps each time, until there were too many for Jaren to capture, and Joans released one lump in Jaren's chest.

"You must know your limits, which I notice have increased significantly since I last tested you."

A free mind of Jaren's accepted the responsibility to feel embarrassed for forgetting to hide his abilities. A neighboring mind, however, asked why he was even trying to hide his abilities. It didn't make sense to most of his minds. Joans didn't pause his lecture for Jaren's internal dialogue.

"A powerful Light-Twister can often defeat a weaker one by overwhelming him. It is probably the easiest way to kill another Light-Twister. However, you cannot know how powerful another Light-Twister is, so this is also the riskiest way to try. Better to release the energy before your opponent can take control. Released energy's direction, speed, and density all depend on what the lump is doing when you release it. A good spin helps to stabilize its direction. A bad spin causes the lump to veer off course."

Joans demonstrated before continuing.

"Density is crucial. Energy dissipates quickly after release, so to have any effect, it's best to compress the lump as you release it or fold the lump in on itself. The timing, however, is difficult to master."

Joans demonstrated, and then explained several more facts, which Jaren could not keep straight. This ultimately meant that when it was his turn to practice, not a single attack of Jaren's came anywhere near Joans. To make matters worse, even without looking Joans was able to announce that Jaren's attack was released too early or too late. Too early made it easy to defeat. Too late allowed Joans to take control of the lump and attack Jaren with it. And Joans never missed.

By the time the session was over, Jaren's minds were exhausted.

"That, boy, was your first good training session yet. I expect that level of performance from now on. Continue practicing attacks. As you walk around Freysdal, imagine that you are surrounded by enemies. Form practice lumps of light and annihilate the foes—but don't unintentionally blind anyone." This last sentence was said with an unexpected glee. Joans' eyes had widened, and a twisted smile bent his mouth, revealing crooked teeth. Despite an abuse free lesson, Joans was still crazy.

"Oh, and one last thing. When you notice something about your sources that I haven't taught you, you'll be ready for some advanced lessons."

Chapter 26

Feeling Lighthearted

Jaren felt light. The sky was beautiful, the birds were chirping happy songs, and everything was right. Well, not everything was exactly right, but it was immeasurably better. Maullie's reaction blew away the dark clouds and let the sun in. She and Joans might still be wrong—that newest mind was making some pretty awful suggestions, in fact, it was excited about the assignment to practice killing—but, even the possibility of avoiding being corrupted was a glorious revelation.

Jaren cheerily released a low-density lump of light in the head of a Souhain freedman. Grallan, Chorat, Mohis, Arentasher, and Souhain all walked peacefully in Freysdal, national animosities set aside in their unified opposition to Thralldom. Dark skin, short hair, pale skin, long hair, blue eyes, brown—in Freysdal it made no difference. And most importantly, whether freeman, freedman, or thrall, all were one in following Hairth. And for the first time since learning of his new role, Jaren felt joy at being the defender of that peace and unity.

Jaren ignored an uneasy mind that opposed practicing violence, but he didn't silence it. It had a good point. If he only used his radiance for violence, even in defense, would all of his new minds be born violent? He wanted to do good with his radiance, but doing good seemed like tricky skills to learn, and mistakes were very costly. The image of a dead squirrel came to one mind.

Jaren smiled at a pair of attractive Arentash Oranges as they walked past. One had her long black hair in a braid over her shoulder. The other wore colorful strips of fabric in her hair. They smirked at him, and then laughed once they were past. He kept smiling, having burned their lungs with practice lumps. He let his unused minds wander, until one pointed out that someone was smiling back at him. He dropped his smile, and she did the same.

"Oh." Her face pouted, "I thought you were happy to see me."

"Uh...yeah, of course I'm happy to see you."

Tobie's frown deepened a little, and her thick, brown eyebrows furrowed over her slightly too-far apart eyes. She ran her fingers through her hair—it was unusually tame.

"No, your smile was clearly not for me."

Jaren shrugged. He knew better than to try to talk his way around Tobie. She had probably just read a book about interpreting people's smiles.

"You are happier."

"What makes you say that?"

"Well, I just finished this book on body language..."

Jaren laughed. Tobie eyed him uncertainly.

"...that was not the reaction I expected."

Jaren felt free. That laugh had taken the last bits of burden and just tossed them into the air. He threw his arm around Tobie's little shoulders and said, "You're headed to dinner, right? Of course, you are. Why don't you join us?"

Chapter 27

Squirming at Dinner

"Thank you for saving my son's life!"

Tobie blushed as Maullie wrapped her in her arms, then she held her so long that Jaren felt embarrassed. Haerlee and Orthania arrived just as Maullie released her, but then Haerlee also threw her arms around Tobie.

"It's been too long. Where have you been?"

Tobie's blush deepened. "I've been busy..."

Jaren recognized both Haerlee's curiosity and Tobie's discomfort. Tobie did not talk about her job—whatever it was—and he had not brought her to dinner to be interrogated. Though upon reflection, he couldn't really say why he had invited her.

"Tobie, have you met Orthania?" he interjected.

"Oh, I'm sorry. Tobie, this is my mother, Orthania."

"Tobie, what a beautiful name. You have such lovely hair. How do you get so much volume in it?"

Orthania took over the conversation, saving Tobie from Haerlee's examination.

The front door opened again and May walked in wearing a broad smile. Jaren reached behind her to close the door she had left open, but then a hand grabbed the door and a man followed her in. He was familiar to Jaren, but he couldn't recall his name or why he knew him.

"Let's move out of the entry way," Orthania suggested.

Everyone made space and waited for May to introduce her friend, but she just smiled, and then looked down. During the shuffle, Kehvun had arrived and was glaring at the back of the man's head. He caught Jaren's eye and with a questioning look jerked a thumb at the man. Jaren shrugged.

157

Ella and Haerlee resumed getting the food ready. Orthania joined them, taking Tobie and the conversation with her. Maullie took May by the arm, glanced at the man's blue-green ropes, and said, "Hello, I'm Maullie. I don't believe we've met."

"Mosj, in maintenance. I hope I'm not intruding." That's right, Mosj, Jaren remembered.

"Oh no, not at all. Please, have a seat." Maullie led May back to the kitchen, whispering to her as they went.

Kehvun put a sturdy hand on Mosj's shoulder as he stepped in. Jaren had personal experience with that grip. Mosj's face tightened for a second before relaxing and turning to Kehvun.

"I'm Kehvun."

He took Mosj's hand, undoubtedly showing him how strong he was.

"May's brother?" Mosj asked.

"Pretty much," Kehvun replied. Then before Mosj could ask what that meant, he asked, "So, May invited you for dinner?"

"Well, strictly speaking, I invited myself."

Kehvun scowled. Jaren did, too.

"Not that I meant to," Mosj said with a smile, hands up in a placating gesture. "I suggested we could eat dinner together. She told me that she ate here at home, and I told her that sounded nice—then, somehow, I found that I was coming, too." He smiled, almost apologetically.

Jaren narrowed his eyes. Why was this guy pursuing May? She was amazing, but most of what made her amazing was still emerging from the protective shell she'd surrounded herself with. May was in a delicate state—he was not going to let someone take advantage of her. He started...but Kehvun got there, first.

"What do you know about May?"

His voice carried a challenge. If he didn't feel the same way, Jaren might have found Kehvun's protectiveness amusing. As it was, he wished he could throw his own weight behind the challenge.

"Hey, look," Mosj said, bristling a little, "I didn't mean anything by it. My first owner was..." he trailed off, disgust curling his lip. Jaren hadn't noticed that Hallumon was his *second* owner. "I have some idea what May's going through. The Peace of Freysdal doesn't easily penetrate the thick wall that thralls like us erect to take refuge in. I just thought I could help her escape more easily than I did."

While he was still talking, Maullie joined them, wiping her hands on the white, flower-embroidered apron.

"Boys, let Mosj through."

"Thank you," Mosj began, then glancing at Kehvun, continued, "but I was just going to head out. I can see you've already got a full house, and I don't mean to intrude."

He turned to go, and Jaren felt relieved—until he saw the look of pain and confusion on May's face. She weakly raised a hand as if to stop him from leaving, but it fell limply to her side. Jaren dropped a small lump of force against the door. Mosj was struggling to pull it open when Jaren took him by the arm.

"Please stay," he said.

Mosj met his eyes, then nodded. Maullie stepped up, took Mosj's arm and began peppering him with questions.

"Why'd you do that? I thought we were on the same page," Kehvun said, then added before Jaren could respond, "Did you see him pretending like he couldn't open the door? The guy's a snake."

"Yeah, we were on the same page. But if he can help May..."

Kehvun just shrugged and began talking about the troubles of his day. Jaren listened with a couple of his minds, but the bulk just watched Mosj, and a darker few repeatedly dropped light in his chest.

The table was decked with roast beast and vegetables, potatoes with a savory red sauce, twisted rolls, and a fluffy cream mixture with syrupy fruit in it—all his favorite things. Had Maullie come straight home from her conversation with Hairth—or rather, after her "conversation" with Joans? Jaren wished he could have seen that.

The conversation at the table was almost like at the dining hall.

"Yes, but he still hasn't recovered," Haerlee told Orthania and Tobie.

"Have you tried scalpmoss?"

Haerlee took a deep breath. "Yes, and silver mint, blaylock, rumfoil, and spiceleaf."

"Dear—those are the exact things I would have tried!"

"I know." Haerlee muttered.

"And how do they know who the father is?" Maullie asked, a scandalized look on her face.

"Well, it doesn't matter. All adults help take care of all the kids in the home." Mosj was shrugging his shoulders as May, Ella, and Maullie stared at him. "I call four men 'Father,' though there's clearly one I resemble." Maullie just shook her head. Jaren didn't think she would be comfortable in Butanogato.

"And then Pabst told me that Caidron's own civil defense is going to be used against us, but Callas said it was Oiandan Pirates sailing up the river past Caidron, enticed by supposed jewels hidden in Freysdal's hills and mountains. Of course, I knew it was all rubbish from the start, but I had a hard time keeping them focused on their work."

Rubbish it was, but that didn't stop Kehvun from telling Jaren every rumor he had heard.

Mosj reached over and squeezed May's hand. Irritation surged in a number of Jaren's minds, and while he kept a few focused on Kehvun, he turned the remainder to Mosj who was talking about his parents and his brother.

"...they found him about three months ago, but his owner wanted too much. My reward increased to just enough, but when they went back..." Mosj's mouth took an involuntary downward turn, and his voice shook. He paused and took a deep breath. "Well, someone else had bought him. The seekers are still looking for him, but..." He choked up, and both May and Ella rested hands on his. Jaren's irritated minds suddenly felt sheepish. He knew what it was like to live in Freysdal anxiously waiting to be reunited with a sibling. He stopped killing Mosj with light.

Gerald finally arrived and had the effect of a cold wind blowing across the table as he took his seat. The conversation died off as everyone turned to look at him. His shoulders were slumped, his face fatigued. Kehvun had said Gerald had been called away earlier in the day. Wherever he had gone, it must not have been pleasant.

"What's wrong?"

Gerald looked up from the table, and started, as if seeing for the first time how many people were in his home. He smiled at everyone, but despite the attempt, the smile didn't penetrate the anxiety he wore.

"Gerald?" Maullie asked again.

"There's nothing really wrong, now. Just a couple of mysteries that I can't work out."

"I love mysteries!" Tobie's eyes were eager. Having been the one who had invited her, Jaren felt embarrassed—he hadn't realized that she was worse with social cues than he was. Gerald sighed, then said, "Hairth was attacked yesterday."

Gasps and exclamations joined with silverware clinking on plates.

"What happened?" Orthania asked.

May and Ella both stared at Jaren. Bones of *Re'hal*, could they know? Jaren glanced at Maullie who was looking toward the girls. Haerlee was studiously avoiding meeting anyone's eyes — an unusual behavior for her, as well.

"Two men got through the gate somehow. They attacked Hairth in his office. Both were killed in the attempt, and Hairth is safe." Hairth had decided it would be better if everyone believed both men were killed.

"Why didn't the guards stop them?" Kehvun asked.

Gerald glanced at Haerlee, who was still avoiding eye contact. "The guards were all found unconscious."

"What?" Maullie asked, apparently not having heard the details.

"Was it radiance?" Tobie asked, dismayed. Jaren shot a glance at Ella, and his chest tightened. Ella couldn't remember the crazy things she said, but Jaren worried that deep in her mind the connection would be remade.

Gerald was still looking at Haerlee as he began dishing up food. Jaren saw her peek up at him, sigh, and then lift her head and respond, "I don't think it was radiance. They are in a deep sleep — kind of like what Jaren was in, except they show more signs of rousing. I expect them to wake up any time now."

"You knew about his?" Kehvun asked in surprise.

"Not exactly," Haerlee admitted. "They brought them to me because they wouldn't wake up. They wanted to know if it was something contagious. I knew that was a lie but didn't press the matter. No one mentioned an attack on Hairth, but I matched the lid to the pot when Gerald said Hairth had been attacked."

"And, what did you know, Jaren?" Ella asked, her big blue eyes firmly fixed on him, obviously thinking of Jaren's distress the previous day. The heat in Jaren's face rose and sweat formed on his forehead. His minds searched for some way to obfuscate, but Maullie started talking before they found one.

"Jaren was with Hairth when it happened," she started. His heart beat faster. "He actually saved Hairth's life by stopping one of the attackers."

Mosj began coughing and put his cup of water down.

"You knew?" Gerald asked. At the same time, Kehvun muttered, "Does everyone here besides me have secrets?"

"You killed the attacker." Ella's voice was soft but carried through the surprise. She wasn't accusing or guessing, she was simply putting the pieces together. Jaren closed his eyes and shook his head, the image of the man with the knife and the blood...but then he crushed it. He mumbled, "It was an accident."

Kehvun's mouth dropped open. May inhaled sharply. Gerald turned away from Maullie, and his face softened as he looked at Jaren.

"Killing is an awful business, Jaren. But sometimes you have no choice. It changes a man. Takes something from him no man should have to give up. I'm sorry for you. But, even so, I'm glad you were there and I'm glad you did what had to be done."

His words both helped and hurt. It did feel like something had been taken from him, though he couldn't say what. What made it worse, though, was that if he had been thinking clearly at the time, he would not have had to kill at all.

"As am I," Orthania said. Patting Jaren on the hand, she added, "I hope you get over the harm. The man certainly deserved what he got."

Jaren lifted his eyes, but when he met Mosj's, he saw unease. Everyone else stared at him too, but he didn't want to meet their eyes and see the same discomfort.

The dinner continued, but the conversation didn't pick up again. After a while, Tobie timidly spoke up.

"Mr Gerald, sir," she began deferentially. "You said there were two mysteries."

Gerald cocked an eyebrow at her. "I did?"

"Well, not precisely. You said, '...a couple of mysteries...'" Her impression of him made him sound like an angry man with a deep, gravelly voice. He shook his head.

"So I did. The second won't mean as much to you all." Looking at Maullie, he said, "I saw Artor Joans walking through town today."

Chapter 28

Finding Kinetic Situations

Jaren's eyes returned to the faded stain. It had penetrated the wood. Despite cleaning, it wouldn't come out without refinishing the floor or replacing those boards. Maybe radiance could get it out. Would that be a selfish or charitable use of radiance? Jaren was convinced that using radiance to help others would balance the pressure from the burden to become evil.

Stand-up had been subdued that morning. The story of the assassination attempt was different on every lip. The only constants were that someone had gotten past the walls and all the way to Hairth. The taller and stronger wall being built had not prevented evil from disturbing their peace. All the extra training had made no difference.

To make matters worse, another caravan accompanied by more than fifty guards had been attacked and destroyed. The room had gone from subdued to despondent with that announcement.

The chair creaked as Jaren rocked it back. One mind wondered what he and Hairth would do that morning. Others passed lumps of light around the room, attacking the desk, Hairth's chair, and the partially shuttered lightball. A couple minds studied the sources to try to answer Joans' question about them. One mind prepared to attack Hairth when he came through the door, but Jaren saw Joans' bright sources accompanying Hairth's ring sources.

When they came through the door, Jaren released a lump in Hairth's chest. He hurled six lumps at Joans, releasing them just before Joans could take control. Two swung wide, one plummeted to the floor, but the remaining three went in the right direction. Hairth let out a yelp and shielded his face with a mostly healed arm. A young mind chuckled at startling Hairth with a semi-transparent flying lump of golden light.

Joans responded without breaking stride. In a fraction of a second, he absorbed the three lumps with a mixture of light and heat. At that moment Jaren dropped a seventh lump from above. Joans deftly deflected that attack toward Jaren. He stepped back, and it dissipated before it reached him. But Jaren hadn't noticed the weak lump of heat that Joans had concealed within the light, and that lump did not dissipate. It made a fist-sized circle of Jaren's segg uncomfortably hot. Joans cocked an eyebrow at Jaren.

"Always be ready for the counterattack."

Hairth gave the pair a reproving frown and he took his seat. "I have found a solution to our problem."

"And which problem is that?" Joans asked, contempt clear in his voice.

"You've told me, those lumps of light are good for practice but are not the real thing."

Joans nodded. Hairth continued, "Jaren needs practical experience using radiance in..." Hairth paused, "... kinetic situations."

Jaren frowned. Kinetic?

Joans snorted. "Indeed. And how do you propose to simulate these 'kinetic' situations?"

"I don't propose to simulate at all. Every single wagon train I send out gets attacked. It doesn't matter when they go, or whether they use the main gates or the back pass." Jaren didn't even know there was a back pass.

"And it makes no difference if they stay on the main trails or if they cut across through the drier lands. Someone is discovering the route and timing of each of my wagon trains. I can't figure out how, but I'm going to turn it to my advantage."

"I see," Joans said, tapping his bony finger on his thin lips. Jaren, however, did not see.

"Does this not let the rooster in with the hens?"

"It does, but the defenders with the caravan will be a small group, personally selected by Levi. They will be men I can trust to keep a confidence. My enemies will learn of my secret weapon but letting them know may be exactly what I need to convince them to give up any plans they have for a direct assault on Freysdal."

Jaren jerked in surprise. He had never heard Hairth acknowledge the possibility of an attack. It made him feel queasy. Then one of his minds comprehended what they were saying. "Wait! You're going to send me out with a caravan?"

Hairth and Joans turned to Jaren as if they had forgotten he was present.

Joans rolled his eyes. "As always, your powers of discernment are extraordinary."

Hairth kindly said, "Yes, but not alone. Joans and Mastiff will both be there—to continue your training and to ensure your safety."

The painful thud on Jaren's rear startled him. He hadn't even realized that he had sat down. The guards would learn he could use radiance. And then how long before all of Freysdal knew? Hairth said they would be trustworthy, but how could he trust anyone with this secret? On the other hand, Jaren did trust Maullie, and he thought he could trust Gerald. And oddly enough, he even trusted Joans to keep this secret—not because he actually trusted Joans, but because Joans' arrogance made it unlikely for him to actually converse with anyone else. In truth, he didn't trust Joans beyond that. He couldn't understand how Hairth could trust him, either.

"Very well. When do we leave?"

"The train will be ready in a couple hours."

"Then, if you'll excuse me." Hairth nodded, and Joans strode out of the room.

Jaren sat there, each mind looking to the other minds, wondering what to think. Leaving immediately? Bouncing bones! How long would he be gone? What did he need to bring—what did he even own that he could bring? Where were Ella and May—could he get to them and say goodbye in time?

As if he were reading Jaren's mind, Hairth said, "I figured this would be easier for you than giving you time to stew over it. I've told Gerald that you'll be traveling. He'll tell Maullie and your sisters. I'm sure I'll get stiff bones from Maullie when she hears it, but she'll thank me when you return able to defend yourself and Our Family."

Jaren hadn't heard Hairth say Our Family in all their time together. It was something he said in speeches on high days and feast days to refer to the people of Freysdal. For many, the people here were the only family they had—and for some it was the only family they had ever known. Hairth was their father, and the Peace of Freysdal was their mother. *And I'm to be her defender.*

Though he knew what answer to expect, Jaren dared ask, "Are you sure you can trust Joans?"

"I am sure. I can't explain it to you, but I need Joans, and he needs me. We both understand this, so despite the history between us, neither of us will make a move against the other. In fact, I believe that Joans would go to great lengths to save my life if given the choice."

Jaren didn't know how Hairth could be so confident. Joans was like a large boulder precariously perched on a ledge. A gentle breeze could send it crashing down, destroying whatever was in its path, and Hairth, though sturdy, was no more than a gnarly tree doggedly clinging to the mountainside. If it were in the path of the boulder, Jaren couldn't see any way for it to survive.

He wished he could say goodbye to his sisters, but maybe Hairth was right that it was better this way. If they were leaving tomorrow, he would not have been able to sleep. Maullie and Ella would have tried to talk him out of it, which would have made it more difficult when he actually had to leave—and he knew he *would* leave. He had committed to this, and he needed real experience. He would be attacked, and he would then have to defend himself for real. The practice lumps he held at the ready felt suddenly sinister.

Chapter 29

Leaving Freysdal

The sun was halfway to its peak when Joans arrived. The wagon drivers directed thralls bearing food and water where to put their loads in the wagons and on the donkeys. Mastiff spoke with the armored men. Jaren couldn't hear what he was saying through the din, but the men stood erect and listened. They were all Oranges or above—an experienced party that even included two freedmen. Familiar faces glanced at him, but Jaren didn't actually know any of them. They wore long blades on their backs, and each carried a large pole in his right hand. The leather armor covering their seggs did not look comfortable.

When Jaren had first arrived, Mastiff had momentarily frowned at him. Jaren worried that Mastiff would treat him differently now that he knew he was a Light-Twister, but aside from that initial frown, Mastiff seemed the same.

A sun-darkened driver with leathery skin commented to another driver, "This isn't a very big group to defend a critical supply wagon." The pair of drivers wore coarse robes and wide-brimmed hats. One was a freeman, the other a freedman.

"By my bones, not big enough at all. But Hairth says we're more than enough."

"That he does. I trust him, I do. But I also like to know what I'm getting into, I do."

Jaren looked at their small party of nine defenders, four drivers, a Light-Twister, and himself. That didn't seem like enough—especially Joans, with his bony limbs and stringy hair. He looked the least capable of defending himself, but anyone who thought that would be in for a big surprise. Joans caught Jaren staring and arched an eyebrow in question.

"Joans, how many men can you defend against?"

Joans' lips quirked, and he donned a mask of mock effrontery. "That is not the kind of question you ask in polite company." Jaren wondered what kind of company that question would ever be brought up in besides this one. Then Joans sighed and answered anyway.

"Alone, with good sources, and prepared? Who can say? It depends on how well they knew how to fight me. But, with middling soldiers, probably several hundred. But considering the bag of sodden bones I have to protect," Joans' gray-eyed glare made it clear who that was, "fifty to a hundred. But a single man who catches me unawares and slips a knife in my back can kill me as easily as anyone else."

Jaren nodded as he watched the drivers check straps, not surprised by the response. They inspected the wagons and tallied bags, containers, and chests. The train wasn't large compared to those Jaren had seen before—only twelve donkeys and two wagons—but Jaren had overheard that they were going to pick up a large and very important cargo. Some of the donkeys brayed back and forth, but mostly they stood patiently as the men worked.

Jaren turned and saw Mosj looking at the party. The sun made his golden hair glow, and he wore a big smile which made him look like a mischievous little boy. As he walked toward him, Mosj called out, "Are you seeing the wagon train off?"

"I'm going along with it."

"Really? Why?"

Jaren shrugged, "Hairth says that as his apprentice I should know all about the business. I guess this trip will teach me about supplies and trading—and wagon trains."

He and Hairth had discussed their cover story for this trip. But there was truth to the shrug he offered—he wasn't exactly sure what, if anything, he was really going to learn about supplies and trading.

"Wow. You didn't mention this at all last night. I would have offered to help you get ready."

"Yeah, I didn't learn about it until this morning. And...well, I didn't really need to get anything ready. I just grabbed a few extra seggs from supply, and here I am."

"May must have been pretty worried when she heard the news."

"Actually, she hasn't heard. Aside from you, I haven't told anyone yet. But Gerald knows—Hairth told him—and he'll tell the others. I figured this would make it easier on everyone."

"If you say so. If it were me, I'd want to be able to say goodbye just in case...well, just in case something happened."

Jaren squashed the minds that were conjuring up images of "something."

"Well, I really didn't have time."

"Look, if you want me to, I can look after May while you're gone...and Ella."

"Thanks, but they'll have Kehvun, Maullie and Gerald," Jaren said, feeling uneasy about Mosj's intentions. Mosj frowned and Jaren wondered if maybe he had judged Mosj too harshly. May would struggle, and since Mosj was around her during the work day, maybe he could help her cope. After all, he did have a better understanding of what she was going through. Jaren grinned at him, and added, "But you looking out for May during the day would mean a lot to me."

Mosj smiled again, nodded, and continued on his way. Jaren watched him for a moment, then shouted at him, "Tell them I love them!"

Mosj turned and waved in reply.

Jaren turned back to see that Joans was speaking with Mastiff. Maullie and Gerald knew Joans and what he was like, but Jaren wondered if Mastiff did. He began worrying again that Mastiff would treat him differently because of his association with Joans.

The guards were fidgety, checking the straps on their armor or adjusting the blades on their backs. They shot uneasy glances at Joans as he spoke with Mastiff, and then shot the same glances at Jaren. They had been told that Joans was coming to evaluate the quality of a new ore for cold source, but apparently, they'd also been told about Jaren.

As if to confirm what he suspected, a short bald man walked up to Jaren. He moved deliberately like a man would approach a lion when he was all that stood between his family and the hungry beast.

"Now, you listen carefully, young man," he began slowly. Jaren looked him in the eyes. The man flinched, so Jaren looked down.

"I understand that you're Hairth's apprentice, and that you're...uh...*special*." The man glanced right and left to see if anyone had overheard him, then he stiffened and continued, "But on this trip, I am in charge. You'll do as I say and when I say it."

Jaren nodded. So, it wasn't a secret. He opened his mouth to reply, but Joans suddenly sidled up and spoke with undisguised disdain as he looked down his crooked nose at the man, "And you, good wagon master, will understand that this is my pupil, and while his first loyalty is to Hairth, his second loyalty is to me. He will obey you when it does not contradict what I have told him to do."

The man jerked back. Sweat beaded on his forehead, and he began fanning his robes desperately, as if trying to cool down. To everyone else it looked as if Joans' was intimidating the wagon master, but Jaren could see the diffuse lump of heat Joans was maintaining around the man.

"Yes, sir. Of course, sir." The man clumsily bowed to Joans and backed away. Joans didn't make the lump follow him, and as the wagon master stepped free of it, he began barking out orders to the others.

"Force, while useful, isn't the only answer," Joans commented. "*Persuasion* is often just as effective." Jaren ran his hand through the lump. It was just hot enough to be uncomfortable, but not enough to be noticeable by someone not aware of it.

After a final shout, the whips cracked, and the creaky wagon wheels began turning. Even covered with baggage and pulling against the harnesses, the donkeys didn't seem to struggle with their loads.

The first step beyond Freysdal's wall was like walking out of a cool, shaded room into a stifling desert. Jaren felt vulnerable and exposed, and a little melancholy. The dry, windswept plains of Pinnutuck stretched before them as gray and black birds darted off of the half-white, half-red wall behind them. He envied them their freedom. He was bound to his duty, whether in peace or conflict.

Chapter 30

Walking for Days

The bright sun beat down on Jaren, his head ached from squinting, and, despite the cowl he wore, he was sunburned. Hard-packed red earth stretched into the hazy distance in every direction. The few shrubs that dotted the red lands were no taller than Jaren's waist. According to Griff, the irritable wagon master, they were also covered with long, sharp thorns and inhabited by poisonous creatures.

The heavily-loaded donkeys drew the carts at a slow amble, and the fifty-foot long wagon train felt confining. Griff expected everyone to stay close, and he cursed at anyone who strayed. Despite being worried about his family the whole day, Jaren had slept well that first night. But the next morning started early.

Mastiff handed Jaren a stick about a foot longer than Jaren was tall, and just over the thickness of two fingers. It was heavy, but smooth.

"It's not the best first weapon, but it's the safest to learn while on the move. Plus, you can use it as a walking stick. We'll start with stances."

Mastiff led Jaren out in front of the train as far as he could—that is, until Griff started yelling. He showed Jaren how to hold the staff and position his body. It was similar to the stances he had learned for grappling.

"Good—that's stance one. There are eight basic stances. Once you master each one, I'll teach you how to transition between them." Mastiff showed him the other stances, and Jaren practiced as the train made its way past him and Mastiff. Once the train was as far ahead as Griff would tolerate, they walked to the front and resumed.

The staff was not heavy, but after an hour Jaren's forearms ached, and he was covered in sweat. Mastiff eventually took the staff from Jaren and let him rest. After a walking lunch of dried meat, bread, and vannfruit, Joans laid his claim on Jaren's time. They used the same technique of walking ahead of the train and then standing to practice as it passed them by.

"In a 'kinetic' environment, the most important thing will be keeping yourself alive." Joans' use of "kinetic" was clear mockery of Hairth. They walked on the opposite side of the train from Mastiff. Other than that first morning, Jaren had not seen Joans and Mastiff together.

Joans erected a large spheroid of force around himself.

"Strike me."

Jaren hesitated, trying to decide whether obedience or disobedience would hurt more.

"Good. You aren't always dense. Why didn't you obey?"

"Your force vectors are all pointing out. Hitting you would be like hitting stone."

"That's right. We call this a shield. We'll start by practicing with light."

Everything they did started with light because, except when very dense or released in someone's eye, it did not harm people. It was also the most abundant source that Hairth had. That, in part, was why this trip was so important. The material they were collecting, if it was as described, amounted to hundreds of times the cold source in Hairth's inventory. The newest product he was developing depended on cold, so it was critical they bring it back.

"Use the light to copy what you saw me do."

Jaren formed an ellipsoid around his body.

"Now, maintain the ellipsoid as you release."

Jaren carefully released the energy, and a glowing egg of golden light surrounded him. A few of the guards turned and stared as they walked by. The light-egg quivered as Jaren folded and added more energy to the ellipsoid while releasing the energy already in place, matching the release to the feed.

"That was tolerably well done. You will need to improve, if you expect to survive without my protection. Explain to me what would have gone wrong if you had done exactly this with force instead of light."

Force always pushed in the direction of its vectors, and items within the lump tried to move out of it. The pushing stopped once an object was no longer in the lump, and the denser the force, the harder the push. Everything seemed right, except...

"The light ellipsoid is not hollow. As force, if the vector were outwardly directed, the lump would be trying to push my body out in all directions."

"Yes. And if you made it very strong?"

Jaren grimaced, "I would tear myself apart."

"Indeed. Not something I'd recommend. Do it right this time."

Jaren repeated the exercise but made a hollow center. Balancing the feed and release was tricky, but after a few seconds he had it stabilized.

"Drop it and do it again once we get to the front." The two walked to the front of the train. Jaren was sweating again, but Joans didn't seem to notice the heat. Once to the front, Joans had Jaren repeat dropping and forming the hollow ellipsoid until he could stabilize it instantly.

"Finally. Let's hope no one attacks us anytime soon. Now, try it with a weak lump of force."

Because force was so much more difficult to control, they had not used it often previously. Bio was the only source with which he had even less practice.

He took a deep breath and formed the hollow ellipsoid around himself. He ignored the young mind producing images of him tearing himself apart. He carefully checked to make sure he was not within the lump anywhere and then slowly tried to balance the release and feed. What should have been a small release almost drained the lump, so Jaren staunched it and filled the lump back to quarter-density. This time he let the release just dribble, but the energy in the lump dropped again. Instead of stopping it again, he simply began feeding at the rate of the drop. The process was touchy. Jaren had to put all his minds into it, which engaged those that had been wondering whether a finger or a toe could be ripped off more easily. After a few minutes of struggling, he had the feed and release balanced.

Joans shook his head. He picked up a small pebble and tossed it at Jaren. The pebble accelerated downward as it passed through the shield and slammed into the ground. Jaren experienced the drain as the pebble passed through and struggled to match the feed to the shield. Sweat ran down his back. Bones it was hard!

"A perfect shield if you'd like someone to strike you slightly lower than where they are aiming. Drop it and try again but watch your vectors."

Jaren obeyed, but the vectors kept pointing in the same direction. He couldn't tell how they decided which direction, but they all drifted to the same way.

Joans picked up another pebble and tossed it at Jaren. This time, the pebble slowed and reversed direction before the shield collapsed. How could a pebble that size draw so much power?

Joans had already turned and was walking to catch up with the train. Casually he called over his shoulder, "Look at your feet."

Jaren glanced down and saw deep furrows in the red soil in a circle around him. He had formed the ellipsoid all the way around his body—including under his feet. He had been dumping energy into moving the earth around him—no wonder it had been so hard to maintain and stabilize! He ran to catch up with Joans.

Jaren practiced again and again while Joans scoffed, and after over an hour of practicing he was able to get the shield up and balanced, stopping at his feet and mostly orienting it in the outward direction.

"That's acceptable. You are ready for some of that 'kinetic' action," Joans said as he gave Jaren a handful of bright orange stones, each about the size of a large walnut. Jaren had never seen their like. They were smooth and marbled with greens and white streaks, and they seemed to sparkle in the sunlight.

"Where did you get these?"

Joans smirked—obviously aware of how unique the stones were.

"I found a small pile of them where the Nogato river runs into the Southern Ocean."

Jaren had never heard of the Nogato river, but he knew the Southern Ocean was far to the South.

"Now, give one stone to each guard on this side of the train. Tell each man to throw it at you as he passes you. Once you get in front, put up your shield. After each stone, drop the shield then raise it again."

There were four guards on this side of the wagon train. Near the back on Joans' side was a squat man named Desot from Chorat—or was it Grallan?—Jaren couldn't remember. His freckles looked like dirty smudges around his cheeks and nose.

"You want me to do what?" Desot asked as he studied the peculiar stone in Jaren's outstretched hand.

His thick accent was hard to understand. Jaren explained again, pushing the rock toward Desot.

"I will throw it at you…" Desot repeated slowly, wiping sweat from his forehead, "to help you train?"

Jaren nodded and handed him a stone. Desot took it and rolled it in his fingers. Jaren turned and took a few steps toward the next guard when pain flared in his back.

"Ouch!" he yelled, turning around to see what had happened. He glared at Joans as he bent down to pick up an orange stone, but Joans cocked an eyebrow at him, and shrugged.

"I don't see how this helps you," Desot called in his peculiar accent.

Joans' crooked smile spread across his face. Jaren walked back to Desot, put the stone back in his hand and explained a third time.

"Oh, when I pass you, not when you pass me." Could Hairth really have confidence in this man?

Cosren, Yates, and Iambret all understood the task without issue. Jaren got out in front and turned to face his attackers. The slow-moving train crept toward him. The wagon drivers, by now used to him practicing as the train passed, stared at him as he stood without a staff and without Joans. Their sun-darkened, freckled faces showed only slight interest in what he was doing, but compared to an endless stretch of red earth, patchy yellow grass, and gnarly scrub brush he was relatively interesting.

Jaren put up the shield. The burden pressed lightly against his heart. Iambret's smile sported missing teeth as he gave a gentle, underhand toss toward Jaren. The stone arched up and bounced off the top of Jaren's shield. Jaren grinned at the wide-eyed, smile-dropping astonishment in Iambret's face. He released the shield then put it back up before Yates could get his toss off. At least, that's what he tried to do. He did get the shield up but didn't get the vectors right. Yates also threw an underhand toss, which also struck the shield above Jaren's head. Unfortunately, Yates' toss picked up some extra oomph as it was pushed through the shield, striking Jaren's shoulder. Jaren yelped and Yates and Iambret both chuckled. He dropped the shield and rubbed his shoulder, but quickly threw up another shield, trying to ignore the pain. This time he didn't even get the shield up before the orange stone was arching through the air. He was surprised at how clearly the orange stood out against the bright, cloudless blue sky. He knew he wouldn't get the shield up in time, so he threw the lump he had folded into the path of the oncoming stone and shot it straight to the ground. All four guards gave out a shout for that trick, two of them even clapped, but Joans hollered, "That's cheating!"

The drivers and the guards on the other side of the train moved to where they could see the source of the commotion. The sound and movement had distracted Jaren from putting up his next shield. He looked toward Desot, who was drawing his arm back like he was throwing for his life. Jaren raised his own arms to try to ward him off, but Desot was already in motion. Jaren threw himself to the side, narrowly dodging the orange streak as it zipped past his head.

A mix of boos and laughter, slapped thighs and clapping sounded in the desert as Jaren lifted himself from the hard ground. He stood up, checked to make sure the sources were all still in their pockets, and then brushed red dirt off his segg. He tried to wipe the sweaty, reddish mud from his arms and face, but it did no good.

"You may have to walk a bit to retrieve that last stone," Joans said, as he walked past Jaren. The man wasn't even sweating.

Jaren gathered the nearby stones, and then set off after the fourth. The stone was not difficult to find, its white and green stripes sparkling against the dark reddish earth. As Jaren walked back toward the group, he noticed something odd about Joans.

"You've got a lump of cold inside you," Jaren said, shocked.

"Yes—apparently stupid people don't notice heat."

"I thought..." Jaren didn't finish. He hadn't thought to cool himself, but if he had he would have expected Joans to berate him about wasting his sources. Jaren slowly released a diffuse lump inside his chest. It was incredibly refreshing—like a perfect, cool breeze. Jaren looked at the train of sweating guards and wagon drivers, and an idea of how to stave off the cruelty of radiance occurred to him.

"No."

"No."

"No, thank you."

" . . . "

"No."

"That's thoughtful of you, Jaren," Mastiff said, "But what if you just cooled my water instead?" Jaren did and went back to all the others and offered that instead. Only Desot took him up on his offer. He understood everyone's discomfort with radiance, but he wished they'd let him help.

The previous night they had burned scrubbrush to keep the cold at bay, but it produced a sickeningly sweet smoke. That night, Jaren dumped heat into a rock and invited others to join him around it instead of lighting a fire. Most accepted this—nothing touched by radiance was going inside them. Just like in Freysdal, they experienced radiance around them, but were only indirectly affected by it.

The next few days followed the same pattern—training with the staff in the morning, followed by strength training using his own body weight, a brief break during lunch, and then training with Joans.

His forearms strengthened, and he developed calluses on his hands. The staff started to feel natural in his hands. His ability to throw the shield improved, and by the second day he was giving stones to the four guards on his side plus the four drivers. Jaren had to get the shield up almost as soon as he dropped it. The men sometimes coordinated their tosses to get through his shield. It was like a game for them—a game where their points were Jaren's bruises. He didn't mind—the guards and drivers seemed to be warming up to him at least a little bit, and it served as a good motivation to get the shield right.

By the end of the third day, however, the dried meat, dried bread, and dried cheese were no longer even marginally satisfying. The vannfruit was going sour and would soon be inedible. The animals smelled bad as usual, but by then the people were smelling as ripe as the vannfruit.

Chapter 31

Seeing Light-Twisting

The pile of small stones glowed red. They emitted a steadier heat than the fire, but Jaren had to frequently replenish the energy. He could have just warmed himself directly, but the stones brought everyone together, and let him serve others, too. Within a half-hour after sundown, the air chilled and cut through the summer segg. Jaren would seek the warmth of his stone fire or crawl into his blanket. Sleeping curled up in a blanket on the ground was not as comfortable as sleeping on a pallet, but it wasn't as bad as sleeping chained to other people. He pushed the mind holding those images out to the periphery.

Seven days walking and the scenery had not changed. Jaren looked up at the starry sky. He often wondered which twinkling stars his parents looked through. He could never tell—there were so many windows into the great harvest, but from this side it was impossible to see who was watching.

"Sure is a small guard this run, eh, Ranma?" Agshot said.

"Yeah, very small." They had had this conversation before.

Ranma and Agshot could have been brothers—same height, same slender build, dark deep-set eyes, short hair, and rough curly beards hiding their cheeks and necks. They seemed to have the same thoughts too—at the very least Ranma always agreed with Agshot. Agshot was older, with heavy wrinkles across his dark tanned face.

"Why do you think that is?"

"Was wondering that same thing myself. What do you say?"

"What I says is that Hairth's putting us out as a decoy."

"Sounds right to me."

"A decoy, you see, to draw all the bandits and what-nots to us, so a more important train, prolly, say Trankard's team, or maybe Bultip's can take another route without any real aggressions."

"We draw the attention, and they go smoothly."

"That's right. But if that was the plan, doesn't seem like we'll get real far."

"Nope."

"Now, Griff did say these were the best of the defenders, and I've worked with a few and tend to agree, but even so, eight defenders is a mighty small guard for the route to Cresswand."

"Too small by half or worse, as I reckon."

"Now, Jaren, I see you working on your radiance. Don't go mistaking me for some fool who thinks you a servant of *Re'hal*, like as some say."

Ranma squinted at Jaren in the moonlight and smoothed his beard around his mouth, like he had to decide whether he agreed with that. "Not what I think, neither."

Agshot nodded, then continued, "And I don't mean no disrespect, but from what I can tell, you just aren't that good yet."

"I'm not offended, Master Agshot. I'm still learning." Jaren smiled. The glow from the stones cast peculiar shadows against people's faces, and he hoped the smile looked friendly.

"Just Agshot, just Agshot. Like I was saying, though, you don't seem to be in much of a position to add to the common defense here. Ranma and me, we can hold our own against bandits, but during an attack we focus on keeping the animals calm and stopping those as who gets past the guard."

"They don't get past often, but Agshot and me'll stop 'em if they do."

"What I'm not sure of, is what to make of that fellow... Joans. He's not the most sociable of folk. Except for to you, I haven't heard him say more than a few words, and most of them have been, 'You're in my way' and...well...maybe that's all I've actually heard him say. Now, I'm not saying being quiet means a guy is bad. Take Lexer, for example. I could count on one hand how many times I've heard him say more than 'yep' and 'no.' Maybe Joans' momma never taught him how to be polite. But what I'm trying to get at, in a roundabout sort of way, is, well, does he make up for the twenty guards I reckon we're missing?"

"Twenty or more?" Ranma added.

Jaren looked out at Joans again, standing off by himself. The cool breeze blew through his dark robes, making him look like a shifting shadow in the dark. Jaren shivered.

"In truth, I'm not sure. He says he can handle hundreds of soldiers...more if he didn't have to protect me. I don't think he's exaggerating, but I don't know. Hairth trusts him, and I guess that's enough for me."

"That's enough for me, too," Ranma agreed. Agshot raised an eyebrow at him.

"I trust Hairth as much as any man here, I do. And I'm not about to start questioning his intentions. I just hope they line up with mine—which are to stay alive." Agshot paused, then turned to Jaren.

"Will we be helping you practice tomorrow?" Agshot really enjoyed getting a stone past Jaren's shield.

Jaren smiled. "I think so."

A faint twang and a whistling were all the warning they had, but for Mastiff it was enough.

"Guards up!"

An arrow embedded itself in Ranma's arm. More arrows whistled through the night air, overshooting the camp. The guards pulled wooden-panel shields off the wagons. Agshot helped the wide-eyed Ranma to the cover of the wagon and the other drivers followed.

Jaren stood and formed his shield. He ran toward Joans, but his foot touched the inside edge of the shield, and the misaligned vector pinned it down. Momentum carried his flailing arms through the shield, which shoved his whole body to the ground. He hit hard. There was a huge drain on his shield, and he instinctively increased his feed to balance it. It felt like the wheel of a loaded wagon was on his back, and he couldn't breathe until he realized he needed to release the shield.

With his radiance-sight he could see lumps of all sorts and shapes in the distance. With his eyes he saw the guards staring dumbfounded with their shields resting on their feet. Even Mastiff, who was holding his shield aloft, was completely still.

"How is that possible?" Cosren asked.

"It isn't," Mastiff replied.

Jaren looked for Joans' lumps, but they had all been released. Joans' sources were slowly coming toward them. He was in no hurry, as if returning from a leisurely stroll.

"*H'ust*, he moves like lightning!"

"He moves like death on the wind."

"Bones...I counted ten men."

Jaren strained his eyes to pierce through the darkness. He could make out over a dozen prone shadows in the distance.

"Keep your shields," Mastiff ordered, almost perfunctorily. "This could have been a feint." No one moved, except to turn their heads to watch Joans as he walked back into the camp.

"Excellent work, Jaren. Perhaps next time you'll orient the vector inward to keep you in place. You're fortunate you didn't tear yourself in half." Jaren blinked. He *was* lucky he hadn't hurt himself.

"An arrow slipped past me. I presume from the shout I heard that it struck someone. Is he alive?" With contempt in his voice he added after a moment of silence, "Mastiff, will you please have someone answer me?"

Mastiff stiffened, but replied, "Ranma was hit in the arm. Agshot is tending to him by the wagons."

"Jaren, come with me." Jaren roused himself and followed Joans to the wagons.

"Healing is a delicate art. It is easy to heal what you can see, but trying to mend torn flesh below the surface can be deadly. A good healer leaves no scars, and the best can heal well below the skin, but I'm not a good healer, though I can do passably well with myself."

Joans knelt to inspect the Ranma's wound. A gentle glow appeared around the arm, illuminating the damage. The arrow had pierced his forearm, and blood was dripping off the barbed tip onto his leg. Joans placed a lump of inward-facing force around the entire length of exposed arrow above and below his arm, essentially locking it in place. Then he used a blend of heat and cold to saw through the shaft, dropping small specks of sawdust as it went. To Jaren's eyes it looked like a narrow slice of the shaft was disintegrating. When the shaft was cut, Joans dropped the force lump and the back half of the arrow tumbled to the ground.

Next, Joans put a half-density lump of cold into Ranma's arm. He released and fed it at a slow rate. Ranma gasped, then his breathing slowed. Joans maintained the chilling for a minute or so before abandoning the feed to form a pair of force lumps. One he placed within the shaft. The other he placed in the air a few inches below Ranma's arm. The lumps were very dense. Joans released the energy, and the arrow shot free from Ranma's arm, stopped in mid-air, and then fell to the ground. Ranma grunted softly.

"Grandfather's bones," Agshot cursed.

Blood began running down Ranma's arm, but Joans dropped a mixture of bio energy on the entry and exit wounds. This elicited a yelp from Ranma, but he then quieted again. Scar tissue now covered the wounds.

"You'll have a big bruise tomorrow, but you won't lose much blood. The biggest worry now is infection."

Both men stared wide-eyed at Joans. Ranma gingerly felt the pink scars that were still illuminated by the light Joans provided. He grimaced and held the wounded muscle.

"Thank you, Light-Twister," Ranma said, reverence filling his voice as he bowed his head.

Uncharacteristically—and totally shocking to Jaren—Joans placed a gentle hand on Ranma's shoulder and smiled at him. A real smile that even crinkled the skin around his eyes. Then he stood, and his scowl—which better matched his sunken eyes and narrow lips—returned as he walked to where he had been standing prior to the attack.

Iambret walked up and stared at the arrow on the ground. Then, looking at Ranma, said, "I once knew a man who got an arrow through the arm. He went for his shield, like a good guard does. But when he grabbed it, he only got one hand on it. He dropped the whole thing on his toes. He cried out and swore on his pa's bones. He bent to pick it up, but again he only got one hand on it. It was then that he realized the arrow had gone through his arm and right between two ribs. His arm was pinned to his chest, and he couldn't move it. I couldn't help but laugh. Well, he grunted and with a mighty heave he tore the arrow free from his chest and lifted his arm—like a little child showing how proud he was that he had gotten free. The arrow was still embedded in his arm, but now also had a big chunk of flesh hanging off the end. Then he dropped dead."

Iambret laughed so hard that Jaren was startled and stumbled backward. Iambret then slapped his belly, smiled his five-tooth grin, and walked away, continuing through his laughter,

"Dropped dead, right in front of me. Proud as a rooster, and he had killed himself."

Jaren raised an eyebrow at Agshot and Ranma, but they both looked as confused as Jaren felt.

"He's always had a darker sense of humor."

"Likes to joke about death, he does."

Jaren walked to Joans. "That was amazing," he said.

"Yes, and completely unnecessary," Joans replied in irritation.

"What do you mean?"

"I mean that even that first arrow should not have struck our party. I made a mistake. Perhaps Hairth was right—sending us out on this fool's errand is exactly what we need."

"How could you have stopped the arrows? We didn't even know they were there until the arrows were loosed."

Joans raised an eyebrow at Jaren.

"Wait, the *first* arrow...did you make the other arrows miss?"

"Yes, I made them miss. It was a simple matter of putting a little upward force on them. I could have done other things, but that worked...at least mostly," Joans stated. "And I most certainly could have stopped the first arrow. Worse, though, I could have prevented them from ever being fired. But I had placed my ward too close to camp and didn't have enough time to react."

"Your ward?"

"Yes. It is much more complicated light-twisting—the kind you may never be able to master." The harshness in his criticism was expected. Joans turned to Jaren, however, and said more gently, "You have recognized the drain that you feel on your shield when it acts on something? Imagine something like a shield, except that it forms a giant bubble around our camp so that you can feel when something passes through it. That is a very basic ward."

"You've placed a bubble like that around us?"

Joans nodded, but his eyes were once again scanning the darkness.

"Why could I not see it? Or the force on the arrows?"

"A number of reasons. First, you don't know what to look for, so if you did see it, your minds would most likely interpret it as something else, such as twinkling stars or the wind moving in the distance. Second, it's a very, very weak blend — think one one-hundredth density. You're unlikely to be able to see it until you have developed thin radiance skills."

Thin radiance? Wards? And what else had Jaren never heard of or seen?

Chapter 32

Moving the Shield

The next morning the trip resumed almost as if the attack had never happened. Mastiff and Iambret had inspected the bodies. They had taken the weapons and coins, but there was nothing else of value. The attackers appeared to be a roving band.

The only changes were Ranma's wicked bruise and new scars, and the awe with which everyone watched Joans. What changed in Jaren was a new motivation to master the shield.

They were attacked again a few days later. Jaren formed and oriented his shield correctly, then stood there slack-jawed, with everyone else, as Joans killed the attackers in a matter of seconds. But more impressive than the carnage was how Joans used force to accelerate and control all of his movements.

Jaren's skill with the staff continued to increase. The forms began to feel natural, and his arms hardened with use. The guards took turns sparring with him, which both helped him improve and made the guards more comfortable being around Jaren. They commented on his improving skills and asked about his family. They teased and joked and expressed worry about the rumored pending attack on Freysdal. A couple even let him cool them as they passed by while he practiced with the staff. Joans didn't seem to mind since, "You're still exercising your skills," but he warned, "If you freeze someone's organs, they are as good as dead." But Jaren was careful, and the action soon became second nature. One particularly hot day, Agshot asked to be cooled, and within an hour everyone else had asked, too. Griff even asked him to cool the donkeys, which he gladly did. Their water consumption dropped, and they were able to increase their daily distance. Joans scoffed at all of it, muttering about wasting resources, but from time-to-time Jaren also saw him surreptitiously cooling the guards' water before they would drink.

"With this speed and water consumption, we could take fifteen days off our trip," Griff said, fanning his sun-darkened face with his hat. "We could go straight from Rascoe Spring to Marrett Spring."

"Have you identified anything different about the sources?" Joans asked again, as he had every day of the trip. But for the first time, Jaren had an answer.

"The color of your force source has changed."

"The 'color?'"

"Well, no, but that's how I think of it. It's almost like there's another form of energy coming from your force source."

"That's it!" Joans said. Jaren felt pleased with himself until Joans continued, "And, it only took you several weeks and a severe drain to notice it." Jaren stiffened, surprised at how a simple insult hurt when he used to tolerate physical abuse.

"Now explain why."

"The source is dimming because the energy within it is being used up."

"Yes, of course. Your brilliance is astounding." Then louder, as if to the guards, "Get this boy a philosopher's quill!" Jaren's face turned red.

"What of the heat energy from my force source?"

Joans pulled out the source for Jaren to see. Of course, it didn't look any different to his eyes, but to his radiance-sight the flow of heat was feeble and felt different from the energy of his heat source.

"Why does the heat energy feel...weak?"

Jaren carefully picked the heat out of the energy, and folded it into the source.

"Fool child..." Joans scolded.

He ripped the lump from Jaren's control, as if tearing a waterbag from his hands. The burden in Jaren's chest recoiled and jarred his concentration. The lump throbbed with an angry color. Joans split the lump into two. The smaller one was like heat energy, but with a muted color. Warmth flowed out as Joans released the lump, though less than Jaren expected. The other lump, however, was new to Jaren. It was like seeing a new color. It wasn't exactly angry, but it did have more...motion... action...something to it. Joans sent the lump high into the air and then released it. A deep *"Thuwump!"* sounded as a percussive stiffening of the air passed over them. The donkeys brayed and the men shouted, as they spun around to look at the sky.

"Folding one energy into another can have unexpected results."

Joans did not deign to explain further.

Over the next few days, the scenery began to change. Long undulating hills replaced the flat ground. Grasses began to appear in larger and larger patches as the soil color shifted from red to brown. Unlike the limp and sickly greenery of the desert watering holes, here the grasses grew as dense turf and bushes followed along rivulets. The change in scenery was interesting, but it was nothing compared to the change in Joans.

"It truly is a gift from *Hel'dig*. We are a privileged few, and while we do deserve some special...compensation...for our efforts, we are also under a great obligation to use the gift for the benefit of others. If you can remember that, you will find greater joy than you will ever extract trying to take it away from the powerless. Now put up your shield and walk."

Jaren threw up his shield, vectors oriented outward. He slowly shifted the shield as he took a small step. The shield pulsated, and a large wobble threatened to collapse it. He took the minds that had been trying to figure out what had happened to Joans and directed them to stabilize the shield. It remained in position. He had taken his first conscious step. Joans gave him an encouraging nod. It made Jaren uncomfortable, but Jaren wasn't going to squander the opportunity.

"So how did you meet Hairth?"

"That's a long story, but to keep it short we crossed paths at a time of great need on both our parts, and our ability to mutually fulfill the other's need created the foundation for a long-term relationship."

It wasn't a terribly informative answer, but it also wasn't accompanied by a biting comment or a radiant blow.

Jaren took another step and touched the shield. The force grabbed his boot and yanked his leg forward, pulling it into the shield. That applied more force, which caused more of him to lurch forward. If that were all, he would have simply been spat out of the shield, but at the instant his foot was grabbed he had also tried to move the shield for his next step. This brought the shield along with him and sent his entire body lurching forward. The ground zipped several feet under him faster than he could process. He hit the ground rolling in a cloud of dust.

"And that is how you speed walk," Joans said, nodding, as if Jaren had done it purposefully. "Typically, however, when you exit the force lump you try to do so a little more gracefully by reversing the vectors. Perhaps you should focus on mastering the shield first, though." His smile curved naturally without a hint of a sneer, and even more surprising, it showed amusement bereft of cruelty.

Jaren was pretty scraped up, and it felt like someone had just tried to rip his leg off, but he hardly noticed. That had been incredible! His minds were racing with the possibilities. Looking at Joans' un-twisted smile, he asked, "Can you fly?"

Joans eyes lit up. "In a manner, yes."

He formed a force lump like a shield, but it was solid rather than hollow and had an upward-oriented vector. He rose into the air. The excess force in the bubble around him made a gentle breeze flutter his robes as he floated. He sideslipped to the left and then to the right, and then returned to the ground.

"It's difficult to do well, but it can be done. However, in general it is a complete waste of a rare source. Speed-walking will get you where you need to be much faster without all of the dangers associated with falling from the sky."

"Is there a limit to how fast you can speed-walk?"

"Yes, your ability to avoid running into things. Now, try the shield again."

Jaren imagined soaring with birds then realized he had forgotten that Joans' behavior was totally wrong. He needed to be careful.

"How did you learn so much about radiance?"

"I had excellent teachers."

Jaren formed the shield and carefully took a step. The shield moved without too much wiggling. He took another step, with the same result. A third step ended with him being thrown butt-first out of the back of the shield. He tried again, took six steps, but dropped the shield when it grabbed him. It made him stumble, but he didn't fall.

"One question I've had since learning about radiance. During the accident, why was there a ball of swirling light? If I was containing the energy from the source, why was it visible?"

"You were only partially containing the energy—that's why Hairth described 'puffs' of heat, and the light was probably decay products from the rapid exchange within the two balls of heat. At least, when I mimicked the ball in Hairth's office, I put a little light in it to make it look like Hairth described it." Decay products? Jaren did not want to get side tracked.

"Have you known Hairth since you learned you were a Light-Twister?"

"Oh, no. Hairth and I didn't meet until many years later." Joans pushed a clump of windblown hair from his narrow face. "That last one was good—now try to make the shield move smoothly as you walk rather than moving it each time you step."

Jaren shifted the shield very slowly and walked like an old man who didn't trust his legs—one tiny step at a time.

"Try widening the shield."

Jaren did and found that he could take full-length steps and still keep the shield with him. He smiled up at Joans. Joans' smile slid from his face like the peel from a rotted vannfruit.

"Finally. Now, hand out the stones to the men and tell them I'll throw something at *them* if they don't throw hard at *you*." That was better—more like the Joans Jaren was accustomed to.

He took the bright orange stones and walked toward Yates. The Choratan was tall for his people, which made him almost as tall as Jaren. Jaren had mistakenly asked him about Grallan once and had been called something like a freckled rat. Handing him a stone, Yates smiled, "Another round of Stone Jaren?"

"Yes, and this time you need to throw it really hard or Joans says he'll throw something at you."

Yates' smile dropped from his freckle-free face as he looked wide-eyed at Joans. Joans was just standing there, seemingly unaware of their conversation; however, he was lightly bouncing what looked like a ball of fire in his hand. Jaren knew that it was just a construct of light, but it looked intimidating.

Yates stammered, "I...I'll do what I can to serve you and Joans."

Jaren just shook his head. Joans did not deserve the honor that the men gave him. Yes, he was powerful, and he had saved their lives, and though some of his minds politely pointed out that this alone meant they owed him all the respect they could muster, other minds argued that he was simply fulfilling his assigned role. In addition, he showed them no real respect or favor or kindness—he didn't actually seem to care about any of them.

Cosren and Iambret had the same reaction to the instructions.

Desot looked a little uneasy as Jaren relayed the message.

"Are you okay?"

"Yeah, I just wanted to ask you something."

"Sure. What is it?" Jaren had come to understand the man's accent more easily, and while he didn't seem as dumb as he once had, he wasn't the most intelligent man.

"Well, you see, my wife and I have been married for four years." He paused and looked directly at Jaren.

Jaren nodded, not sure where Desot was going.

"And, well, we haven't had children."

Jaren nodded again, and waited, but Desot didn't say any more.

"I'm sorry, Desot. What are you asking?"

"You know—can you talk with...*him*...about, you know, healing my wife?"

Jaren was stunned. Joans couldn't heal his wife. And why was Desot hesitating to call Joans by name?

"Desot—he can't heal your wife. He's not a god."

"I know, but could you ask him anyway? Maybe he can do more than he's told you. Just ask him for me, please?"

"Yeah, okay."

Jaren's minds were in a frenzy as he reached the front of the train. Desot wasn't the first to ask Jaren to approach Joans with some request. They were all lunatics! Maybe Joans' sudden bouts of kindness were because of all the praise he was getting. Jaren preferred it when they disliked Joans, and he was a jerk.

Mastiff was the only one with sense. He didn't bow and scrape when Joans walked by, and he didn't hesitate to meet Joans' gray-eyed glare with his own thick-lidded, brown eyes. Jaren had heard Griff try to reprimand Mastiff for his "insolence," but Mastiff had shot a glare at him that would have withered him — if he hadn't already been so desiccated by the sun.

Jaren formed the shield as he turned around and saw that Desot's thick arm was already hurling forward. Jaren watched the stone zipping right at him. He flinched as he took a step toward it, but the stone sank into the shield only an inch before stopping and popping back out. As the train passed by, the stones bounced harmlessly off his shield. When he reached the end of the train, Joans was still holding the ball of fire, but there was heat in it. He smiled at Jaren, and then launched the flaming ball at him. Jaren knew the shield would do nothing to stop the heat, so he dove to the side — right through the shield — and was expelled like a bar of soap being squeezed between wet hands.

Heat brushed Jaren's feet before he hit the ground and tumbled to a stop. The guards and wagon drivers cheered.

"You've got to keep the shield with you!" Joans shouted. Jaren again picked himself up out of the cloud of dust and brushed at the torn-up skin on his knees. Joans would heal him when the train stopped, but Jaren wondered if there would be any part of him that wasn't scraped or bruised by the end of this session.

Chapter 33

Chatting with Mastiff

That evening Jaren found Mastiff standing some distance from the fire. More trees meant more pleasant fires, more animals to eat, and better shelter. They also meant more creatures to fill the night with croaks and chirps. Mastiff had left the group around the fire when Desot again proclaimed that Joans was almost a god incarnate.

"Why doesn't Joans do something about this?" Mastiff asked as Jaren walked up.

Jaren kicked a clod of dirt and shrugged. The breeze pulled at his segg.

"Sometimes I wonder if he believes it himself," Jaren muttered, hoping Joans wasn't somehow listening from where he too stood alone in the darkness. Mastiff let out a deep belly-laugh that silenced the noisy bugs. Jaren was not trying to be funny.

"Perhaps he does. And when you are as skilled, will you think you're a god?"

"No,"

The hard look Mastiff gave Jaren, with his brow narrowed over his squinting eyes, could have squeezed truth from a stone.

"No, I don't think you will." Mastiff smiled, then lunged at Jaren.

Jaren gripped Mastiff's robes, rolled backward, and tried to throw Mastiff. Mastiff anticipated the move and twisted off of Jaren's bent legs. Jaren continued to roll with him but was too slow—Mastiff had Jaren strung out and could break his leg or arm.

"I give."

The two disentangled and brushed off their clothes. Mastiff pulled a long stalk of grass from the ground and began chewing on the end. Jaren wrapped his arms around his knees.

"You were too slow—time to revisit grappling."

Jaren nodded. He felt slow.

"Have you ever thought about using radiance when we fight?"

Jaren hesitated, then said, "No."

"Why not?"

"Well, Hairth says that I'm learning from you for those times when I don't have a source."

"Yes, I understand that, but when you do have a source, you could use it to your advantage."

Jaren took a deep breath, and slowly blew out the air.

"What?"

"It's just that...well...if I had a source, I wouldn't need to fight with my hands or even with a staff, I could just kill you."

Jaren felt embarrassed saying it. Mastiff could kill him a hundred times over with or without a weapon. But with a source, Mastiff didn't stand a chance.

Mastiff nodded. "And if you didn't want to kill me, just stop me?"

Jaren shrugged. "I could make the air around you solid, or lift you up into the air, or pin your feet to the ground, or..." Jaren stopped and shrugged. Mastiff was quiet for a moment.

"Why didn't you do something like that when Hairth was attacked? I had assumed you didn't know how to use radiance well enough, but, after watching you the first few days, I realized that was not the reason. Then I figured you didn't want to kill them because you wanted to capture them. I wondered if perhaps Joans was only teaching you how to kill."

Jaren hoped that it was too dark for Mastiff to see the red in his cheeks.

"At the time, it didn't even occur to me to use it. I was so shocked and scared, I just stood there until Hairth shouted for help. And even then, I didn't use it—I just tackled him like you had taught me."

"Don't be embarrassed. Everyone has the same reaction—freezing, the inability to think, reverting to their simplest training. The only way to overcome that is to repeatedly put people in stressful situations and demand them to react. That's why I started the surprise attacks."

Jaren kicked the clod again.

"Ah. And that's why you're here. I hadn't seen it before." Mastiff stared out across the darkness. "Well, while we told everyone else that both assassins had been killed, I'm glad you didn't actually kill both. "

"Why?"

"We questioned the attacker. He didn't have much information for us, but we learned some." Mastiff whipped at the grass with the piece in his hand.

"The pair came from Monrarmon, a town not too far from Trargarsul, in Bongardon. They have a large population of Troer there. I assume you have never heard of Troer before?"

Jaren shook his head.

"It might come as a surprise to someone like you, but there are people in Thadren who believe radiance is evil. It's not just that it makes them uncomfortable, or they think Light-Twisters are bad like the rest of Bongardon does, they believe it is against the will of the gods, even *Re'hal*, for man to use the energy from the sources."

Jaren nodded again, "I remember Hentoya talking about his people getting chased out of Trargarsul."

"That's right. Well, after that, Hentoya sent some men to learn more about the people there. They found Trargarsul as expected, but Monrarmon was frenzied, like sick with animosity toward radiance. A man named Tro had traveled a great distance—having crossed the Traegar mountains."

"There's nothing beyond Traegar mountains," Jaren interrupted. "Where could he have been coming from?"

Mastiff shrugged. "That's the story they were told. They say that he had prayed to *H'ust* for guidance, and he stopped to preach his message in every town, but in each town, he felt the people were not fervent enough in their response, and so he moved on. When he finally reached Monrarmon, *H'ust* told him that the people were prepared. In less than a year, almost the entire town had covenanted to worship only *H'ust* and began living as Tro taught them."

Jaren was astounded. Only worship one of the gods? That would undoubtedly offend the other gods and bring down their anger against the town. He wondered how a whole town could be so foolish.

"The two assassins were from this town. They had both been murderers and were worried about how *H'ust* viewed their past actions. Tro had moved on, so there was no one who could tell them if they could be forgiven for what they had done. They were certain they were doomed to suffer in the Frozen Waste and had planned to die alone so they would never be buried."

Jaren couldn't imagine having lived a life so bad that you'd prefer to be trapped in this world with an unburied body instead of moving on.

"One evening, while discussing their plight, a missionary of Tro arrived. He taught them that they could absolve themselves by doing a great service to the Cause—which is what they call their efforts to spread Tro's teachings. The man told them of Hairth and Freysdal, where they manufacture sin and sell it to willing buyers throughout Thadren. He told them that Hairth was corrupting the world and that they would be absolved of all past sins if they could kill him."

"The two men were told to meet a man named Trocks in The Lucky Tavern in Caidron. Trocks gave them darts that could put people to sleep. You know the rest of the story."

"What did you do with the man?" Jaren wasn't sure why that was the question that popped out among all the questions in his minds.

"He's locked up. Hopefully we'll get more information out of him."

"Were you able to get any descriptions from him—of the missionary or Trocks?"

Mastiff nodded, "Not a lot, but enough to start a search in Caidron. It's unlikely that we'll find anything, but it's the only lead we've got."

Jaren asked a dozen more questions, but Mastiff had no more answers. Jaren's minds kept mulling them over, regardless. How would this missionary know Hairth? How would he have a man inside Freysdal?

"Mastiff, who are Hairth's enemies? Why would someone want to kill him?"

"Hairth is powerful and wealthy. That's enough for some people to hate him. People have different reasons for hatred—jealousy, a past injury, scorned love...or maybe they think radiance is evil?" The last was said in half-jest.

"Has Hairth done things to people to make them hate him?"

"Of course. The better question is, how is Hairth still alive given how many powerful enemies he has? More than one person is out to kill Hairth, and right now we're one of his arteries they are trying to open up."

Chapter 34

Discovering Limits

The few days they had eaten fresh meat had been unbelievably good, but once the train arrived at the main road, the animals knew to stay away. Jaren would have skipped the meals of salty meat and dry bread, but Griff made him eat.

Six days earlier, the grassland had given way to forest—thin at first, with grass and bushes between individual trees, but growing dense the further they went. By the time they got to the road, it felt like they were cutting through unexplored woods. The road, however, when they found it, was wide enough for two wagons to pass. But on either side the thick undergrowth obscured the view into the dense forest. The air was cooler and smelled of soil and wild blooms.

They had been attacked the second day in the forest, but Joans had given the train early warning. Jaren had been moving inside his shield before the first enemy appeared. The speed that had been so impressive in the open was dangerous to use in such close quarters. The attack got close enough for Jaren to ready a lump of heat against the last attacker.

"Let him go," Joans had said before Jaren released the energy.

"Maybe he'll spread word to leave us alone," Mastiff said as the man scrambled back into the woods.

"My sentiments, exactly," Joans added.

The next few days had been uneventful, until the forest had opened up to reveal a large river—the Eldvar—which made Hairth's river look like a stream. Jaren tried to throw a stone across it, but it plopped into the water near midstream.

The party turned upstream. The wheels of the wagons rolled easily over the hard-packed earth, and the donkeys snacked on the patches of green grass that grew between the wheel ruts. They stopped at a place where the road curved past a low elevation surrounded by a shallow depression.

Jaren explored their little green hill. The slow-moving Eldvar ran past it on one side, bordered by a pale sandy bank. The hill was covered in grass except at the very top, where a large clump of broad-leafed trees grew. If the water were just a couple feet higher it would have filled the depression and the hill would have been a tiny island.

On the upstream side, the river reached into the depression, making a large pool of almost still water. It was a perfect place to wash off the weeks of dust. But before he could step in, he heard a hiss behind him.

"Don't disturb the fish," Joans said. "If I have to eat another bite of that salty dried meat, I just might kill one of those guards and eat him instead."

Jaren flinched in revulsion. Joans rolled his eyes.

"Let me show you a trick I learned just outside of a little town called Monrarmon."

Jaren's heart skipped a beat, "Monrarmon?"

Joans folded out lumps of light, heat and cold, and sent them down over the surface of the water to the center of the pool. He compressed the lump of light into a sphere the size of a pea. Below it he placed the heat and cold that he had blended and spread out like a large bowl.

"Yes, I passed it on my way from the coast to respond to Hairth's summons. Have you ever seen the ocean? It's an amazing sight—filled with a diffuse mixture of sources—so that it has a faint radiance-sight glow. It's beautiful to see—both with your eyes and with radiance-sight." Joans wore a wistful stare that looked out of place on his face.

"But Monrarmon was full of strange people. They hate radiance." Joans released a fraction of the light, causing a brief flash, like a star on a clear night. He did this repeatedly, though Jaren couldn't see why.

"It wasn't your daily pot of hatred. No, this was a special variety of hate, like you feel for someone who betrays you or kills your family. It would be unfortunate for Hairth's business if that sort of belief spread." The grin on his face said he did not think it would be "unfortunate."

A jumping fish startled Jaren. It lunged toward the pea-sized lump of light, but of course it just sailed right through. As it fell downward, Joans released the heat and cold mixture, catching the fish in a bowl of solid air. It flopped about, but Joans had trapped it. A lump of force brought the air-bowl drifting across the water.

"I ran into a pair of men who were fishing in a most peculiar manner. They had a polished piece of brass that they twirled above the water. The metal caught and reflected the sunlight. Attracted by the light, a fish would leap from the water, and the second man would catch it with a net. They were quite proficient. When I copied their actions in my own way, however, they attacked me. I subdued them and kindly asked about their hostility. They told me of their town's peculiar beliefs." Jaren could imagine what "kindly" had looked like.

Another lump of force lofted the fish into the air, a blade of air removed its head and opened it up. Force cleaned the innards, and a lump of heat cooked it. The fish floated to Joans, where it landed on a plate of air. Jaren's stomach growled as it floated past. Joans, with a knife and fork of air, began cutting the steaming fish like he was standing before a dinner table.

"The men were criminals. Their belief system suggested that killing me would pardon them from some former misadventures. I was amused and hoped they might stumble upon my enemies, so I let them go." Joans' countenance as he ate reminded Jaren of a large, predatory bird.

Jaren's shock at how close Joans' story matched Mastiff's recounting of the assassins' history was interrupted by a shout from behind.

"Praise *Hel'dig*!"

Jaren turned to see Desot prostrating his short body a few feet away, his large arms outstretched, and his face pressed firmly against the ground. Others in the camp turned at his shout. He continued in his thick accent, "Even the fish reverence him. They throw themselves from the water, reject their own heads and entrails, heat themselves in his divine radiance, and then break themselves into bite-sized pieces which they gently place in his mouth so that he doesn't have to sully his holy fingers."

Jaren groaned as the rest of the party approached. The scene would have been peculiar to someone without radiance-sight, but Desot was taking things too far. Joans, however, simply inclined his head and took another bite—which, to the natural eyes, did look like the fish was coming apart and floating into Joans' mouth as he gestured with his hands. The other men looked uncertain, but Mastiff didn't hesitate.

"He's not a god, Desot. It's just radiance. Get off the ground and get back to work. Those tents won't put themselves up regardless of how much they revere Joans."

Joans scowled at Mastiff, and said, "Jaren and I are as much beyond simple men as the gods are above us," then stuffed a hunk of fish in his mouth with his invisible fork.

Jaren stiffened and took a step away. The gawking guards returned to their tasks, and even Desot got up and returned to work.

Jaren's minds went over everything Joans had said about Monrarmon but came to no conclusions beyond needing to talk further with Mastiff. But first he turned back to the water and copied Joans' technique as best he could. Within fifteen minutes he had enough fish to feed the entire camp. He let a grateful Agshot and Ranma clean and cook them, though. He didn't want anyone thinking he was a god, and he wasn't sure he could do it with air anyway. The pair finished preparing the fish just as the sun sank below the treetops across the road.

The fish improved everyone's mood. Griff's scowl softened and Iambret's jokes became less gruesome. But everyone stayed mostly quiet, enjoying the fresh food and security provided by the river. Except for Mastiff. He was off standing in the depression, looking across the road into the forest while gnawing on a piece of stiff dried meat. Jaren carried a hot fish in a broadleaf over to Mastiff.

"There's enough for everyone," Jaren said as he proffered the fish.

Mastiff scowled toward the group and said, "Too many of these men think that Joans is a god. It's foolishness. And worse than that, it's dangerous. See how relaxed they all are? They've lost all fear—and caution—because they believe Joans will protect them." He took the fish and stuffed the dried meat into a pocket.

Jaren wasn't sure what to make of Mastiff's comments. Especially in their current location. Iambret had pointed out how having the Eldvar on one side of them meant that they didn't need to worry about an attack from that side. This location was more secure, so why stay so tense?

The twang of released bows sounded in the twilight air. Jaren threw up his shield, encompassing Mastiff to avoid having the heavy draw of the shield push him away. As usual, Joans deflected the arrows over the main party, but they dropped right toward Jaren and Mastiff. With no time to react, Mastiff's eyes widened. Jaren grabbed the larger man's leather armor, holding tight as he attempted to dive away. The arrows glanced off the shield.

The men stood and looked toward the opposite shore where the arrows had originated. Jaren's heart was pounding. He was glad for all the practice with his shield. He watched with the others as Joans streaked across the river. Water curled to either side in massive waves as it was pushed aside by Joans' incredible speed.

Joans cut down, burned, and destroyed the attackers, but the dense trees slowed him. Shouts and screams said the attackers were surprised by someone suddenly on their side of the river. One of Jaren's minds had already been wondering why they were attacking from that side of the river when a sudden and severe drain on the shield almost caused Jaren to drop it. At the same instant, shafts streaked past Jaren and Mastiff, a few of the arrows burying their heads in the ground just outside his shield.

"Up Defenders!" Mastiff bellowed. "Rouse, you radiance-stilted fools!"

Jaren turned and in the fading light could just make out a party of attackers poised inside the edge of the forest nocking another round of arrows. Mastiff rushed through the shield toward the wagons. The incredible draw caused it to collapse, but not without first propelling Mastiff forward. Impressively, the broad man kept his feet. Jaren froze, but a few of his minds pushed through the paralysis. The howling behind him made him move almost instinctually. He threw up the shield again and sent dense lumps of heat at the attackers. They were beyond his range of control, so he set the lumps spiraling before he released them. Three of the six lumps stayed true and hit their targets. Three men's bodies went up in flames, shrieking out their last breaths. The other three lumps veered off target and ignited the brush lining the forest wall where the men were hidden. A hailstorm of arrows, loosed right as he released the heat lumps, sailed toward him. His shield deflected them without a single wobble. The momentum of the attack drew his other minds out of their stupor.

Jaren rushed toward the attackers, his legs and arms pumping, careful that the shield didn't catch his limbs as he dashed. He folded out heat and cold and readied the blade that Joans had taught him. One of his minds sketched out the attack. Five men stood with bows and arrows. They were shaken by the sudden burst of flames and were likely panicked by the death screams of their comrades. Two were close enough that a single blade could catch them. Another pair were not far, but a few more steps and he could send heat directly into their heads if they didn't move. No, they probably would move—better to target the chest. The fifth appeared to be backing away. He would be out of range for a controlled brute-radiance assault. Jaren's feet ate up the distance and he closed in on the first pair. They had nocked a third set of arrows. The bows and hands that held them fell to the ground as his up-stroking blade sliced through them. Their short-lived screams were halted when their chests were partially severed before the blade lost its cohesion. Their open but silent mouths did not distort the surprise in their eyes. They collapsed to the ground like sacks of rocks.

The lumps of heat he had loosed found purchase in the chests of the second pair. He released the energy, and the men's eyes widened as they clutched at their smoldering chests and collapsed to the ground, their partially drawn arrows releasing harmlessly. Smoke came from their mouths and nostrils, and an awful burnt pork smell filled the air. One of Jaren's minds briefly wondered what their insides would look like after an attack like that.

Jaren slowed his mad sprint. One mind had mapped out how to go after the final man, but others had recognized that there was no need. Yet others wondered about the situation at the wagon train. He could hear the howling of the injured behind him. The whole attack had lasted less than a minute, but Jaren felt exhausted.

As he stopped at the edge of the road, a loud roar came from the trees. He saw twenty or more men garbed in mottled cloaks rushing madly out of the undergrowth. Illuminated by the sputtering flames from his initial volley of heat, he saw they were armed with battle-axes, clubs, and swords. They vaulted over their fallen companions or burst through smoldering bushes. Jaren took an involuntary step back and was thrown several feet backward by his shield, landing hard on his rear near the bottom of the depression. The men nearest him slowed, surprised by the rapid retreat, but then pressed on. Jaren reformed his shield over his sitting body as the first man stabbed a sword at Jaren's face. The blade penetrated the shield, and Jaren screamed as he increased the flow to his shield. The force stopped the blade inches from his neck and shoved it backward. A few of the cooler minds kept the shield in place, though they struggled as another blade was brought down in a ferocious arc, drawing more of the energy. The first man's face scrunched up as he tried to drive his rusted sword through the barrier again. Other men arrived, surrounding him and striking at his shield. Jaren's free minds began frantically folding and throwing energy while the majority struggled to maintain the shield. There was no coordination to it, just lumps of heat, cold, force, light and bio being flung indiscriminately into the mob. Shouts and screams accompanied their release. Burns and ice appeared, chunks of flesh were ripped from bodies, startling flashes of light did little of use, and random growths caused feet to burst boots and hands to swell and drop weapons. But despite his radiant flailing, the attacks continued. The shield gave way and he knew he was going to die.

The first attacker probed at the border of where the shield had been, and finding no resistance, jabbed forward. But another blade swung in from the side and deflected the thrust. The guards slammed into the attackers. They moved into a defensive ring around Jaren, pushing away the attackers. He stopped his flailing and worked to gather his many wits. Wooden shields deflected blows and the guards returned the attacks. Jaren began thinking straight again and resumed his controlled attacks. He took down four more men before Joans showed up and within a few brief seconds reduced the remaining attackers to corpses. The defenders carefully lowered their weapons, wary eyes darting toward the tree line. Jaren took rapid, shallow breaths, his eyes trying to penetrate the darkness of the forest.

Mastiff called out, "Iambret, check for survivors. Cosren, watch those trees. Everyone else, treat the wounded."

Jaren scrambled to his feet in stunned silence, looking at the death surrounding him. How many had he killed? The faces of the dead still showed surprise. They had no idea what had killed them—no idea what they had been facing. Jaren knew he shouldn't feel sorry for them—after all, they had been trying to kill him—but in a way he did regret what had happened. He wrapped his arms around his own stomach. Despite the warm evening air, he began shivering and couldn't stop shaking.

"You're okay," Mastiff told him, gripping his shoulder with a beefy hand.

But he wasn't...it wasn't. He tried to keep his body still, but he couldn't do that either. All he could do was look at Mastiff. He had a cut near his right eye that had left a smeared trail of blood down his face, over his prominent jaw, and down his neck onto his segg.

Mastiff pulled Jaren into an embrace. He wrapped his large arms around Jaren and just held him. Jaren began and then couldn't stop sobbing. After a few minutes of crying like a small child, he tried to talk.

"It looked so easy when Joans did it..." A few minds replayed memories of Joans dealing death and destruction to those who threatened them and then returning to camp as if nothing had happened.

"...he just killed people as if it was nothing."

"It's never easy, even for Joans. He's just dealt with it so often that he can hide it better."

The thought appalled Jaren—it was like being used to dipping yourself in the latrine pit because you'd done it so often. His heart ached from all the radiance, and it felt...soiled. He kept his eyes closed, buried in Mastiff's segg. He could hear the other men moving around, but he didn't care if they saw him bawling.

"They were going to kill me. I thought I would die."

"That is something everyone feels during battle—the fear of dying. It's a cold that goes down to the bones."

"But you fought your way through them to me without radiance to protect you. You weren't afraid."

"That's what training is for. It kicks in when the fear prevents thought. Fear isn't a sign of cowardice, it's the sign of a functioning mind."

Mastiff continued, "Cowardice is when you do everything possible to avoid that which you fear. Tonight, you're the hero. You ran right at those men who were attacking us, and you saved lives."

Chapter 35

Marking the Spot

The sun hadn't peaked over the horizon, but the sky brightened after the darkest night of Jaren's life. He stood by the still-fresh mound of earth. He wondered if Desot's soul traveled across the water or in the opposite direction. He hoped that he had gotten to walk on water. His lasts words had been misplaced confidence.

"I saw him walk on water. He can heal me. He's a god."

Others had looked expectantly at Joans, but Jaren knew better. Joans had looked at the arrow through Desot's chest and the pooling blood, glinting red in the moonlight, and just shook his head. Agshot and Ranma's faces dropped as Joans turned away. Desot smiled and stretched his hand toward Joans, but his soul slipped away before he could catch Joans' robe.

A thin mist rolled along with the Eldvar, drifting up onto the island where they had slept. It obscured the guards as they broke camp. It swirled around Agshot's feet as he came to the grave.

"He was a good man—none too bright, but always good." Agshot bowed his head. Then he looked right at Jaren and asked, "Why didn't Joans heal him? Had he done somethin' to make him angry?"

Jaren tried to keep the anger from his voice as he replied, "He couldn't heal him. He's not a god."

Agshot furrowed his brow, looked at the mound of earth and then, head still down, turned and walked toward the camp, kicking the mist as he went.

"Agshot, can I ask you a question?"

Agshot stopped and nodded.

The question had been burning in his mind since seeing the light leave Desot's eyes.

"Why do you stay with Hairth? The work you do is dangerous—you could lose your life. Why not leave Hairth and go set up your life somewhere safer?"

"And where would that be? Thought my home was safe 'til my family and I were taken. I met thralls from all over Thadren in Freysdal. There's no safe place as long as Thralldom exists."

"Why not move into Caidron? Or one of the other big cities? They don't take thralls from cities. Just working for Hairth makes life more dangerous."

"It does that, but working for Hairth also gives me purpose. I had a family once. My wife and son were captured same as me. Our three daughters were too young, praise *Hel'dig*, so I hope they were left with my parents. My son, he tried to escape and lost his life. He was close to your age. My wife was sold to someone else, but her new owner wouldn't sell her to Hairth. The laws were different back then—twenty years to free a thrall. First thing I did was went and found my wife. Her owner let me talk with her. She wouldn't look me in the eyes. She had...like I said, the laws were different then...she had had ten children since we had parted. One had her arms wrapped around her mother's legs, one was running around, still too small to be given serious work, and the youngest she was holding in her arms. The others had all been taken from her and sold off as soon as they could be put to work. I told her I'd buy those children and her, too, but she wouldn't have it, said if I did, she'd run away. For twenty years I nursed the wound of my lost son and worked and lived looking forward to the day I could see my wife again—to when we could go find our daughters together. In a few minutes she broke my heart worse than I knew was possible. Twenty years, well, it changes a person. I found my daughters, they had happy lives without me. I went back to work for Hairth, but I visited my wife. After a couple times, though, she told me to never come back. I didn't see a reason for living and was apt to give up. But then Ranma showed me the truth. I had a reason for living, something to get me up in the morning. I had a family, though I didn't recognize it as such, in the people of Freysdal. I had a purpose in the fight against Thralldom. The peace of Freysdal, which I had seen come upon so many people, finally sank into my heart that day, and I've been committed ever since. Just like Desot, I'd gladly give my life if it helps defeat Thralldom."

Thralldom hurt everyone it touched. It destroyed families, like Agshot's. Ruined individuals, like May.

Agshot put a firm hand on Jaren's shoulder.

"Even a life of pain can be one worth living—and one worth giving for a great cause." He smiled at Jaren with his sun-browned face, and then resumed his path back to the camp.

"I envy them sometimes."

Jaren's shield came up at the unexpected voice.

"Their lives are so simple, their pain so simple."

Jaren burned with indignation.

"You have no right to demean him in that way. What do you know of pain?"

Joans recoiled and raised his eyebrows in shock.

"After you've lived forty years with radiance, then ask me of pain."

The response was not what Jaren had expected—it *did* sound pained. Joans shared so little about his life, and his demeaning, inconsiderate, smug behavior suggested a life devoid of feelings, free from regret-forming introspection. If he understood pain, why was he so awful? Jaren's anger smoldered.

Joans looked over at the grave poking up through the fog. "He was a good man."

"A *good* man? He worshipped you, and you did nothing to disabuse him of the insane idea that you are a god. Even with his dying breath, he was proclaiming you."

Joans raised a hand as if to strike, but Jaren wouldn't back down. Joans hissed through clenched teeth, "Do you think I didn't hear? Do you think that it didn't hurt me to have someone who looked up to me with so much faith suffer and yet not be able to do anything about it? Do you think that I haven't beaten myself up all night for failing to protect him?"

Jaren hadn't thought of any of those things, but his temper was already turned loose and the abuse Joans had heaped on him rushed through his minds.

"Why would I expect you to feel sorrow or regret? You've *never* shown concern for anyone but yourself."

Jaren stomped away from Joans back toward Desot. He folded heat as he went, over and over, using as many minds as he could spare until he couldn't hold any more. An intense ball, brighter to his radiance-sight than the sun, rested in the air in front of him. The burden on his soiled heart ached, but he pressed every bit he could hold in. He compressed it and spread it out like a blanket into the exposed soil. He released the energy and steam hissed from the earth. The low mound rose a couple of inches. Heat radiated from the ground, and the mist recoiled as if touching the grave caused it pain. A dull red light grew from the dirt, and the bulge sank downward. Heat seared Jaren's exposed legs and arms and he had to step back, but he kept adding heat, and kept up the release. The grave glowed brighter and brighter until it was an intense burning white. The surrounding trees were as clear as they had been in the sunlight, and Jaren cast a long shadow. The fog was dispersed twenty feet in all directions, and even at several feet away Jaren had to shield his face from the heat.

Jaren stopped pouring energy in. The light diminished as did the heat. In the receding light he saw that the molten earth had solidified into a smooth, almost polished, dark mottled glass capstone. A fitting monument for one who lost his life in the service of so great a cause.

Chapter 36

Entering Cresswand

The dark gray walls of Cresswand stood as tall as the ash trees. Uniformed men, their faces small spots under gleaming helmets, looked out across the surrounding fields and river. They wore green tabards over shirts sewn with metal disks. Not the most comfortable-looking clothing, Jaren thought.

The gate stood at least as tall as Freysdal's old wall and was made with thick iron straps across enormous timbers. The two halves were held to the wall by six hinges, each the size of Jaren's thigh. Where they met in the center, they rested on iron-bound wagon wheels as tall as Jaren. Years of use had worn two deep grooves across the paving stones

A short guard with a pinched face approached the wagons. Griff intercepted him.

"Is there something I can do for you, Commander?"

"Move aside, all cargo entering Cresswand must be inspected." The man's voice was nasally and gruff, but despite his words, he made no effort to go past Griff. Jaren left one mind focused on their conversation and continued exploring with the rest.

Mastiff spoke with Yates and Iambret. They nodded, then crossed an open square into a tall, white-plastered building. Dark brown wood beams showed through the plaster, and the roof was made of wooden shingles. A blue and yellow sign proclaiming "Grapes and Honey" hung over the arched wooden door.

Griff continued his conversation with the guard. "No, sir, no catching sicknesses, no weapons beyond what we wear, no silks or oils." Griff handed the guard a small purse.

"Everything looks in order with this half of your train," the guard said, pocketing the purse.

Griff frowned, as the guard stood there unmoving. He reached under his seat and handed the guard another small purse.

The buildings butted up against one another, lining the street. Stout women in pleated white blouses leaned out past brightly colored shutters to tend dainty flowers in long, narrow boxes. They smiled and called to passers-by as they poured water from pails.

"If you've come to trade, you must also declare the quantity of the gold."

Griff winced. "We do not have a lot of gold with us." He handed the guard yet another purse.

The guard stepped aside and waved Griff in.

Mastiff continued sending the guards into Cresswand in pairs. Once done, he walked to the edge of the square and purchased an apple from a wizened, gray-haired farm wife.

Griff drove the donkeys through the gates. The walls looked even taller from inside. The city was huge—and crowded. The people had light hair and pale skin with the slightest yellow cast. They were shorter than the people of Caidron, and had sharper, more angular features. Most of the women wore their hair in a twist pulled over their shoulders.

"Stay close to me," Joans said. Jaren stiffened.

In the days since Desot's death, Jaren had had limited interactions with Joans. They had not practiced and Joans hadn't tried to speak with him. There was a perceptible rigidness to Joans' radiance use. Jaren had grown uncomfortable with the tension but refused to try to diffuse it.

Their train moved along a broad cobbled road between three- and four-story buildings. Some men rode on horses and wore trousers and shirts instead of robes. Jaren had seen a horse once in Freysdal. But it had died within a few days of its arrival.

While many in Cresswand wore robes, half wore long tunics with high stockings or shirts and trousers like the riders. The women wore colorful blouses with patterned skirts. Jaren had seen these styles in Caidron, and even a few of the freemen and freedmen in Freysdal experimented with the fashions, but here they were everywhere.

Blinkered bones! He saw sources moving toward them from up the road. Jaren craned to look past people and carts to see who was carrying them. He glanced to Joans to see if he could tell who it was, but he wasn't even looking toward them.

Jaren thought about climbing up on their cart but decided against it. The sources had a muddy quality to them. They stopped, and then darted to one side, away from the main thoroughfare. Of course! That Light-Twister could see their sources just like Jaren could see his, and probably better because their sources were so bright.

"Up ahead! A Light-Twister that just crossed our path!" Joans said.

His eyes had narrowed, staring down his long nose toward the retreating sources. Squinting didn't help radiance-sight, but Jaren—and apparently Joans, too—still did it when trying to "see" sources from a distance. Just *crossed* our path? Joans must have only noticed the sources when they moved to the side.

"It may be possible that he hasn't seen us yet. Our sources are significantly brighter than his, but he may be weak."

"What does his strength have to do with whether he sees us or not?"

"The distance at which you can see a source depends on your strength and your affinity for a type of energy. The greater either is, the easier it is for you to pick out a source further away."

Affinity?

"There! Can you see him?" Jaren watched as the sources stopped, as if the person was waiting.

Jaren stumbled as a tall man in a rough brown robe pushed past him. A shout ahead drew Jaren's attention. A woman wearing very fine robes was pointing at Jaren.

"He cut my purse!"

Jaren stopped and looked at the woman in dismay.

"Someone stop him! He's getting away!" she shouted.

She shook her fist and then began moving toward them. Jaren heard a commotion behind him and whirled around to see the taller man that had pushed past him pushing faster through the crowd. He broke free and sprinted through an opening in the masses.

To the people on the street, the man's sudden fall must have looked peculiar—the way his feet and waist continued moving forward, while his head stayed in place. But Jaren had seen the lumps of heat and cold Joans had placed in front of the running man's head and recognized the solid air that had knocked him down as if he had run right into a stone bridge.

City guards swarmed the man and hauled him to his feet. They glanced around, searching for what had stopped him. The man was doing the same thing, though he was doing it through tears of pain and a swollen bleeding nose. One guard walked up to the woman who had been robbed.

"Magistrate Siltemrah, Hel'dig does watch over you. Here is the coin we found on the scoundrel."

The woman took the money and counted, then in a loud voice announced, "I have my money and there is still some left over. Perhaps someone else will report a cut purse and you can also return their money." Many within the watching crowd nodded their heads, and the woman smiled at them.

"Looks like he has had some training," Joans said, nodding toward the sources up ahead.

Jaren returned his attention to the other Light-Twister.

"Is he lying on the ground?" Jaren asked before recalling his feelings for Joans.

"No." Joans turned to him with a raised eyebrow, but Jaren couldn't tell if it was because Jaren asked him a second question after days of silence or if it was because the question was so stupid. Well, Jaren had started, he might as well continue.

"How can you tell he's had training?"

"He's offered the trade," Joans said, as if that explained the whole of it, but then continued, "He's obviously seen our sources. As bright as they are, it's a wonder he didn't see them much earlier. He assumes from the strength of our sources and the fact that there are two of us, that we are..." Joans paused, as if he were about to say something else, "...more than a match for him. Not knowing our intentions, he's submitted to us, offering his sources in exchange for his anonymity."

Jaren nodded in understanding—if he put his sources down before his face was seen, it would be difficult for them to identify him.

"How does he know we won't take his sources?"

"He expects we will. That's the deal—we get his sources, and he remains anonymous."

"But couldn't it also be a trap? He's laid them out, we go to retrieve them, and then he attacks us to steal ours?"

Joans gave him that same cocked eyebrow. "And, how would he do that? We've got our sources on us. By necessity, he is separated from his. He doesn't have any others accessible, or he's discovered ploomun and is hiding them, which makes no sense at all. The best he could do for a trap would be to have a large guard—rather, a small army—just waiting to attack us when we go to retrieve his sources. That is highly unlikely."

"But, didn't you say good sources were hard to come by?" Joans continued to stare at him with that "you're an idiot" look.

"Then why would he give them up so easily? Why not turn and run?"

The crowd was moving again after the excitement of the theft, and Griff began driving the train forward.

"He could have tried that—it's always an option—but if we had been looking for sources, we would have pursued him, and he may have been killed. It's a much safer choice to offer the trade. In a town like this, where Light-Twisters neither control nor advise the ruling class, someone might keep their sources in a bath of water, deep underground, in a thick metal chest, or more likely, in a secret place far from normal traffic to hide them. There are different approaches to radiance. One is that you only carry a source when you expect to need one, and only carry your best sources when you know you will need them. Generally, it is best to not carry sources, as other Light-Twisters could not identify you and take them from you. If this Light-Twister follows this approach, then it means that he thought he had need of his sources today."

Jaren noted that Joans had called the city a town but decided that correcting him on that mistake wasn't worth the potential consequences. What he described sounded like reasonable cautions, but the whole practice felt a little bizarre—until he remembered they were talking about Light-Twisters.

"Then is it dangerous for us to carry ours?"

"It's always dangerous to be a Light-Twister, but less dangerous than carrying around a fat purse of money. There are not many powerful Light-Twisters in this part of Thadren. That's partly why Hairth chose this *H'ust*-forsaken region for his enterprise."

Joans turned down the road that led to the sources.

"What are you doing? We don't need to take anyone's sources!" Jaren hissed as he dashed after Joans.

"Of course not. I just want to see them."

They found the sources sitting on dry, caked soil in a narrow wooden box that must have fallen from a window. The sources were heat, cold, and light, but they weren't pure—each was giving off a mixture of different energies. Joans picked them up and examined them. Unlike Hairth's smooth metallic sources, these just looked like regular stones. He folded lumps out of each of his five sources, twined them together in an unfamiliar mixture that was reminiscent of a ladder twisted around a tree. He spun it tight into a fine rod, like a needle at one end, then touched each of the stranger's sources at a number of places.

"Hmm."

Jaren glanced around. He wondered what all the passers-by thought of them staring at stones. The shutters to the building were open, but it was too bright outside for Jaren to see if anyone was inside. Joans released the rod and replaced the stones.

"What were you doing?"

"Probing them. They are common sources. They appear to be from somewhere nearby, though that's surprising since this area is largely devoid of solid sources. They have not been used much."

"You can tell all of that?"

"Yes, and even more under more favorable circumstances, but in sources so close to their origin, there's not much more to determine."

Joans reached into his cold pocket and extracted a small cold source. Jaren had not noticed it there before because its radiance had merged with the light of the larger, refined source. He placed it next to the other sources—it was higher quality than the stranger's cold source—and then walked away.

"What are you doing?" Jaren asked.

"Showing our good will and inviting him to talk."

Jaren frowned.

"If he is interested in talking with us, he will approach us. We'll be able to recognize him—even if it's in the future—because we now know what sources he will have."

Chapter 37

Exchanging Valuables

"Come feel the finest silks!"

"Dyed wool—will not fade!"

The cries of merchants could be heard over the clomping of horse and donkey and the rhythmic thunking of the wooden wagon wheels on the paving stones. Jaren walked to the front of the train, amazed at the variety of fabrics on display. Griff looked irritated, probably by the slow pace.

"Are there no thralls here?" Jaren asked.

"No thralls?" Griff scowled. "Of course, there—don't you see them?"

Jaren looked around but couldn't see a single segg. He shook his head.

Griff gestured toward a short, plump man in heavy robes. "She's a thrall."

She? Jaren looked closer. It was a woman! Thick robes hid her figure, and her hair was cut very short—almost like Levi's. All of a sudden, he saw thralls all around him. They wore heavy robes plainly cut, with no belt, and each had little to no hair.

"Why is her hair so short?"

"It's the law here in Cresswand. Thralls must wear heavy robes, keep their hair short, and wear a nose hoop."

Jaren saw a small gray ring hanging from the nose of a thrall. It was not obvious, but now that he knew what to look for, he saw them on all the heavy-robed thralls.

"That looks very uncomfortable." Jaren reached up and felt his nose.

"I'm sure it is, but their *owners* don't care." The way he spat out "owners" made clear Griff's feelings about the situation.

"Will they put one of those on me if they learn I'm a thrall?"

Griff scowled and gestured at Jaren's wrist, "No, they already know you're a thrall, and they can tell you're not from here. We've got a writ that permits you to travel. Cresswand and Pinnutuck have an agreement to abide by their respective thrall-law. They'll not harm another man's *property*." Jaren nodded and tried to keep his hand from going to his nose. He stared as one particularly attractive thrall walked past, wondering how he could have ever mistaken her for a man.

Griff grabbed Jaren's arm and shoved him against the wagon. A dozen armored men on horses pushed past the train. One man's metal-clad boot brushed Jaren's arm. He would have been trampled if Griff had not pulled him out of the way.

Griff glared after them once they had passed, and then smirked at Jaren. "You can get killed by letting a pretty face distract you."

Jaren's cheeks burned. He turned to look for her again, but she was gone. As they moved back to the center of the narrow road, Jaren saw the other Light-Twister's sources move. It looked like he had picked them up and was moving away from their wagons. So, he preferred to avoid them. Jaren didn't blame him.

A distance ahead of them he saw a dull glow in the form of an oblong...blob. It was difficult to identify because of how dim it was. It also seemed to be rippling. Jaren focused more minds on it but couldn't figure out what he was seeing.

Griff led the train through the town, taking a road to the left, then to the right, then to the left again. They were moving toward the dim source, which, Jaren reasoned, was probably their cargo.

They stepped past a large building and their view opened wide as if they had stepped outside of the city walls. But the open expanse wasn't land, it was the Eldvar. Oared boats skittered across the water like multi-legged bugs. The smell of fish and water filled the air. Wooden platforms jutted into the water from the stone walkway. Some had boats beside them, with thralls loading or unloading materials, sweating in their heavy robes under the hot sun.

The diffuse source was within a short, wide boat gently rocking beside one of the platforms. A man sat on a stool beside it, staring at the passers-by. He had long braided hair that was the dark orange color of the flowers that bloom the day after rain. His skin was olive, and he had bright blue eyes that gazed past thick slanted eyelids. He had a long knife under his belt and a narrow mustache turned up at the ends in points.

Joans moved to the front of the wagon train. Griff lowered his head in deference and walked behind Joans while slowing the train to a stop in front of the boat.

"My name is Artor Joans. Hairth has asked me to evaluate the quality of your material."

He inclined his head to Joans and then to Griff. The man glanced at Jaren before dismissing him as unimportant. Then, in a deep and smooth voice, he stated, "I'm Auyus Roosji. You may inspect my hold." It took Jaren's minds a moment to work out what the man had said. His accent made it all come out like a single word.

Joans nodded and climbed a small ladder into the boat. Jaren was surprised when Joans disappeared behind the side of the boat. Joans was a tall man, and his head and shoulders should have been visible. Jaren studied the boat and the source more carefully and realized that the source was also present beneath the surface of the water. He had not been able to see it from afar because water obstructed radiance-sight. The boat appeared to be small, but Jaren now saw that it rode very low in the water.

"Are you Cayrentall or Falstreycheck?"

A woman's voice spoke softly at Jaren's side. He jumped but stopped himself from forming a shield. His radiance-sight recognized the sources he had seen earlier. He had been so focused on the boat that he didn't even notice...her...approaching. The top of her head reached to Jaren's chin. She appeared to be in her early twenties, though Jaren wasn't sure. Her light brown hair in broad curls reflected golden sunlight. She wore deep red robes cut to fit her shape. Her eyes were vibrant green, and she stared into Jaren's eyes. She stood so close, if Jaren inhaled, they'd be touching. He took an involuntary step back.

Working to regain some composure, Jaren asked her, "What did you say?"

"Are you Cayrentall or..."

Joans' sharp voice cut in. "Madam, with whom do you stand?"

As he spoke, Joans stepped in front of Jaren, looming over the woman. Now, it was her turn to step back.

"I'm unencumbered," she said, dropping her gaze from his piercing eyes. Her accent was very slight, and she sounded friendly. Joans stared down his hooked nose at her, as if trying to put her in her place with just his eyes.

He continued, "And how were you trained?"

"I was trained by Rudaltro."

"Rudaltro?" Joans' eyes briefly widened, but narrowed again, "Describe him for me."

She folded her arms and met Joans' gaze, a defiant look in her eyes. "He looked like you, Artor Joans."

Joans nodded, showing no surprise that she knew his name. "When did you last see him?"

"It has been a while."

"Tsk. Rudaltro surely trained you better than this."

She pursed her lips and narrowed her eyes, then an impish grin spread across her lips. She spread her arms and said, "He did the best he could with what he had to work with."

Joans laughed with real mirth, and Jaren frowned. Joans laughed at suffering or crazy thoughts. He would laugh as he described getting revenge on unnamed enemies or at Jaren's mistakes—especially those that hurt Jaren—but not at things other people found funny.

"I'm sure he worked very hard with that." Joans smiled an almost pleasant smile. "We are also unencumbered. It has been years since I've seen Rudaltro. Do you know where he is hiding?"

"How do you know he is hiding?" she asked, a broad smile now on her face. She was quite pretty. Joans chuckled again.

"Rudaltro is always hiding. He was hiding even when he was here training you—I assume you are from here?"

She nodded. "He was always looking over his shoulder. The last time I saw him, he was running from a pair of very short men." Joans stopped smiling but nodded.

"I told him to be careful around the Shamear brothers. They were not quick to…forgive." Joans glanced at Jaren, then continued, "He did not convince you to join with Cayrentall?"

She became serious, too. "No…" she trailed off. Joans just looked at her—not a hard look, but he expected to hear more. She shrugged.

"He said that I could trust them more than those who professed Falstreycheck, but also said I could not trust either… or those who claimed to be unencumbered."

Joans grinned his normal, crooked smile. "Good advice— trust no one. Why did you approach us?"

"I have not seen another Light-Twister since he left. I had begun wondering if I ever would. Then yesterday this boat docked, and today you arrived with such powerful sources, and then you proffered…this…" she said, gesturing toward the small bright cold source in her robes.

Joans studied her. "What do you want of us?"

She looked at Jaren, then the boat, and then back to Joans. "I'm not sure. Answers, I guess."

Joans continued to stare at her.

"It's lonely here, I guess. But I'm afraid to leave and I don't know where I'd go if I did. My sources aren't great, and...I just...I feel a little lost."

Jaren was surprised by the vulnerability in her answers. He glanced over at Griff, who was studiously not listening, and the orange-haired man, who was paying close attention. Why would she trust Joans?

"What's your name?"

"Lesarra."

"What do you want for yourself?"

She studied him. "I want to be part of a community."

Joans nodded. "Which one?"

"Neither."

"Then you must remain unencumbered. Perhaps one day there will be another community—one for those of us who are unencumbered."

Her shoulders drooped along with her eyes. "So, there isn't one now?"

"Not that I have discovered."

She looked at Jaren with her big green eyes, "Then, can I join you?"

His heart raced—Of course!

"No," Joans said. Both she and Jaren turned to look at him.

"Are you sure?" Jaren asked, and she turned to him hopefully.

Joans let out another laugh, but this was of the normal, mirthless variety. "No Jaren. Your *owner* would not appreciate that."

Jaren's face went red as Lesarra looked at him wide-eyed.

"You're a thrall?" she asked incredulously.

Jaren could see her trying to reason it out—and he reached for the non-existent ring in his nose.

"He must be an extraordinarily powerful Light-Twister to keep you as a thrall."

Joans grunted, "Extraordinarily powerful? Yes. Light-Twister? No."

"Then why...?"

Jaren knew what she was getting at. The orange-haired boatman was leaning so far he was almost out of his stool. The loose robes the man wore hung open and Jaren could see the top of a blue tattoo on his chest.

Jaren tried to explain, "Because I believe in him and what he's working for. He will release me when the law allows it, but for now I choose to serve him."

She shook her head. "I would never let someone own me."

"If you knew him, you might."

She just continued to shake her head, the broad curls swaying gently.

Joans reiterated, "You may not join us, but if you are willing to wait, I will return when I get the opportunity."

She looked as though she might cry but tried to put a smile over it. "Rudaltro said the same thing when he left so long ago. I guess I don't really have a choice." Then turning again to Jaren, "Will you be coming with him?" The eyes she made at Jaren made his stomach flip.

"I will."

"You will?" Joans asked, the mocking tone returning to his voice. She shot Joans an irritated look, then looking past him at the boat, and taking a deep breath she asked, "What is all of this cold source? Not a stone of it is worth carrying."

Joans suddenly turned coldly serious. "That is of no concern to you."

"Oh, but it is. This is my guarantee."

Joans cocked an eyebrow at her.

"If you don't return within three months, I will set out to find one of the factions and will tell them everything I've seen. I understand both factions are after you and I bet they would be very interested in whatever it is you are doing here."

A wicked smile crossed Joans' lips briefly. It was the same smile he sported when he was abusing Jaren.

"That's a bold threat from a little girl." Her eyes narrowed and a slight twitch in her hand was all that betrayed fear...or maybe it was anger. "But," Joans continued, "I like someone who can stand up for themselves. While it would be easier and safer to just kill you, I give you my word. But I don't believe I can return in three months. You must wait six."

"Six it is—and you might have found it harder to kill me than you imagine." She and Joans glared at each other as if they were both imagining the duel.

"I will come, too—if I can," Jaren said, as much to break the tension as to get her to look at him.

"That's sweet of you, umm...

"My name is Jaren."

"Jaren."

It sounded so nice when she said it. Then she continued speaking to Joans, "Six months. Then I walk."

"I look forward to our next meeting."

She turned and walked away, swaying her hips as she went. She glanced over her shoulder and winked at Jaren before she walked around a public house and disappeared from sight. Jaren continued to watch as her sources moved farther and farther away.

"Quite the woman," the man on the stool said. Jaren turned to see that he had resumed his relaxed posture on the stool.

Joans looked at him, and then turned to Griff. "I presume you'll take care of this man?"

Griff nodded, and Jaren saw the orange-haired man tense up. He gripped the hilt of the long knife in his belt and glanced toward where Lesarra had gone.

"His merchandise is what we came for."

Griff nodded and gestured for Lexer to come to him. He removed a lock from a large box in Griff's wagon. They struggled together to lift it out of the bed, muscles in their arms bulging. Griff let a few choice phrases fly as they carried it toward the river, eventually placing it at Auyus' feet. Griff pulled his own knife from his belt and pried the lid open. Jaren's eyes bulged as he saw more gold than he could have even imagined. A single coin was more than Jaren's yearly reward. Just how wealthy was Hairth? Auyus was trying to hide his astonishment but couldn't quite manage it.

"This is for the merchandise. And for your good will. Bring another delivery like this in five months…"

"Six months!" Joans piped up. Griff scowled. Then realizing the target of his ire, he lost the scowl and lifted his hands in apology.

"In *six* months. And you will be rewarded likewise."

The man reached for the end of his blade and pressed his finger onto the point. He squeezed a drop of blood onto his other hand, and pressing it to his chest said, "Auyus agrees."

Griff nodded, but then added, "If you want more business with us, you will keep everything you have heard here today to yourself."

"I, too, value privacy. You will of course extend the same courtesy and not mention the value of this transaction to the city guard." Griff nodded. Auyus made a hand motion, and six armed men with the same olive skin and thick orange hair filed out of the public house Lesarra had disappeared behind. They began loading the wagons, and before the two were full, Agshot and Ranma had arrived with two more empty wagons and more donkeys laden with supplies.

Chapter 38

Taking Reports

The red lands were ugly. That's the most generous description Jaren could offer. Passing from them into the forests had been pleasant, but going the other way was depressing. There had been so much to think about during the first few days of their return trip, but finding himself now surrounded by thorny bushes, dry red dirt, and poisonous creatures he regretted not having enjoyed the forest greenery more.

The first night outside Cresswand, everyone had reported on what they learned in the city. As Mastiff had explained to Jaren, "All trips are information-gathering activities. I'll report everything we learn to Levi or Hairth." This trip had been particularly informative.

"Potatoes are going to be scarce," Cosren relayed. "Crop failures from bad weather."

"It's already driving up the prices of other tubers as well as grain," Yates added.

"Tunkstan and the silk guild are on the verge of all-out war. Both think they could do better without the other," Iambret reported.

Jaren turned to Agshot and asked, "What's he talking about?"

"Tunkstan's a powerful house that owns all the farms of mulberry—the only thing silkworms will eat. The silk guilds claim authority over any silk that is produced, but the Tunkstans produce some on their own."

"There are thrall uprisings in the Dural iron mines and quarries," Vorlen said.

Before Jaren could even ask, Agshot explained to him, "Troubles at the mines and quarries may impact Freysdal if they are widespread. Hairth does a lot of business with the mines because the lightballs are safer than torches."

Mastiff took notes as everyone spoke, then relayed his own information.

"Orders for wood from Cresswand haven't changed since our last team was here."

"That means boats are being built, people are gaining wealth, and lightball sales to coastal cities should remain steady."

Even with all his time apprenticing with Hairth, Jaren still had no idea how interconnected everything was.

"What of the call for men?" Agshot asked.

Everyone—except Jaren, of course—had heard that in Cresswand.

"I spoke with Recrutal to find out more," Mastiff began. "'A coin per day for new recruits, two for those who can handle a weapon, five for a sergeant, and more for an officer.'" Mastiff impersonated the man, "'And you, my good fellow, have the look of an *officer*.'" The guards laughed and Mastiff smiled briefly, but then his smile dropped.

"An odd business—hiring strangers to fight."

"Merchantaries," Briaben said in his light, almost feminine voice. Vorlen and his twin brother Veerlen nodded.

"Merchantaries?" Mastiff asked.

"In Souhain, powerful houses only have a couple dozen men under arms. It is the Merchants of Men who maintain men under arms, and the lords hire these men—merchantaries— to augment their small forces as necessary. Merchantaries get paid for fighting—a daily rate like you heard—but also receive a portion of the spoils when they win. It's a dangerous profession, and most find out that the easiest way to get out of their commitment is to die."

"Or get sold to thrall-takers for flirting with the Merchant's daughter," Vorlen chuckled, elbowing Veerlen.

Veerlen scowled. "Curse you...and our *Hel'dig*-blessed good looks!"

Mastiff ignored this exchange and continued, "Yes—he did say something about spoils. It sounds like *merchantaries* could stand to make a great deal of money."

This began a conversation about merchantaries—what type of men would join, how to ensure loyalty, the various groups or factions that might employ them, and for what purpose. Mastiff brought the conversation to an abrupt end when he added, "Recrutal said a large force was already underway, and they could use a good man like me."

No one wanted to say what Jaren was sure was on all their minds—were they heading toward Freysdal?

Chapter 39

Making Accusations

"I know who's trying to kill Hairth."

"How were you able to figure out which of Hairth's many enemies it is?"

A few of Jaren's minds latched onto that question. How *had* he identified which one? Others laughed at the answer—Jaren only knew one enemy, and that's how he figured it out. Mastiff stopped about fifty paces ahead of the train and whirled on Jaren, practice blade flashing through the air with a whoosh, but Jaren was ready. He always expected an attack from Mastiff, though he was still trying to transfer that same vigilance to other dangers.

Mastiff struck at Jaren's chest, but Jaren side-stepped and brought his staff down on the outstretched sword. Mastiff lowered his shoulder with the momentum of the falling sword and drove it into Jaren's body. Jaren tried to use his momentum to roll with Mastiff, hoping to get the advantage in the tumble, but Mastiff continued to push forward, taking Jaren's staff in one hand and leaning his weight on it. With his shoulder in Jaren's chest and his weight bearing down on the staff, Jaren was unable to maintain his grip on the staff and was forced into a backward-toppling fall. He tried to roll backward to spring back to his feet, but Mastiff was already up, sword leveled at Jaren's throat.

"You're dead."

He reached down and helped Jaren to his feet.

Jaren relayed the story Joans had told him about his visit to Monrarmon and his interaction with the two criminals. "They must be the men who attacked Hairth."

Mastiff nodded, and then attacked Jaren with a downward strike. One of Jaren's minds goaded him to jab Mastiff in the ribs with the staff, but the majority again told him to step out of the way of the strike and deflect the falling blade. His muscles had a mind of their own, reacting as soon as—if not before—the majority of minds had selected the appropriate response. This time Jaren also kept his focus on maintaining his balance and regaining his center after the move.

Mastiff stepped forward with his momentum and reached out to snag Jaren's staff, but Jaren knew it was coming. He pulled back and gently kicked Mastiff in the gut. Mastiff dropped the sword, then reset. Mastiff showed Jaren how he could have deflected the kick and then showed him how to better respond to an overhead attack. He set Jaren to practicing that combination, then continued their conversation.

"And that's why you think Joans is trying to kill Hairth?"

"That's not the only reason. He also comes from the region where those snakes are from, and the snake attack came the day Joans arrived."

"You're letting your elbow drop too soon," Jaren repeated the form and Mastiff nodded.

"So, the evidence you have is that Joans passed through the town the assassins came from—a town where radiance is viewed as pure evil—where he met with and *abused* two criminals before leaving. And that he comes from a place where the snakes used in the attack originated. Right?"

"Yes. Exactly. The question is, how can you take him? If you can separate him from his sources, I'm sure we can stop him."

Mastiff shook his head, "Jaren, that's not enough information to arrest someone. Those are very likely just coincidences."

Mastiff attacked again—the same cutting, downward blow. He moved faster this time, and Jaren was barely able to sidestep and deflect the blow. Mastiff took hold of the staff, but Jaren didn't pull back this time, instead he followed the forms Mastiff had showed him and continued to drive the practice blade to the ground, taking Mastiff's grip with it. Twisting the staff toward Mastiff's thumb, he broke the grip and brought the other end of the staff down across Mastiff's back.

Righting himself, Mastiff nodded his big head.

"You've taken to the bow much better than I thought you would."

Jaren nodded. "The bow feels natural in my hands. It's like holding a shovel or a rake."

Several of Jaren's minds protested the change in subject. They couldn't believe how easily Mastiff had dismissed his suspicions.

Jaren broached the subject again. "I don't understand. You don't like Joans. Why are you defending him?"

"I'm not defending *him*. I'm defending fairness. The connections you've identified between Joans and these attacks are too weak. You need stronger evidence showing Joans was actually involved in one of the attacks, if you want justice to be on your side."

Jaren tightened his lips. He hadn't expected Mastiff to arrest Joans right there. He thought they would wait until they got back to Freysdal and had a plan to overpower him. But based on Mastiff's response, Jaren wasn't sure Mastiff would bother bringing it up with Levi. Fortunately, Jaren knew he could personally bring it up with Hairth, and if he could convince Hairth he wouldn't need Mastiff's help. The problem was that he didn't think he'd be able to convince Hairth either. Jaren admitted to himself that he would need more evidence. In the meantime, he still had to work with Joans.

Chapter 40

Being a Target

"If there are enough regular men, they can be a threat, but another Light-Twister is the real danger. Now defend that plant."

Jaren stood beside a fragrant wind-twisted scrub brush. Joans sent lumps of energy zipping toward the bush, and Jaren plucked them out of the air as easily as he might pick apples from a tree.

"Good. You continue to grow in strength and quantity." "Quantity" was the word Joans used to describe how many minds Jaren had.

"Of course, a Light-Twister wouldn't attack you with unreleased energy—and once it's released, it's much harder to stop. The best course often is to deflect or dodge it."

Mastiff had taught him the same thing about physical attacks. Jaren nodded, suppressing the minds that still resisted light-twisting.

"We start with the simplest deflection: an angled wall of air between you and the incoming attack."

Jaren formed an angled wall of air in front of the bush as Joans launched and released a lump of heat. It hit the wall, slid along the angle past the bush, and dissipated, but not without leaving a streak of glowing hot air in the wall. The heat radiating from the wall caused the bush to smoke and then burst into flames. Jaren stepped back in surprise.

"The wall of air will deflect most of the energy, but not all. You must be moving away from the attack, and you must put enough space between you and the wall. Try again at the next bush."

Jaren formed the wall and stayed well away from it. Joans lobbed a lump of force—vectors oriented forward—and released it. It slammed into the wall with a "Whomp!" and shoved the stiffened air ten feet—right into and through—the small plant, leaving twigs and splintered kindling on the red earth.

"Force is best dodged, but anchoring the air will help deflect it. If you can't anchor it, place a counter force on the back side of the air wall. Either will give more time and space to dodge. Time and space are interchangeable. If you have more of one, you have more of the other." Jaren nodded, even though he didn't understand what Joans was talking about.

"Try again."

Joans' lump of heat transformed into a glowing, roaring fireball just before Jaren could take possession of it. Jaren folded heat and cold, forming an angled wall of air as he threw himself to the side. The fire smeared across the wall, still roasting Jaren but not doing any damage. Next time, he'd put the wall even farther away from himself. He wiped sweat from his forehead and wished he had enough minds to maintain some cold while working with Joans.

"Good. The more solid the air, the less heat will penetrate. Now it's your turn."

Jaren followed Joans' example and formed a very dense lump of heat. He hurled it at Joans as fast as he could while trying to hold a steady spiral and curl. He continued to control it until he thought that Joans would be able to take it from him, then he released it. The lump blazed to fire and flew true for fifteen feet, then took a sharp turn and headed right for the wagons. Jaren's heart sank.

"Pox-riddled bones!" Joans cursed.

Jaren watched in horror as the guards dove out of the way of the incoming fireball. Joans reached out with a blend of cold and bio energy and quenched the ball in midflight. A mist like a fogbank washed over Agshot and his wagon. Cosren let out a low whistle and everyone in the train watched the mist as it dissipated.

"Radiance-twisting fool! You will use light!"

Jaren's radiance-sight saw another attack coming. He threw up a wall and sprinted sideways. When he had the wall in place, Jaren reached out to take the lump. Joans released the energy the instant Jaren touched it, and a ball of fire blossomed right in front of his wall. Jaren took another step to the side and saw a second lump coming at him. The heat from the first ball burrowed through the wall and warmed Jaren's exposed skin as he threw up a second wall and dove away. A third attack followed shortly after, and other minds prepared the next wall. Jaren rolled to his feet as Mastiff had taught and continued running, preparing a wall that he released only when the ball of fire flared to life. He kept running and forming walls to deflect more and more attacks. The last two had curved over Jaren's walls, and he wondered if Joans was trying to trick him, but when he looked back, he saw that the wagons were far in the distance.

A soft scraping sound made Jaren's ears perk up. He looked toward the sound, expecting a brush spider or one of those burrowing lizards. He stared across the red wasteland, but the only motion was the waves of heat from the afternoon sun. Jaren cooled the air around him and began a gentle trot back to the train.

A second sound—like something dragging across dirt— made him whirl around. A twang reached his ears mid-spin, and Jaren immediately threw up his shield. He felt a draw the instant he got it up. It quivered, but he maintained it. He saw red-clad men materializing from the ground, drawing their weapons as they ran toward him. Memories of being pinned down near the Eldvar flooded his minds. The archer had another arrow nocked, and now a second archer was lifting his bow. Jaren turned to the train and shouted, "Attack!" He did his best to maintain his shield as he ran toward the train but struggled to keep the vectors aligned. He kept shouting as he went. More arrows were loosed and deflected. The shield wobbled and he felt a bite in his neck and a jolt of pain down his arm as an arrow zipped in front of him, and then veered off through his shield. He stumbled and was partially thrown through his shield before he dropped it and then reformed it around his sprawled-out body. As he fell, he saw a blur move past him.

"Guards up!" he heard Mastiff shout in the distance. Jaren rolled over and saw Joans delivering death in large and small packages. The fallen men blended in with the soil, almost disappearing into the ground, except where smoke rose from them or pools of dark red blood collected beside them.

Joans slowed, but for some reason he didn't return immediately—he was instead poking around at the bodies. Jaren dropped his shield and tried to stand, but as he leaned on his arm, he felt a sharp shooting pain in his neck. He reached up to feel for damage and got blood on his fingers. That arrow had penetrated his poorly formed shield and grazed him. Some minds began berating the others, like a row of screeching blackbirds chivvying another row on another branch. Wiping the blood from his fingers onto his segg, he stood and waited for Joans.

"You're lucky your shield didn't correct that man's aim. You might be dead."

His cheeks turned red. He needed to work on shielding while running. He tried to consider the problem, but the pain in his neck was too distracting for most of his minds.

Joans folded out a small blend with bio and healed the wound. A little damage remained beneath the skin, but most of the pain was gone. Jaren wiped the blood off the soft new scar.

"Thank you."

They made their way back to the stationary wagon train. The setting sun washed the whole sky in a reddish hue that was the same color as the soil, making it hard to tell where the soil stopped and the sky began.

"What are you holding?" Jaren asked.

"I'm not quite sure, but I have a guess."

Joans handed Jaren a piece of cloth. Blood covered the edge of an intricate piece of black and white embroidery on a red background. The stitches depicted what looked like a bear in manacles. As Jaren ran his fingers across the stitching, a couple of minds laughed at the idea of trying to put a bear in chains. Jaren had not seen this emblem before.

When he handed the rag to Mastiff, the long shadows from the last sliver of sun made the man's grimace ominous.

"House Krandor."

Jaren had heard the name before, but he couldn't remember the context.

The guards had put their wooden shields back on the wagons and were starting to set up camp, and the train drivers were pulling food and fodder from the donkeys' packs. Mastiff looked out over the horizon, a frown still on his face as he rolled the red cloth between his thick fingers. Jaren stretched his shoulder, feeling at the wound in his neck.

"Is something bothering you?"

"It doesn't make sense that Krandor would be attacking us. And especially not here."

"Who is Krandor?"

"House Krandor started Thralldom here in Caidron...before there was a Caidron. It's a long story, but they became very powerful by selling thralls. Prestare, head of Krandor, sits on the council of Caidron, and frequently is the executive. His is a powerful name in Pinnutuck."

"So, why would he be attacking us?" A mind provided an answer that Jaren spoke out loud, "Because he hates Hairth." Another mind added, "Maybe because Hairth is trying to end Thralldom?"

Mastiff nodded, his eyes still searching the darkening horizon for something.

"Oh, yes, he hates Hairth, but I can't see him sanctioning let alone sending his own men out to attack Hairth. He's more likely to have someone put a knife in Hairth's back or poison his drink. An outright attack, if it were made known, would weaken his support among the lower houses and push more people toward Hairth. Like I said, it doesn't make sense."

"Maybe something has changed to make him more aggressive," Jaren suggested. Mastiff in turn shot a wry glance at Jaren.

"Something like you?" He shook his head. "Unless you've been telling people what you are, I see no way for Krandor to have learned. I spend hours with you every day and I only learned right before we started this trip."

Jaren felt a twinge of guilt at that comment and hoped the waning light made the color in his face hard to see. He regretted having deceived Mastiff all those weeks. It had been Hairth's instruction, but Jaren hadn't wanted to tell Mastiff anyway.

"No, it's something else. How did they know we were coming through? Prestare's men wouldn't be robbing travelers. They were here just for us." Mastiff narrowed his eyes toward the thickening darkness ahead of them. "And the way they came at us from behind. That's what's really getting at me." His eyes widened. "Guards up!"

Startled heads turned toward him, but then their disciplined bodies rushed toward the wagons. Shields were up and the men were forming their wall by the time Mastiff and Jaren rushed past the half-erected tents and the partly unhitched donkeys.

"What's this all about?" Griff demanded, pushing his prune-like face from behind Cosren's shield. Pale moonlight reflected off his bald head. "I don't see any attack. Is this some sort of drill? Dusty bones, Mastiff, this ride has been rough enough. We don't need any drills."

"This isn't a drill, Griff. That attack made no sense. I think we sprung a trap early and I want to be ready when the rest of the teeth clamp shut."

Aside from a gentle wind blowing through the scrub brush and Joans' impatient pacing, the night was still as they waited. Jaren had to remind himself to breath. There usual warning from Joans was only a few seconds prior to an attack, so, as the minutes wore on, Jaren found that he'd just as soon skip the waiting. He wasn't the only one.

Yates and Cosren were quietly chuckling at something about an Arenti rice girl. Iambret was trying to convince Mastiff with hoarse whispers that it wasn't a trap, just a poorly executed attack. Jaren listened but wasn't sure what to think. The night continued to darken, and even with the moonlight and a sky full of stars Joans was little more than a shadow. Those who were still vigilant strained to search the surroundings, but it was difficult to seen anything.

Iambret's and Griff's protests steadily grew stronger, and Mastiff's certainty waned.

"I guess..." he began.

The twang of dozens of bows and the whistling of arrows cut him off. An eyeblink later, there were arrow shafts sticking out of Joans' shield like pins in a cushion. Why hadn't Joans detected the attack and deflected the arrows? Another set of minds wondered why the arrows stuck in the force shield, but those minds who had been watching explained that there was thick air around Joans on the inside of the shield, like the flesh of a vannfruit under the peel. An interesting configuration Jaren would need to ask about after Joans dispatched these attackers. Other minds had put a shield around the guard block, ready to drop it if the guards moved.

"It appears I am a target," Joans said to the huddled group. He spun out a dozen small lumps of energy and placed them on the tips of the arrows. He reversed the direction of the arrows in his shield, and then placed force along the length of the shafts. When he released the lumps, the arrows shot back to where they had originated. The energy lumps stayed with the arrow heads, and Jaren watched them with his radiance-sight as they disappeared from his vision. Each lump was mostly heat, but also had a tiny odd lump inside of it, like an egg with a tiny yolk. The energy stayed coherent long outside of Joans' range. The yolk disappeared, and the heat released with a bright flash followed by loud pops and screaming.

Joans took off toward the attackers while the rest of the train stayed under Jaren's shield. Another volley of arrows came down on the wagons and deflected off the shield. At Mastiff's shouted command, the block reoriented. Jaren watched Joans, who was folding, and shaping, zipping and releasing, all the while leaving screams and flashes behind him. With his radiance-sight and the glow from Joans' sources, he could see the silhouettes of falling men. Joans kept attacking, and Jaren realized there were more men than any attack they had previously experienced.

"*Jaren!*" Mastiff shouted. "Fight!"

A huge draw pressed on his shield, and he dropped it as the guards moved forward. Hordes of red-clad men rushed in from the darkness. Jaren replaced the shield around himself as a man swung the butt of a spear to strike him. The shield repelled the blow, and with a shove from a free lump of force, Jaren drove the spear into the man's chest. Jaren kept up with the guards, lobbing lumps of energy and slicing the attackers with blades of air. He froze them, burned them, and pulled them to pieces, but the attackers were everywhere. Jaren's heart was pounding, and his minds were shouting between each task he gave them. The burden pressed hard against Jaren's chest, and he became sluggish with his lumps. Men reached for Jaren, but their hands were repelled by his shield. Those who touched his shield became his next targets.

He tried to drop a lump of cold into the brain of a bearded man, but his aim was slightly off. The man let out a horrendous scream, and his hands went to his face. A blow from a shield shattered his nose and cheek, and pieces of his face dangled at his chest, still tangled with the hair of his beard. The man fell to the ground, writhing in pain.

Four men tried to separate Mastiff from the bloc. Jaren formed the air blade and drove it forward at neck height. It removed the first two heads but wobbled toward the third. It couldn't go entirely through his head, instead leaving a gash from the top of his ear across his face to the bottom of his jaw. He jerked back, shuddered, and then collapsed. Mastiff was as surprised as the fourth attacker but recovered first and cut the man down.

Jaren was able to keep his shield up and oriented, but it required more and more minds as he became fatigued. The attackers kept pouring in. For each man that fell, another stepped in. The press was incredible. Jaren's heart pounded against the burden, near to bursting. He burned the lungs of a wiry old man wielding a short sword in either hand, and a giant of a man moved forward to fill the gap. He wore a cruel, gap-toothed smile as he hefted a hammer that could have been a small anvil on a thick pole.

A stocky man shouted "*That's* the boy, idiot!" as he batted at the giant with his shield. Recognition crossed the giant's face and he lunged toward Jaren. His outstretched hand and anvil-on-a-stick pushed against Jaren's shield. It felt like a blow to his head that shot down to his heart. He kept the shield in place, but lost control of the vectors, and they all pointed downwards. The giant was jerked to the ground, and Jaren drove his knee into the man's nose on the way down. He felt and heard the crunch of the man's facial bones, and his leg went numb. He stumbled. Three more men pressed against his shield, and it collapsed.

Rough hands grabbed his arms and neck. More hands went over his face, covering his eyes. His minds went frantic—he couldn't see, and he felt like he was being torn apart. They were pulling him away from the guards. He tried to shout, but a hand clamped over his mouth. He bit down on the hand and tasted blood. A fist connected with his side, then another with his stomach.

"Get his sources!"

"What are they?"

"Search his pockets for stones."

His minds unified at the thought of losing his sources. He began folding and hurling lumps based on his radiance-sight, but he was exhausted and found it a struggle to control the lumps. He dropped force directly onto the hands holding him, successfully tearing two hands apart before splitting his own skin right below his bruised knee. As blood spilled down his leg, he screamed with pain. Every grasping hand he removed was replaced by a new one, and soon his cold, bio, and heat were taken out of their pockets. Then something struck him on the head, and everything went black.

Chapter 41

Surviving Captivity

Jaren woke to creaking wood and a throbbing head. He tried to open his eyes, but the light was blinding. He ached all over. The sun burned his exposed skin. His minds moved sluggishly, and he felt disoriented. His sources weren't anywhere nearby. His nose and throat were painfully dry. When he finally managed to open his eyes, he wished he hadn't.

"He's awake!"

The man who shouted wore a red robe. A twisted smile, more gaps than teeth, flashed on his weathered and stubbly face.

Rough wood dug into Jaren's skin as he struggled to sit up. Manacles weighed on his wrists. He fought down a sudden panic as memories of the thrall march resurfaced after being buried so long.

Before him rolled a long train of wagons, several filled with motionless men. Beside the wagons marched scores of red-clad men. Several limped or cradled injured arms, but most walked with straight backs. A few turned and glared at him.

A tall thin man with a strip of green fabric on his red shoulder walked down the train, accompanied by a younger man. The thin man wore his sword with the same ease that the younger man wore his scowl. Jaren felt his dread deepening when he recognized Olis, a boy who had bullied Jaren during his last trip to Caidron.

The older man stopped, glared at Olis, and stated firmly, "The answer is *no*!"

"No one says 'no' to me."

"Yes—and that is the problem. You are in this company to learn discipline. Your father told me to treat you like any other junior officer, and I'll shear my sheep with wood before I'll disobey Prestare."

Olis glared at the older man and said, "When I take my father's place as head of this house, I will have you striped for how you are treating me."

"When you take your father's place, if you have not yet outgrown your childish ways, you will be killed in your sleep before you can carry out that threat, and another better-respected heir will lead House Krandor while your unburied carcass molders, and all will rejoice that we are not being led by an addled *pisspot*."

The blood drained from Olis' face. Jaren would have laughed had his own situation been different. Instead, he hefted the manacles and tried to rotate his hands so that the metal wasn't cutting into his wrists. The world tilted, but Jaren kept himself upright.

The officer turned to Jaren.

"Thrall, you have been accused under the authority of Caidron of escaping." The man adjusted the green strip of authority on his shoulder with surprisingly delicate hands.

"Escaped?" Jaren's voice was rough, and his mouth didn't work. His minds were fuzzy, and he felt sick to his stomach.

"Yes, you idiot," Olis growled. The officer raised a narrow eyebrow at the boy.

"You will keep silent." He said it matter-of-factly rather than as a command. Then turning back to Jaren, he continued, "Do you have your papers on you?"

"No, Mastiff has them."

The officer glanced left and right over his narrow shoulders, and said, "I don't see anyone named 'Mastiff.' The law allows you two hours to find the holder of your papers while being accompanied by a responsible freeman. Your time starts now. Olis will accompany you."

Olis' sneer changed to a grimace. "Accompany *him* for two hours?"

"That is what I said. I will return in two hours." Then turning back to Jaren, he added, "If you cannot obtain your papers within the allotted time, you will be placed under arrest."

There was no harshness in his eyes— just a man doing his job. He turned and walked away.

Olis muttered under his breath, "Tavlar, I swear I'll kill you one day!"

Jaren's throat felt like it was on fire.

He squeezed his eyes closed, as much to block out the bright light as to try to wake himself from this nightmare.

"Can I have some water?" Jaren croaked. He didn't see the blow coming until it landed on his cheek. He pitched over and hit his head on the edge of the wagon. His vision darkened.

When he awoke, he saw Tavlar standing beside a sweating and sulking Olis.

"Your two hours are up. By the authority of the magistrate of Caidron you are now under arrest for escaping. You will be executed upon our return."

Jaren opened his mouth to speak, but only a ragged gasp came out. Tavlar gestured at a guard, "Give him some water."

A guard brought a waterskin and poured some water into Jaren's open mouth. It spilled all over his face, but he didn't care—he gulped as much as he could.

"Do not let him die before we arrive in Caidron. Olis, you will come with me."

The water helped to clear Jaren's head. The land they traveled was the same flat red with a sparse scrub. The train was kicking up dust as it went, so Mastiff should be able to find him—assuming Mastiff was alive. One mind wished Joans would appear to save him, though others believed that Joans was working with these people. Why hadn't he warned them before the attack started? And what took him so long during the attack?

The sun was nearing the horizon. Jaren knew he had to escape. But how? His minds generated ideas, but none were of any use. He couldn't run. He couldn't fight. Aside from the lightballs, there was no radiance nearby. He glanced at the guards standing near him.

"Hey," he hissed at one. The guard turned to him.

"If you help me escape, Hairth will make you a rich man."

The man's loud laugh jolted Jaren.

"But if I help you escape, Tavlar will have me executed right next to *you*."

Though his minds generated more ideas, each was less feasible than the one before. If he were as good with light as Joans, he could make some sort of distraction—or he could just blind the guards around him. But then what? Eventually all his minds realized that the situation was hopeless. Except one. It had found his sources—they were sitting in one of the wagons toward the front of the train, far outside his reach. They were surprisingly dim and must have been in a large tub of water. That one mind reached and strained, and eventually an older, strong mind joined in. Together, they touched the source.

Jaren stretched as far as he could, and, with all the minds working together, set a weak net around the heat source. He slowly folded the energy back into the source, but it slipped through the net. *Brittle bones!*

Jaren started over. He collected, folded, collected, and then lost it again. He tried over and over as the sun dipped below the horizon. The guard changed, and he had to employ one of his minds to drink and eat the crust of bread they gave him. Because he couldn't use all of his minds, he didn't fold at all, he just pulled the energy closer while he ate.

He could have kicked himself. When he finished eating, and could devote all of his minds to it, he began drawing the energy toward him after just two folds. Getting the energy out of the water made it much easier to hold. If he could have kept the third fold he would have done so, but he lost most of it. One of his minds dropped out and calculated that he needed a little over five hours at his current rate to be sure he'd melt one of the links in his chains. He sighed and continued to gather energy. The mind performing the calculations suggested that it be allowed to continue to compute other options instead of joining the gathering effort. It considered how many men could be stopped with a lump of that size. Could he possibly get free and then get his sources back? He didn't think so. There were too many men between him and the sources. Could he slowly inch toward the sources during the night? If so, maybe he could maintain the third fold, and gather more lumps.

The train stopped and the red-robed men began setting up camp, pulling tarps from the donkeys, rolling out pallets, and distributing dry meat and vannfruit. Except for a few dark glances, the men ignored Jaren. He moved as close as he could to the edge of the wagon he was in. The two feet of proximity he gained by doing this made a small improvement in his ability to collect energy.

An olive-skinned man with short graying hair and two yellow strips of fabric rapped on the side of Jaren's wagon.

"Get out. We are still a week out from Caidron, and well over five days from the last watering hole. I've got men who need to ride in the wagon you're riding in, and aside from that cut on your leg I don't see anything wrong with you. We can't wait for you to hobble along with those manacles, so tomorrow they'll be removed, and you'll have to carry your own weight. Don't run—we'll catch you. And if we don't, you'll die of thirst." The whole instruction was delivered with cordiality, as if the man were talking to one of his men rather than a captive.

"If I stay, I'll be executed when we reach Caidron."

Jaren wasn't sure if he was more surprised by the steadiness of his voice or by the fact that he had said it at all. At the same time, other minds were drawing another lump from the source into the lump he was holding near the wagon.

The man smiled, adding to the wrinkles around his eyes.

"A boy who faces death with a steady hand." He nodded. "Tavlar presented the law as he is supposed to. But there are powerful men who would much rather have you in their service than feeding the flies in Caidron."

Jaren continued to fold as soldiers chained him to the edge of the wagon and he ate his dried meat and bread. He only stopped collecting when they allowed him to relieve himself. He briefly considered killing his three guards but doubted he could find water.

When they brought him back, he moved out to the full length of the chain and laid down with his head pointed at the distant sources. He continued folding as night bugs began their noises, as the stars came out, and as snores joined the chorus of night bugs. He added to his lump again and again, and when he finally had enough energy to melt a link of chain, he let out an exhausted sigh. He had never continuously maintained focus like this. It was painfully hard—like holding an arm straight out—easy at first, almost impossible after a long period of time. Jaren relaxed his minds, except those holding the lump.

The moon was high in the sky. Guards patrolled the camp, but no one was watching him. As soon as the patrol passed him, he compressed the lump of heat as tightly as he could manage with his weary minds and released it in a link used to chain him to the wagon. The metal glowed bright white. He pulled it apart, and the link fell to the ground. Jaren remained motionless.

After the next patrol passed, Jaren inch-wormed himself toward his sources. He set his minds to collecting heat again—doing his best to ignore the pain from the resumed effort. He stopped by the next wagon, hoping the guards wouldn't notice the change. The folding had become easier as he had gotten closer. The guard walked by but paid him no mind—he was just a boy chained up to a cart. As he scooted closer, he used the gathered energy to split the chain between his ankles. He was doing it! Just a few more feet—another minute—and he'd be able to free himself completely and retrieve his sources.

Something sharp poked into his chest.

"And what are you doing here?" Tavlar asked, amusement in his voice. He pressed the tip of a spear into Jaren's chest. Jaren froze. As he began stammering, minds started offering suggestions, but none were worth saying. One mind shouted above the rest to keep folding, and Jaren realized Tavlar couldn't see what he was doing anyway. His next thought was, 'Keep him talking!' so he tried his best.

He looked from side to side, scrunched up his face as if he had just woken up and sleepily replied, "I was trying to sleep until someone poked me with a stick. Now, if you don't mind." Jaren gently pushed the tip of the spear away and put his arm over his eyes as if trying to go back to sleep, but his minds were folding for all they were worth. He couldn't see what Tavlar was doing—the sources were too far for him to use his radiance-sight—but the spear point then rested against his neck.

"So, I'm supposed to believe that you crawled this far in your sleep."

Jaren folded and collected as he replied, "Crawled? What are you talking about?"

Jaren reached out to fold again, but as he made his second fold the source grew bright. He almost cursed. The sources were moving! They had realized what he was doing and were taking the sources farther out of range. He almost cried.

"Do you take me for a fool?"

Jaren moved the lump he held to the center of Tavlar's chest, but a shout from farther up the train made Tavlar shift just as Jaren released the energy.

Tavlar's scream pierced the night as his robe burst into flames, illuminating his horrified expression while burning his chest. He dropped the spear and batted against the flames. Other shouts ran up and down the train. Jaren rolled over, quickly crawled under the next wagon, and was surprised to see the sources coming toward him. The fools! They didn't understand how sources worked. He reached out and began folding heat again, but the possession of the lump was taken from him. It was released, yielding screams from another soldier. Other, denser lumps were formed and released just as quickly. More screams, then a general cacophony filled the air. The sources were still moving toward him. Had Joans found him? Why wasn't he carrying his own sources?

Jaren couldn't think of an answer, but he knew if he were going to escape, this would be his only chance. He crawled out from under the wagon and moved to intercept the sources.

"Run!"

Orange and red tongues from burning wagons licked the sky. Dancing lights filled the camp with eerie shadows of men running about wildly, some in their robes, but most wearing only nightclothes.

Then he espied Lesarra running toward him with the sources. She threw out a lump of heat at the wagon he had been under and a set of cold lumps at the donkeys. The loud braying and sudden scattering of the animals added to the nighttime pandemonium. Jaren turned and ran to keep pace with her, wincing at the pain in his leg. He folded the force source and erected a large shield around the two of them. In the moonlight and amidst all the shouting, few people noticed them. Those who did were met with a lump of heat or cold from Lesarra.

Within a few minutes the pair were beyond sight of the camp. They kept running in a mostly straight course, dodging gnarly brush that were highlighted by the reflections of their radiance-sight and moonlight.

"Do you think they will follow us?" Jaren asked. Lesarra couldn't run as fast as he could, so it wasn't hard for him to speak. But the pain in his leg and the cracked and bleeding wound made him grateful he didn't have to run faster. Lesarra, however, seemed to be wholly unaccustomed to running. Through huffs and puffs she replied, "Probably," so they kept running until she said, "I know...we need to keep...moving, but I...can't run...another step." Jaren nodded and slowed to walk beside her.

"I'm sure they're tracking us."

She nodded, still breathing heavily. She pushed a breeze in swirling patterns all around them, then formed air into four-foot-wide blocks and laid out a path perpendicular to the direction they'd been running. Ingenious! Jaren thought. The air blocks would spread their weight, eliminating any trace they had passed. They moved off silently into the night, angling this way and that as they went, but they didn't stop moving until the eastern sky began to lighten.

Chapter 42

Accompanying Lesarra

Jaren's back felt stiff from laying on hard ground. He hadn't intended to sleep, but the drool he wiped from his cheek said he had slept deeply. Lesarra stared out through the veil. A leather cord that had been holding her hair back hung loose. She wore sturdy tan pants—now covered in red dust—and a red shirt.

The "veil," as Lesarra had called it, hid anything inside it. From the inside you could see out, though it obscured things a little. It also reduced the sunlight that passed through, which was a blessing considering how high in the sky the sun was.

"You snore," she said, still staring out.

"Yeah, sorry. Kehvun says it's not bothersome. I hope it didn't keep you awake."

"No, I couldn't sleep, but it had nothing to do with your kitten-purr snore." Despite the joke, her voice was flat, and in the veil-dimmed sunlight, some of the sparkle seemed gone from her green eyes.

"Are you okay?"

She continued to stare. "Their faces keep coming back to me. The look of surprise, their pain as I..." She shuddered. "Rudaltro taught me how to defend myself—how to..." She trailed off, looking at nothing at all.

The image of a man with a knife in his chest appeared in one of Jaren's minds. Others dredged up memories of the men at the river and from the night before. He watched again as they split in two or exhaled smoke, wide-eyed. He raised a hand to put on Lesarra's shoulder, but then stopped, uncertain how she would take it.

"What if they had families? Wives now widows, children without fathers...all because of me. Mothers weeping for their sons. Fathers swearing to avenge their deaths. Siblings waiting for their brother to come home...waiting, though he never will."

Another mind pulled up images of Ben as he had left their starving family to hunt. Yet another recalled all those nights watching the darkness for Ben's return. Those men were Ben to someone—gone off to do something important and never returning.

One of Jaren's minds objected. Those men tried to kill him and that was all that mattered. He wouldn't just die to prevent someone else's heartache. But how many hearts had he broken?

A gentle hand on his shoulder pulled him from his thoughts. Lesarra had turned to him, her eyes laden with unshed tears.

"What other choice did we have, though?"

The gesture made Jaren feel even worse—now *she* was comforting *him*? He shook his head but managed a half-hearted smile—the other half of his heart refused to participate.

The veil flickered and then winked out. Lesarra had made a small blending of energy with many tiny shapes and layers. When attached to another lump, it somehow doled out the energy without the Light-Twister's attention. Jaren had been fascinated, but it was too intricate and too delicate for Jaren's minds, especially as tired as he was.

"I guess that means it's time to move," she said.

They walked in silence heading west where they would eventually run into the river, which they could follow north to Freysdal. Jaren worried about running into Krandor's men again, so they watched for dust plumes. Lesarra's air pavers were hard against worn boots and tired feet, but thirst and hunger bothered Jaren more than anything else.

As the sun touched the distant horizon, Lesarra stopped. She folded out a lump of force and dropped it into the ground. When she released it, a shower of red dirt and dust shot into the air, raining down pebbles and clods of soil.

"Watch it!" Jaren yelped as he threw his arms up to protect his head.

Lesarra just chuckled, brushing the dirt from her tangled hair. The laughter eased some of the strain—from a lack of sleep, from running, and from killing—on her face.

"I'm sorry. These sources are so strong!" Color rose in her cheeks. She paused, looked down at the ground, and then up at Jaren with her deep green eyes. "Did you get these from the source trail?" She still carried the sources—she hadn't offered to give them back, and Jaren hadn't asked.

"Source trail? No."

"No? Then where?"

He looked away—it was hard to think straight when looking into those eyes. He couldn't tell her about Hairth. Joans had warned him what would happen if other Light-Twisters learned about Freysdal. Joans was probably protecting what he believed would be his once he killed Hairth. But regardless of his motivations, Joans' advice seemed sound.

"I'm sorry. I didn't mean to pry."

Jaren realized he had been silent too long. He nodded toward the hole she had made.

"What were you trying to do?"

"Well, if we don't get water soon, we're going to die. I was digging a well."

Jaren shook his head. "There's no water down there. Once you're more than a couple hundred feet from the river, there's no water."

"How far are we from the river?"

"At least a week. Maybe longer."

Her face sagged, and her lost stare returned.

"But," Jaren said, "I can get water." He formed a bowl of air and used one of the stones Lesarra had ejected from the ground. As the water began to drip from the rock, Lesarra's eyes widened.

"How does that sum make water?"

"It isn't making water, it's pulling water out of the air." And it was taking a lot longer than it had in Freysdal.

"Try some."

Lesarra took the transparent bowl from Jaren and drank deeply, relief spreading across her face. She exhaled, then gushed, "I could just kiss you!"

Jaren's face went as red as the ground. All of his minds stood still and stared at her through his eyes. The light of the setting sun made her face impossibly beautiful. One mind sketched an image of her kissing him. The others scrambled to copy it.

When her smile quirked into a mischievous grin, Jaren realized he was staring and quieted his minds. He turned away and muttered, "It's nothing." One mind brought up an image of Haerlee, and the rest abashedly turned away.

Lesarra copied what Jaren had done and filled another bowl. They resumed walking, and Lesarra transformed her bowl into a cup to make drinking easier as they walked, and Jaren copied her.

"Do you have any tricks to pull food from the air?"

"I wish!" Jaren replied. Even dry bread and salty meat sounded good.

"I guess we will have to get food the normal way."

Jaren wasn't sure what that was. They continued to walk in silence. Not only was Lesarra able to maintain the air pavers while pulling water from the air, she was also able to pull the water faster than him.

Jaren wanted to talk with Lesarra but had a hard time finding something to say that didn't sound dumb. He wondered about her experience learning radiance, about her family, about her plans—about her rescuing him. He wondered about being "unencumbered"—that seemed like a better topic than whether she had a boyfriend, which a few of his minds had hinted that he ask. He turned to look at her, but saw that she was staring into the slowly fading sunlight with that same lost look.

As the red sun dipped halfway below the horizon, Lesarra folded a blend of bio energy. She formed it into a hemisphere, and then expanded it so there was a hollow center, as if she was making a shield. She kept spreading it out, until it became impossibly thin and then disappeared.

"What was that?"

"I'm looking for food."

She squeaked, then folded out a small, dense lump of cold, which she deposited into the earth some sixty feet from them.

"Jaren, you might be better with force than I am. Can you pull a chunk of the ground up— about so big—where I dropped that cold quantity?" She indicated the size of a large basket.

Jaren set a large lump of force with the vectors pointing upward and then released the energy. A chunk of red soil lifted up into the air a few feet and then dropped back down, crumbling as it hit the ground. Running over, Lesarra dug through the soil and pulled out a stocky, dead lizard the size of Jaren's forearm. She carried the mottled brown and red creature by its tail back to Jaren. Lesarra made a blade from air and neatly cleaned it.

"Those are poisonous," Jaren said.

"Yes, I know, but the poison is up in the head. As long as you stay away from that, they're fine to eat."

Jaren was impressed both that Lesarra knew that and with how the scaly skin peeled off under Lesarra's concentration.

"Not as easy as a treecat, but with self-sharpening sources it is easy to keep the blade together."

Treecat? Did she mean treebunny? But another mind got its question out first.

"What do you mean, 'self-sharpening sources?'"

She raised an eyebrow, and then folded a broad lump of heat and slowly released it into the lizard on a plate of air. The roasted meat smelled like scrub brush and fish, but his mouth still watered.

She folded out another lump of heat and brought it out between the two of them.

"What do you see?"

"A lump of heat."

"Lump?"

"Yes, lump."

"Right, well I say *quantity*. But that's not the point. What do you see in the quantity?"

Jaren furrowed his brow. He looked at the quantity...lump...

"All I see is heat."

Lesarra nodded. She stared at the lump, and Jaren watched as the lump separated very slowly into a large and small lump. His eyes kept darting at the steaming meat, but Lesarra's attention was on the energy, so he tried to ignore his growling stomach.

"Now what do you see?"

"Two lumps."

"Don't just look. Feel them. Use all of your radiance senses, not just sight."

Jaren wasn't sure what his other radiance senses were, but he took control of the lumps and tried to "feel" them, not just look at them. He shaped them, brought them together, and pulled them apart. They were different, but he couldn't quite say how. It was like recognizing a segg made from two different fabrics. The energy was heat, but there were two distinct kinds of heat.

The larger lump was stiffer, spicier, more vibrant—but just a little.

"They're different," Jaren said, looking up from the lumps.

Lesarra nodded as she chewed a mouthful of lizard. A small pile of bones sat beside her. Jaren gaped. She had eaten nearly half of the lizard!

She pushed the plate over to Jaren and he tore off the muscular tail. His minds knew that lizard did not taste good, but it was the most delicious thing he had ever eaten.

"Self-sharpening sources, as they get used, shift to another variety of the same energy. They are incredibly valuable. Your heat source seems to self-sharpen at least three times. Most sources, as they get used, shift to another kind of energy, so you have to constantly filter out the energy you want."

"That sounds difficult."

"When it's all you know…" she shrugged. "How long have you been studying under Joans?"

"A few months."

Her ears shifted back, and her eyebrows rose. She tried to cover her surprise by pushing her hair back and retying the leather cord. Why was that a surprise?

"And how old are you?"

He had wondered that same question about her. She was clearly older than him, but young enough to be only a little older.

"I'm seventeen," Jaren lied. "And you are…?" "I'm twenty-one."

Jaren had hoped she would only be about nineteen. His lie hadn't reduced the age gap much at all. She probably thought of him like a little brother.

They each took another chunk of lizard. Lesarra reformed the plate into one with a curved surface and drank the meat juices.

"How long did you know you could control radiance before you began training?" she asked.

"I didn't know I could until I started training. There was an accident..." Jaren trailed off as the memory of the burned men and women in the clinic surfaced in his minds. "Joans had to prove to me that I could actually do it. What about you? How did you learn you could control it?"

A smile crossed her lips as she pulled her legs underneath her. "I was in Cresswand when I saw a man with a lightball. It was the strangest thing. I could somehow see it with my eyes closed and even when it was behind me. It was the strangest thing," she repeated.

Jaren nodded. He could only imagine how unnerving it would be to discover radiance-sight without a guide.

"The man left, and I assumed it was just the lightballs. I asked..." she paused, "a friend if he noticed anything strange about them, and he laughed when I said I could see them with my eyes closed. That was a little before I turned nineteen. Then a few months later a man came to Cresswand, and he had lightballs hidden in his robe—but I could see them too. They were different from each other, though—almost like they were different tones of music. I was able to get one from him."

Jaren looked at her questioningly, and even in the dusky light he could see her blushing, but she rushed on.

"I was sure he wasn't following me, but as soon as I pulled it out to look at it, he was right there behind me. I could see what looked like clouds of light swirling out of his lightballs, and then settling around me and vanishing. I was trapped in something solid, and I was sure I was going to die. But instead of killing me the man merely asked, 'How many of those do I have?' I told him five, and then he released me and asked me if I...wanted to learn..." she trailed off.

"So, he trained you." Jaren finished. She nodded.

"For two years. He taught me about radiance, and about myself too." She went quiet again. Jaren was enjoying listening to her voice, and had even more questions, but she preempted him.

"Jaren, what do you know about Joans?"

"Not a lot."

"Did you know he was expelled from Cayrentall for releasing a powerful prisoner?"

Chapter 43

Facing a Dilemma

Lizard lost its appeal after two days, and without Mastiff and Griff there to force him, Jaren ate very little for the next six. Lesarra ate less. The water was quenching, but bland. The heat and hunger enervated. They walked a lot and spoke little, but when they did talk, Lesarra always had startling revelations.

Joans had been exiled from Cayrentall for releasing a Light-Twister despised by both factions. They had worked together — putting aside their theretofore insurmountable differences — to capture him. Joans had thought he could pry information from him when no one else had been able to.

Both factions viewed Light-Twisters as superior humans. One believed in helping people as advisers to rulers while the other believed in subjecting people and becoming their rulers.

Lesarra's father had left when she was little, and her mother had been horrified by Lesarra's radiant abilities. She had a hard time talking about her past. Jaren apologized for asking, but she brushed it off, wiping tears from her eyes.

"We've got to talk about something to pass the time." They had walked in silence for three hours after she said that.

Lesarra asked about the sources again, but Jaren refused to tell her anything. Instead, he told her about his sisters and his Freysdal Family — Maullie, Gerald, and Kehvun. He did not mention Haerlee.

Lesarra had followed them from Cresswand, staying within Joans' detection field, or carefully passing through it if she was outside. Their bright sources made them easy to follow. She had left hers in Cresswand. When she ran out of water, she just stole theirs. Mastiff would not be happy when he discovered how easy it had been for her—that is, if Mastiff was still alive. Jaren tried to push that worry aside.

The most startling thing he learned, however, was that he was powerful—maybe even *very* powerful.

"What do you mean by powerful?"

"I mean *powerful*."

"No. I can't even control lumps like you, let alone Joans."

"True, but you've only been using radiance for a few months. How many streams of thought do you have?" Jaren liked thinking of them as minds better, but streams of thought flowing through his mind and then moving out to control energy was also a good description.

"Around thirty-five. Sometimes the number goes up and down."

"Sure, like when you're rested and fed, the number is higher. Kind of like how strong your body is. The total number that you control is not, by itself, a good measure of how strong you are, but the number will go up as you use radiance and as you get older." So far, her explanation was all familiar to Jaren.

"The younger you first control radiance, the longer your initial burst of growth will be and the greater your total strength will be. Rudaltro said that it's kind of like how young children can learn new languages so much more easily. He explained that most first learn at the end of their eighteenth year and have an initial burst of a year or so. Those who learn closer to twenty have an initial burst that may be as short as six months. He knew someone who learned when he was almost seventeen and his initial burst had lasted four years. In that initial burst, you grow very fast, then you slow down. That's why it's important to use radiance as much as possible early on."

Maybe that is why Joans had been aggressive—*abusive*—in training. It was not right, and Jaren wouldn't forgive him, but it did make some sense.

"But…" Jaren started to ask a question, but Lesarra wasn't done.

"You started when you were seventeen—just think of how long your initial burst will last. And…" she had stopped walking and turned to stare at him. "You are already stronger at four months than I was after my first year. I'm guessing it has something to do with the quality of the sources Joans found for you."

Jaren realized that this was another sneaky effort to get him to talk about the sources. Initially she had just delicately probed, saying she "respected" Jaren's quiet. Now it was like a game she played to try to catch him off guard. She was playful, but she clearly wanted to know where the sources came from.

If what she said about power was true, and not just an attempt to learn about his sources, then Jaren was going to be even more powerful than she knew—she still thought he was older than he was.

Power prediction was just one of the many things that Joans had kept from Jaren. Others were thin radiance, cross-source blending, pumps and timers, and the factions. Some were simply advanced topics, but others felt like Joans was intentionally keeping him ignorant.

"I can't wait to drink real water and eat some fish," Jaren said, knowing the river was close.

Lesarra nodded but didn't reply. They walked on in silence. Jaren's mouth watered at the thought of fish. He reached out and folded a lump of light. Lesarra still carried the sources, but she never stopped him from using them. She would not voluntarily return them, and Jaren wasn't going to try to take them. Maybe if Joans had been there, she would have.

They had taught each other things as they walked. Well, mostly Lesarra taught Jaren, but he had shown her a few things, too. She mastered each as soon as she saw them. Jaren had been trying to do thin radiance, with impossibly skinny shapes, but he was still too clumsy. He folded out a small lump of bio and striated it within a lump of light. Then, ever so slowly, he worked the blend thinner and thinner, spreading it wide like water poured on a polished stone. But then he lost control and the energy released in blue and green sparks that zipped and twirled like bees around a flowering bush.

"Slow *down*."

She said that every time, and every time he knew that if he went any slower his minds would cramp. But he dutifully started over.

"Do you think Hairth will let me stay in Freysdal?"

Jaren's minds jumped at the question he had been avoiding all morning. He didn't even get the striations completed. The energy plunked out in thick pulsating clumps of blue and green that sank to the ground.

A better question would be, would Hairth even let Lesarra *into* Freysdal? He had been hinting to her that Hairth might not. Hairth was very concerned about security, and he didn't let just anyone in. He had told her that Hairth was fabulously wealthy—that he owned an entire town and most of the people in it. But he hadn't told her where his wealth came from, nor that the sources belonged to neither Joans nor him, but to Hairth.

"Maybe if you first remove the tiny amount of cold that is in the light it will be easier to control."

Lesarra had taken Joans' lesson on sources changing and expanded it tremendously.

"In Joans' source that you said produces force and a small amount of heat, when he folds he is folding a lot of force energy into a lot of force source, a lot of force energy into a small amount of heat source, a small amount of heat energy into a large amount of force source, and a small amount of heat energy into a small amount of heat source. Each cross-source sum produces a different energy that depends on the energy and the source. Then, if you fold multiple times, the situation is just compounded. In a mostly pure source, the extras are still tiny amounts even after multiple folds. When evenly mixed throughout a lump, they do make the lump a little volatile, but not so much that it is difficult to control. As more of the pure source is changed to a secondary source, the more complicated it becomes to control."

"And," Lesarra continued, "as you use the source, you can end up with tertiary, quaternary, and even fifth-level sources all within that single source. Each of the separate energies could be extracted from the lumps and used alone, but that seriously slows you down—which is fine for calm situations, but problematic in an emergency."

Jaren nodded and began folding out the light and bio again. He extracted a lump of cold that at single-density was only the size of a grain of sand—hardly worth the effort—but he hoped she would forget about her original question...at least, until he needed to bring it up again. But his hope was in vain.

"I mean, I know he's already got...*you*...working for him..." she was still incredulous that Jaren didn't just take his sources and leave with Joans—especially considering how powerful Joans was. Her view of Joans, based on stories from Rudaltro, was very different from what Jaren had experienced with him. "But, surely, if he's as wealthy as you say he is, he'll have something for me to do, too."

"He is that wealthy. But it's not a question of whether he has wealth or even work for you. It's..." Jaren wasn't sure how to finish the sentence—*That he can't trust you? That he doesn't know you? That he didn't trust people he didn't own?*

She released a lump of force she had been twirling. It hit Jaren like a punch in the arm. He kept his wits, though, and continued to slowly turn out his lump—so slowly, he didn't think he'd finish it by the time they reached the river.

"What is it? Why won't he let me stay?"

"He doesn't know you."

"No, he doesn't. But you do. Don't you trust me?"

"Of course, I do, but…"

"Then you can explain to him that he can trust me."

Jaren shook his head. "It doesn't work like that."

"Why not?" The heat in her voice was like a double-density lump released near his face.

"Because, I'm not that important." He was scrambling.

"Not that important—does Hairth own many Light-Twisters?"

"Well, no, but…"

"Then how can you say you aren't important?" Jaren's face turned red. He knew she could get fiery but hadn't seen this before…and her heat was rubbing off.

"Because I'm *not*!" He glared at her. "No one but Hairth knows I can use radiance." He turned to walk away. She started to say something else, but he cut her off. "*I'm just a thrall!*"

He hadn't meant to shout, but that was how it came out.

They walked together in silence again, following their shadows. Lesarra folded out a corridor of cold for them to walk in and Jaren tried to make the veil again. When it burst into sparks, she didn't say a word. Why didn't she understand? He had no influence with Hairth, and he couldn't explain why he wouldn't let her come. Jaren ran through different ways to finish the conversation, but none of them worked.

When they reached the river, the greenish-yellow grass felt nice beneath his feet. Jaren had calmed enough to try again.

"I'm sorry for shouting at you."

"Well, you should be!"

His anger flared up again, but he tamped it down by allocating more attention to the cooler minds.

"I don't know what Hairth will say, but I will talk to him for you."

"That's all I'm asking," she said curtly. She had not calmed down yet.

Jaren pulled some light, made some air and started fishing.

"That's incredible!" Lesarra said as she watched the fish pile into the basket. The wonder must have pushed the anger aside.

"Too bad it looks like the nestros are the most excited to jump."

"Nestros?"

"Yeah, the ones with whiskers and stripes. They taste like vomit." Lesarra wrinkled her nose.

After sorting out the good from the bad and cleaning and cooking them, Jaren and Lesarra sat to eat. They ate until they could hardly eat more.

"Why were they after you?"

Jaren tensed up. "What do you mean?" He knew exactly what she meant—he could still hear the voice, "That's the boy, *get him!*" How did they know about him and why were they trying to capture him?

"I guess you wouldn't have seen it. As soon as they got you away from the wagons, the fight there mostly stopped."

Jaren took his time chewing his last bite. Did that mean that his friends had survived? His minds provided some reasons for why the fight would have stopped then, but nothing he could share with Lesarra, and, in truth, none were likely. He nudged a rock with his toe and shrugged.

"I can't imagine they were really after me—it must have just been a coincidence."

"Right. They only decided to take *one* captive, and they just *happened* to know that he had sources on him. Either that or they were just somehow lucky enough to keep the sources away from you."

"Yeah, that doesn't seem likely. But I can't think of why they would be after me." Except, maybe, to get at Hairth—because they know that I might one day be a newly sharpened weapon in his hand. But he couldn't say that. He needed to change the subject...

"Lesarra, why did you follow me?"

"I already told you. I wanted to be around other Light-Twisters."

Jaren shook his head. "That's not what I meant. I mean... when you saw them capture me, why didn't you just wait for Joans to get back and stay with him? Why did you follow *me*?"

Now it was her turn to shrug. "Maybe I was worried about you. Joans was still off doing his 'death in the night' thing. You were getting to the edge of where I could see, and...I guess...I guess I just didn't want you to get hurt any worse." She stood up abruptly, kicked off her boots and walked down into the river. Her steps caused reddish mud to swirl through the clear water around the riverweeds, scattering a group of darting little fish. She hiked up her pants and walked in until the water hit her knees.

"It's cold, but it feels nice. I haven't had a bath in...I don't even know how long we've been traveling."

She flung herself—clothes and all—into the water. Jaren shook his head at her as the reddish soil swirled around in a muddy cloud. She splashed around, wiping her face and arms down. When she finally came out, she used air to dry herself off, and when she was done, she said, "Let's get to it."

Following the river north, it took three more days before Jaren could make out the mostly white wall of Freysdal. They had to hide from thrallchasers once, but with Lesarra's veil, it was easy to go unnoticed.

The mountains filled the view from East to West, and Freysdal—nestled in the gap between the two ranges—never looked so beautiful. The peace radiated out to him from there, and it was almost enough to calm his nerves for the final confrontation with Lesarra. He touched her elbow and stopped. She turned to him.

"Is that Freysdal?"

"It is, but I need you to…" Jaren wasn't sure how to say this, but he pressed on, bracing himself, "…stay here…until I can talk with Hairth."

Jaren was getting tired of that look—the one filled with anger and stubbornness that seemed to question his intelligence.

"You think I'm just going to stay here and wait for you?"

"Yes—that's what I think you are going to do."

The look shifted from anger to outrage. Jaren swallowed hard.

"And what if I decide I don't want to wait? Do you think you can stop me from going into Freysdal?"

"No. I know I can't…" Jaren started, but she hadn't finished.

"I rescued you! I walked all this way with you when I could have taken the sources and left you! I should be getting a hero's welcome, and instead you're treating me like a hound, telling me to 'Sit!' and 'Stay!'"

"It's not like that," Jaren began, and hurried on so she wouldn't interrupt. "I know I can't stop you, but I'm telling you it would be best for you to wait here. I can't stop you—and I wouldn't try—but Joans can, and if he's there and sees you coming, he wouldn't hesitate."

That certainly brought about a change. She wasn't happy about it, but the fire was gone from her eyes. Between what Rudaltro and Jaren had told her, she knew to be wary of Joans.

"I'll be as fast as I can."

"I'm keeping the sources."

Jaren just nodded his head. "That's fine. Just, don't go anywhere." She nodded and he was off.

Chapter 44

Reuniting Family

"What took so long?" Lesarra demanded, hands on her hips. The posture drew Jaren's eyes to Lesarra's narrow waist, but his eyes didn't linger. He knew a biting comment was in the offing, and only a quick reply would forestall its delivery.

"You can come."

No point in saying how quickly he had run—faster than anyone he knew. Or how he had found Hairth almost immediately upon entering the gates and how, much to his own surprise, Hairth hadn't hesitated in welcoming her to Freysdal.

"It was that easy?"

"It was. I just have to bring you right to him so he can introduce himself."

"Well, let's go then. I've seen all this spot has to offer. Lead on."

Jaren couldn't hear Hairth and Lesarra as they talked in his office. With his radiance-sight he could tell she was sitting across from him, but not much more. After just a few minutes of talking, he saw her stand up and hurriedly walk toward the door.

The heavy wooden door swung open and Lesarra rushed out. Her ashen face and wide eyes made her look like she'd just received the fright of her life. She didn't glance at Jaren, and she didn't stop. She just continued walking down the hallway.

Jaren watched her as she went. There was no strutting in her walk. She just left. Jaren stood and looked to see Hairth.

"Jaren, go home and let Maullie know you're alive. She's been very...concerned...about your safety. I'll want to talk with you more tomorrow. And bring Lesarra. But tonight, you should be with your family."

Hairth's instructions were more businesslike than Jaren had expected.

"What's going on with Lesarra?"

Hairth glanced past Jaren toward the empty hallway and smiled slightly.

"I made clear to her what would happen if she tried to steal from me or revealed what she saw here to anyone else. In all their years of radiance use, no other Light-Twister has thought to artificially concentrate sources. I'm not sure why, but if it ever occurred to them, Thadren would be a much more dangerous place. I helped her to understand that and the lengths to which I am willing to go to ensure that this secret stays safe with me. She took it kind of hard, but she should be back to normal in a few minutes. I believe she'll fit in nicely here if she chooses to stay."

Jaren tried to imagine what Hairth could have said to Lesarra to get that kind of reaction. He figured he should pay more attention to how Hairth dealt with women.

Lesarra was standing outside with her back against the wall.

"Why didn't you tell me?" Color was returning to her face, but her eyes still looked like a wild animal caught in a trap.

"I did tell you he's a hard man. You just didn't believe me."

She glared at him. "Well, you did tell me that..." She said it as if waiting for him to say more, but he couldn't quite tell what she meant.

"I can take you straight to your room," Jaren began, then added, "Or, you can come home with me to meet my family first."

She pushed off the wall and turned toward Jaren. The wild look in her eyes was mostly gone. "I think I'd like to meet your family."

Jaren had forgotten how wonderful Freysdal smelled at dusk. His heart raced as he got closer to home, Lesarra following right behind him. He wondered if she could hear the pounding in his chest. He wanted to dash in and shout that he was home. At the same time, he wanted to quietly sneak in and see everyone before they saw him.

What he did, though, was muddle between the two, slowly opening the door and then rushing in. Everyone was at the table, and most of the plates were eaten clean. The spicy smell of Arentash hung thick in the air. Gerald was leaning back, resting his hands on his curly brown hair. The sleeves of his blue and maroon robe were slid back, exposing thick arms. He looked content. Maullie was sitting next to him, but there was more gray in her hair than Jaren remembered.

Jaren couldn't see Kehvun's face, but he had his arm on the back of the seat next to him, where Haerlee happened to be sitting. Jaren could only imagine his self-satisfied grin. Haerlee was leaning back against his arm, her brown hair coursing over it. Jaren's exhilaration was momentarily deflated by a stab of jealousy. He knew that in his absence there had been no competition for her attention. Some minds had believed that Haerlee would ignore Kehvun and wait for him, though most had mocked those minds. But just as his minds were being humbled, Haerlee grabbed Kehvun's wrist and tossed his arm off her chair.

May sat next to Haerlee, and though Jaren couldn't see her face either, her head was held high, and her laughter filled the room. Her hand rested on the hand of the man sitting at the foot of the table. It was Mosj, the maintenance man. He was smiling at her. An enormous weight lifted as Jaren realized she had not relapsed in his absence. He would have to thank Mosj for taking care of her.

Ella sat directly opposite from the doorway. She wore a tired smile that didn't reach her eyes. She had pushed her chair away from the table, but her plate still held most of her food.

And sitting between Ella and Maullie was an empty setting, with a plate, cup and silverware waiting for him. Jaren's throat tightened and tears came to his eyes.

"Jaren!" Ella was up and out of her seat before anyone else noticed him. Chairs scraped on the hardwood floor as everyone stood. Ella wrapped her arms around him, and she cried into his neck.

"You're safe! You're safe!"

"Welcome home!"

"Jaren!"

The voices and expressions of welcome were a din of joy. Tears streamed down his own face, but he didn't care. He hadn't realized how much he had missed everyone. Arms reached out and wrapped around him, while Gerald patted his back and gripped his shoulder. Haerlee stood back a little, her delicate hands clasped together in front of her. Mosj stayed at the table, an uncomfortable look on his face, probably from the intense outpouring of emotion.

Everyone was crying—well, at least the women and Jaren were. Kehvun's face was red, and his eyes glistened with unshed tears. Gerald just had a huge smile, though his eyes did sparkle a little more than usual.

"Let me breathe!" Jaren shouted out in laughter. The pressing embrace lessened, and the sobs of happiness lightened, but no one let go. It was like they were making up for all the missed hugs from the months of separation. After a bit, Gerald withdrew and returned to his seat, followed by Kehvun. Mosj continued to watch—the discomfort gone, and a broad smile in its place.

"Let the man in!" Gerald called from the table. Maullie shot him a disapproving glance but made her way to her seat. Ella and May stepped back, though May reached out and cupped his face in her hand.

"Look at you!" Then they also moved to go back to the table.

Jaren glanced behind him—Lesarra was still out in the dark, her hands behind her back. She was looking up like she was inspecting the night sky. Jaren smiled. She was uncomfortable. Jaren stepped through the door and pulled it the rest of the way open for her to follow.

The happy noises stopped as she stepped in. The smiles slid off faces—except for Ella, who was smiling even more.

"Everyone, this is Lesarra."

No one made a sound. Kehvun's eyes went wide, looking Lesarra up and down. Jaren doubted he had ever seen a girl in pants. Haerlee split her scowls equally between Kehvun and Lesarra. The same dynamic could be seen in Maullie and Gerald, though Gerald wore a smirk and Maullie's frown was less conspicuous.

"Hi." Lesarra raised her hand in a slight wave, but then let her hand fall back to her side. Her cheeks grew red as she looked at everyone. She started to turn back to the door, but Jaren grabbed her hand. Her skin was much softer than he had expected. Tingles rushed up his arm and warmth filled his cheeks. She looked down at his hand and raised an eyebrow at him. Maullie sat up straight in her seat and mirrored Lesarra's reaction, but said, "Welcome to our home." Then, turning to Kehvun, continued, "Go get her a seat, please. Would you like something to eat?"

As if in answer, Jaren's stomach rumbled, and his mouth started watering. The Arentash dish smelled delicious. He only hoped she had enough.

"Yes, please. Thank you," Lesarra replied.

She squeezed Jaren's hand, smiled at him, and then let go. He could still feel her touch on his fingers as he rubbed them together. She straightened her shirt and smoothed down her pants. Jaren tried not to grin at the look the girls were giving those pants and the glares they directed at the boys who were looking at the pants.

As Lesarra and Jaren ate, everyone introduced themselves. The food was delicious, but Jaren couldn't eat as much as he expected, and Lesarra didn't eat much at all. Which was just as well, since everyone had questions for her—Where do you come from? How did you meet Jaren? Will you be staying long in Freysdal?

With each question, Jaren's anxiety increased. Lesarra knew that no one knew he could control radiance. But would she remember that while being bombarded with questions? He could have kicked himself—they should have come up with a story. His minds gave a collective shrug.

"Why, exactly, are you here with Jaren?" That was Maullie. She somehow made it sound like a nice question, but the words were clear to Jaren, and his stomach rolled itself up into a knot.

"Well..." she started, but Jaren jumped in.

"She..." except, he didn't have anything to say, either. Everyone's eyes moved from him to her and back again as sweat beaded on his forehead.

"It must have been nice to have someone you could relate to during the trip back," Ella said, still smiling and oblivious to Jaren's stress. Jaren wasn't sure what Ella was talking about, so his minds continued scrambling for an explanation.

Maullie's eyes narrowed and then widened in what Jaren hoped was understanding. "Would anyone like some cake? I had made it for Leyunell, but I can make another tomorrow, and well, this *is* a better reason to celebrate." Maullie was up before anyone could respond, telling May and Ella to help get the cake and Kehvun and Gerald to clear the table.

Mosj also stood up. "Please excuse me, I have to be up early tomorrow. Jaren, it's good to have you home. And it was nice to meet you, Lesarra." He gave May's hand a squeeze as he left.

The cake was delicious, and made everyone forget the awkward moment, but Jaren really did not have room for more in his stomach. He instead took small bites and savored the flavor while answering questions and asking some of his own. There was a lot of catching up to do. Jaren told about the journey, giving only scant details about the attacks they had been subjected to. He said nothing about the people who had died or the injuries he had sustained. He would need to talk with Haerlee about his leg, but it was mostly healed now and could wait another day. He of course said nothing about his own captivity. Somehow, he knew that they would all eventually find out, but it didn't feel right to bring it up yet.

He told about Cresswand and all the things he had seen — people riding horses, the strange clothes, nose rings for thralls, and the tall buildings. Ella asked Lesarra about her pants and Lesarra simply explained that they were necessary for riding horses.

"You own a horse?"

"Well, not exactly, but I have ridden them before." Lesarra's face colored slightly, and Jaren could hear in her answer that she had stolen horses before. She did not mention her profession.

Maullie told them about her classes and the new teachers who had joined the school. Hairth had acquired a very large number of new thralls since Jaren had left, and most could not read or write, but the few who could were excellent at it and were all good teachers, too. As for Gerald, he didn't have anything new to relate.

"Gerald!" Maullie scolded, but he just shrugged his shoulders. "Anything I tell him he will have to listen to again tomorrow when he and the train are debriefed by the Associates."

Jaren glanced at Lesarra, who was also looking back at him. He gently shook his head, and they both returned their attention to Maullie and Gerald, who were still looking at each other. Maullie rolled her eyes and turned to Lesarra.

"I hope we're not boring you."

"Oh, not at all. Jaren has told me so much about..." she glanced at Haerlee, "his family. It feels like I already know you."

Maullie gave Lesarra a look and she seemed to understand its meaning.

"I am getting rather tired, though. Perhaps I should go find my lodgings." Women were able to say so much without saying a word.

Maullie nodded, "I'd offer for you to stay in our home while you're here, but we do not have extra pallets and there really isn't space."

"I should be getting home, too. Mother is probably ready to go to bed," Haerlee added, perhaps picking up on the same wordless message.

"Have you found anything to help?"

Jaren wasn't sure what his feelings toward Haerlee were—she was just as beautiful as before and her smile was just as kind. But with Lesarra there, too, Jaren was all mixed up. Regardless, he still cared about her and knew how much she cared about her mother.

She gave him a sad half-smile in reply. "I did read about a particular vine whose leaves might help, but as near as I could tell, it only grows in a place thousands of miles away."

"Oh." Jaren didn't know what else to say. "I'm sorry," he added after a moment. Lesarra's green eyes settled on him. Maybe he should have told her about Haerlee.

"Gerald and I will walk with the two of you," Maullie told them as she looked directly at Gerald. He arched an eyebrow, but agreed when he saw her face.

Goodbyes were exchanged, and the group stepped out.

With just the four of them left in the room, they settled into the couch and chairs. Jaren felt a little vulnerable without any sources near him, but he pushed that feeling aside. He was safe here in Freysdal.

"So, you're hiding things and so are we," Ella began. May gave her a disapproving look. Kehvun just grinned.

"How did you ever convince Lesarra to follow you here?" Kehvun asked. Ella batted at his arm.

"That's not what I was asking."

Jaren looked from Ella to Kehvun but wasn't sure what to say. He could deny that he was hiding things, but the last time he tried that, Ella had called him on it. They were all staring at him, waiting for his answer. He settled on telling the truth.

"I am hiding things, but I can't tell you them now. I promise I will when I can."

He was pleased with how good it sounded when it came out and surprised by how steady his voice was. Ella narrowed her eyes. May sat quietly.

Kehvun broke the awkward silence. "Well, then let us tell. The day you left, someone poisoned Hairth. He was sick for weeks. Nothing Haerlee did worked. I thought he was dead, for sure. Tobie began quoting every mention of poison in the library, and eventually they determined it was from a poisonous salt-water fish."

Ella smirked, then. "I had to explain to Kehvun that you don't need to bring the whole fish. You just extract the poison and bring it."

"Once they knew what it was, they were able to figure out a cure for it, but Hairth looked really bad for a long time. It's only been the last few weeks that he has gotten back to normal."

Jaren nodded, his minds processing the information—Hairth had looked less robust. And Joans had been at the ocean.

"Have there been other attacks?"

"No. But there are some strange people visiting Freysdal right now."

"Strange—in what way?"

"Well," Kehvun shrugged, looking from Ella to May, "We just don't have many visitors other than peddlers, and we've had at least a few dozen in the past week. They're staying in the barracks, too. Some came with large, covered wagons pulled by long trains of donkeys. When I ask about them, I'm told to keep quiet and mind my own business."

"It doesn't sound like anything dangerous," Ella added in a voice that said they had been over this before.

"No, not dangerous. Just strange," Kehvun's agreed, with a slight trace of excitement in his voice.

"What else has been going on?" Jaren asked.

Ella glanced at May. "I've been having very vivid... thoughts? I'm not sure what they are. It's like I can remember that I had a very vivid dream, but I can't remember what the dream is. Sometimes, if I start talking about something, the memory becomes clearer, and I can almost see things in my mind."

"What do you mean?"

"Well, when you left, we were all pretty upset. You didn't even come to say goodbye or let us know what was happening, so we talked a lot about why. While we were talking, it was like I could see you. You were walking, and you were tossing rocks over your shoulder."

Jaren narrowed his eyes.

"I know, I know, it sounds strange, and most of what I... remembered...was so vague, except there were always a few details that were so clear—like the brilliant orange and green striped rocks. Maullie was upset and worried, so I started telling her about the things I saw. At first, it seemed to comfort her, but then..."

Ella trailed, but May stepped in. "Then Maullie asked her to stop because the stories were making her worry even more."

Ella took a breath and continued. "Yes, so I only shared them with May—and Kehvun, when he was around. I saw so much, but most of it didn't make sense. You were constantly running, almost like you were racing someone. You learned to make glass. You stood by a shining boat. Sometimes there were other people with you, but they were usually indistinct. Often you were alone."

Jaren wasn't sure what to say.

"I thought it was all crazy—you know, like when you all tell me I say things that I don't remember saying. Except, this time, I was the one seeing things and no one else could. Like I said, I thought I was crazy, but then when Lesarra came through the door...well, I *recognized* her. I had seen the two of you all alone—it was like I could see all the plains of Pinnutuck, and you were the only two people there."

Jaren just nodded, still trying to wrap his minds around what he had just heard.

"I'm not making it up!" Ella's face was growing red, and her eyes were tearing up. Jaren realized he was grimacing and relaxed his face.

"No one said you're making it up," Kehvun said in a soothing voice, reaching out and gently patting Ella's arm. That was new—he was much more the one to tease than appease. A lot had changed while Jaren was gone. "It's just that we couldn't see the same things."

"But it's true. I saw her!" Ella wiped the tears from her eyes.

"I believe you," Jaren said.

The other three turned in unison and said, "You do?" Then they glanced at each other in surprise.

He wasn't exactly sure what he was doing, but he was tired of hiding so much. He could be honest about other people, even if he couldn't be honest about himself.

"Yes. Like I said, I can't tell you exactly what happened on this trip—again, just trust me—but I can tell you that I experienced something like everything Ella just described."

Kehvun was shaking his head. "She said some pretty... unbelievable...things about what she saw you doing. I'm not sure if I'm convinced..." Tears began welling up in Ella's eyes again. "No, Ella, I don't mean anything by it. It's just that... May?" Kehvun turned to May, looking for some support. May just looked from him to Ella and back again.

"You just think I'm crazy." Ella stood and hurried to her room. Kehvun made to follow after her, calling her name, but May caught his wrist.

"Let her go." Then she said to Jaren, "It was really hard on her when you left. She'd been working so hard at keeping up a happy front for me, but after you left..." May shrugged her shoulders. "Like I said, it was really hard on her."

"And on Mom, too," Kehvun added.

"She saw things that she didn't tell you just now—people hurting you, you being tied up, you cutting your own leg, people screaming all around you, strange lights dancing on your face." Jaren shook his head in wonder. He then pulled up his segg and rotated his leg to expose the puffy tear in his skin. May's hands went up to her mouth as she shook her head. Kehvun simply cursed. When she finally recovered, all May said was, "You've changed."

Chapter 45

Debriefing the Train

Jaren could recall the attack as if it had just happened. He had been sitting in this same chair and Hairth had been sitting just the same behind his desk. The image of the knife protruding from the attacker circulated among the minds. But new images circulated, as well—men at the river and in the red lands cut, mangled, burned, and frozen. Jaren's growing file of lives taken weighed heavily on his minds.

"What did you see while following Jaren's captors?"

Hairth had quietly listened as Lesarra gave her account—just as he did when Mastiff, Joans, and Jaren had given theirs. And now it was Hairth's turn to ask questions.

Just as her pants and blouse had been replaced by what Maullie would call a decent robe, her haughtiness had been replaced with proper respect when Hairth had entered. More than respect—she appeared to be wary, like a cat crouching as a large dog crossed its path. She provided more details.

"You say all of the men had these sigils on their robes?" Hairth held one of the sigils cut from a red-robed man.

"Yes—at least, all those that I saw. I only approached in the dark, so..."

"And Joans, you said the men you fought were not bandits?"

"They wore the Krandor sigil, and they fought like soldiers—soldiers trained to fight a Light-Twister."

"You said that before. What do you mean by that?" Hairth's long, wiry eyebrows knit together. He had lost weight, and his hair had dulled. An effect of the poison?

"I mean they knew what they were doing. They fanned out before I got there, used heavy-headed arrows and stones to burden my shield, crowded me when I got close, and used spears."

"So, they were expecting you to be there, and they drew you out to capture Jaren."

"I believe so. Based on Mastiff's account, the initial attacking force was three times as large as the group that grabbed Jaren, and because of their tactics they were able to keep me occupied for a long time."

"Didn't you see when the smaller group attacked the wagon?"

"I did—I saw Jaren fending them off, though not with my eyes. I hadn't recognized it was a coordinated attack, so when his sources started moving away, I assumed he had driven them off and was chasing them. I was ready to chastise him for his foolhardiness, but..." Joans shrugged.

"Mastiff, what do you make of the whole situation?"

"I think Krandor has somehow learned about Jaren and our trip and sought to take advantage of it. They knew how we had been defending ourselves—that Joans sallied out to intercept attackers—and built their plan around that fact. They wanted to capture Jaren and they did it with relative ease."

Turning to Levi, Hairth asked, "And you?"

"I agree with Mastiff." The man scratched his leathery cheek. "I think that first encounter was an accident—they hadn't expected Jaren to be so close. That group was supposed to be part of the second pincer coming from the rear to finish off the guard."

Mastiff nodded. "If they had been there at the right time, I don't think any of us—except maybe Joans—would have survived."

Hairth asked a few more questions, and Mastiff and Joans answered. Following Jaren's capture, Joans had continued fighting until the attackers broke and ran. When he returned to the wagons, he found that everyone had been injured. He searched for Jaren but couldn't find any sign of him in the dark. In the morning light, they searched again to no avail, so Mastiff decided to try to get back to Freysdal before his injured men died. He'd already lost Yates, Briaben, and Veerlen and wasn't willing to continue what looked to be a hopeless search and risk losing more men. They had arrived only a few hours before the debriefing. When Jaren heard about the lost guards, it felt like a punch to his stomach. They had died because of him.

But the final question was for Jaren.

"Are you certain that one of your captors was Olis Krandor?"

"Yes."

"Well, this complicates things. Let's hope to *H'ust* that he wasn't killed when Lesarra rescued you." Hairth pushed back from his desk, his rings thumping on the solid wood as he did so.

"Why would they risk attacking so openly?" Mastiff asked.

"Because, they didn't expect anyone to survive," Levi replied. "Dry bones can't sing."

"Did any of your men have family here in Freysdal?"

"Yes. Yates and Desot had wives but no children," Mastiff replied. Jaren thought of poor Desot importuning to have Joans help his wife.

"Go and let them know what happened." Levi and Mastiff nodded and walked out of the office.

Turning to Joans, Hairth asked, "What can you tell me about the cold source?"

"It's pretty evenly spread throughout the ore. Can Gerald concentrate it?"

Lesarra's eye's narrowed as she listened, but they slowly widened. Hairth and Joans casually discussed what Jaren had worked so hard to keep from her.

"He can—at least as well as what I gave you."

"They are better than anything I've ever seen before."

"Concentrated sources?" Lesarra covered her mouth when she realized she had spoken aloud. Hairth and Joans glanced at her before resuming as if she hadn't said anything.

"This is good. Very good." Hairth was rubbing his hands together, his rings clacking as they moved past each other.

"That load you bought. How much cold source will it produce?" Joans asked.

"Gerald got about one part per eight from the first sample we had."

Jaren considered their wagon train and his egg-sized source. Half a wagon full of that source, if put all together, would freeze...what? —maybe all of Freysdal in a second? His own eyes widened as he considered the potential.

"What about the other purpose of the trip? It sounds like it was successful." Joans also looked at Jaren as if he were weighing him. They clearly knew he was there, so why were they talking as if he weren't?

"It was—he doesn't hold back when fighting, and he is a much more competent fighter now. He can obviously still be overpowered, but he can defend himself. Yet I think his strength is less than what it could be. He hasn't been working hard enough."

Jaren looked at Hairth, wondering what he thought of that. It was true. He had been holding back.

"That's fine—the strength can come later. My worry had been whether he could survive being attacked."

Hairth waved his hand dismissively, but Joans' mouth tightened. He obviously didn't think Jaren's lack of effort was "fine."

"And what about her?" Hairth nodded toward Lesarra.

At that, Jaren felt indignant. Hey, we're both sitting right here, listening to you talk about us! He thought it but didn't dare say it.

"She's a student of Rudaltro. I've told you of him previously."
Hairth nodded. "He was a decent man. He had good values and
was someone I trusted." Joans turned to Lesarra, though he
continued to speak to Hairth. "However, I told her to stay in
Cresswand and she disobeyed. I'm not sure how much you can
trust her. I will not vouch for her."

Jaren's blood boiled.

"She saved my life! *I* trust her!" He almost shouted it. He
knew he should stop, but he continued. "I already vouched for
her yesterday."

Joans let out a mocking laugh. "You should probably be a
little more discriminating in whom you invest your trust. You
barely know her."

Hairth did not join in the derision.

"I trust that she won't double-cross me, Jaren," his voice
was smooth yet firm. "However, the people here in Freysdal are
united in purpose. If she can't get behind that purpose, then she
doesn't belong here."

Globs of anger, like handfuls of hot tar, were being tossed
back and forth between Jaren's minds. A few stayed above the
fray and recommended caution, but Jaren didn't want to listen.

"Belong here? What about *him*? Does *he* support our vision?"

Lesarra took hold of his wrist. "It's okay," she said quietly.
A few of Jaren's minds scraped the sticky anger off in response,
but most continued to cling to it.

"It's *not* okay," he insisted.

"Ah, the vagaries of youth," Joans said, a thin, cruel smile on
his face. "And I do have a purpose, even if I don't particularly
care about your...vision."

"Joans," Hairth said. There was no anger in his voice, but
somehow it carried more weight than all the yelling Jaren had
done. Joans' unpleasant smile disappeared and the mischief in
his eyes melted away.

"But he's right, Jaren. Joans has a clear purpose which supports our vision, so despite his ambivalence toward our goals, he is welcome here. Just like the Leyunell performers camped out on Chartriece field, they will leave once their purpose is fulfilled. When Joans' purpose is fulfilled, he will also be on his way."

The surprising—and conspiracy-free—explanation regarding all the strangers visiting Freysdal calmed the anger in a few more minds. The remainder of the tarry substance cooled into a solid determination.

"Fine! Then I'll find a purpose for her."

Chapter 46

Eating Lunch

Lesarra didn't belong in Freysdal? Joans was the one who didn't belong! *Bones*! He was trying to kill Hairth! He almost got Jaren executed and would have succeeded had Lesarra not been there. That story about a group trained to fight Light-Twisters sounded as truthful as a snake explaining the lumps in his body to a hen searching for her eggs. And, not being able to follow the trail of the men that had captured him? They left giant plumes of dust behind them!

As Jaren stomped out, Hairth told him to take the day to relax. Tomorrow would be Leyunell, and maybe training would resume a few days after that. Jaren hadn't replied.

Lesarra grabbed his arm. He wanted to roundly curse at her and ask why she hadn't stood up for herself, but he knew that wasn't fair. She feared Hairth. He couldn't tell why. She hadn't returned his sources, and if Joans weren't present she could have easily put Hairth in his place, but she didn't.

"Are you okay?" she asked.

"Yeah. I'm just frustrated." He tried to keep the heat out of his voice. He wasn't angry at her—not really.

"Maybe we can find me a 'purpose' here."

"Yeah."

He needed to find evidence against Joans to show Hairth, and now he needed a purpose to keep Lesarra around. But at least it sounded like she wanted to stay.

"Hey, rail!" Kehvun was walking down the street with a cold source in his hand.

"What are you holding?" Jaren asked, confused about why Kehvun would have a source.

"It's a cold source. Just got it from storage. Dad's working on improving the refinement process and said he needs one." Kehvun stopped as he reached them and did a double-take of Lesarra.

"Oh, hey, I didn't...uh...recognize you in...robes." Color bloomed in his cheeks. Lesarra smoothed the robes, pulling them tight around her waist as she did so, and then gave him a big smile. His cheeks darkened. Jaren just shook his head.

"Is he working on that lot we brought back?"

"Yeah—said he couldn't wait to get into it. There're a couple new devices that research and development have designed that use cold. I've seen them demonstrated. One just keeps a box cold so foods can last as long in the summer as in the winter. The other freezes anything almost instantly. It's incredible. Dad says Hairth will let Mom have a set, like with the oven, before he starts making them for sale. Can you imagine? Cold drinks all summer long!"

"Yeah, that would be pretty incredible," Jaren let one of his minds reply while the others were still grinding away at how to deal with Joans.

"What do you think, Lesarra? How'd you like to share a cold drink with me in this heat?" The blushing had gone. Confident Kehvun had returned.

"Ask me when you have to shave every day, and maybe I'll think about it."

Kehvun just smiled at her.

"If you two aren't busy, we've been eating together during first lunch. You can tell us more about your trip, Jaren. And, I'm sure everyone would like to get to know Lesarra better and learn more about Crosswind."

"*Cresswand.*"

"Right. That place. I've got to take this to Dad. I'll see you in half an hour." Lesarra watched as Kehvun continued down the street.

Then she folded a little lump of cold and sent it toward Kehvun, releasing it in the source he held. He yelped and dropped the source, rubbing his hand on his robes. Lesarra chuckled.

"Cheeky kid. If he were about ten years older, I'd consider that drink offer."

When Jaren didn't respond, she said, "I can see why you thought Hairth might not want me here. Concentrating sources. I never even imagined it. If either of the factions could do that, it would be impossible to challenge them."

"Come on, there's someone we need to find," Jaren said.

Jaren could smell lunch as they stepped out of the library. Tobie was nowhere to be found, despite a thorough search. Lesarra had been quiet—even more than Jaren expected in the library.

"Are you okay?" he asked, as they approached the food district.

Lesarra just shook her head. "I just had no idea there were that many books in all of Thadren."

"Yeah, I was surprised, too. What's even more amazing is that you can borrow any of them that you like."

She didn't respond.

"What's wrong?" Jaren asked.

"Can I borrow someone to read them to me too?"

It hadn't occurred to Jaren that she couldn't read. That would make finding her a purpose in Freysdal that much harder.

"Maullie runs a school where you can learn to read. But until then, I'd be happy to read to you." Jaren said with a smile, though he wasn't sure how much he was joking versus how much he was hoping she'd agree to it.

"I'll talk to Maullie."

Yeasty sweet rolls, savory roots, spiced meats and vegetables— it was enough to make a person stand still in awe. Jaren also felt a strong sense of nostalgia. Prior to the accident, he had eaten all his meals here. For over two years he had been exposed to the wide variety of foods Thadren had to offer—spicy, sour, squishy, sweet, savory, bland, earthy, nutty, chewy, crisp, stiff, dry, moist, delicious, and inedible—with folks from the admin shop. They had—at least in some ways—helped him through the bitterness of Thralldom and to find the peace of Freysdal. It had been many months since he had last visited his old shop.

"Hey, are you lost?" Lesarra asked.

"No. I was just thinking."

"Well, you've got lots of minds to do that with, so why not let a few of them keep you moving through the door."

Jaren took one of the sweet rolls in a bowl—he didn't like to have the other food touching his desserts—and filled his plate with the Votnaan food. He got a large portion of yogurt to help combat the spice. Lesarra followed his lead, though based on the curious looks she gave the food, she'd probably never seen Votnaan food before.

Haerlee waved at him from a long, mostly empty table. Her smile faltered when she noticed Lesarra.

"I'm surprised to see you here. After this morning's stand-up, I thought Hairth would be drilling you all day long."

"Yeah, well, the drilling only ended thirty minutes ago. We ran into Kehvun, and he told us to meet him here for lunch. He said you all had been eating together?" Jaren asked as a half-question.

"After you left...well, May and Ella were pretty upset. When I came to eat, I would look for them and we'd talk. Then one evening we mentioned it to Kehvun, and he started coming too. Since then, whoever can..."

"Jaren!" Before he could turn, two arms wrapped around him. But he recognized that high-pitched voice.

"Tobie! I was just looking for you."

"You're back! It's so good to see you. All of Ella's crazy stories made me so worried for you." Then, as if she finally heard what he had said, asked, "Wait—you were looking for me?"

Lesarra allowed the lumps she had folded to expand and dissipate. He caught her eyes. He tried to give her a look that said "We're safe here," but for all he knew what she might have gleaned from it was, "I like cabbaged-donkey buns." Girls could talk with a look, but he wasn't sure he could.

Jaren looked at Tobie as she sat down beside Haerlee. She had grown taller and filled out some since he last saw her. Her face was more mature, and overall, she looked more like a woman and less like a little boy. Her eyes still seemed to be set a little too far apart, but it wasn't as noticeable.

"Yes. I need your help." Jaren paused as Ella joined them at the table. Tobie mouthed "Jaren's back" and pointed with her index finger. Ella nodded in reply, eyes sparkling and smiling as she mouthed back, "I know."

"I'm sorry. You said you need my help?" She returned her attention to Jaren, and then seemed to notice Lesarra.

"Who needs help?" May asked, as she arrived and sat on the other side of Lesarra. "Oh, I like the robes on you!" she added. Lesarra made a face that could have been interpreted equally as a smile or a grimace.

"Jaren needs Tobie's help," Haerlee told May.

"With what?"

"I was just asking him that."

Jaren realized he was outnumbered five to one. He wasn't sure he could make it through this conversation if it kept up like this.

"Well, Jaren, what do you need help with? And who's this with you?" Tobie asked.

"I..."

"Looks like I'm late," Kehvun announced as he plopped down next to Ella.

"Nope, we just got here, too," she replied.

"I haven't been here long either."

"Did you all hear about the wagons?" Kehvun asked. Jaren sighed.

"They're performers for Leyunell tomorrow!"

"Really? So, they aren't a secret army Hairth hired to defend Freysdal?" Ella elbowed him as she asked.

Kehvun's face turned red, but he replied, "Umm, no. Hairth wanted to make this the best Leyunell ever because it's the twenty-fifth one that has been celebrated here. There are jugglers, a tightrope walker, animal trainers, and more!"

Everyone was excited—except Jaren, who was frustrated. But truthfully, most of his minds were excited, too. He just had something more important on the rest of his minds.

"Did you see the man with the odd mustache?" Ella traced curling lines across her upper lip.

"I was too busy noticing his well-formed shoulders." Tobie smiled, but her face turned a little red when Kehvun gave her a suspicious glance.

"Tobie!" Ella laughed, and then continued, "Well, I can't blame you. His arms are as big around as my head."

The group went on laughing and guessing at what the different people they had seen might do tomorrow. Jaren tried to be patient. Lesarra sat like a spectator rather than a participant, watching everyone with a little quirk in her smile.

"Jaren, who is that?" Tobie hissed at Jaren, nodding to Lesarra. She tried to do it surreptitiously but ended up talking over everyone. They all stopped to listen.

Jaren ground his teeth, but replied, "This is Lesarra, from Cresswand."

"Cresswand?" Tobie asked excitedly. "I read about Cresswand once. Is it true that during Leyunell people swim across the Eldvar while holding pies up out of the water?"

Being brought into the conversation highlighted Lesarra's bemusement. She stuttered as she tried to explain, "Well, I... that is...uh...I was only able to go to Leyunell in Cresswand one time." She left it at that, but with everyone looking at her, Lesarra squirmed and then continued, "My mom wouldn't let me, and when my...when I finally did go, I wasn't in the best of moods."

Jaren understood, though he knew the others wouldn't. Lesarra's opportunity to attend Leyunell in Cresswand would have been shortly after her mother had disowned her. No doubt that would have cast a gloomy shadow over even the finest celebration.

"I didn't go near the river, but there were all kinds of entertainers—acrobats, singers, storytellers, trainers. They each did amazing things and if I had been in a better mood, I'm sure I would have loved it." Lesarra's smile at the end was better than her attempt with May, but it still wasn't very good.

The brightness in everyone else's eyes was dampened by her subdued report. It was the perfect opportunity for Jaren to retake the initiative.

"I'm sure the festival will be great, but aren't any of you worried about there being another attack with all of these strangers here?"

Everyone slowly pulled their eyes away from Lesarra to look at Jaren. He was ready for the weight of their stares.

"Kehvun told me about the poisoning attempt the day I left, and I think I know who's behind everything." That got their attention. "A man named Artor Joans. He's an old... acquaintance...of Hairth's who was on the trip with me."

"Is that what you want my help with?" Tobie asked between bites of fried carrots.

"Yes," Jaren quickly replied before anyone else could jump in. "I was able to talk with him while we were traveling and he told me..."

Mosj appeared and quietly sat beside May as Jaren explained about the snakes and Joans' hometown, the assassins and Joans' visit with the radiance-haters, and the poison and Joans' time near the ocean.

When he paused, Mosj asked, "Are you talking about the guy with the hooked nose and the scraggly black hair?"

Jaren nodded. Haerlee went wide-eyed and covered her mouth.

"What?" Jaren asked.

She looked at the others at the table. "I know who you're talking about, and I just realized something. I can't believe I didn't see it before."

"What?"

"The guards that were knocked out by those assassins — they each came to me a few days after the attack complaining about bug bites that wouldn't go away. When I looked at the bites, I could see that they were reactions to plate-weed — one of the herbs I dispense for people who need help sleeping. In a mild tea it calms the nerves and helps people fall asleep. In a more concentrated form, it puts people to sleep very quickly."

"What does that have to do with...Joans?" May asked.

"Well, I found him in the clinic prior to the attack. I should say I caught him poking through my containers. When I asked him what he was doing, he said, "Admiring your vessels." Then he asked if I had something for sleeping issues. If he is trying to kill Hairth, then he must have been the one who gave the assassins the mixture."

"Did the bug bites look like two red rings around a small bump?" Jaren asked, as a few minds were holding up an image of a disheveled Joans arriving late while scratching his arm.

"Yes, it does."

"I saw the same thing on Joans' arm a few days before the attack. He must have tried it on himself first."

Mosj whistled. "That guy creeps me out. I had just finished up my work on the stage this morning when I saw him snooping around. I didn't think much of it at the time—like I said, he creeps me out, so I just thought he was being creepy—but now I wonder if he was up to something."

"What do you mean?" Jaren asked, not following Mosj's point.

"Hairth is scheduled to deliver a speech and make a demonstration from that stage tomorrow. I just wonder if he's sabotaged the stage somehow."

"We need to tell Levi," Kehvun said.

"And what did you need my help for?" Tobie asked.

"Well, you know a lot," Jaren started.

"She's a walking library," Kehvun said. All the girls except Lesarra glared at him, but he didn't notice. "Literally! She has memorized half of the books in the library and is working on the other half. It's her job!"

Based on his facial expression, Kehvun obviously thought that it was a strange job. Jaren thought it was strange, too. Tobie shrugged her shoulders and explained to Jaren after she had finished glaring at Kehvun.

"Hairth learned about my ability to remember…everything… and asked me to read all of the books, both in the library and in the admin office. Once I'm done with those, he'll have me go around all the shops and watch their processes. He hopes I'll be able to help out in research, and he said if anything ever happens to Freysdal he won't have to worry about bringing all of his records with him as long as he could take me along."

"So, you're like an extra copy of everything?" The disgust in Lesarra's voice was clear.

Tobie bristled. "I'm not just a copy," she said, raising herself upright to her new, slightly taller, height.

Haerlee came to her aid. "She has helped save dozens of lives by knowing obscure pieces of information."

Jaren added, "And hopefully you'll know something that can help us save Hairth's life now."

Lesarra lifted her hands in defense, "I didn't mean anything personal. Everyone keeps telling me how wonderful Hairth is, and that just doesn't sound like a wonderful use of a person."

Kehvun nodded, "Hairth's a good leader. Sometimes being a good leader means asking people to do things that they wouldn't otherwise choose to do."

"Being a strong leader is convincing them to do it," Mosj added.

"Tobie—what do you know about Artor Joans?"

She sat quietly for a minute, then shook her head. "His record is restricted—they never let me read it. There is a mention of an Artoros Joans in a small volume about the temporary alliance of the normally warring factions of Light-Twisters, but all it says is that his actions and subsequent exile led to the collapse of the alliance."

"Well, that's not our guy," Kehvun said. "We're looking for a real person, not some made-up Light-Twister alliance person." The smirk on his face and mocking in his voice said he didn't believe in the factions. No one else spoke up.

"We need to do something about this," May spoke into the silence. "Jaren, you need to go to Hairth and tell him what you know."

Jaren shook his head. He had already approached Mastiff and had been told he needed more evidence. Was the information about the sleeping powder enough? Jaren doubted it.

"I have a plan. Tobie—is there any way you can read that restricted file?"

Chapter 47

Taking the Stage

A raised wooden platform with an angled cover overhead sat in the fields surrounded by the performers' tents and wagons. Men and women milled about, preparing for Leyunell. Jaren and Lesarra had examined every square inch of the stage, and by the time Haerlee and Kehvun arrived, they were convinced there was nothing dangerous about it. Lesarra had been convinced for over an hour.

"Maybe Joans was really just interested in the construction of the stage."

"Yeah, and you're just interested in working for Hairth."

"Look, I'm out here with you trying to save his life—not because I actually care about what happens to that monster, but because I've finally found people like me, and at any time other than right now, I like to be around them."

Hairth? A monster? But, before he could ask, Haerlee and Kehvun showed up.

"Any luck?"

"Not on either front. You?"

"Hallumon said he knows Joans. He said he wouldn't be surprised that Joans would like Hairth dead, but he also said he would be surprised to learn that Joans was trying to kill him. Tell me how that makes any sense."

"Dad said essentially the same thing—about how Hairth and Joans' relationship was a lot more complicated than it seemed, but that neither was likely to kill the other any time soon."

Jaren scowled. "Mastiff said the plate-weed and the skin reactions were good additions to the evidence, but that none of them actually showed that Joans was involved in any of it. He said we needed indisputable evidence."

"That's frustrating."

"He did say that if we found anything here to come tell him. He also said he'd tell Levi what we had told him." Haerlee was shaking her head. "This is ridiculous. Have you found anything here?"

"The most dangerous thing here is a protruding nail and the twelve-inch drop. Whatever Joans was up to, he didn't leave any trace of it."

Kehvun walked over to the demonstration. It was a contraption about as tall as Jaren, with two parallel plates of cold source.

"These things are really cool," Kehvun said, laying his hand on the contraption. "Dad let me watch as they demonstrated it for Hairth. You stick something in this space, right here above the bottom plate, then you crank up the spring. When you let it go, the top plate spins around. When it is right over the bottom plate, it gets really, really cold—you can even feel it on your face from a distance—for just a second, freezing whatever you have put there."

What Jaren knew, but Kehvun didn't understand or care about, was that the reflectors above the top plate and below the bottom plate would fold the cold energy whenever the plates overlapped.

"Watch this."

Kehvun fished an apple out of his pocket and placed it on the bottom plate. The other three came over to watch him. He ratcheted down the handle several times to prime the spring, and then he released it. The top plate shot out in a swinging motion, causing the cold energy to grow brighter.

Then there was a loud clunk, and the cold energy grew impossibly bright. Jaren flinched. It was like looking directly at the sun after sitting in a dark room. His minds worked in unison trying to deflect the huge amount of cold energy pouring from the device. The burden pressed down on him like a rushing river, threatening to sweep away his consciousness, but he held on. The cold energy coursed around them like a waterfall divided by a small outcropping of rocks. The suddenly frigid air on either side was still bitterly cold. There was another loud "clunk" as the plate finished its swing. Lesarra collapsed to the platform. Kehvun yelled and grabbed the side of his head. It was all over in an eyeblink, but echoes of the intense burden still reverberated in Jaren's chest.

A thick fog enveloped the platform and extended in every direction. There were misty outlines of working men and women who were shouting and writhing. Jaren inhaled for the first time, and the frigid air froze his nose hairs and stung his lungs. Haerlee rushed to Lesarra's side and began examining her.

"What under the soil just happened?" Kehvun shouted, still holding his ear, his face scrunched up in pain. But Jaren was too concerned with Lesarra to answer.

"Is she...?"

"I don't see anything wrong. But we need to get her to the clinic." Haerlee looked up and saw all the people moaning and shouting and added, "And those people, too."

The shouting drew the attention of people outside the affected range. Frost had built up on the entire platform except in a wedge where it had been blocked by the four of them. The fog slowly sank off the platform to the ground.

Kehvun removed his hand from his ear, and Jaren saw that his ear ended in a sharp line of exposed flesh. Kehvun held a frost covered piece of his ear in his hand. He reached up and fingered the wound, grimacing as he did so.

Jaren's minds were drawn to Lesarra. The sources she wore were pulsating, like they were being folded and partially formed, but then were being released. The lumps were jerking and twitching. The sources stopped pulsating momentarily and then started again. Only this time the folding was more intense, and the energy moved out, releasing away from her. One lump of heat compressed right before being released, causing a coin-sized spot on the frosted platform to melt and sizzle. Jaren didn't understand what was happening, but he knew he needed to get the sources away from her.

The burden on her must have been too great. It was far more than Jaren could have controlled on his own. She had saved their lives, but she was paying for it now. The color had drained from her face and Jaren would have thought she was dead if it weren't for the random lumps streaming from her.

Haerlee glanced impatiently at Kehvun and Jaren. "I need to go check out those other people. Get her to the clinic. I'll be there as soon as I can."

Jaren nodded, but most of his minds were trying to counter the energy Lesarra was flinging about. She had a lot more minds than he did, and she was closer to the sources. Haerlee moved toward the other victims, slipping on the frosted stage as she went. Before Kehvun could even respond to her instructions, Jaren reached into Lesarra's robes and pulled out the sources. His face burned red as he felt around for the pocket openings.

"What are you doing?" Kehvun asked reproachfully.

"She's carrying some rocks that will make her heavier to carry." It was the best suggestion any of his minds came up with, though he knew it was not a very good answer. "Help me get her up."

Once the sources were in his pockets, it was easier to put a stop to her unconscious forming, though she was still able to push and pull at the energy.

One of Jaren's minds dredged up a comment Joans had made—Jaren was not as strong as he should be. If Jaren had embraced the training as Joans had wanted him to, would he have had the strength to stop this? Could he have carried enough of the burden to keep Lesarra from getting hurt?

As Jaren and Kehvun struggled to get Lesarra off the stage, a wagon rolled up and they were able to load her onto it. Haerlee began directing the more seriously injured people toward the wagons that were arriving and urged the others to walk to the clinic.

"You can walk to the clinic, unless you're hurt somewhere else," Haerlee said to Kehvun after examining his ear. Kehvun shook his head.

"Are you hurt?" she asked Jaren, "No? Good. Walk with Kehvun. He's a little dazed." Jaren nodded and looked at the scene around him.

The fog was mostly gone, but the frost continued to grow thicker. People walking toward the clinic were staring at their hands or rubbing frost off their bodies. Those in the wagon had frost building up on their legs. An unconscious man in the wagon had a thick layer of frost building up on his face.

"Jaren!" Mosj came running toward the pair, breathing hard. "What happened? Did Joans do this?"

"There was an accident."

"It doesn't look like an accident to me."

"It doesn't feel like one either," Kehvun said. He was coming out of his daze, still tenderly fingering his damaged ear.

"I was going to show you this tonight at dinner, but since I found you...I've got another piece of evidence for you to show to Hairth." Mosj held up a small metal pin with cotton on the end. "It's a dart. I found it in his room."

"You went into his room? How'd you do that?"

Mosj smiled, "Maintenance—we've got keys to everything."

"What if he found you?"

He shrugged. "I'm maintenance. I'd just tell him I was checking the room. I do it all the time and no one ever says anything about it." That seemed odd to Jaren until he remembered a maintenance thrall working on his bed in the barracks—he hadn't thought twice about it either.

Kehvun was staring at the dart. "Jaren, we need to show this to my dad. He'll believe us after what just happened and if we show him this dart."

Gerald shook his head as he replied, "I hear what you're saying, and I know it all looks pretty obvious, but you need to understand that I've known Artor Joans for almost twenty years. He's a self-serving scoundrel and a liar, and he wouldn't blink at killing a man, but he's not a murderer. He only kills when he believes he must. He doesn't steal, and I can't imagine him killing Hairth to steal from him."

Jaren's jaw ached from clenching it. The adults listened. They accepted the evidence. But they were unwilling to follow to the logical conclusion.

"What else do you need? Mosj saw him messing with the stage, and then the demonstration Hairth was supposed to do tomorrow almost killed us. He also found a dart in Joans' room. Isn't that proof enough?" Kehvun pleaded.

Gerald shook his head. Kehvun held a cloth to his ear to stop the bleeding that had started on their way to the shop.

"Look, I'll bring it up with Hairth and Levi when we meet tonight, but I'm pretty sure they'll feel the same way I do. In the mean time, I can't believe you were foolish enough to play with an unfamiliar machine. You're lucky you weren't killed. I can't decide whether to send you to your mother or the clinic first. You need the clinic now, but you'll probably need it more once she's done with you."

Jaren felt despondent. They were just going to have to find more evidence against Joans and hope that no one died before that happened. Jaren turned to go when he heard bells. *Gong—gong, gong, gong—gong—gong, gong, gong.* That was odd. Leyunell bells were supposed to be rung at midnight to announce the start of the celebration. The sun had only just set while they were walking to Gerald's shop.

"Those aren't Leyunell bells," Gerald said, as if he were reading Jaren's mind, "That's the attack bell."

Chapter 48

Being Attacked

Gerald picked up three stout hammers and handed one to each of the boys. Kehvun shook his head and said, "Dad, I need a pair of knives."

Gerald lifted an eyebrow. Jaren added, "And I would be better with a staff."

He wouldn't use the staff much, but something about holding one just felt right to him. The bells kept ringing.

"Why do you need knives and a staff?"

"Well," Kehvun began, "When Jaren left, Laodosus agreed to teach me dual knife wielding if I mastered the grappling skills faster...so I could show Jaren up when he got back." Kehvun grinned at Jaren.

"Son," Gerald shook his head, "that sounds really impressive to me, but if your mother found out she would teach you how a paddle is used. Let's not mention it to her." Then, turning to Jaren, "I suppose you've got a similar story?"

Jaren just smiled. He had not learned the staff to outdo Kehvun but showing off in front of him had crossed his minds. *Gong—gong, gong, gong—gong—gong, gong, gong*

While Gerald searched the shop, Jaren helped Kehvun fashion a headband to hold the cloth to his ear. Gerald returned with two knives and a staff. One was a kitchen knife, the other one was a small, heavy bladed work knife.

"These are the best I could find."

The "staff" was a couple feet shorter than what Jaren had trained with—it was probably the handle of a shovel. It wouldn't be much use if he needed it, but it was better than nothing and much better than holding a heavy hammer. Gerald carried the longest of the hammers as the three rushed to the sounds of battle.

Warning pyres flamed and lightballs flickered along the city wall and the ridge line that defined the valley of Freysdal. The smell of burning oil filled the air. They headed toward the wall, following the sounds of men shouting. Jaren felt surprisingly calm. He wondered what Kehvun and Gerald were feeling.

He maintained a shield around them as they went. Jaren skimmed heat off the force as he fed the shield. Lesarra must have done a lot of practice with force.

"Keep close to Gerald," Jaren told Kehvun, who kept getting close to the shield. Kehvun frowned at him but obeyed.

As they turned southward, scores of men streamed out of buildings and toward the wall. They wore seggs or robes and fear on their faces. They carried kitchen knives and farm tools uneasily. But the few with real weapons held them like they knew how to handle them.

A sudden whistling snapped Jaren's minds to attention. The whistling stopped with a thud. Jaren balanced the energy. Gerald stared at an arrow buried in the ground in front of him. If Jaren hadn't been there, that arrow would have been sticking out of Gerald's chest. Gerald recovered and moved to charge the attacker.

The archer, with a look of confusion on his face, drew another arrow from his quiver. Before Gerald took more than a step, though, Jaren dropped a lump of heat in the man's chest. He screamed out black smoke and collapsed to the ground.

"Shards of broken bones. What happened?" Kehvun asked.

"Watch your mouth." Gerald said, popping him on the back of the head.

"Look out!" Someone shouted and the crowd scattered.

Dozens of arrows skirted and rebounded off the shield. People around him cried out in pain. Jaren released additional lumps as Gerald shouted, "Out of the center of the road!"

A dozen attackers fell, unnoticed by Kehvun or Gerald as they stepped behind a building. Gerald stared at Jaren and put his hand on Kehvun's shoulder.

"I had no idea you were capable of that."

"What do you mean?" Jaren asked, anxiety in his voice.

"You can control radiance. I had wondered why Joans showed up and why Maullie and I were asked to take you in. It makes sense now. Does Maullie know?"

"Wait—you did that with the arrows and the smoke?" Kehvun moved his hands like arrows turning and smoking coming out of his mouth.

Jaren couldn't speak. He just nodded, and held his breath, waiting for their response.

"Hel'dig Bones! I knew it! Ella's stories, and those rocks you carry around—who carries rocks?—all makes perfect sense now! And then I saw that Lesarra was carrying them, too. I knew it!"

Jaren's anxiety peaked as he waited. Kehvun hadn't looked horrified, but he hadn't looked pleased.

Then Kehvun blurted out, "Can you teach me?" His eyes were wide, and his mouth hung open in anticipation. He looked like a boy whose dad had just brought home a dancing weasel. Jaren felt a wave of relief that Kehvun didn't despise him.

Gerald shook his head. "It isn't something that can be taught."

Kehvun looked crestfallen "Fine—but can you show me the cool things you can do?"

As Jaren began to reply, a man stumbled around the corner of the building. Jaren had a lump of heat positioned within his lungs, but noticed the man was a citizen and that he had an arrow jutting out of his neck.

"Brittle bones!" Gerald turned to the man, catching him as he fell. "Let's get him inside."

"I've got to go find Hairth," Jaren said as Kehvun helped lift the man.

Gerald looked him straight in the eyes. "Are you sure you can take care of yourself?"

"Yes."

Gerald nodded.

Jaren turned and repositioned the shield around himself before rushing around the corner. A steady flow of arrows was streaming down the road. Segg-wearing thralls left and right were ducking behind buildings, unable to move forward. Others lay unmoving in the street. A dozen sword-bearing attackers interspersed with as many archers were moving down the street in a tight block. They shot anyone that moved toward them as well as anyone hiding behind buildings at the intersections. The men were dressed in thick leather armor like thrall raiders. Their legs were protected from the knees down by dark boots.

Jaren released heat and cold in every chest. The attackers fell in unison, screaming and clutching at chests. Smoke and fog rose from the collapsed pile of bodies in small streams where final "breaths" were exhaled.

Jaren walked past, ignoring the stench of charred internal organs. Along the edges of the street, cautious citizens poked their heads out. Exclamations of surprise filled the air, but no one stepped out. He was the only one moving down the road, and everyone else stared at him, but his normal self-consciousness was overwhelmed with the task before him. In the distance, his radiance-sight could see Joans spinning out an incredible number of lumps. They were like huge fireflies zipping back and forth through the air. Jaren had seen Joans like that before—dealing death with every move, but was he killing defenders or attackers? Jaren dashed toward the light show.

The battle raged on as Jaren passed. He helped where he could, but his focus was on getting to Joans. On the edges of the fighting, groups of armored defenders battled attackers. At street corners, larger mobs of citizens overwhelmed invaders. But as Jaren moved closer to the wall, large groups of attackers were cutting through citizens. Jaren produced a constant flow of heat and cold, taking down as many as he could, but he knew he needed to stop Joans. He was attacked a few times, but the attackers soon learned their mistake. The smell of burnt flesh followed him wherever he went.

Jaren rounded a corner and knew Joans would be there. What he didn't expect was the number of bodies surrounding him— both defenders and attackers. He watched as Joans spun out dozens and dozens of complicated lumps. He saw as one near him went up behind a defender's head. It made a soft "pop" when it was released, and the man crumpled to the ground. Other more basic lumps entered defenders' bodies and killed them where they stood.

Jaren's rage boiled. All his minds were engaged and focused. He rushed forward, stepping over the fallen bodies, and spun out simple attacks, rolling and folding to keep straight, then releasing before Joans could take control.

But, despite his effort at good placement, most of the attacks veered off wildly, and those that went toward Joans were easily deflected into oncoming invaders.

"Brittle bones, boy! Work on your aim!" Joans shouted, never taking his attention off the battle in front of him. "Stop wasting your time on the invaders and help me with these bone-dragging Glow-Benders."

Jaren rushed toward Joans, preparing additional attacks and readying defenses, but once he stepped past the buildings, he stopped. His minds reoriented and he saw three other people with sources and shields. *Glow-Benders?* Was that some sort of insult among Light-Twisters? In the strange light of the radiance, he couldn't make out more than their outline. They each carried several impure sources. Jaren hadn't noticed them because of all the lumps moving around the battle, but now he could see them clearly. It was like looking at a painting and seeing only random colors at first, but then suddenly being able to see the clear image of a person.

These invaders were attacking, and Joans was defending the defenders. They were also attacking Joans, and he was defending himself. Joans was not killing anyone.

Joans knocked out a released lump of heat that would have taken Jaren. *"Pay attention!"* Jaren threw up a wall of air to deflect further attacks.

"Bone-headed defenders, stay away!" Joans shouted. Then he yelled to Jaren, "Go distract those Glow-Benders. I'll knock out enough of the defenders, so I won't have to worry about them being killed. Run around and attack from the side. And keep moving! Your sources are like blazing torches to them."

More defenders collapsed as Joans' strange lumps popped behind their heads.

Jaren dashed to the side. The pain in his wounded leg distracted two minds but was ignored by the rest. None of his minds were available to think about what had just happened, but they tried between the assignments he gave them. Jaren had been sure that Joans was responsible for this attack, but here he was—fighting the attackers.

A spiraling cone of flame shot at him. Jaren rolled across the ground, keeping his staff in his hand like Mastiff had shown him. He pushed against the incoming energy a split second before it was released and diverted it from its path—probably saving his own life, as it punched right through the wall of air he had erected. The end of his staff was smoldering as he stepped out of the roll, but he had not been touched.

As soon as he righted himself, an explosion a few feet behind him hurled him forward. He hit the ground with a thud but scrambled back up and kept moving. His force shield had reduced the effect of the blast, but his side hurt, and he was sure the wound on his leg had reopened. A crackling mass of energy, released just outside of his range, snapped in front of him and tunneled into the ground. He leapt over the deep furrow—three feet wide and at least fifteen feet long—where the ground had collapsed into the tunnel. As he ran he threw a few poorly aimed attacks.

Jaren dashed behind the dining hall. The attacks abated once he was behind solid walls. He could still see the battle between Joans and the three invaders, though it was dimmed by the stone. The parties appeared evenly matched, though Joans had the clear advantage of quality sources. While the three attackers had to slick off their impure energies, Joans was able to use almost the full power of his folds. However, there were three of them, and they each controlled more lumps than Lesarra could. A single mind briefly worried about her, but Jaren quickly put it back on the task of folding lumps.

Jaren ducked as a dancing blend of energies flashed toward him. It inexplicably sailed through the dining hall, walls and all. Compared to the speed of the raw energy, this released attack just drifted like a leaf on a meandering river.

Jaren glanced up as he crawled away from the spot. The blend continued to glide out of the building and Jaren reinforced his shield. He had no idea what the attack was going to do. Oddly, it just continued gliding. Jaren kept moving but glanced back as it moved into the backs of a group of fighters. A terrible sloshing noise erupted as liquified flesh splashed to the ground throwing up a spray of blood. Jaren wiped his face and tried to ignore the stench. The fighters who weren't hit ran in terror while those who were hit but survived reached for limbs that were no longer there, screaming in agony. Jaren stood and kept moving.

He rounded the dining hall. The attackers could see his sources, but at least their attacks wouldn't get to him—unless they had other tricks that passed through walls. He peeked around the corner. The four were still facing off, but there were no attackers or defenders left near them. All three were concentrating their attacks on Joans and appeared to be pressing him backward.

One of Jaren's minds provided a good idea. He dashed out behind the attacking Light-Twisters, and once he cleared the building, he hurled half of his lumps at the nearest one. Before he even let the lumps go, he dove behind the building. When he felt the lumps responding to someone else, he released them. As fast as he could, he pulled his segg over his head to remove it. His radiance-sight saw the attacked Light-Twister stop his forward movement and begin moving toward him. Jaren pushed the staff through the shoulder holes of the segg, and held it up, stretching it far from his mostly naked body toward the corner of the building. He folded out additional lumps and sent them around the corner. The approaching attacker countered them. Jaren waited, folding the sources and positioning them for another attack.

The man sent an attack at the corner of the building. It blasted through the red stone and tore Jaren's segg from the staff. At the same time, Jaren released all the lumps he was holding. He pulled the staff back to his body. A large pile of rubble partially buried his segg several feet in front of him.

The attacking Light-Twister continued forward. Jaren took a deep breath to calm his nerves. He tightened his grip on the staff, pressing back against the wall as if trying to sink into it. As the attacker walked around the crumpled corner, Jaren jabbed the staff at the man's head with all his strength. He focused all his free minds on diverting the flow of energy to open a hole in the man's shield. His lumps lunged at Jaren as the end of Jaren's staff connected with the man's temple. There was a loud crack, and then the Light-Twister collapsed. Jaren took control of the closest lumps and as quickly as he could, Jaren burned out the man's lungs. As the shield dropped, Jaren slipped under the sagging body, dragged it toward the pile of rubble and laid it down. He retrieved his segg, slipped it on and then walked around to the front of the building.

Joans had been able to stop the forward movement of the attackers once they were without the help of the third man. Their attention was focused on him, but they could see Jaren's sources approaching. Jaren's heart was racing.

"When this is over, you're going to have to share those sources with us, Trallcus!" one of the Light-Twisters shouted over his shoulder. His voice was gravelly, and his accent was unfamiliar to Jaren.

Jaren kept walking closer. The other man then shouted, "If what they told us about this place is true, we won't need to share!"

They both laughed as they pressed against Joans. Jaren formed up his lumps, and while still behind the two Light-Twisters he sent a volley of attacks against the nearest one. The Light-Twister responded too late and took a dense ball of heat to the shoulder.

He screamed as his arm tore free like a stick burned in the center breaks in two. His lumps winked out as one of Joans' attacks caught him in the head. The final attacker speed-walked away from Jaren, but Joans caught the man in mid-stride with a blade of air. The man sped right through it, and the momentum sent the two halves of his body tumbling several yards down the street.

Joans said, "I thought you were dead! You'll have to explain to me what happened."

Jaren just looked at Joans. If not Joans, then who was trying to kill Hairth?

"And remind me to never let you behind my back," Joans commented as he toed the still-smoldering, headless man. "These were not inexperienced fighters, and their sources were not insignificant. I wonder how they were recruited."

"I heard them mention the sources here in Freysdal."

"Yes—if they knew what Hairth kept hidden here, they would certainly want to come. Too bad for them they didn't know I...*we*...were here. What's all over your face?"

An arrow bounced off Joans' shield.

"Where's your shield, boy?" Joans snapped, as he whirled on their attacker.

Jaren reformed the shield he had forgotten after faking his death. The attack continued despite the defeat of the enemy Light-Twisters, as invaders poured in through the open gates while others dropped down from the tops of the wall. The gap around Jaren and Joans shrank, and a tight unit of spearmen moved toward them.

"One thing at a time, I suppose," Joans said.

He folded and blended faster than Jaren could track, forming muddy lumps into twisted rods. Each man they touched stiffened and fell to the ground. The unit broke and ran.

"We'll need to close those gates," Joans said.

Jaren nodded, steeling himself to wade upriver through the stream of oncoming attackers.

"This force source is better than anything you'll find in nature," Joans said, like they were back in the old house, and he was delivering a lecture. He folded out a lump the size of two wagons as they moved toward the open gates. He split the lump and formed two side-by-side half arches, almost like a tree with the top branches cut off. The vectors were mostly pointed up and out, but at least a fifth of them were pointed in the wrong direction. Joans held the arches in front of him as they pressed into the massed attackers.

Every attacker that ended up between the moving arches was lifted off the ground and thrown to the side. It was like an enormous bull tossing its head right and left to throw men out of its path. Except, the men weren't just being tossed aside. The misaligned vectors tore both clothes and skin, pulled fingers from hands, removed noses from faces, and broke bones. But the ripping, cracking, and crunching sounds were hard to hear over the shouts and screams.

Joans maintained a thick flow of energy to the arches. Instead of folding the energy out, he somehow streamed energy out and then back into the source. It was like loops from a knotted ball of yarn, with each loop denser than the last. The last stream, as thick as a log and denser than Jaren could have managed, fed the arches as they drew in and chewed the invaders up and spat out human carcasses.

Jaren dropped heat and cold into as many invaders as he could reach outside of Joans' onslaught. The two walked on a smooth, empty path toward the wall, building piles of dead and damaged bodies on either side. As they neared the gate, crackling bursts of light appeared in the arches.

Joans' expanded his shield, but the snapping, hissing, and burning made it unstable. His source had turned into a muddy mixture of energies.

"Blasted bones!" he shouted, pulling the shield back and skimming the impure energies and flinging them at invaders. The resulting explosions destroyed bodies and were almost deafening.

"Use mine!" Jaren shouted over the din, but Joans was already on to something else.

Swirling energy from one source to another, Joans dropped a half-circle of sharp-angled filaments into the ground. When he released the energy, the red soil lifted up like a wall and pushed the invaders away from the gate. Joans blended a huge lump of what looked like air with bio in it, and filled the space left by the traveling wall of earth. The invaders who scrambled over the earthen wall were caught in the air mixture and moved as slow as sap running down a tree on a warm day. Jaren watched as they struggled against the thick air. Joans reached down into Jaren's force source and then pushed them away from the wall as he forced the gates closed.

Joans then created another earth-shoving wave and piled thousands of pounds of dirt against the gate.

"That should hold it. Now we stop the men on the walls," Joans said. As an arrow deflected off his shield, he caught it with a lump of heat that turned it into a cloud of smoke and ashes that coated the defender behind them who otherwise would have been impaled. The man coughed, eyes wide in surprise.

Joans didn't even seem to notice what he had just done. He was instead staring at the invaders piling down the stairs on the interior side of the walls. "I'll take one side. You take the other. Remember to keep your shield up."

Joans turned and delivered death as he made his way to the white side of the wall.

Jaren ran in the opposite direction, cutting men down as he went. A loud crack drew his attention, and he turned to see an invader screaming and covering his eye. Levi pulled his whip back while cutting off another attacker's arm with his short sword. Jaren finished off the half-blind man and ran over to Levi as he drew his sword from the other man's chest.

"We've got the gate closed."

Levi raised an eyebrow at him. "With just that short burnt staff?"

An invader rushed toward them, and Levi turned to face him. However, the man suddenly stopped and screamed out stinking smoke, clutching at his chest before falling dead. Levi eyed the man, then looked at Jaren.

"So, it's not just Joans out here." He paused, then nodded. "Excellent! The next step is to get those ladders off the walls and get our archers back in their positions."

"That's where I'm headed. If you can find our archers, I can clear the wall."

Levi started shouting orders.

Jaren rushed toward the stairs and began climbing, killing the invaders as they spilled down. Their bodies piled up so high he couldn't climb the steps. Worse yet, the invaders behind the pile were climbing over it and attacking from above.

Jaren took a dense lump of heat and folded it into his force source. The resulting angry energy was hard to control, but he set it in the center of the pile of bodies. When he released it, a deafening roar filled the air as the pile of bodies exploded, knocking Jaren backward. The response was so fast he couldn't keep his shield oriented around him, and, as he passed through, it accelerated him even faster out the back. He hit the ground hard, but kept enough minds to reform his shield, which protected him from the body parts raining down on him.

When he stood, he saw that several stair steps were missing as well as a large chunk of the wall. Jaren was relieved to see that the hole didn't go completely through the red stone. He glanced toward Joans and saw that he was using a wedge of air pushed with force to shove people off the stairs, so he copied him.

Jaren hopped over the missing steps and pressed the wedge to the top of the stairs, tossing bodies as he went. He threw the men at the top over the wall with lumps of force, ignoring their screams as they fell, and then turned down the length of the wall. Parapets on the outside of the wall were crowded with men scrambling over to join the press moving toward the stairs, heedlessly trampling the bodies of the dead defenders. The passage was wide enough for three men standing shoulder to shoulder.

Jaren formed a dense fist-sized cylinder of heat and burned through a number of invaders. They collapsed, clogging the already full wall. As more men surged forward, Jaren copied Joans' arch as best as he could, which threw the men up and over the wall. Some men fell straight to the ground. Others slammed into ladders as they fell, taking additional men with them.

At the first ladder, Jaren swung a blade of air and removed the hands of the man at the top. He slid forward, unable to catch himself, screaming in pain. A large lump of cold directed down the center of each rung caused them to shatter under pounding feet and hands. The two poles, no longer connected to each other, twisted free, and men fell shouting to the ground below. Jaren looked out over the edge of the wall and felt sick to his stomach. Torches extended as far as he could see in the darkness. The sheer number of men was overwhelming, and Jaren could feel exhaustion spreading through his body and the burden pressing against his heart.

More men reached the top of the wall and poured toward him. Arrows from behind deflected off his shield. He turned to see confused defenders who were trying to shoot past him.

"Hold!" he shouted, surprised to hear himself using Mastiff's commands.

The next attacker wore grim determination like a familiar coat. He moved toward Jaren with the assurance of a man accustomed to battle, axe held firmly, and shield raised. Jaren froze his brain and he collapsed. The man behind him went wide-eyed but continued forward. He stepped over the fallen man, his curved sword raised high, ready to strike Jaren down. Jaren pushed his shield out and reinforced it. The man rebounded off the shield and was impaled on the spear held by the man behind him. Both careened over the edge.

The battle across the top of the wall continued slowly. Jaren grew more and more tired with each foot gained. He cut down a trio of attackers with a wide blade of air and was surprised to see a man crouching behind with a spear thrusting at him. The spear pushed through the shield, and only Mastiff's staff training saved Jaren. He knocked the spear aside with his staff and burned the man's brain.

Finally, after five more ladders, Jaren met Joans near where the red wall was being expanded with the white stone.

"Excellent work. Now, for our last act." Joans rubbed his hands together, apparently enjoying the slaughter like someone else would have enjoyed a gala event. He folded his light source into a stream and poured the resulting massive amount of energy down over the wall, allowing it to surround the invaders like fog.

"You might want to look away."

Jaren clamped his eyes shut and turned his head as the night sky turned to day. The invading force fumbled about in blindness, trying to run away but uncertain which way to go. Jaren wondered if the condition would be permanent. Men on the wall were also blinded, but Jaren was sure theirs was only temporary.

As the defenders who could still see continued to put arrows into attackers within range, the attackers collapsed to the red soil of the plains of Pinnutuck. Jaren knew *their* state was permanent. He watched as Joans formed another unknown lump. He spread it thinly, like a giant sheet in the night sky over the attackers. When he released it, it looked to Jaren like nothing was happening.

Joans then spoke. "Flee...or die painfully!" Jaren could see his mouth moving, but the sound came from the sky above the attackers in a voice that echoed like thunder.

Jaren watched as the men in the front dropped their weapons and turned to run. He could hear officers shouting at the men to get more ladders up and to continue pounding the gate, but those shouts were silenced by no-longer-friendly blades. The men in the front fought the men behind them to escape, and the battle for Freysdal was over.

Jaren turned to walk off the wall but found himself face to face with defenders holding swords and spears. The first was the hulking Blue who sat outside the security building. He was staring down at Jaren. When Jaren met his eyes, the Blue stepped back in fear. Jaren looked down the row of faces— some bleeding, some blind, all dirty and sweaty, all shocked. He dropped his own eyes, and despite the horror he had just participated in, he couldn't help but think of the fear and disgust people would feel toward him.

He turned to look away from all those eyes when a wild cheer broke out. The men pressed in on him, overwhelming his shield, reaching to clasp his hand and pat his back. Shouts of praise and gratitude rang out. Behind him, he could hear the same acclamation from the other side of the wall.

Then both sides dropped silent. Jaren looked, expecting to see Hairth, but instead saw Joans walking down a staircase of air with flames billowing out on either side. The light from the flames cast large shadows of Joans across the ground and on the wall. As Joans threw his arms up into the air, bolts of sparkling aural light shot into the air. The cheering went wild again. One mind suggested that he copy Joans, but the rest of the minds mocked that idea. Instead, Jaren threaded his way through the defenders, shaking hands and acknowledging thanks as he passed by.

Chapter 49

Revealing the Truth

Jaren's tired muscles struggled to carry him down the stairs, stepping on or over the dead and dying that littered the way, wincing at his pain as he went. While a few people still cheered for him, most did not pay him any more attention—probably because he wasn't walking on air, surrounded by flames. That was fine by Jaren. His secret was out, but maybe they would attribute everything they'd seen to Joans.

More important at that moment, was Jaren's worry about his family. He moved past the pockmarked and destroyed buildings that had been caught in the crossfire of the radiance fight. He told himself that the thralls he stepped over had been simply rendered unconscious by Joans. He was tempted to stop and look for Gerald or Kehvun's face but resisted. He used the edge of his segg to scrub at the blood on his face, hoping he could get most of it off.

Defenders were rounding up the few remaining invaders who hadn't been killed, but no one paid Jaren any mind. He was just a thin teenager making his way across the battlefield.

"Jaren!" It was Gerald. He was holding a large satchel and wrapping a defender's bleeding arm.

"Are you okay?" Jaren asked, relieved that he didn't have to search through the bodies.

"Praise *Hel'dig* you're safe!" He embraced Jaren for a moment, and then pulled away.

Jaren asked, "Is Kehvun...?"

"Kehvun's fine. Haerlee drafted us, and we've been helping stop the bleeding of wounded for the past three hours. There's no end to them!"

Three hours? Had it been that long? It had only felt like a matter of minutes—until his body reminded him of how fatigued he was and he noticed how dark the sky had become.

Gerald continued, "Can you run home and let the women know we are okay?" Jaren nodded and tried to ignore the destruction as he passed out of Freysdal proper.

As he approached the house, he could see the women sitting on the front porch.

"We're all okay!" he shouted, waving his hands up in the air. He felt giddy at their survival. "We're all okay. Not a scratch!" At least nothing serious, anyway.

Maullie was shaking her head. In the glare of the lightball, he could see tears streaming down her face. Not only hers, but all the girls.

"It's okay—we're all safe. You don't have to cry."

He put a hand on May and Ella's shoulders. Ella took his hand and placed a rolled-up paper in it.

"Jaren...Haerlee is..."

"It was Mosj! How could he? How could he?" May sobbed.

Jaren read the paper.

Jaren, I've taken Haerlee. If you ever want to see her again, walk farther into the valley. You'll receive more instructions. Come alone. We are watching you. Come now.

Jaren had to reread the message, but then anger replaced the confusion. He tightened his fist and crumpled the paper. Through clenched teeth, he said, "Ella, go find a defender and tell him what happened."

Without further words, Jaren walked up the path in the moonlight. He passed the last of the houses and continued on to where the path grew rougher and the river was just a stream. He walked for another two miles as both worry and anger fought to consume his minds. He planned his attacks and readied his lumps. Mosj? It made no sense.

He came upon an arrow sticking out of the ground with a note on it. Lighting a small ball, he read:

I know what you are. Take off your segg and hold up each of your sources so we can see you place them on the ground. To your left you'll see a small fire burning on the hill, walk to the fire. If you don't leave your sources behind, Haerlee will be killed.

A few of Jaren's minds berated the rest for not taking the dead Light-Twister's sources and tucking them into his undergarments. The others defended themselves by pointing out how stupid that was—who would have guessed that something like this was going to happen? He shivered as he pulled off his segg and set out the sources.

He considered using force to carry the sources far behind him, but he didn't know where Mosj's people were, or how many there were with Mosj—and he wasn't sure he had the skill to do it. Unless Mosj was a Light-Twister himself, he wouldn't be able to see the lumps Jaren carried, so he folded out as many as he could hold as densely as he could, then began trudging through the stream. The water was freezing, and his boots sloshed as he began walking up the hill.

After a few minutes of climbing, Jaren found himself in the darkness of dense forest. He almost released one of his light lumps before remembering that he didn't have his sources. At times he lost sight of the fire and had to search for it, but he continued making his way toward it. As he neared the fire, he saw motion out of the corner of his eye. He sent his attacks toward it. Because he wasn't streaming energy to his shield, the downward blow punched right through it and connected with his head.

Jaren regained consciousness with a moan. He had an enormous headache, and his eyes wouldn't focus. His lumps were gone, of course. His back and neck were scratched up, and the rough ground poked into his bare chest and cheek. He blinked a few times to clear his eyes. The stars and moon peeked through the canopy overhead. Haerlee was sitting beside him with her hands tied behind her back. Sitting in front of them was Mosj, busily cleaning under his fingernails with a long-bladed knife. There was no fire anywhere near them.

"Well, your luck's finally run out," Mosj said, but he didn't sound pleased. "Look, I didn't want this. But you left me no choice. The army arrived ahead of schedule."

Most of Jaren's minds were spouting nonsense, and it was difficult to understand Mosj.

"What are you talking about?" Jaren asked, squeezing his eyes shut in an effort to concentrate. He tried to lift himself, and only then realized that his hands were tied behind his back.

Mosj punched his fist into his hand. Was he crazy?

"I was so close! Time and time again! But each time you were somehow there messing things up, and now I've run out of time. The source 'accident' should have killed Hairth, but it didn't. Why? Because of *you*! The assassination should have worked too—the schedule showed Hairth was alone. Even when I was trying to pin Hairth's 'accidental' death at tomorrow's fair on Joans, you somehow managed to spring the trap early! But since the attack began early anyway, I guess it wouldn't have mattered, but still, it would have succeeded, except, again, for *you!* I couldn't understand what was going on until I saw you and Joans dueling with those other Light-Twisters—*you* are a Light-Twister. That's how you've been stopping me. But now I'll be turning you over in exchange for my brother and I can be done with this wretched place and finally go home."

"What?" Haerlee asked, a horrified look on her face. "You're a Light-Twister?"

"Yeah, he is, and he thinks very fondly of you. Picture that, you holding hands with a dirty Light-Twister."

More of Jaren's minds were functioning correctly, but he was still confused. And terrified. He was tied up wearing only his underclothes and boots—completely defenseless. Haerlee was involved because of him, and she was horrified by what he was. He could see his sources down at the base of the hill—small pinpricks of light on the ground—much too far to even touch. Jaren wasn't sure it could get any worse.

"Don't worry, I won't hurt her. The truth is, I like you—I like all of you. It breaks my heart to do this to you, but they've got my brother."

"Then don't do it, Mosj," Haerlee pled. "Let us help you. We can find your brother and save him."

Mosj laughed. "Right. You guys—who had all convinced yourselves that Joans was the one trying to kill Hairth—are somehow going to find my brother. Hairth's searchers can't even find him. No. I wish it was that simple, but I have no choice. Don't you see it? I have no choice."

Jaren could have shouted, but he tried to keep his voice steady. "You always have a choice."

Mosj just shook his head. "You're still deluded by the false idea of the 'peace of Freysdal.' Haven't you learned yet that there is no peace, even in Freysdal? Surely after spending months with Joans you know it's a lie."

It was another kick to the stomach. The peace of Freysdal was not for Jaren to enjoy—he was a protector of the Peace. While his minds struggled, one pointed out the faintest glow in the earth beneath—a weak, very low concentration of light source flowing down the mountainside. That mind showed the others and they stopped debating and began the excruciatingly slow process of gathering the energy.

"See! Even you can't deny it!"

"So, what are you going to do now?"

"I'm going to hike the two of you out of here and trade you for my brother."

Jaren's most observant mind shouted in alarm. If they moved much further up the mountain, he wouldn't be able to reach this weak light source at all, and there were no other sources.

"How did you do it all? How did you swap out the source, and get the herbs, and everything?"

Mosj smirked. "Everyone thinks I've got the least glamorous job in all of Freysdal—I clean, I remove refuse, I fix broken things. But as you know, no one ever notices me. I'm in maintenance. I've got keys to everything, and no one ever questions why I'm where I might happen to be. I can get into any building, look at any record, touch anything, and no one says a boned word about it."

"The secretary's desk...."

"Yes. I got into that desk every night. I knew Hairth's schedule better than he did. I planned each attack carefully, so that no one would know it was me, and no one ever did."

Jaren's minds were still collecting, and he had enough for a very small pop of light, but not enough for anything useful.

"Hairth was spending a lot of time at the research facility. I followed him there—actually, I was there before him, waiting. I learned what he did. I watched the researchers and learned what they did. I studied their notes at night. I understood—maybe better than they did—how radiance works, and I swapped out the sources on a demonstration I was sure they would show to Hairth, and they did!"

"But, why? Why are you doing this?"

"I've told you—to get my brother back. They have him. The seekers found him, but I didn't have enough reward to get him. When I finally did, someone else had bought him. Then one day a piece of paper showed up in my room. It said they had my brother, and they would kill him if I didn't follow their instructions. I was to communicate by pigeon—there would always be one or more with a purple band tied around its leg. I was pretty shaken by the note, but figured it was some cruel joke. If Hairth's people couldn't find my brother, then who else could? Two days later I found another note in my room with the name of our pet dog... and it was wrapped around a pinky finger."

Haerlee let out a low moan.

"A pinky finger!" Spittle flew from Mosj's mouth as he shouted, "What kind of monster does that to a little kid? He's only ten years old."

Mosj stabbed at the trunk of a nearby tree with the knife. "So, I just had to do what the notes said. They told me to kill Hairth, and they gave me ideas and told me where to find resources."

"What about the snakes?" Jaren asked, stalling for still more energy.

"I don't even know who has him." Mosj paused to digest what Jaren had said. "What snakes?"

"The ones you tried to kill me and the Associates with, but almost got Kehvun instead?"

Mosj shook his head. "That wasn't me. I just thought it was bad luck."

"Maybe it was Joans, then..." Jaren couldn't make any sense of it.

"You're so obsessed with that kooky old guy in the room next to mine that you can't even see who he really is. I hear him talking to himself all the time—he thinks pretty highly of you— seems jealous, though, that Hairth found you instead of him. One night I got so irritated with his talking that I used Haerlee's sleeping blend on him."

"You stole my mix?"

"Yes. I didn't want to kill the guards to let those assassins in, so I used your herbs." Then returning to his previous rant, "And if Jaren hadn't been in the office then they probably w..."

Jaren released two small lumps inside Mosj's eyes. Beams of light shone out through his pupils. He shouted, dropped his knife, and covered his eyes. Jaren rolled over and got to his feet, ignoring the awful pain in his leg. He speared Mosj in the stomach with his shoulder. One of Jaren's minds laughed and shouted to the others—"It's a fight between a boy with no arms and a blind man!" The others told it to keep quiet.

The two struggled, but arms were more important than eyes when it came to wrestling, and despite Jaren kneeing, kicking, and biting, Mosj was able to get on top of him.

"You infernal bone breaker!" Mosj wrapped his hands around Jaren's neck and squeezed. Jaren writhed, fighting against his bonds. Darkness began to close in. He couldn't convince his body to fight any more and the pain in his leg was now gone.

Mosj screeched. He jerked upright and clawed at his back. Jaren gasped in fresh air. Mosj's face contorted in pain as he arched his back and toppled sideways. Behind him, covering her open mouth with both hands, Haerlee stared down at Mosj with wide eyes. Jaren turned to see Mosj lying face down with a knife protruding from his back. Behind him lay the remnants of Haerlee's cut ropes.

Haerlee was quietly repeating "No! No! *No!*" to herself, and Jaren's relief was tempered by the empathy he felt for what she had been forced to do. An image of a man with a knife protruding from his chest was Jaren's constant companion, and now she had a similar one, except she had stuck a knife in the back of her friend.

Chapter 50

Finding Peace

Jaren stared across the ornately carved heavy wooden table. A small cut on Levi's rock-hard jaw was the only evidence of the previous night's battle. The room felt empty without all the apprentices and Associates. Jaren's eyes felt dry and sandy. He struggled to keep his minds focused. Most were sleeping. Would they wake refreshed? Or would they just stay asleep until the rest went to sleep, too? Maybe he could let them...

"Jaren?" Hairth's voice brought Jaren back into the conversation.

"Oh, right. No, he said he didn't know."

"But it must have been someone here in Freysdal," Levi continued.

He gestured toward the notes spread across the table. They were written in different hands with different ink and on different kinds of paper. He had put them in order as best he could. The leather-bound journal Mosj had kept revealed the story of a young man in bitter anguish. A bowl of sleeping powder, several darts, and an enormous set of keys made up the rest of the items Levi's men had found. Like most thralls, Mosj did not have many personal possessions. But the keys had allowed him to give himself a private room, which was more than most single thralls had.

"You never saw anyone going into his room?" Levi asked Joans a second time.

"I did not," Joans replied.

He had come down pretty hard from his high of the night before. In addition to looking greasy, he now looked ragged, and his eyelids were drooping.

"To be honest, though, I didn't pay any attention. I had no idea someone lived in that room."

He glanced at the darts and scratched at his hand. Levi had found a small hole in the wall between the two rooms, just big enough for a dart to pass through. He had begun asking Haerlee about the powder with great interest before Hairth had returned the conversation to the attack.

Levi turned to Hairth. "I don't think we'll learn anything else until the search party returns. Unless you have other plans, I'd like to ask the merchantaries some more questions." Hairth shook his head, and Levi left the room.

Jaren thought of all the men he had killed that night. The thought as well as the smells evoked by the memories made him feel slightly queasy. And he wasn't just recalling the smells from memory. The smells from the clean-up fires—that's what they called the fires where they burned the merchantaries' bodies—were not all that different from the smells of heat burning someone's chest. They deserved it, though—let their bones burn and scatter in the wind. After years of wandering Thadren as trapped souls, their bodies would eventually settle into the soil and get turned under, and then their souls would finally proceed to the Frozen Waste.

Hairth watched Levi leave, then turned to Joans.

"Where did they find three Light-Twisters? I chose this place because it's so far removed from Light-Twister communities and natural sources."

"I don't know. They weren't trained in any discipline I'm familiar with, but they weren't inexperienced."

"Could they have been connected to Lesarra?"

Hairth had been under the impression that Lesarra was one of the attacking Light-Twisters. He had been visibly relieved when Jaren and Haerlee had explained what had happened with the freezer earlier that evening.

"I don't believe so. As I said, I know her mentor and he would not have been associated with those scoundrels." Joans' scowl deepened even further. "I will need to investigate to find out where they came from."

"You'll come back when you've found your answers?"

Joans nodded in response, then asked, "Do I take him with me?"

Jaren's alarm spiked. Hairth hesitated, but then shook his head.

"No—unless he cannot continue to learn in your absence. I think he needs to spend some time with his family."

Joans smiled. It might even have been a real smile—it was hard to tell because of how tired he looked.

"He's at a stage where he is safe to experiment, and I don't think he will develop any bad habits over the course of a few months. He's seen enough now to know what he needs to work on. And I won't be leaving for a few days anyway. I believe Lesarra will want to come with me, but she won't wake up for at least three more days."

That had been one of the few reliefs that came from this early-morning meeting. When Jaren and Haerlee had described what had happened with the freezer, Joans had explained that Lesarra succumbed to the burden. In other words, that Light-Twisters—when they try to do more than they have strength to do—are pulled from consciousness. Jaren also learned that it had been a good thing he had taken the sources from her. Light-Twisters in that state experience the equivalent of muscle spasms and can cause serious harm with any sources left near them.

Finally understanding what Joans had said, however, Jaren's still awake minds sat down in sadness. Lesarra understood him, and sitting next to Haerlee, who was being uncharacteristically quiet, he thought it might be nice to talk with someone. One mind pointed out that it was unfair for him to think that. Haerlee had just been abducted by a friend and had then been forced to kill that friend. That was probably why she was quiet, rather than an aversion to Jaren's radiance. He hoped that proved to be the case.

The investigation was still ongoing, and there were some ominous unanswered questions. One of the most perplexing questions was how such a large army had traveled all the way to Freysdal without being detected, but Jaren and Haerlee's debrief was over. Hairth asked Jaren to stop by the following afternoon. When he asked Haerlee if she would like someone to stay with her and her mother that night, she answered with a curt, "We'll be fine." He smiled graciously in reply.

"Haerlee, wait!"

She didn't. Jaren's minds couldn't agree whether to chase after her or let her go, so he just stood outside the building and watched as she disappeared into the darkness. With his head hanging down, and with only enough energy to walk, Jaren headed back down the valley road. The sky was lightening to his right—the sun would be rising soon.

Jaren watched as two men carefully placed a segg-covered body onto a board. The man's hand dragged on the ground as they carried him. The stage and a few of the tents that were to have been used for Leyunell had been converted into temporary morgues. The dead were brought there, and a sprinkle of earth was placed upon them so their souls could begin their journey. They would be buried once they were identified and their family was able to...actually, Jaren wasn't really sure what people here did with their dead. The only dead Jaren had ever directly dealt with had been his parents and Desot. The small graveyard that held Hairth's son and wife would need to be enlarged. This was surely the worst Leyunell in the history of Thadren.

A hand on Jaren's shoulder startled him—especially because he had been staring at the limp dragging hand of the body.

It was Gerald.

"Don't worry, Jaren. Once she's had a chance to work through all of this, she'll be ready to talk."

"What if it's more than just that?" Jaren couldn't bring himself to ask about what he was really worried about. What if she wasn't the only one? What if his sisters were also like Haerlee or Lesarra's mom and didn't want anything to do with a Light-Twister?

"Well, sometimes we grow up thinking one thing and later in life learn that we were mistaken. I used to think that all Oiandans were thieves. When I met Deaelestran, I knew I had to be careful around him, but after a few weeks I realized that what I had been taught was simply wrong. Some things just take time."

Some hours later, Jaren woke up on his pallet. The sun was shining in through his window, catching the dust floating in the room. Kehvun was sitting on his pallet across the room, holding a bio source in one hand and fingering the bandage over his ear with the other. He was staring at Jaren.

"So, you can use radiance?" The question sounded like it had been rehearsed.

"Yeah." Jaren's thigh was throbbing, and his head hurt right behind his eyes. His mouth was dry, and he felt weak all over.

Kehvun's face brightened.

"That is so incredible! I am so jealous." He tossed the source in the air and caught it. "After the fighting had stopped, defenders streamed past talking about the two Light-Twisters—how they had walked in the air and shot out flames and had thrown the invaders off the wall. I heard a couple of people talking about a radiance duel filled with strange lights, buildings exploding, and…" Kehvun kept going, but Jaren didn't know whether to laugh or to cry, so he kind of did both.

Ella poked her head into the room, "You're awake?"

Jaren wiped the tears from his eyes. His heart raced and he tried to brace himself for her reaction. They had grown in the same home. He knew what she thought of Light-Twisters—that she despised them. But she had come here to see him, so he inwardly hoped…

"I'm glad you're okay," she said as she slipped in and sat by Kehvun. Her hair was disheveled, and her eyes were red with dark bags beneath them.

"Great Leyunell journey."

"Great Leyunell journey," Kehvun and Jaren both replied, though Kehvun's was more enthusiastic than Jaren's.

"Kehvun told me what happened last night—with the freezer and with the battle. I overheard Gerald telling Maullie about Mosj and Haerlee. I felt like I was listening to a fable, except that I had seen parts of it with my own eyes. When you and Haerlee and the two guards walked back to Freysdal, I wanted to run to you, but I couldn't leave May behind." Ella's face wore the pain she was trying to express.

"How is May?" Jaren asked, working a little moisture into his mouth, hoping to move the subject away from himself. He felt bad for thinking about it that way—everything always seemed to be about him—but he hadn't really even thought about May and that made him feel worse. Ella just frowned in response.

"I haven't heard your parts of the story, though. I'd like to… when you're ready to share them."

Jaren was sure they could see his segg moving with his pounding heart. Better to get it over with.

"I can control radiance. I've been doing it for months."

Ella's face drooped a little, "Of course you can—you've always been able to do radiance—like the time you tripped yourself and slammed into the ground, or when you and Kehvun fought each other with power." Then turning to Kehvun, she said, "Oh, Kehvun, I'm not sure if I like that ear better fixed or broken." She paused for a second, her face returning to normal, and then continued, "Kehvun told me. Jaren, I'm not sure...What?" She furrowed her brow and glared at them, then her eyes widened.

"Did I just do it? What did I say?"

"You said he could always do radiance, and that we fought with power and something about my ear." Kehvun was feeling at the bandage with his free hand again, but he was staring at the source.

"Oh, kitten bones!" She closed her eyes and was silent for several minutes. Jaren started to talk, but Kehvun signaled for him to wait.

"I can see Jaren taking a step and being shoved hard to the ground. He can't breathe—it's like something is crushing him—but there's nothing there. Then it's gone and he is able to get back up." She opened her eyes.

Jaren was staring at her, slowly shaking his head. "That happened to me. I made a shield, like the one that stopped those arrows." Kehvun nodded in understanding. "Only at that time I was still learning, and I ended up falling through it and it pinned me to the ground."

"Does this mean that I'm going to learn to use radiance?" Kehvun's eyes were wide, but not nearly as wide as his smile.

Ella just shook her head, "I don't know. I didn't see anything else when I closed my eyes. Someday I'll figure this all out."

He and Ella talked for a while longer—Jaren told her about his experience, trying to reduce the danger that he had been in and minimize what he had done. She didn't give any sign that his ability bothered her. When he asked about May again, however, she just said he'd have to see for himself.

May was sitting at the table, staring out the window. Or maybe she was staring at the window. Jaren hugged her head to his chest. Her only response was to put her hand on his.

It was disheartening to see her like that. It was as if all the progress she had made in the months since being purchased by Hairth had been wiped away in a single night. The sight of her like that stoked his anger against Mosj and whoever had been manipulating him, but deeper than that there was a slow burning determination. When Jaren had arrived in Freysdal he had been a helpless victim. With time, he was eventually buoyed up and strengthened by the Peace of Freysdal. He had no choice in his ability to control radiance, but he did have a choice in what he would do with it. He had made his choice. He had given up the Peace of Freysdal to become its defender—*the Sword of Freysdal.*

Epilogue

Jaren's distracted minds hadn't processed the loud noise before he had formed a shield and folded out a score of lumps. The shield shoved the door against the wall for a split second before he dropped it.

"Surprise!"

Maullie flung open the shutter on the lightball and illuminated the room. Everyone was smiling—except May, of course. She hadn't remembered how to smile yet, but she would at least look people in the eyes again. Progress. That's all he could hope for. Ella threw her arms around him. Kehvun patted him on the shoulder. Maullie roughed his hair. Tobie and Haerlee stood in the back, and even Haerlee was smiling at him, which hadn't happened since before that terrible night. Everything was either "before" or "after" that night.

"What's this all about?"

"It's your four-year anniversary. Tobie mentioned the date a couple weeks ago, and I've been planning it ever since."

A couple weeks ago had been one month "after." Maullie had made a huge dinner spread and invited everyone over. She had called it a "getting back to normal dinner." It had been anything but normal, with an amazing assortment of foods—from Grallan white-sauced duck to Chorati stew, from Souhain pastries to Tragarsulan cheeses.

Things were finally getting back to normal. Repairs were underway, work schedules were normalized, and routines reestablished.

Hairth had given up on pretending Jaren was his apprentice. He had attained a rare, though temporary, popularity. For the first week or so, people thanked Jaren when they passed him on the street and pointed him out to others who did not know him. It took him twice as long to get places because of all the stopping he had to do, and he had been embarrassed the entire time. But after that first-week people stopped stopping him. People smiled at him less often, and some even began avoiding him. It was disappointing, but not surprising. Plenty of people still smiled and waved at him, but almost as many crossed the road to avoid walking near him.

Lesarra had left about a week "after." Jaren no longer felt her absence quite as keenly. It had been bad at first, despite the fact that he had only known her for such a short time. Oh, but he missed her. After she'd been gone a few days, one mind had pointed out that because the hours they had spent together were so intense, they had created an outsized place for her in his heart. That space was still empty, over a month later, but its emptiness wasn't so painful. She and Joans had departed at the same time, leaving him as the sole Light-Twister in Freysdal.

Maullie interrupted Jaren's thoughts. "When Gerald and I first came to Freysdal it was customary for people to celebrate their anniversary. It was kind of like a countdown—six years left until freedom."

Everyone sat down at the table, and Jaren noticed that Maullie had prepared his favorite dish—crisped and sweetened pork belly. His mouth was watering before he got to his seat.

Gerald reached out and stopped Jaren's hand as he reached for the pork. "Wait—before we start, there is more to this tradition than just a celebration. You must share with us your goal for this next year, and what you will do when you are free."

Jaren looked around the table at the people he loved. Half of them thralls, the other half already free, all celebrating his progress toward freedom together. He did not have to think long about his answer.

"In one year, I will be the strongest Light-Twister possible. And when I am free, I will end Thralldom."

The End

From the Author

Thank you for reading *The Peace of Freysdal*! I remember the day I had the idea for this book. I was studying in the D'Azzo Research Library while working on my master's degree in Nuclear Engineering. I believe I was reading a book on nuclear physics, and I was fascinated by how radioactive materials worked. Materials can emit several different kinds of radiation. Some materials produce radiation naturally, while others produce it only when they are struck by some other radiation. I thought about how cool it would be if there were a world where magic behaved like radiation. I wondered what it would be like if some people could control that magical radiation energy. From that initial thought flowed the book you have now read. I have great thoughts about future stories, explorations for new sources, Jaren learning more light-twisting, Kehvun, Ella, Tobie, and everyone else growing into their own, furthering the fight against Thralldom, and discovering more about Joans' great mistake. There's so much more to tell and I hope you're as excited to read it as I am to tell it. If you have enjoyed this book, and especially if you'd like to hear the other stories from this world, please consider adding a review to your favorite online book site. Additionally, send me a message and follow me on Facebook @authormichaelrichards or Instagram @michaelrichardsauthor. You can also sign up for my newsletter at www.michaelrichardsbooks.com to hear about the progress I'm making on the books I'm writing. Again, thank you for spending your time with me.

Very Respectfully, Michael Richards

Acknowledgments

I'd like to thank all the people who have helped me as I've worked on this book. My wife, Adrianne, and our children have been a tremendous support and have always encouraged me to pursue my dreams. My oldest, William, in particular, has been my best reader and has helped improve the quality of my storytelling with his thoughts and insightful questions. My other children, Isaac, Eli, Piper, and Felicity, have been great at encouraging me all through this process. My parents and siblings have also been a huge support. My sisters, Mandy and Jess, both read early versions and provided me with encouraging feedback. My brother Andy connected me to several resources that helped improve my writing, most especially the podcast "Writing Excuses" which improved the quality of my storytelling. My brother-in-law, Jason, gave me some invaluable ideas early in the process that changed the trajectory of the story, and my mother-in-law, Chris, who doesn't particularly like fantasy, nonetheless read the very first version of this story and encouraged me to keep at it. My friend, Louis Floyd, trudged through what I thought at the time was a finished product and helped bring my book to the next level. Several other people read the story or pieces of it at various stages and provided me with good feedback. Finally, a big thank you to all the folks at John Hunt Publishing who believed enough in my work to help take it from a dream to a reality.

LODESTONE
BOOKS

YOUNG ADULT FICTION

Lodestone Books is a new imprint, which offers a broad spectrum of subjects in YA/NA literature. Compelling reading, the Teen/Young/New Adult reader is sure to find something edgy, enticing and innovative. From dystopian societies, through a whole range of fantasy, horror, science fiction and paranormal fiction, all the way to the other end of the sphere, historical drama, steam-punk adventure, and everything in between (including crime, coming of age and contemporary romance). Whatever your preference you will discover it here. If you have enjoyed this book, why not tell other readers by posting a review on your preferred book site. Recent bestsellers from Lodestone Books are:

AlphaNumeric
Nicolas Forzy
When dyslexic teenager Stu accidentally transports himself into a world populated by living numbers and letters, his arrival triggers a prophecy that pulls two rival communities into war.
Paperback: 978-1-78279-506-3 ebook: 978-1-78279-505-6

Time Sphere
A timepathway book
M.C. Morison
When a teenage priestess in Ancient Egypt connects with a
school-boy on a visit to the British Museum, they each come
under threat as they search for Time's Key.
Paperback: 978-1-78279-330-4 ebook: 978-1-78279-329-8

Bird Without Wings
FAEBLES
Cally Pepper
Sixteen-year-old Scarlett has had more than her fair share of
problems, but nothing prepares her for the day she discovers
she's growing wings...
Paperback: 978-1-78099-902-9 ebook: 978-1-78099-901-2

Briar Blackwood's Grimmest of Fairytales
Timothy Roderick
After discovering she is the fabled Sleeping Beauty, a brooding
goth-girl races against time to undo her deadly fate.
Paperback: 978-1-78279-922-1 ebook: 978-1-78279-923-8

Escape from the Past
The Duke's Wrath
Annette Oppenlander
Trying out an experimental computer game, a fifteen-year-old
boy unwittingly time-travels to medieval Germany where he
must not only survive but figure out a way home.
Paperback: 978-1-84694-973-9 ebook: 978-1-78535-002-3

Holding On and Letting Go
K.A. Coleman
When her little brother died, Emerson's life came crashing down around her. Now she's back home and her friends want to help, but can Emerson fight to re-enter the world she abandoned?
Paperback: 978-1-78279-577-3 ebook: 978-1-78279-576-6

Midnight Meanders
Annika Jensen
As William journeys through his own mind, revelations are made, relationships are broken and restored, and a faith that once seemed extinct is renewed.
Paperback: 978-1-78279-412-7 ebook: 978-1-78279-411-0

Reggie & Me
The First Book in the Dani Moore Trilogy
Marie Yates
The first book in the Dani Moore Trilogy, *Reggie & Me* explores a teenager's search for normalcy in the aftermath of rape.
Paperback: 978-1-78279-723-4 ebook: 978-1-78279-722-7

Unconditional
Kelly Lawrence
She's in love with a boy from the wrong side of town...
Paperback: 978-1-78279-394-6 ebook: 978-1-78279-393-9

Readers of ebooks can buy or view any of these bestsellers by clicking on the live link in the title. Most titles are published in paperback and as an ebook. Paperbacks are available in traditional bookshops. Both print and ebook formats are available online.

Find more titles and sign up to our readers' newsletter at http://www.johnhuntpublishing.com/children-and-young-adult
Follow us on Facebook at
https://www.facebook.com/JHPChildren
and Twitter at
https://twitter.com/JHPChildren